Garters

Garters

Pamela Morsi

GARTERS

A Jove Book / published by arrangement with
the author

ISBN 0-515-10895-2

Jove Books are published by The Berkley Publishing Group,
200 Madison Avenue, New York, New York 10016.
The name "JOVE" and the "J" logo
are trademarks belonging to Jove Publications, Inc.

PRINTED IN THE UNITED STATES OF AMERICA

DEDICATION

*In memory
of Howell Robert Sylvester,
a one-time resident
of the original Vader, Tennessee*

February 26, 1888

Mr. M. Cleavis Rhy
Vader, Tennessee

Mr. Rhy:

   It is with a good deal of excitement that I take up
my pen for this correspondence. I have just
Thursday past received of my good friend from my
days at Yale, Benjamin H. Westbrook, now
employed with Dr. Phythe in Washington, the
exciting news of your work with pisciculture. I
believe your efforts may prove a genuine boon to
my research here.

   I concede difficulty in believing that in such a
desolate highland place as I have heard Tennessee
to be you would be blessed with such riches as
three different species of Salmonidae. Surely, your
little spring-fed mountain creek must be the
southernmost home of the Appalachian Brook Trout.

   I sincerely hope that I am not too forward in
suggesting that I would very much love to visit your
valley and see for myself that work that you have
accomplished there. I write this very day to Dr.
Westbrook suggesting same.

                          With greatest sincerity,

                          Theodatus G. Simmons
                          Springfield, Massachusetts

❧ 1 ❧

Tennessee, 1888

Winter was still enough of a memory to whip a distinct chill into the morning breeze, and the smoky-gray haze had not been burned off by the sun. Yet on this inhospitable morning Esme Crabb made her way down the mountain, her threadbare coat pulled tightly about her. Her thoughts, however, were not on the weather.

In the valley below her, through the dark barren trees of winter, she spied her destination, Vader. The tiny little crossroads on the Nolichucky River was the nearest thing to a town that Esme had ever known. Four houses, a church, a livery stable, and the tiny "graded school" that Esme had attended only a half-dozen times were in sight. As was the building that was her destination.

A false front made the building appear two stories high, but from Esme's perspective it was clearly only one floor, built long and narrow. Though she was still too far away to see it, she knew the sign emblazoned on the front read: "M. Cleavis Rhy, Jr. General Merchandise."

When she reached the foot of the mountain, Esme made

a quick stop to right herself. Hiking up her skirt, she pulled at the much-mended black wool stockings that now clung precariously at her knee. After first carefully smoothing the material up her thigh, she rolled it down about two inches. Grabbing one edge of the roll, she twisted it until the material tightened, painfully digging into her flesh. The near-knotted twist was carefully tucked underneath the roll. It was a makeshift solution, not as good as garters, but such trifling matters didn't concern Esme.

Stockings straight and skirt brushed, Esme raised her chin, proud. She was wearing her Sunday best and bravely assured herself that if she did as good as she looked, she'd do all right. With a determined stride she headed for the store.

Her sisters had really gotten her into this, she supposed. The twins were now seventeen and, to Esme's thinking, the prettiest girls in the county. Most considered them to be identical—even Pa couldn't tell them apart—but Esme found that difficult to understand. To her they were as different and distinct as any two persons, and they sure to graces had the same shortcomings!

Presently, both of them were calf-eyed and mooning over Armon Hightower, and a more worthless piece of Tennessee manhood never existed, except maybe for Esme's own pa.

Ma had been just like the twins, all starry-eyed over a handsome face and broad shoulders. Well, Ma had won her handsome face and broad shoulders, and then she'd worked herself to death for them. Esme was determined that her sisters wouldn't meet the same fate. That's why she was here.

"Mornin', Mr. Tyree, Mr. Denny," Esme said as she stepped onto the porch of the store. The two men sat on the long bench in front of the store swapping stories and spitting tobacco.

"Who are ya?" Tyree asked, squinting at her as his jaw continued to work its tasty wad.

"Esme Crabb," she answered simply.

"What she say?"

"She said, 'Esme Crabb,'" Denny hollered to Tyree. "You know, she's one of Yo's daughters."

"She one of the pretty ones?" Tyree asked, squinting again.

"Nay," was the definitive reply.

Esme felt herself flushing as she stepped through the door. Being compared unfavorably to her sisters was as common as slugs in springtime, but this morning she needed a bit more of what God had granted the twins so liberally.

The tiny bell over the door tinkled loudly in the quiet of the store when she stepped inside. *He* was standing behind the north counter, papers and ledgers strewn before him. He raised his head and glanced politely at her.

"Good morning, miss. Have yourself a look around. Let me know if you see anything you like."

His attention immediately went back to his papers, and Esme began to wander as casually as possible around the store. Two long narrow counters ran the length of both sides. On the walls behind them were shelves of tobacco jars, kitchen wares, and canned goods. Near the front there were cupboards full of cloth and ready-mades and drawers with notions and hair tonic, suspenders and fishhooks. Above her, dangling from rafter hooks, were harnesses and baskets, washtubs and chamber pots. In the far corner was a latticework of cubbyholes and a counter with different plates of ink and rows of carved wooden stamps that represented the official U.S. Post Office of Vader, Tennessee.

Usually Esme considered a trip to the store an adventure, but today Esme's mission precluded any careless frivolity.

She looked back toward the man behind the counter. He was tall and lean looking. It was obvious that he didn't spend his life pushing a plow and looking at the back end of a mule. His shoulders were, however, nicely squared in his crisp white shirt and bisected neatly by gray suspenders. His long arms, now resting elbows against the counter, were not heavily muscled, but were thick enough, Esme thought, for him to defend himself in a row. His hair was dark, but not black. A rich brown color, it was parted in the middle with distinctly pomaded curls facing each other across his forehead. As she moved closer, she saw that his pencil was held by long graceful fingers crowned by the cleanest fingernails she'd ever seen.

"There!" she heard him whisper under his breath as he marked one of the numbers in the long column of figures he was working on. As he made his correction, he smiled, and the sight of his warm smile made something inside Esme go real still.

"Cleavis Rhy! Are you crazy?" She could still hear her sisters laughing at the suggestion.

The discussion last night had begun, as had all discussions for the last several weeks, with the name Armon Hightower.

"The man is strictly up to no good," Esme told the twins sternly. "He's not at all the kind of man I want for either of you."

"Armon Hightower is the finest-looking man in these mountains," Adelaide protested.

"Every dang girl in this part of Tennessee is after him. Why shouldn't we be?" asked Agrippa.

Esme put her hands on her hips and sighed loudly. "Because after all these years of living with Pa, you ought to know that sweet talk and a comely visage don't put beans on the table."

The two quieted at that. Food was always in short supply this late in the winter, and hunger was not to be taken lightly. Since Esme was the undisputed breadwinner of the family, as well as the brains, what she had to say on any subject, especially about eating regularly, always bore listening to.

"Well, what kind of man were you thinking of?" the pretty blond sisters finally asked her in unison.

Esme's brow furrowed in thought for a moment. "Well, I was kind of hoping for Milt Newsome, before he up and married that Maud Turhell."

The twins gave each other a wild-eyed glance that Esme didn't catch. Gratefully they both raised their eyes in thanks to heaven on Milt Newsome's fortunate marriage.

"Milt's farm was the best run in shouting distance, and I was real hopeful about that." Esme shook her head sadly.

"Also, it's got to be someone that's got a big house. I ain't willing to live in this hole forever." Esme gave a pointed look around at their less than ideal surroundings. "We'll need room for all of us to come live with the bride." Beginning to slowly walk back and forth across the room, Esme was thoughtful. "It would be best if the man had some money stuck back for hard times. The way our luck seems to go, hard times are always cropping up."

Stopping her meditative pace, Esme stared sightlessly into the distance, mentally examining each man in the community and subsequently discarding him. Her sisters were very special to her, but the welfare of the whole family counted on one of them marrying well.

Her eyes suddenly lit with excitement. "Of course! I should have thought of him first!"

"Who?" the twins asked in unison.

"The storekeep, Cleavis Rhy!"

"Cleavis Rhy!" Their reaction was immediate. "Are you crazy?"

"He's perfect," Esme declared. "He's not nearly so old as Milt Newsome, and think of that house! There must be a half dozen rooms in there. And getting down off the mountain might be good for Pa's health.''

"There is nothing wrong with Pa's health," Adelaide said.

"You can't really expect us to marry up with someone like that?" said Agrippa.

"And why not?" Esme demanded.

"He's not like us, Esme," Adelaide wailed. "He don't even talk like us. I wouldn't even know what to say to him."

"You don't have to say nothing to him, you just have to look pretty. That's all men want anyway."

The two pretty sisters refused to listen. "You don't know a blooming thing about what men want," one declared honestly. "You ain't never let one get within a stone's throw of you."

"None that was worth a poot ever tried," Esme said, then quickly she moved the subject back to the problem at hand.

"If either of you'd just give that storekeeper a second glance, the whole bunch of us would be living in a big white house and feasting on fried chicken for the rest of our lives!"

The sisters shook their heads obstinately.

"Not me," Agrippa proclaimed.

"Me, neither!" Adelaide parroted.

"You like Cleavis Rhy so much, then *you* marry him!"

"Why, he must be thirty years old!" the twins remarked incredulously.

"May I help you?" Cleavis Rhy had raised his head from the compelling pile of papers before him to look at his customer. His "gift-from-heaven" smile was still in place, and added to it, Esme found herself being watched by the warmest, palest blue eyes she'd ever seen.

Her throat went dry. Her heart pounded like a blacksmith's hammer. She blurted out the first thing that came to her mind.

"How old are you?"

Cleavis Rhy was momentarily startled by the question but quickly recovered himself.

"Twenty-six," he answered, his look now quizzical.

Esme nodded. "I thought you weren't as old as you act."

Cleav blinked at the curious statement, then looked at her more closely.

"You're one of Yohan Crabb's girls, aren't you?"

"Yep," Esme replied, raising her chin a bit defiantly.

He looked slightly uncomfortable now. "You understand that I can no longer extend credit to your father. However, if there is something vital that you need—"

"Don't need a thing," Esme answered quickly, swallowing the lump of shame that formed in her throat.

His smile returned, but it was a more kindly expression now. "There's cheese and crackers back on the barrels. Go help yourself."

"I didn't come 'cause I was hungry," Esme insisted, pride evident in every word.

"Of course not," he said. "But you can have a bite just the same."

Embarrassed now, Esme took one step away and saw him immediately return his attention to his papers.

It was now or never. She had come all the way down the mountain to say one thing. If she didn't say it now, she never would, and her family would be grubbing for toads and eating poke salad forever.

"You wanna marry me?"

"What?"

Esme stood ten feet away from him, their gazes were locked. Across the man's face she saw nothing less than shocked horror. Her face flamed like a fire, and she made a hasty prayer that the heavens would open up and strike her with lightning.

"I said, you got any huckleberry jam?"

A momentary strained silence followed. Finally Cleav's brain absorbed the question.

"No, no huckleberry," he said quietly. "There's peach preserves and some plum butter."

Esme gave a slight nod and hurried toward the rear of the store. As she fished a cracker out of the barrel, her hand trembled. She doused the thin wafer heavily with plum butter, realizing that it was very unlikely that she would be able to swallow.

Cleav watched her go, his thoughts spinning crazily. *Had she said what he thought?* Of course not, he assured himself. But could his ears play such tricks on him? He clearly heard her ask him if he wanted to marry her. No, he *must* have misunderstood.

She stood next to the cracker barrel now, with her back to him. Her hair was wild and curly, a dark blond color that was plaited in three or four strokes at the nape of her neck, the rest hung in disarray down her back just past the rim of her shoulder blades. The ragged wool coat she wore reached just past her hips and her heavy serge skirt had seen better days. Even at a distance Cleav could see the frayed hem, which was a good two inches shorter than fashion and good taste dictated. But the shoes were the worst. The black hobnailed work boots belonged on the feet of a plowman, not a young woman.

Had she really said . . . ? No, Cleav reassured himself. His ears were just playing tricks on him these days.

He forced his eyes to return to the bookkeeping. He'd found the three-cent error that had plagued him all morning, but he still needed to balance the books. Even as he worked, his eyes continued to stray from the neat rows of penciled figures to the female person standing warming herself at the stove and munching on crackers.

Esme was trying to decide what to do. She'd taken one bite of the sweet-smeared cracker but found it totally tasteless. The cane-seat chairs around the stove looked comfortable, but she remained standing. All the chairs were turned to the front, and she just couldn't bear the thought of having to face Cleavis Rhy again.

She should have planned more carefully. Instead she just blurted out her offer like a madwoman. Maybe he hadn't heard her. He *had* to have heard her. She prayed that he hadn't.

Truth to tell, all last night she'd lain awake struggling with her decision, trying to convince herself it was for the best. After all, here she was willing to sacrifice herself, her personal happiness, on the altar of a loveless marriage for the sake of her family. It had never occurred to her that he might not be interested. But she began to fear that he might not be.

Especially now that she'd really taken a good look at him. He wasn't so old, after all, and he was fairly good looking. Not like Armon Hightower, of course, but the face of Cleavis Rhy would never curdle milk. And that smile . . . Esme was surprised to hear herself sigh. It was just dog-it unfair for a man to be rich and pretty, too!

She took another bite of her cracker and shook her head. If just one of the twins had shown the slightest interest in him, they'd already be swimming in gravy!

The curvaceous cotton-headed Crabb twins caught the eye of every man they passed, young and old, and each and every one of them would be proud to have such a beauty walking at his side.

Esme was different. She always had been. From the moment that she had been old enough to understand anything, she'd realized that the twins didn't know "come here'' from ''sic 'em.'' It was clear that God had put Esme on this earth to keep those two beautiful, feather-headed creatures safe. Neither of her older sisters could be counted on to keep from drowning in a spring shower by closing her mouth, let alone coming in out of the rain.

Esme had taken on the job immediately, gladly, lovingly. She could hardly remember her ma. And Pa, well, he was simply Pa. Her sisters were the most important thing in Esme's life, and only on rare occasions did she envy their perfect complexions and their extravagant bustlines.

This was one of those rare occasions. At least a full bosom would be something to offer Cleavis Rhy. Esme's was decidedly lackluster.

Well, she was sure to graces smart as a whip! she reminded herself. But would Cleavis Rhy be impressed with a smart woman? Esme knew that he'd been all the way to Knoxville to school. In a big town like that he had probably met dozens of smart folks; some of them might have even been women.

She knew that when his pa died, he had had to give up his education to come back and run the store. But Pearly Beachum at the church said that he'd managed to finish his high school diploma by mail. That was nothing to be sneered at.

Pearly's latest gossip was that he was paying call on Sophrona Tewksbury, the preacher's daughter. Sophrona played the piano at church. She'd always been right civil to Esme and the twins, but Esme didn't understand her much. She studied the Bible almost constantly, and just about everything she said was quoted verse. Esme thought there was just something you couldn't trust about a person who never had anything of her own to say. She wondered if that was the way to impress Cleavis Rhy. Esme'd memorized her share of Bible verses; in fact she could recite the whole thirteenth chapter of First Corinthians. At least she thought she could, as she quietly began to murmur to herself.

" 'Though I speak with the tongues of men and angels, and have not charity, I am become as sounding brass or a . . .' " Wait a minute. She stopped herself abruptly. Charity. Charity was *not* one of her favorite words. She'd certainly heard it more than she wanted. And it would never do to remind Cleavis Rhy that last Christmas he had forgiven $42.73 worth of credit that he had extended to Pa over the past few years.

How about Proverbs 31? Maybe that would impress him. " 'Who can find a virtuous woman? for her price is far above rubies.' " Oh, turd-buckets, Esme thought, money again. This would never work.

She'd never be as beautiful as her sisters, and it was sure to graces she wasn't Sophrona Tewksbury. She was just plain Esme Crabb, and the kind of things she knew how to do—skin one possum and feed four people with it for a week—would probably not make a fancy fella like Cleavis Rhy sit up and take notice.

How was a nothing-special woman supposed to get a man anyway? It was a question she'd never bothered to ask herself in the past. Now it was suddenly of utmost importance.

Lost in her thoughts, she felt the nagging discomfort of her stockings beginning to sag again. With an exasperated sigh, she propped her foot on the edge of the nearest chair and jerked up her skirts. As she leaned over to grasp the errant stocking, she froze in place. She felt his eyes upon her. Unwilling, yet unable to stop herself, she turned her head to look at him.

Cleavis Rhy stood stiff and silent twenty feet away, his warm blue gaze locked on Esme as if mesmerized.

Her eyes widened at his appraisal and her first instinct

was to right her skirts and run from the building. But something stayed her.

As she watched him watch her, a hot honeyed glow seemed to envelop her. Her breathing became labored and her lips parted slightly. She looked away from him, looked at the leg she bared before him and suddenly wanted him to see her.

All her years she had wondered about the thing between men and women, never truly understanding it. It was all necessary, of course, to have babies. But it had always seemed a decidedly embarrassing thing to do and a deucedly stupid way to act.

Now suddenly, in the middle of a Tuesday morning in the M. Cleavis Rhy General Merchandise, she felt for the first time the sweet, dark rush of desire.

Glancing back to Cleavis, she saw that his gaze had never left her. With pleasure she watched the rise and fall of his chest as if he too found the interior of the store suddenly short of life-giving breath. His powerful-looking hands lay flat on the counter, as if bracing himself. And the pencil he had been using now stood, in silent testament, broken between his fingers.

Esme turned her attention back to her stocking, carefully, and oh, so slowly smoothing the black wool up over her thigh. She sort of accidentally pushed the skirt a little bit too high, giving a momentary glimpse of the frilled hem of the leg of her white cotton drawers. Then she gently rolled the stocking down into place, revealing her smooth white satin skin. She twisted the corner and tucked it into place casually. With unnecessary drama she slapped her skirts back down into place before removing her foot from the chair.

Esme turned to face Cleavis Rhy. With a lazy, hip-rolling swagger she approached the counter. Never in her short, busy life had Esmeralda Crabb ever had the opportunity to feel such power, such confidence. Standing before him she saw that his hands trembled slightly and that sweat had beaded on his upper lip. Desire. Ah, desire. An unexpected weapon.

With feigned wide-eyed innocence, she cocked her hand on one hip and said to him, "Let me know if you see anything you like."

His own oft-repeated phrase falling so glibly from Esme's lips shook Cleav from his trance. Quickly, he squared his shoulders. Nearly choking from the inexplicable dryness in his throat, and tortured by the very understandable discomfort elsewhere, he attempted an apology.

"Miss Crabb, I . . . I didn't . . . I'm sorry that . . . I . . ."

Her smile was triumphant. "Please, Mr. Rhy, you have my permission to call me Esme."

Without another word she turned and marched out the door, her backside swaying provocatively. As far as Esme was concerned, it was all settled. She'd be Mrs. Cleavis Rhy before the turnips were sprouting.

Yohan Crabb was the laziest man in Vader, Tennessee. That was an accepted fact. Some thought he might be the laziest man in the world, but so far nobody could prove it.

It would have been bad enough if Yo Crabb were *drunk* and lazy. But, as a God-fearing man, Crabb had never allowed demon liquor to pass his lips. He was lazy for the mere sake of *being* lazy.

It was said that when Yo was born and his strange, foreign-speaking mother asked with her last breath to name him Yohan, what she was really trying to say was, "Son, I can already see that you ain't never going to turn Yo han' to no good purpose."

When Yo married Providence Portia, the community had felt a spark of hope. Miss Providence was as hardworking as the day was long, and most thought she might be a good influence on Crabb. Unfortunately, most of Yohan's new-found energy was channeled elsewhere. The twins were born barely a year after they wed, and Esme eleven months later.

To Esme's knowledge, Yo had never stirred himself again.

Except, of course, to play the fiddle. And thank goodness for that. Were it not for the fine way that he played, Yohan Crabb would have been *totally* worthless instead of just *practically* worthless.

Pa *could* play that fiddle, Esme thought as she listened, walking back up the mountain. The sound got louder and clearer with each step toward home. How sweet and romantic it was, she thought, her heart still pounding from the memory of Cleav's warm blue eyes fixed upon her.

"Evenin', Pa," she greeted him as she stepped into the clearing next to the house, though *house* was an exaggerated term for the place the Crabbs called home.

Esme remembered when they had first come to live up on the mountain the year after Ma died. They had been sharecropping on Titus Mayfield's place, but without Ma to do the work, Pa had almost let the crop rot in the field. Mayfield had ended up picking it himself and then told Pa to vacate the house so he could get somebody who wanted to work.

They had come up the mountain, Esme at her father's side and the twins running up ahead, laughing and picking flowers.

"It's a fine, sturdy house, Esme," he'd told her. "I guess you'd call it a stone house. And it's not about to fall down. And the best part is that it's ours, all ours. Nobody's ever going to take it from us."

Even at eight years old, Esme had known her father well enough to be skeptical.

"It's a cave!" Esme had cried in horror as she stared at what was to be their new home.

"I'm sorry, darling," Pa had apologized. "Believe me, Sugarplum, I hate moving you children into a cave as bad as you hate moving into it. But there ain't no help for it."

Esme felt tears of despair welling up in her eyes, but she fought them back.

"We're going to live in a cave!" Agrippa's voice squeaked with excitement.

"I'm a cave girl," Adelaide insisted, pounding upon her chest.

"See," Pa had whispered to her. "It's gonna be all right, Esme. I never lie to you."

It was a stone house, of a sort, Esme had to admit. And bears had been living in it for hundreds of years, so it probably wasn't about to fall down. And he was telling the truth: nobody was going to take it from them. No other human would be willing to live there!

The cave now had a split log front for protection from the wind. The logs, culled from fallen trees and scrub brush, were chinked together every which way and supported, where possible, with rocks, mud, and anything else that Esme could drag up the mountain. There was also clearly a front door which made it seem almost like a house. Esme had cut a window one summer, but it was covered over and chinked up now. The cave was never too hot, but it surely could get cold. For that reason a stovepipe now came through a hole near the top of the logs. The stove made cooking possible and living bearable.

"That's a pretty song you're playing, Pa," Esme told her father.

The old man smiled up at her. Even nearing sixty, he was still handsome and a charmer to boot. "You like that, Esme-child?" he asked. "I thought up that little thing today."

She smiled briefly before a worried frown creased her face. "You wrote the song today? I hope it didn't take you all day."

"Purt near," he admitted.

"You promised you'd head down to the river and see if you could catch us a fish for supper."

Yo sighed and shook his head. "Esme-girl, I clean forgot it and that's the truth."

She felt the annoyance rise up within her. "Pa, how could you forget. We don't have a blame thing to eat in the house!"

"I just forgot, Sugarplum," he answered. "You know how it is with me, I get to playing and I forget what time it is, I forget about eating and sleeping and purt near everything."

"Didn't Adelaide or Agrippa remind you?"

"Ain't seen neither since early this morning. Right after you left, that Hightower boy showed up, and they went running out to have a picnic with him."

"A picnic!" Esme's voice was incredulous. "Well, I sure hope he brought the food."

"Nope," Pa said shortly. "They both were carrying a basket of vittles."

Esme's spark of vexation quickly flamed into a full-fledged anger.

"Well, sure to graces, I bet there is not so much as cornmeal dust left in the house. How am I supposed to feed this family anyway!"

Her father had the decency to look embarrassed and hastily rose to his feet. "I'm sorry, Esme-girl," he told her cajolingly. "I'll head down to the river right now."

Esme sighed in exasperation and shook her head. "Pa, it's late afternoon. It'd be dark afore you even got to the river."

Her father glanced up, surprised to notice the sun had nearly disappeared behind the mountain.

"You're surely right, Esme. Lord, girl—where you been all day?"

A flush of embarrassment stained her cheeks. She should have come straight back home and gone to work. Instead she'd wanted to hold those moments in the store more closely, to think about them, to inspect them, and she had spent the afternoon wandering along the river, daydreaming about Cleavis Rhy and the way he had looked at her.

"I went to town, Pa. I told you that."

"That don't take all day," her father said. "And you didn't bring nothing back. That young Rhy wouldn't give you nothing? He was always fairly generous to me."

Esme's chin came up defiantly. "I will not stoop to begging."

Yohan shook his head slightly in disbelief. "Accepting Christian charity ain't begging," he told her. "Believe me, Esme, it makes those folks feel downright warm inside to be able to help those less fortunate, like ourselves."

"Well, it don't make me feel 'downright warm inside.' It makes me feel downright queasy!"

Her father nodded. "I know. Your ma was the same way. She hated taking anything from anybody. Why, that woman worked herself down to a nub. Always thinking about what we were gonna eat and where we were gonna live."

"Well, somebody's got to worry about those things!"

Yo seated himself back on the ground, leaning against the rough wood of the house, and drew his bow sweetly across the strings of the fiddle.

"You've got the right of it there, and I cain't deny it," he admitted. "But sometimes it appears to me that you've been considering the practical too much. You're neglecting to live and breathe. Feel that breeze stirring, Esme-girl? You can almost smell spring in the air. Spring's a-coming. Flowers gonna bloom, birds is a gonna sing. And plenty of young gals like yourself is going to be falling in love. That's what you ought to be considering."

Esme jerked the front door open with disgust. "I think a gal would be a good deal more likely to fall in love when she's got a full belly and a pantry full of food put by for the winter. Now, if you don't stop talking that nonsense and let me get to my work, I'm going to break that dang fiddle over your head!''

Yo chuckled slightly at the idle threat. "Just like her ma," he whispered to himself. A wave of sadness crossed his face. Putting the fiddle to his chin, he returned to his music, filling up the growing shadows with beautiful sounds, sounds of spring and romance.

Cleavis flipped open his gold watch and checked the time. "Six o'clock, precisely," he said to himself, smiling. Slipping the fancy timepiece back into the watch pocket of his trousers, he picked the sign up from under the counter and went to hang it on the door.

It read, CLOSED. ASK AT THE HOUSE. It was not a good sign. His father had painted it, and the big block letters were formed like those of a child and all the *e*'s were upside-down. It didn't matter, however. Very few people on the mountain would actually bother to read it. And every living soul in and around Vader knew that if Cleav wasn't at the store, they should ask at the house.

After grabbing up his thick wool coat from the hook and dousing the light from the one coal-oil lamp, Cleav headed for home.

He took a circuitous route, walking along the ridges of the numerous small ponds that he'd dug in the marshy bottom land between the store and the river. The fish swimming in those pools were his true work, or at least he liked to think so. Storekeeping might be his vocation, but natural science was his avocation.

Darkness precluded any investigation this evening, but he already knew what was going on beneath the surface of each still, small pool. He smiled to himself, thinking of the gentle silence of the water and the scores of trout eggs to be harvested next fall. Someday he hoped his work with trout would be known to fish culturists worldwide. Perhaps in the distant future a new species might carry his name. The Nolichucky Rhy Trout, he postulated. The idea brought a whistle to his lips.

When he approached the house, he noticed a lamp was lit in the parlor. Clearly it meant guests for dinner, and he hurried his walk. Taking the porch steps two at a time, he saw a young woman's head inside the parlor window, her crowning glory neatly twisted into a topknot of flaming red.

Not red, he corrected himself quickly. Ladies do not have red hair, only strawberry-blond.

Stepping into his foyer, he hung his coat on the elaborate wooden hall tree and checked his reflection in the mirror. His hair on his forehead had formed errant curls, and he hastily pushed it back into place. He hesitated only momentarily to run his hand across the fine mahogany finish of the hall tree's umbrella rail. Like every piece of furniture in his house, it had been brought over the mountain for the specific purpose of conveying fashion and good taste.

"Good evening, ladies," Cleav said to the three women as he stepped into the door, but his eyes immediately sought only the lovely Miss Sophrona.

"Cleavis, dear," his mother said. "Finally you're home. I feared we'd be waiting dinner on you all night."

Cleav didn't need to check his watch to know that it was no more than a quarter after six, his usual time to return from the store.

"I'm here now," he commented agreeably and seated himself in a stuffed horsehair chair, near—but not too near—Miss Sophrona.

"The Reverend Tewksbury has gone to sit up with Miz Latham," his mother continued. "Poor old thing, she's about dead herself, and now her man's took sick."

Cleav nodded with appropriate gravity.

"We, of course, are blessed that dear Mrs. Tewksbury

and her precious daughter can therefore spend the evening with us.''

''Doubly blessed,'' Cleav said and then cast a glance at Miss Sophrona, who was blushing prettily.

Unbidden, an image sprang to mind of a long slim leg encased in black wool. He was so surprised at the unexpected and inappropriate image that it must have shown upon his face. Miss Sophrona glanced at him curiously.

Quickly trying to recover himself, Cleav turned to Mrs. Tewksbury. ''So what pleasant pursuits have you ladies been discussing? A new quilting pattern, perhaps? Or something more serious, such as . . . ah . . . the actual versus the symbolic meaning of John's Revelations?''

Mrs. Tewksbury beamed with approval. She was very proud of her deep and sublimely metaphysical understanding of the Bible. In fact, the woman was virtually certain that her husband, Reverend Tewksbury, knew absolutely nothing by comparison.

''Mrs. Rhy and I were just discussing the parable of the twelve virgins and how such careful Christian planning could be translated to charity to the less fortunate of our own community.''

Smiling politely, Cleave turned to the attractive strawberry-blonde on the divan. ''And Miss Sophrona, what bit of wisdom did you offer to this discussion?''

Lowering her eyes humbly, Sophrona's voice was sweet and almost childlike in its clarity. '' 'For I was hungred, and ye gave me meat. I was thirsty, and ye gave me drink. I was a stranger, and ye took me in. I was . . .' ''

Sophrona stopped, her face flaming with color. She glanced toward her mother without uttering another word.

Cleavis realized immediately that Miss Sophrona's hesitance concerned the next line of the verse: ''Naked and you clothed me.'' It was without a doubt not to be spoken by one such as Miss Sophrona. He was sure no one could ever imagine such a thing!

Like a heroic knight for a damsel in distress, Cleav quickly covered the gaffe. "It's interesting that you ladies should be discussing charity this evening. I had a visitor to the store today, sorely in need, I believe."

Grateful for his rescue, Sophrona showed an inordinate excess of interest. "Whoever could it have been?" she asked.

"One of Yohan Crabb's girls," Cleav answered, then he discovered to his surprise that he didn't wish to elaborate.

"One of those twins!" Mrs. Tewksbury shook her head in exasperation and gave Mrs. Rhy a concerned glance. "I don't know whatever we will do with those two."

"No, not one of the twins," Cleav hastily corrected. "The other one, Esme she's called."

"Ah." Mrs. Tewksbury shook her head wisely. "She's a good girl, that one. Must be a throwback to her mother's side of the family."

Eula Rhy's forehead creased into a frown. "I do hope that you haven't allowed them to run up more credit. There is no chance in the world that they would ever pay." Smiling at her guest, Mrs. Rhy added, "Dear Cleavis is so soft-hearted, I swear he'd give away the store if he thought somebody needed it."

Cleav bristled slightly under the criticism. "If folks are hungry, we have to feed them, Mother, that's not even a question for discussion."

"If the Crabbs are hungry," his mother suggested coldly, "it's because that old man won't work. The Bible says the Lord helps those who help themselves."

"Actually, that's not in the Bible," Sophrona corrected gently. "But it does say to 'consider the lilies of the field, they toil not, neither do they spin. Yet Solomon in all his glory was not arrayed like one of these.'"

Mrs. Rhy was so dumbfounded by the unexpected rebuke that she didn't respond.

"Actually, the young woman didn't ask for anything," he told them. He gave his mother an appeasing glance. "Nonetheless, I clearly let her know that business with her family would have to be on strictly a cash or barter basis."

"Then whyever did she come down the mountain?" Mrs. Tewksbury asked.

In his memory Cleav distinctly heard the words *"You wanna marry me?"*

"I have no idea," he answered. "But she was certainly looking poorly. It occurred to me that this late in the year they must be pretty low on winter stores. It's a good two months before they'll get so much as a potato from the ground."

"Oh, then we must get up a basket for them," Sophrona said with genuine sweetness. "Thank you so much for mentioning it, Mr. Rhy." Her voice lowered to a shy whisper. "I will make it my personal duty this week to bring this need to the attention of the Ladies' Auxiliary."

Miss Sophrona's sincere goodness was so powerful that Mrs. Rhy quickly forgot her previous irritation. Once again she beamed at the young woman.

"Such a precious daughter you have," she told Mrs. Tewksbury.

"'Raise up a child in the way he should go,'" the preacher's wife quoted proudly. The two women gazed fondly at their children. The handsomely dressed Cleav was nodding approvingly at the sweetly blushing Sophrona, who smiled back at him shyly.

"Mayhap we should leave these two alone," Mrs. Rhy suggested in a whisper. "Would you care to help me get our supper on the table?"

Cleavis rose politely as the women left the room and then,

with only a moment's hesitation, seated himself on the divan next to Sophrona.

The young lady continued to face the front, her eyes on the pale lavender hankie that she nervously twisted in her hand. Her hands were beautiful, pale and unlined, with tiny little childlike fingers. It was not, however, her hands that captured Cleav's regard. Miss Sophrona was a diminutive woman, no higher than a fence post. If she'd been standing next to Cleav, the top of her head would have come no higher than his heart. But what heaven had robbed from her in stature, it had repaid in abundance. As with every opportunity Cleav had to observe her, his gaze unerringly went to the overgenerous outpouring of firm feminine flesh that was Sophrona Tewksbury's bosom.

This evening that blatant attraction was modestly covered with a lavender dotted-swiss bodice, its neatly stitched pleats designed to disguise the beauty that just couldn't be hidden.

Remembering propriety, Cleav tore his attention from the lushly rounded curves of the preacher's daughter and forced himself to speak civilly. "Do you think we'll be seeing any more snow this year?" he asked.

She gave him a shy glance. " 'It's not for you to know the times or the seasons which the Father hath put in his own power.' "

Cleav nodded. "Just so." After a moment's hesitation he began again. "Mother told me that the ladies of the church are planning a social."

"Yes," Sophrona admitted. " 'For where two or three are gathered in my name, there am I in the midst of them.' " When the gentleman at her side raised a quizzical eyebrow, she added, "It's still too cool for ice cream, so we're thinking of a taffy pull."

Cleav cleared his throat slightly and then issued a polite

invitation. "I would be honored, Miss Sophrona, to be allowed to escort you."

Sophrona twisted the handkerchief to such a state, it by rights should have been torn to pieces. "'Thou has given me my heart's desire.'" Her voice was barely above a whisper.

Uncomfortable with the sudden serious turn of the conversation, Cleave grasped at his thoughts, searching for potential topics of conversation.

"I received a letter today from a Mr. Simmons. He's a gentleman from New England, who's with the American Fish Culturists Association."

"Oh?" Sophrona's reply held only the mildest pretense of curiosity.

"Yes," Cleav continued eagerly. "It seems that Mr. Simmons heard about my trout-breeding experiments from Mr. Westbrook of the U.S. Deputy Fish Commissioner's office. The two were fellows together at Yale."

"How nice."

"Wonderful, actually." Cleav leaned back against the cushions of the divan and comfortably crossed his legs. "Mr. Simmons is active in the Fish Restoration Movement and is very excited about the prospects of what I've been able to do here on the Nolichucky."

"We're all very proud of your work, Mr. Rhy," Sophrona said gently.

Looking across at the unmistakably bored expression on the young woman's face, Cleav's lips broadened into the wide smile that had the power to melt her heart.

"My dear Miss Sophrona," he said. "How generous you are to allow me to ramble on about my fish. You are much too polite to remind me that ladies care nothing for the spawning and rearing of piscis Salmonidae."

Her answer was an impish little giggle that further endeared her to him. Slowly and with due gravity and consideration, Cleavis took her tiny hand in his own and brought it to his mouth, very lightly grazing the first knuckle with his lips.

"Oh, Mr. Rhy!" she protested breathlessly. But she continued to allow him to hold her hand until they were called to supper.

"Well, it's about time you showed up!" Esme said, greeting her sisters less than favorably as they walked through the front door only a few seconds before full dark.

"Evening, Miss Esme," a male voice called out behind them.

"Saves to graces! I thought you two would have more sense than to invite him to dinner," she scolded the twins.

Armon Hightower gave a good-natured laugh as he walked through the door. "Now, don't get in an uproar, Miss Esme."

Hightower was long and well muscled, as fair of face as any girl ever dreamed, and his coal-black hair was only slightly less dramatic than his heavily lash-fringed dark blue eyes.

"I don't come to your table empty-handed," he said proudly as he threw the dead carcasses of two squirrels upon the kitchen table. "I shot these for the girls while we were out."

"I would have thought you'd have had time to clean them," Esme said unkindly.

Hightower laughed as if Esme had just told a good joke. "Now, Miss Esme, you needn't take on so. Next time we'll take you with us."

It was as blatant a lie as ever was told, but Esme chose to ignore it.

She glanced over at the two stiffening squirrels with distaste. Food, however, was food, and she was grateful for it even when it came from a no-account like Armon

Hightower. "Thank you for bringing the meat," she choked out politely. "I'll have them skinned and a-roasting in two shakes."

The evening was a long one, with Armon's gift for gab and way with a story keeping both the twins and her father rousingly entertained. Esme didn't have an opportunity to speak to her sisters until the young man finally left and the girls began their preparations for bed.

"Why in the world would you two run off from your chores like that?" Esme demanded.

"Esme, we just couldn't help ourselves," Agrippa said in protest.

"That Armon." Adelaide pulled the cotton flour-sack nightgown over her head. "I swear he could talk the leaves off the trees. It's just pure-d hard to say no to the man."

"Well, I hope you both still are!" Esme exclaimed in an aggravated whisper.

The twins burst out in giggles and collapsed joyfully onto the worn straw tick. "Esme, I swear, you're too silly," Adelaide finally had the breath to tell her. "If anyone knows about handling men, it's me and Agrippa."

Agrippa sat up on the bed and took Esme's hands in her own. "Little Sister, if you're thinking to give us the 'won't buy a cow when milk's for free' lecture, you're a little late," she said. "Adelaide and I have been practicing what you preach since before you knew what made men's trousers so downright interesting."

Giggling again, the two began to tease Esme mercilessly. "You may know all about putting in a garden and running a house and cooking and such, Esmeralda," Adelaide told her. "But when it comes to the male of the species, there's no chance that you'll ever be more than our baby sister."

"Adelaide and I have already *forgot* more about men than you'll be able to learn in a lifetime."

Pulling on her own threadbare nightgown, Esme decided

that she had heard quite enough. "Well, Sisters," she told them, "in the next few months I'm going to be learning what you know. And"—she paused for emphasis—"*you* are going to learn what I know."

"What on earth do you mean?" one twin asked.

"Learning what you know?" the other questioned.

"You two are now in charge of the house," Esme said firmly.

"What!" the exclamation came in unison.

"I won't be able to take care of the house and find the food and see that you two and Pa are clean and fed and looked after. Somebody will have to do it; it has to be you."

"Now, Esme," Adelaide said gently, "we told you that we were sorry for running off today."

"Yes," Agrippa agreed. "You did leave us in charge and we promised to take care of things for you, but . . . well—" She looked at her twin for guidance.

"We just forgot," Adelaide said.

Agrippa nodded eagerly. "That's right. We forgot, just like Pa does. I guess it's in the blood."

Esme snorted in disbelief. "In the blood? Well, I suspect that in the future it will be in the stomach instead." She pointed her finger sternly at them. "The next time you forget, you'll just be going hungry, and not just you—Pa, too."

The twins gazed at each other dumbstruck.

"I'm going to be busy with my own concerns, and I won't be able to fetch and carry for you. I've got important business to attend to—I've got plans to make life better for all of us. And it's best that I get at it."

"Esme, you can't do this," Agrippa said. "This is the worst time of the year. Where are we supposed to find food this late in the season?"

"And who'll put in the garden?" Adelaide asked. "It's

nearly time to turn the ground, and we won't know how to
do it without your help.''

''Somehow you'll manage.'' Esme slipped beneath the
covers next to her sisters.

''We can't manage,'' Agrippa complained. ''I'm almost
sure of it.''

''Well, you'll have to see, won't you?'' Esme said as she
tried to stick her nose in the air haughtily, a gesture not
easily accomplished when lying down.

''What on God's green earth can be so important for you
to do that you can't be at the house anymore?''

''That's for me to know,'' Esme said and closed her eyes.

Adelaide was having none of it. She sat up in bed, her
arms folded across her chest and her jaw stiffened in anger.

'' 'Fess up, Esme, or I'm going to Pa.''

''Me, too!'' Agrippa chimed in.

The standoff lasted at least a full minute.

''Oh, all right,'' Esme said, sitting up herself and pulling
her nightgown high enough to sit cross-legged. ''I won't be
around here much for a while,'' Esme began hesitantly.
''Because I'm going courting.''

The twins sat silently, staring at their sister for a moment
before looking at each other and bursting out laughing.

''Esme, Esme, we said you don't know much,'' Agrippa
began.

''But we never thought it was this bad,'' Adelaide
finished for her.

''What are you laughing at?'' Esme demanded.

''*You* don't go courting,'' Adelaide told her as Agrippa
covered her mouth, trying to hold in the laughter. ''The man
comes courting for you.''

''Not if the man ain't interested,'' Esme told them. ''He
ain't about to come up here.''

''If the man ain't interested,'' Adelaide tried to explain,

"then there can't be any courting. You just have to find another man. One who takes a liking to you."

"I don't want another man," Esme said decisively. "I intend to marry Cleavis Rhy before the summer's out. And it don't matter to me if he likes me or not."

3

The door slammed on a small outbuilding set far apart from
the others on the land that belonged to Cleavis Rhy. Loaded
up like a pack mule, Cleav came across the winter-shorn
meadow carrying his supplies from the "meat house."

It was a beautiful day for March, and Cleav intended to
spend the early afternoon tending the series of ponds and
holding pools that were dug out of the low ground between
the store and the river. The sun was shining brightly,
warming the lingering winter chill out of the air. And the
breeze that lifted and fluttered through his hair was just
enough to stir, but not disturb, the last of winter's beauty.

Cleav was just glad that he wasn't downwind from what
he carried.

The mesh sack of finely ground meat smelled to high
heaven. This was Cleav's least favorite chore. The care and
rearing of trout was a rewarding, but an occasionally smelly,
occupation.

When he reached the ponds, he began distributing his fish
food in a methodical manner. An adamant adherent of the

scientific method, Cleav believed that order was essential for appropriate and documentable study.

Approaching the nursery pond, he unhooked the loop of rope that stretched across the pond from peg to peg. Carefully, holding the rope, he attached a meat bag and flicked at the rope until the sack had slipped to the knotted stop at midpoint. Then he lowered the rope end to the ground and reattached it to the peg. Already he could feel the steady jerk on the line that meant feeding time.

Cleav had always been fascinated with fish. When he was still in kneepants, he had raced away from school each day and hurried through his chores so he could go fishing.

Some might have described his childhood as ideal: He had plenty to eat, warm clothes, a clean bed, and that elusive of all human commodities, leisure. But young Cleavis Rhy filled his leisure not with daydreams of adventure on the high seas, or rough and tumble games of strength with his schoolmates, but with a quiet watch on the ways of nature.

Now for a few moments every afternoon at feeding time as his mother minded the store, Cleav continued this lazy pursuit. Stretching out on the grass beside the pond, his long legs casually crossed at the ankle, he propped himself on one elbow to view the show he knew was about to commence. The fingerlings, so called because of their size, circled excitedly around the mesh sack. They were young trout, alone and on their own in the world. Hungry by now, but fearful. The world was a dangerous place for a baby trout, and they approached their food cautiously.

Circling, circling, the fingerlings would investigate for several moments. Finally a brave soul would find the food so alluring that the daring fingerling would sneak in for a bite.

The trophy clutched firmly between his baby fish teeth, he would swish away, creating a momentary flutter of panic among his siblings. The crowd would nervously reconverge on the beloved but feared mesh sack until the next adventurous trout risked it all for the sake of his belly.

Cleav watched, satisfied. They were learning, these babies of his. Each day the fingerlings overcame their fear sooner and sooner. His brooders were totally fearless, knowing that there was nothing to harm them in these ponds. The fingerlings would learn, too, but by then these would be in the fattening ponds. Fingerlings would always be afraid of the bag, he decided. It was nature's way of helping the smallest trout to protect themselves.

As he watched, the banquet was steadily increasing its diners. The fancy swirling dance of a hundred tiny trout entranced him. It always did. He could think here, imagine, postulate. Nothing would disturb his peace. That is, until he saw a woman's reflection in the water before him.

Startled, he turned. Esme Crabb was standing behind him, dressed in the same clean but worn dress as the previous day.

"What are you doing here?" he asked, surprised. No one had ever disturbed him at the ponds before.

Esme dropped to the ground beside him, carelessly crossing her legs Indian style, and gave a little shrug of feigned indifference. "Just looking for you, I guess."

Cleav had no idea what to make of that. Since that incident in the store yesterday, thoughts, and memories of Esme Crabb, had plagued him. The sight of her raising the dress to adjust her garters was a shocking one. But he had, with great effort, painstakingly come to the conclusion that he had been at fault. He had continued to stare at her naked calf, knee, and lower thigh. Why he acted so impolitely he couldn't imagine. She was hill bred and motherless. Such behavior for her, while not excusable, was understandable. He, on the other hand, should have had the decency to turn his back. A gentleman would have, he was sure.

Esme looked around curiously and watched the tiny fish nibbling their dinner. "What about you? What are you doing?" she asked Cleav.

"I'm working."

Esme's expression lit with amusement. "Working?" she repeated, glancing at Cleav's relaxed pose and then at the quiet bucolic surroundings. "I'd best tell Pa about this. It looks to be just the job he's been praying for!"

His jaw tightening with annoyance, Cleav rose to his feet. He knew people didn't appreciate his work. Even Reverend Tewksbury and dear Miss Sophrona could barely keep the boredom out of their expressions when he talked about it. But it was work, important work, and Cleav bristled with the unfair comparison to the lazy and worthless Yohan Crabb.

"Some men labor with their backs and others with their minds. It's obvious that you're more accustomed to the former." Almost rudely Cleav walked away from the young woman who had interrupted his afternoon. He had things to do, and he couldn't allow a curious hill girl to distract him.

Esme bristled slightly at his scornful tone, but then bit down on her lip and hurried to follow him. "He's got a prickly pride," she whispered to herself, as if making a notation for future reference. She was supposed to be making him coo and pant after her, not getting him all puffed up and nay-minded.

Cleav picked up a pail that he had left near a larger and deeper pond just downstream. Hurrying to catch up, Esme smiled up at him when she reached his side. He was just the right height, she thought to herself. Not so tall as to be clumsy, but plenty tall enough to see over the crowd. She also approved of how easily he'd scooped up the full bucket. His muscles were strong.

These cheery thoughts intrigued her for a moment until

she smelled a distinctly unpleasant odor. She peered into the bait bucket.

"Whew! What is that?" she asked him, wrinkling her nose in distaste.

"It's trout food," he answered.

"What you feeding them, skunk turds?"

Cleav was momentarily taken back by her frank language, but recovered quickly. "Meat," he answered calmly.

"Meat?" She raised her eyebrows. "I suspect you're dang right it is, and sure to graces it's been dead near a month!"

"Trout can't smell," he explained with only slight agitation. "Fish, in natural circumstances, never consume pork."

"And that's just exactly how God intended it. Can you imagine what would happen if every time a pig wandered into the river the fish came up and started gnawing on the poor thing? Why, they'd be pure-d mangled afore we'd get them to slaughter."

Cleav couldn't quite tamp down the ghost of a smile that came to his lips at the image of a squealing hog being attacked by swarming carnivorous river trout. She had humor, this one, he thought in grudging appreciation. Humor being a high form of intellect, he wondered curiously how bright the Crabb woman might be. People in town said she was smarter than her sisters, but in his slight acquaintance with the twins, he thought perhaps even rocks were closer to his intellectual equals than those two.

With a touch more patience he continued his explanation. "It's very difficult for me to provide enough small fish and minnows to feed this many trout. So I'm trying to extend the fish products I feed them by grinding them with pork. As far as preference, thus far they seem unable to tell the difference. But their digestive systems seem to tolerate the pork better when the meat is partially decomposed."

Esme wrinkled her brow seriously, listening to his explanation. "You mean when it's rotten?" she translated.

"Just so," he agreed, suppressing a laugh. Cleav stopped at the side of the pool, and Esme saw to her disbelief that the shadows his body cast on the water was enough to bring a bevy of huge full-grown trout out of hiding.

"Look at that!" Esme's words were whispered in stunned amazement.

"They're coming to be fed," Cleav answered cheerfully. Squatting down beside the water, Esme saw him dip his hand in the pail of coarsely ground, rotten meat. Retrieving a fistful, he put his hand just under the surface of the water and to Esme's awestruck surprise the big proud trout hurried up to get a bite.

"They eat right out of your hand!" Her eyes were wide with amazement. She looked at Cleav as if he'd just accomplished a great miracle.

Her exuberant enthusiasm over his fish delighted Cleav, but honesty compelled him to explain more fully. "It's not me," he told her. "These are my brooders. I've been feeding them at this same time from this same spot for two years."

"So they know you." Esme's eyes were bright with approval.

"They're just fish," Cleav protested good-naturedly. "They don't know anything but eating and breeding."

"That's pretty much life anyway." Esme glanced into the water. "Do they have names? What do you call that kind of grayish looking one with the black mole on her cheek?"

"I don't call them anything," he said.

"You could call her Pearly, after Miz Beachum," Esme told him. "Miz Beachum's got a big mole just like that."

Cleav gave a little chuckle. "You're absolutely right. She does look a bit like Mrs. Beachum."

Esme sighed loudly. "I'm just so proud of you," she

said. "I never knew a living soul that could call the fish to come to them."

Grabbing another handful of the vile-smelling fish food, he offered it to the still hungry swimmers. "When they see a shadow across the water, they just know that there's food here, and it's safe to come and eat it."

"Oh, but it's wonderful," Esme insisted. "The fish know you and trust you."

"No, you're thinking that these trout are like hunting dogs. And they are not."

"Of course not." Esme shook her head with agreement. "The master tames the dog and then trains him. You've got the fish a-coming to you, and they're not trained or tamed. They're still fish. It's like you talk to wild things."

Cleav laughed out loud at that. The sight of his wide, white smile made something catch in Esme's chest. The gentle afternoon breeze had mussed his curls, and his tangled brown hair accented the depth of his pale blue eyes.

"I do not *talk* to fish, young lady," he declared with a mock severity that would have made Esme giggle had her heart not been pounding like a tom-tom. How had she not realized before yesterday how handsome he was? And so smart? And so gentle even the fish weren't afraid of him.

"It's you that feeds the fish and no one else," she told him softly.

There was a fleeting curiosity in his glance, and then he motioned to her. "Come here and you can feed them."

"Me?"

"Sure. It's just the shadow that they see. They don't know the hand that feeds them."

Esme hesitated. "I'm not sure."

For some reason he wanted badly for her to do it. Intuitively he knew she couldn't resist a dare. Glancing down into the food pail, he said, "You have to be willing to put your hand in that bucket of muck." There was more than a hint of challenge to his voice.

She quickly waved away her former objections to the putrid fish food. "A little muck ain't nothing to me," she boasted. "I've limed the outhouse plenty of times, and that's a lot worse than this."

Cleav had the good manners to ignore her indelicate comment.

"I'd wash in this stuff if it suited the fish," she told him.

Cleav smiled. "I don't believe that will be necessary, Miss Esme."

Hearing him speak her given name pleased her. She wanted very much to feed the fish now. She wanted to show him that she could do whatever he asked.

"Here, come sit in front of me," he said. "We need to make the fish think that you're just another part of me."

Esme hesitated just an instant. Then she scooted closer to him. Still squatting, he spread his legs a little wider and made a place for her in between them next to the water.

"Get into my shadow," he instructed her. "If the shadow doesn't change, the fish will have nothing to fear."

She felt Cleav's hand at her shoulder, gently coaxing her into the correct position, directly in front of him, as he squatted on the grass. She felt the warmth of him surrounding her as she sat so close to him; his knee was near her now blushing cheek.

Feeling the closeness of her back to his chest, she glanced down at the shadow on the water. She was invisible. Her form had been totally absorbed in his. As the thought crossed her mind, she felt an unusual fluttering in her abdomen. As far as the trout were concerned, Esme Crabb was now a part of Cleavis Rhy. It gave her a dizzying feeling.

"Just take a handful of food," he coached. "They've

really had enough, but we'll give them an extra treat today in honor of accepting you."

With his warm smile of encouragement, Esme only made a slight face as she dipped her hand in the bucket. Leaning forward, she felt him right behind her.

"Put your hand just a couple of inches under the water," he told her, "and open it up about halfway."

Esme followed his instructions exactly. She shivered slightly as her hand descended into the cold mountain pool. Stiffening herself against the chill of the water, she tried to tamp down an inexplicable trickle of fear. But she failed, however, to control the sudden jerk of her shoulders when the first big brown brooder greedily grabbed a bite.

"Easy," Cleav cautioned as he laid his hands familiarly on her shoulders. "They won't bite your fingers off," he whispered close to her neck. "You've got to trust them, just the way you want them to trust you."

Feeling the warmth of his hands as they soothed her, Esme felt herself begin to relax. The big fish pushed each other aside and tickled her fingers with their fins as they vied for their share.

"Come on, Pearly," she coaxed the mole-faced fish. "My hand's not as big as Cleav's, but the food tastes just the same."

Cleav's breathy chuckle raised the hairs on her neck.

"Oh, it's wonderful," Esme whispered, her heart pounding from more than the exhilaration of fish feeding.

Cleav agreed, however neither his thoughts nor his senses were focused on the fish. At Esme's startled quiver, his palms had so naturally found their way to her shoulders to reassure and comfort. Now his hand sought only to caress.

Her firm, square shoulders felt unerringly feminine under his fingers. With a pretense of carelessness, he moved his thumb toward her collar. He felt a warm stab of desire.

Stop it! he ordered himself angrily. The woman had asked to feed the fish, not be fondled by the fish handler.

"Look at this big one!" Esme's quiet whisper bubbled with excitement.

Cleav leaned forward to follow her gaze. His chest eased up against the back of the worn wool of her coat. His chin was so close to her neck, he could have counted the tiny trickles of errant curls that had escaped the thick blond braid. He took a much needed breath, only to be assailed by the sweet scent of her. Plain brown soap and woman; it was a combination he'd never fully appreciated before.

Quite naturally his hands slid down to her waist—only to steady her, he swore to himself. He couldn't allow the young woman to fall into the water. That the water was no more than three feet deep and that she was seated firmly on the shoreline were facts he didn't bother to consider.

Her waist was not the tiny handspan that was still the rage of fashion, nor was it bound with the usual corsets that both disguised and protected it from men. Cleavis could feel the gentle give of real flesh. And it lay beneath his hands, thinly separated by her coat, dress, and chemise. His fingers tingled with the wish to dispose of those few garments. He knew he should take his hands from her person, but she felt too good.

Her charges fed and her palm empty, Esme took her hand out of the cold water. The warm comfortable feel of Cleav's fingers at her waist so captured her attention that, glancing to the side, she was startled to find his face so close. How could such pale blue eyes appear so hot, so deep?

It was desire. Desire, the same as in those well-remembered fleeting moments in the store.

But then she had felt power, control. Now, surrounded by him, his hands touching her so firmly yet so tenderly, his mouth, his lips so close, she was entranced, not entrancing. Gathering her courage, she forced herself to speak. "Should

I feed them more?'' she asked him, her voice trembling with its whisper.

"No." His answer was brief, but the sound of it continued to linger in her breast.

She met his gaze but couldn't hold it as time and time again his focus dropped to her lips, which warmed so quickly under his perusal that without thought her tongue snaked out to dampen them.

His eyes widened perceptibly, and the grip on her waist tightened. "Esme . . ." The word was a tortured whisper.

She was trembling now. The nearness of him, the desire, the fear all warred together inside her. Would he kiss her? When would he kiss her? What would she do if he kissed her? Should she scream? Should she run? Oh, how she wanted him to kiss her.

He had turned his head slightly to the side. Save to graces, Cleavis Rhy was going to kiss her! Those long muscled arms were going to hold her. That beautiful mouth was going to press against hers. Those long slender fingers were going to touch her, caress her. It was going to happen. He moved closer, only so slightly. Yes, it was going to be a kiss. She was sure of it. Any second now his lips would touch hers. Any second now. Any second. Now! Now!

She couldn't wait any longer.

Esme threw herself at Cleavis Rhy. Clasping her arms tightly around his neck, she slammed her warm wet lips against his.

At her sudden lurch Cleav lost his balance and fell back against the ground. Esme sprawled on top of him, wiggling closer by the minute. Her fingers grasped his dark hair by the handfuls. Her lips stuck to his tighter than a tick on a stray dog.

She heard a strangled exclamation from his throat and felt the strength of him as gently but firmly he tried to roll her off of him.

The feel of his long, strong body against hers and the spicy scent of his skin was more pleasurable than Esme had expected. That ball of tingling anxiety that lay low in her abdomen dropped within her, and the craving it triggered robbed the young woman of the last vestiges of her good judgment.

Instinctively Esme wrapped her strong, work-muscled legs around him and held on for blue blazes. As he rolled her to the ground, she rolled him atop her.

The fight went out of him for one shocked second as Cleav felt the soft feminine curves of her pressed so intimately against him. Then with his masculine strength he thrust her from him. Rolling to his feet, he crouched before her warily like a wrestler preparing for the next fall.

Esme sat on the grass, a look of stunned surprise on her face. Her dark serge was hiked up practically to her waist and gave much more than a cursory glimpse of her long fine limbs. One black wool stocking dangled unheeded about the ankle of her workshoe, the other clung precariously to her knee. The legs of her unadorned cotton drawers were diaphanously thin from much washing and wearing.

Shocked, Cleav turned away, as much for the sake of his own modesty as for her own.

Still stunned by her actions, Cleav struggled to regain his self-control. One minute they were feeding the fish and the next . . . It didn't bear close scrutiny.

How could he have . . . It was impossible. A gentleman did not sprawl on the ground with a young woman. And young women did not throw themselves into the arms of a gentleman they hardly knew. What was this woman up to?

The memory came back in a rush. *You wanna marry me?* Good God, did this little hill girl intend to seduce him?

As his pulse finally returned to normal and his breathing quieted, so did his thoughts. The young woman was obviously too innocent and unsophisticated to formulate such a plan. Cleav reminded himself that in indelicate situations—and this was as indelicate as anything Cleav could recall in recent memory—it was *always* the gentleman at fault.

With that in mind he turned to Esme, but his apology died on his lips.

Esme was standing before him, looking proud, controlled, and not even the slightest bit put out by the impropriety that she had just suffered. "Cleavis Rhy," she said, her voice strong, "I'm really sorry about that. Truth to tell, it's the first time I ever kissed anybody."

If a blush stained her cheek, it appeared more a fear of a loss of her pride than her virtue.

"I'm a quick learner," she told him. "I suspect if you give me another chance, well, I can be kissing better than most any girl before you know it."

He stood silent and staring. No experience in his life with women had prepared him for Esmeralda Crabb. How could he react as a gentleman if she knew nothing of the behavior of a lady?

Esme took an eager step toward him. One step was enough.

He held up one hand as if to ward her off, as if to say stay away from me, Esme Crabb.

But of course, staying away was not part of her plan.

4

The sweet morning call of doves was joined by the splash of warm water filling the washbasin in the south bedroom of Rhy's big white house. It was still too dark to shave. Finding a match, Cleav lit the coal-oil lamp beside the dresser, which brought a warm orange glow to the silver light of dawn.

Carefully opening the tin of Fulton Brothers Fine Shaving Soap, he dipped a pinch into the mug and vigorously stirred it with his brush. Leaning forward, he examined the thick blanket of dark prickles that had appeared on his cheeks and chin. Yawning, he bent his head over the basin and splashed the water over his whiskers. With brisk, swirling strokes he painted the white lather like a crown mask on his lower face.

When the soap was distributed to his satisfaction, Cleav opened his razor and casually stropped it against the long piece of thick brown leather that hung next to the mirror. Testing the edge of it with the end of his thumb, he determined it sharp enough. He leaned toward the mirror again, holding his flesh taut at the earlobe, and began the first long stroke down the jawline.

His mind was blank. Or at least it was as blank as a man's mind ever gets. The day stretched out before him in the vaguest terms, the chores, the store, the fish. Somewhere in the distance a rooster crowed, adding to the serenade of wild birds that stirred along the fish ponds in search of breakfast.

From the corner of his eye he saw a movement outside the window. "Damn!" He flinched as he nicked himself.

She was back again.

In the gray light of the Tennessee dawn, Esme Crabb stood down by the sycamore tree gazing up at Cleav's window.

His first thought was to douse the light. The young woman could undoubtedly see right into the room, and he stood shirtless, his suspenderless pants hanging loosely at his waist. But he stayed his hand. If she saw something she shouldn't see, then she could damn well avert her eyes.

In the past few days Cleav had already learned that Miss Esme Crabb was a good deal like gnats in the springtime, a constant annoyance, difficult to avoid.

Leaning once more toward the mirror, Cleav continued his shaving, albeit somewhat self-consciously. He could feel her eyes on him.

"This nonsense has to stop!" he declared aloud as he rinsed a line of lather and whiskers in the water.

Yesterday she had actually been waiting for him on the path when he came back from the privy!

"Nice morning," she'd said conversationally. As if she had a perfect right to be on his privy path at sunup!

Esme Crabb apparently thought she had a perfect right to act however she pleased, modesty and convention be damned.

It had started the day after that unfortunate encounter by the brooding pond. He had hoped that upon further reflection, she would be scared off, but first thing the next morning she showed up at the store as bold as brass.

"Just came for some of those peach preserves," she told him, sashaying to the back of the store with the provocative loose-hipped walk that she'd affected of late.

He'd tried not to watch her as she fixed herself a cracker with jelly. When she then seated herself by the stove facing him, he had no choice but to look away.

She'd leave in a minute, he'd promised himself. But he'd been wrong. That young woman had stayed virtually the whole day. She was sitting in his chair, munching on his food, visiting with his customers, and every so often, when they were alone, edging up her skirts to adjust those ragged stockings of hers, and although slightly less noticeably than that first time, he'd gotten several good glimpses of her shapely calves and ankles.

It was beyond all human understanding.

If that had been the last of it, maybe he could have just laughed it off. But night after night she stood on the hill and longingly watched him tend the fish. She followed him at a distance wherever he went. And now she even peeped at him in his own house!

Washing off the last of his shaving soap, Cleav determined that he would have it out with her today. What in the name of heaven was she up to anyway?

The memory of those words, *"You wanna marry me?"*, continued to haunt him. It was just a foolish crush, he assured himself. Surely the young woman was not so ignorant that she didn't realize how unsuited she was to be his wife.

Wiping his face and head with a clean white towel, Cleav made a quick perusal of his features. Maybe the girl really did fancy herself in love with him.

Running a comb through the damp brown tangles on his head, he wondered how he appeared to her. She seemed very young, and he had never noticed her in the store until a few days before. Maybe he was the first man she'd taken notice of.

Feminine sensibilities were strange and irrational. He'd heard stories about young women who placed their affections on poets and actors, men with whom there was no possibility of reciprocation. Perhaps her sudden preoccupation with him was a similar species of feminine hysteria. Whatever, it was deuced disconcerting.

Esme stood near the edge of the front path to the big white house. A little shiver ran through her as the north wind blew through the thin material of her coat. Winter was not quite gone. But now, staring at the big white house that belonged to Cleavis Rhy, she was warmed by thoughts of her future.

It should be blue, she thought to herself as she eyed the stately two-story edifice sitting in the little gap between the mountains. Vader had a shortage of sky, Esme thought, so the house should be blue, like a piece of heaven brought down to earth.

Her imagination conjured the sight of the big blue house trimmed in white like summer clouds. She could almost see Pa sitting in a slat-back chair on that wide wraparound porch. He'd be playing the fiddle: a soft and sweet tune. The twins would be sitting in the swing, of course, in matching dresses of white lawn. They'd make a sight so pretty no man could resist. And herself . . . Somehow she could not quite place herself in the picture. She'd be wherever Cleav was.

Leaning tiredly against the sturdy sycamore, she strained her eyes to make out Cleav's form through the window. He was washing up, she suspected, and he'd notice her soon if he hadn't already.

In the past week she'd learned a lot about Cleavis Rhy.

Things that, Esme was sure, a young wife should know about a man if she was hoping to help him. The first thing she'd learned was that he worked hard. He was up every day before dawn and started up his own fire in the kitchen. He took care of the chores and had the store open by six o'clock. Except for an hour or so in the afternoon when he went to the ponds, he worked stocking, helping customers, or doing paperwork until six in the evening. The second thing she'd learned was that he didn't seem to have enough company. After supper, with his mother, he'd sit alone in the back parlor reading until way into the night. Esme knew that for sure, since she'd sat and watched him read the previous evening.

"Where in tarnation have you been!" her father had hollered at her when she'd finally returned home near midnight.

"I been down the mountain, Pa," she told him with a tired sigh. "Don't worry about me, I told you, I'm going to be out and about for a while."

"You told me you was going courting," her fath. corrected angrily. "What kind of man keeps you out half the night and then don't show up here talking marriage proposal?"

Esme had rubbed her head and yawned tiredly. "He didn't keep me out," she clarified. "I kept myself out."

Yohan eyed her curiously. "A-doing what? Is that more than a father can ask?"

"Just watching him, Pa," Esme replied. "I just follow him around and watch him."

"Whatever for?"

"So I'll know him," she answered easily. Then she added, "And so he'll get used to seeing me around. He needs to get the idea to marry up with me. He ain't gonna get it if I ain't standing around getting his attention."

Her father had shaken his head in apparent defeat. "It sure ain't the way we was courting in my day."

Standing before Cleav's house this morning, Esme was pretty sure it wasn't the way they did courting now, either. But she didn't have any other ideas.

The front door opened and Cleav stepped across the threshold. His necktie was neatly knotted at his neck, and his coat was crisp, clean, and without wrinkles; he looked like the perfect man of business, as recognizable in Vader as in Knoxville or Richmond.

Preparing to follow him at a comfortable distance, Esme's eyes widened with concern as he headed straight toward her.

Since the afternoon by the pond she'd purposely kept her distance. Catching a husband was a lot like catching a chicken for Sunday dinner, she figured. Too quick a move would startle and scatter. That wonderful, dizzying, heaven-on-earth kiss they'd shared had been too quick a move. There was no way that she could take it back, and truth to tell, she would not want to if she could. Those few fleeting moments, enveloped in the warmth and feel of him, were relived nightly in her dreams. But he wanted her to stay away. So she had, far enough to let him lower his guard, but close enough to stay in his mind.

Now he walked straight toward her, his face as stern and sour as a preacher at a barn dance. "I'd like a word with you, Miss Crabb," Cleav said as he reached her side.

"I told you, you can call me Esme," she answered, deliberately making her smile bright and welcome.

He raised a critical eyebrow but didn't choose to argue. "Come along, Esme," he replied. "You can walk with me to the store."

Turning in that direction, Esme hurried her step alongside his. *She was walking with him!* The words sang through Esme's veins. He had considerably shortened his stride to match hers, though he kept his eyes straight ahead. But Esme could see the thoughtful expression on his face.

He was tall and stately beside her. And he smelled so good. It had never occurred to her that a man could smell so good. Pa certainly didn't.

She'd never walked with a man before, but walking with Cleavis Rhy was something that she wanted to do. She wished he'd take her arm, the way the courting couples and young marrieds walked from church. He didn't offer it, and Esme didn't have quite enough pluck to reach over and take it.

Cleav looked down at the woman's face, so eagerly turned up toward his. It was a comely face, handsome perhaps, but not truly pretty. Still, it had a great deal of appeal. And there was an interesting sparkle of intelligence behind those muddy blue eyes.

"I'd like to know what this is all about." His tone was excessively patient.

"What's what all about?"

He glanced down at her, a spark of annoyance clearly visible in his eyes. As she watched, he tamped it down, and after taking a deep breath, he continued with renewed composure.

"Miss Crabb, I realize that you are quite young and undoubtedly do not comprehend the social ramifications of your current course of actions."

Esme's smile brightened and her eyes widened in delight. "When you talk all pretty like that, Cleavis, why it pure-d sounds like a poem or some such."

His expression was stunned and confused. Thoughtfully he wet his lips. "I apologize," he said simply.

"Apologize?" Esme questioned with some confusion. "Well, whyever for?"

Cleav cleared his throat and raised his chin slightly and with intent. "The purpose of communication, Miss Esme, is to make oneself understood, not to entertain with flowery phrases."

A cheerful little giggle escaped her. "Oh, I understood you just fine," she assured him. "But I do love to hear that prissy talk."

"Prissy?" The word exploded from him like an expletive.

"Well, I didn't mean prissy, exactly." Esme immediately realized her mistake.

"You think I talk *prissy*?" His eyes were wide with horror.

"I ain't saying that you *are* prissy—"

"Why, thank you very much, Miss Crabb. I can assure you I will cherish your observation eternally."

They reached the porch of the store, and Esme stopped. Cleav stepped heavily toward the door and then turned back toward her.

"Let me speak plainly, Miss Crabb. And I hope this is not too *prissy* for you." His pale blue eyes flashed with fire. "Keep your snooping, spying eyes away from my door and your long, skinny legs out of my sight!"

Cleav jerked open the door of the store, walked inside, and slammed it behind him with a crash that startled the chickens peacefully roosting across the road.

Esme stood staring at the doorway for a minute, her brow wrinkled in concern. Slowly she smiled in satisfaction. With a burst of confidence she whispered to herself, "They may be long and skinny, but it's *my* legs you've been thinking about."

Burnt into the heavy slab of pine out in front of the town's largest white clapboard building were the words: "The First Free Will Baptist Church of Vader, Tennessee." Walking toward the church beside her father, with her sisters lagging behind, Esme smiled over the sign's pretense. It was not just the *first* Free Will Baptist Church of Vader, Tennessee. Truth to tell, it was the only church of any kind in this part of the mountains.

Esme had been attending every Sunday since the month she was born. And this Sunday, like every other, the Crabb family arrived late. The twins just couldn't seem to manage to get ready on time. Or maybe they liked making an entrance. Usually Esme didn't mind. She liked avoiding the preservice gossip of dresses and beaux. But this morning she'd wanted to be there early. She'd wanted to watch Cleav. To find out what his Sunday mornings were like.

"We're a family and we'll attend as a family," her father had said firmly when she'd asked to go on ahead. She didn't mean to defy Pa, and he already didn't approve of her courting methods. She didn't want to give him a reason to interfere with her plans.

As they approached the door to the church, the sweet blend of voices raised in song drifted out to them. Pa opened the door and headed inside first, leading the way. Half the congregation turned to look at the sound of the door opening. The other half turned when Yo, an eager singer and lover of music, immediately added his strong baritone to the raised voices.

> "I'm in the glory land way,
> I'm in the glory land way.
> Heaven is near and the way groweth clear,
> For I'm in the glory land way."

Esme felt her cheeks brighten as she felt the perusal of the sixty-some-odd people congregated in the little church. Following her father, who was now clapping in time with the rousing hymn, Esme found a seat in the very back pew of the church. The Crabbs always sat at the back.

As soon as she was seated, Esme looked straight ahead to

Brother Oswald. The red-faced, balding man stood behind the pulpit, his arm swinging rhythmically, encouraging the congregation in song. Esme didn't have much of a singing voice, not like Pa and the twins. But she managed to quietly move her lips to the words, giving the appearance of participating, as she listened to the twins' harmonious altos and her father's boisterous baritone.

The church was a straight square building, only one room with a raised platform across the front. The piano sat on the left, directly against the stage. When the twins were little, they had called it the "yellow church" because the walls were clear varnished knotty pine, and the white pine and spruce furnishings all appeared amazingly yellow when seen in the sunlight coming through the cheap borate glass windows.

As the last strains of song died away, Brother Oswald took the seat left of the raised platform, and Reverend Tewksbury, who had been seated at the right, took his place behind the pulpit. "Let us pray!" the man's voice boomed across the sanctuary as if the congregation were hard of hearing.

Esme bent her head piously and for a couple of moments gave her own silent prayer. Then stealthily she raised her head just enough to glance across the room.

Cleavis sat in his usual seat, second pew on the left, next to his mother. From the back Esme could see the fine material of his Sunday dress suit. His dark brown hair was neatly trimmed at the nape of his neck. Beside him his mother was fashionably gowned in a black silk with a smart little hat tied neatly under her chin. Mrs. Rhy always dressed better than any woman in town. And not even the preacher had a store-bought dress coat as fine as Cleav's.

Unexpectedly her gaze continued past Cleavis to the young woman seated primly on the piano bench. Sophrona Tewksbury had removed her tiny little white bonnet and placed it beside her. Her dark, flame-colored hair was beautifully coiffed. Redheads look pasty and freckle too much, Esme silently reminded herself, though the pianist's fashionable hourglass figure was undoubtedly much admired by every gentleman of the congregation. Assessing the young woman's rigidly straight back, Esme was sure that Sophrona's waist must be no less than a foot and a half smaller than her bodice and hips!

"Only cows have bigger teats," Esme reminded herself unkindly. "And her backside is half bustle if I don't miss my guess!"

However the beautiful plum brocade and satin gown she wore was not so easily waved away. Fine materials and Sophrona's skill as a seamstress enhanced her abundant assets.

Esme lowered her head again and studied the worn gray serge that covered her lap and limbs. She ran a hand along the material, testing its strength. There was little serviceability left in the fabric. And it hadn't helped that she'd worn this, her best dress, nearly every day since her decision to court Cleavis.

Clothes had never been an important item for Esme, and when dress material or hand-me-downs turned up at the house, she just naturally gave them to the twins. The two beauties loved pretty things, and a dress made for one fit perfectly enough to share with the other. Usually this pleased the economically minded Esme. Glancing over at her sisters today, one dressed in pink-dotted calico and the other in blue gingham, Esme wished that she'd thought of having something pretty for herself.

The "amen" was shouted and heads were raised. Esme couldn't keep her glance from seeking Cleav. She caught his eye and smiled sweetly. With an appalled expression he immediately turned his attention to the preacher.

Brother Oswald led another hymn and Esme kept her

attention focused intently on Cleav. This time he never so much as twitched in her direction, but he knew Esme was looking at him, she decided. That was the only explanation for the bright red hue that crept down his neck. Esme hoped he was thinking about her skinny legs at that exact moment.

Reverend Tewksbury again walked to the pulpit and this time both Brother Oswald and Miss Sophrona moved to take seats in the congregation with their families.

The preacher waited. He stood, hands placed firmly on the sides of the lectern, taking stock of his congregation. Apparently, he liked what he saw, for he was smiling broadly.

Suddenly, startling the congregation, he boomed, "David was beloved of God!"

"Amen." The chorus of agreement came from several corners of the house.

"David was a man after God's own heart, the Bible tells us. Shouldn't we be striving after God's own heart?"

With more "amens" Esme's mind began to wander. Her gaze fixed on Cleavis Rhy's broad shoulders. Vaguely she heard the Reverend Tewksbury giving a quick reminder of the rise of David from shepherd to king. She knew the story well, so she allowed herself the luxury of inattention.

She decided that so far her plan was working well. Cleav had her in his thoughts quite often. He'd even been looking at her in church. For her next move she decided that she should make herself invaluable to Cleav. He worked too hard. A man of business needed help in the store, and a wife would be expected to do her share. Over the past days Esme had watched and learned in her hours of leisure at the General Merchandise. Next week she would show off her quick study and her willingness to help.

It was only when the preacher began reading from the Psalms that Esme's attention turned from Cleav's handsome profile to the pulpit before her.

" 'For he shall deliver the needy when he crieth; the poor, also, and him that hath no helper.' "

Esme felt, rather than saw, the covert glances that turned her way.

"He shall spare the poor and needy, that's what David tells us," Reverend Tewksbury told the crowd. "And that is just what the women of our Ladies' Auxiliary have decided to do."

A pleased murmur went through the congregation, and several of the prominent members of the Ladies' Auxiliary modestly shook their heads at the unspoken compliment. Esme saw Pearly Beachum reach across the aisle to take Miss Sophrona's hand, giving it a grateful and appreciative squeeze.

"Oh, no," Esme breathed the prayer desperately through her lips. "Not here! Not now! Oh, please not today!"

The preacher was beaming broadly now.

"Yohan, can you and your girls come up to the front," he asked with a beckoning gesture.

Pa rose to his feet, obviously surprised but delighted. The twins were blushing and giggling at the attention.

Esme thought she might be ill.

"Come on, girlies," Yo said to them, loud enough for the whole congregation to hear. "Looks like the preacher's found a way to make Christmas come in the springtime."

The congregation chuckled good-naturedly. Esme, following trancelike, walked with her family to the front of the church. She forced herself to turn and face the crowd when she reached the preacher, but she kept her eyes steadfastly set against the knotty pine wall on the left side of the church.

"Amens" were being spoken all around. Clearly the congregation was delighted at this evidence of their own goodness.

Yohan was expansive as he shook the preacher's hand

and then stepped forward to clasp the hands of the deacons in the front row.

"Lord knows," he told the crowd jokingly. "If I'd imagined something like this, I'd a put on my better shirt."

His humor brought out a titter. But the room quieted as Reverend Tewksbury cleared his throat, signaling a more serious turn of events. The preacher waited, drawing out the drama of the moment. The seconds that ticked by seemed like hours.

Esme quickly glanced at her sisters. The pretty twins had locked arms and were blushing and giggling behind their hands. Looking past them, she saw her father, who continued smiling like the village idiot.

Despite the bombardment of feeling that pounded in her brain and into her heart, Esme raised her chin. With deliberate calmness she stared sightlessly before her.

I'm smart and strong and as good as any of them! she declared silently. No one can shame me but myself.

Bending down behind the piano, the preacher pulled out a big three-bushel basket and held it up before the crowd.

"Looky-here what we got, brothers and sisters," he said with obvious pride.

The large basket was filled to the brim, and the sweat popped out on the preacher's forehead with the strain of lifting it. Peeking out the top was a great, big, sweet-smelling smoked ham.

"Look what the good ladies have come up with for you, Brother Yo," the preacher said. "Here's a baker's dozen of jars of the finest fruits and vegetables our ladies can put by."

He held up a couple of jars to show the congregation.

The members clapped with enthusiasm.

"And here's a twenty-pound sack of flour. And soap— heaven knows we can all use our share of that," the preacher continued with a big smile and a playful poke at Yo's ribs.

"Looks to be some fine yard goods in here, girls." He addressed this comment to the giggling twins, who were now hiding their pretty pink faces.

"And there's a couple of hams and a slab of bacon to get you through till spring comes down."

"Amen!" Yo said gratefully, thanking the congregation as the preacher handed him the basket.

"Brother Yo," the reverend began. "David said that the Lord upholdeth all that fall and raiseth up all those that be bowed down."

Yohan smiled broadly at first the pastor and then the congregation.

"I suspect," the preacher continued, "that there is none in our community, none in our church, so bowed down as you and your little girls."

Murmurs of agreement were churchwide.

"This late in the winter, Brother Yo, the ladies thought you-all'd be low on vittles. David tells us that the Lord givest them in due season. So this ham and the rest is yours."

Resounding "amens" and even a couple of "hallelujahs" were heard as the Crabb family stood in the front of the church publicly and subserviently accepting the charity of the congregation.

Esme struggled to keep her eyes unfocused, gazing sightlessly over the heads of the people so willingly doing their Christian duty.

Unerringly, however, her glance was drawn from its secret refuge to a pair of blue eyes on the left side, second pew.

Cleavis Rhy was looking straight at her. What she saw in his face was understanding.

5

"I declare it feels like spring to me!" Reverend Tewksbury announced conversationally.

"Trees are beginning to bud," Cleav admitted. "I hope a late frost isn't going to disappoint us all."

The women quietly added their own agreement to the thought.

The afternoon sun warmed the wide hardwood porch that so gracefully adorned the big white house. These five well-fed, well-clothed citizens of Vader, Tennessee, sat idly on the day of rest passing the time in pleasant conversation.

Reverend Tewksbury was a short, round little man, nearly as wide as he was tall. His sparse hair was a mix of bright carrot and glistening silver. He had an easy smile and sparkling green eyes that could be warm as June or freeze a body in place when he got wound up on hellfire and damnation.

"I truly enjoyed your sermon today, Pastor," Eula Rhy said as she rocked contentedly in her cane-seat chair.

"Indeed, the reverend was in his best form," Mrs. Tewksbury agreed. Although Mrs. Tewksbury nearly matched her husband in height, she retained a youthful figure. Her round face was flat as a pie plate, her nose only a minor protrusion. She was not at all a handsome woman, but she carried herself with dignity and assurance. The small, frequently blunt woman was never hesitant to proclaim herself as the power behind the man.

"When Reverend Tewksbury gets wound up, it pure stirs the heart," Eula Rhy declared.

Cleav nodded absently but refrained from comment. Seated on the slatted porch swing, he languidly stretched his long legs before him. There was something intrinsically placid about a quiet Sunday afternoon spent quietly at your sweetheart's side. Occasionally he would allow his glance to slide across to Sophrona. Adorned so attractively in her Sunday best, Cleav couldn't help but imagine her as the perfect choice for Mrs. M. C. Rhy, Jr.

She was perfect: so young, pretty, and blushing with innocence, the faultless adornment of a civilized gentleman. *His* faultless adornment.

She cast him a shy glance, and he returned it with a warm and welcoming smile. Encouragingly he reached over to pat her tiny pale hand. She looked up quickly, wide-eyed and blushing, to see if her father had noticed.

Reverend Tewksbury was totally wrapped up in a rather long-winded explanation of his choice of verses for the service and hadn't noticed a thing.

Cleav saw Sophrona's shoulders visibly relax. For her sake he clasped his hands casually against his stomach.

"Well, anyway," Mrs. Rhy assured the reverend, "I think the Crabbs were very pleased with the basket, and a good deal luckier than they deserved."

"Yo Crabb has always been a faithful member of the church," Mrs. Tewksbury said. "Although I could never approve of his laziness, I think of him as just another burden that the congregation must assume."

The three elders nodded in agreement.

"The Crabb family is Vader, Tennessee's cross to bear," the pastor declared. "They can't take care of their own selves, and heaven knows, nobody else will."

Sophrona's sweet singsong voice piped in. "'Wealth maketh many friends; but the poor is separated from his neighbor.'"

Mrs. Rhy and Sophrona's parents smiled proudly at the pretty young woman in the swing.

"How correct you are, my dear," the reverend said.

"And how lucky," Cleav added.

"Lucky?" Mrs. Tewksbury eyed the young man curiously. "Whatever do you mean, Mr. Rhy?"

Cleav had gone cold still when the conversation had turned to the Crabbs. In his memory he could still see Esme, her chin up high . . . daring . . . yes, daring the congregation to try to look down on her.

"I was just thinking of Miss Esme," Cleav said with studied nonchalance. He saw the preacher's eyebrow raise.

"I couldn't help but notice," he explained with a casual glance toward Sophrona, "how the gift seemed almost a blow to Miss Esme's pride."

"Pride!" Eula Rhy scoffed. "There never was a Crabb with a lick of pride," she declared, looking to Mrs. Tewksbury, who gave her an answering of agreement. "If she was thinking herself too good for our charity, well, she should have said so, and we'd have given it to someone deserving!"

"That's right," the preacher added. "Pride and poverty don't mix. That girl is looking for trouble, I hear."

"Just like those useless twin sisters of hers," Mrs. Tewksbury agreed.

"Trouble? What kind of trouble could involve Miss Esme?" Cleav asked, genuinely worried.

Mrs. Tewksbury made a tutting sound and looked gravely

at Eula Rhy. The preacher was flushed with embarrassment and silence reigned for a full minute or longer.

"Sophrona honey," Mrs. Tewksbury said finally. "Why don't you step into Mrs. Rhy's house and check your hair in the vanity. I swear the breeze has nearly swept you away!" This last Mrs. Tewksbury added with a cheery laugh. It fell so false that discomfort was universally felt.

Sophrona dutifully rose from the swing and with formal politeness excused herself. Cleav watched her go warily as he found all three pairs of eyes focused sternly on himself.

"Cleav," his mother began. "Mrs. Tewksbury tells me that there has been talk."

"Talk?" Cleav shifted uncomfortably, folding his arms across his chest.

"Folks are saying that Esme Crabb has been seen with you every day for the last week."

Cleav stared dumbstruck. A hasty denial stuck in his throat, and he choked slightly. Of the three the preacher appeared the most sympathetic. Cleav, therefore, directed the reply to him. "Miss Esme may have been seen *near* me," he said distinctly, "but she has not been seen *with* me, I can assure you."

The pastor nodded, willing to let him split hairs. "The fact remains she has been spending a good deal of time in your vicinity."

Cleav shrugged with feigned casualness. "I have no control over where Miss Crabb chooses to spend her time."

The preacher pulled thoughtfully at the scruff of his chin.

Eula Rhy sighed loudly in exasperation. "What in heaven's name is she following you around for?" his mother asked, refusing to couch the question in more politely vague terms.

"She and her sisters are interested in anything in trousers," Mrs. Tewksbury said firmly.

"Now, that's unfair, Mabel," the reverend corrected his

wife. "The twins never seem to seek the attention of the boys, the boys are just drawn to them like flies to honey."

"Well, that's not true of this one," she declared. "She's never had a beau at all. Now all of a sudden she's making herself Mr. Rhy's shadow."

"Gossip," Cleav said bluntly. "You shouldn't waste a minute's time on such."

The preacher gave a slight inclination of the head. "If it were just old Pearly Beachum wagging her tongue, I would have let it go in one ear and out the other. That dear old lady has nothing to do but mind other people's business."

The ladies nodded in agreement.

"But I've heard it from several people not prone to nosiness," he continued. "And truth to tell, this morning I saw it myself. That girl's eyes fairly bore a hole in your back through half the sermon."

Cleav choked slightly, trying to clear the embarrassment from his throat.

"What is she up to?" Eula asked.

"I'm not sure, Mother," Cleav replied. "She seems . . . well, she seems interested in my life. The store, the fish . . . she—"

"The fish?" Mrs. Rhy fairly cackled at that. "No doubt she's thinking to try a pole in one of those pools when you're not looking!"

Cleav's cheeks puffed out in anger. His first thought was to defend her. Esme *was* interested in the fish, and she was a lot less likely to "try a pole in one of those pools" than the people sitting across the porch from him.

What could he tell them? That the young woman in question had openly expressed a desire to marry him? Maybe a week ago he could have told them that, and they could have all had a superior little laugh about the foolish mountain girl. But not now, not after today. When he'd seen her in church, so brave, so unbowed, he'd felt a keen admiration. He understood what she felt. He'd felt it, too. Not for the life of him would he do anything to bring her low. Pride might *not* go with poverty, but it set well on Esme Crabb.

He kept those thoughts to himself and tried another tack. "I think Miss Esme finds me a curiosity. A sort of entertainment, I suppose."

The reverend was momentarily stunned by the statement. Having seen his share of the evil in men, he immediately thought the worst. "What kind of *entertainment* are you up to, young man?" The pastor's voice was stern for the first time.

Cleav was undaunted. In fact, he felt on surer ground now. He was telling the absolute truth, just not *all* of it.

"I think she's entertained by civility and politeness."

The preacher's look was skeptical.

"She told me she loves to hear me talk 'prissy.'"

A momentary silence followed. Then Reverend Tewksbury roared with laughter. "Prissy?" he asked, throwing his head back, laughing. "She actually called you prissy to your face?"

"She didn't say *I* was prissy," he stated firmly. "She thought my manner of speech prissy."

Slapping his thigh with his hand, the reverend actually hooted. "Prissy!" He could barely get the word out. The older man's face was florid, and his eyes had completely disappeared in waves of grinning wrinkles.

The preacher continued to laugh. And laugh. Cleav watched him cackle with growing annoyance.

"There is nothing wrong with Mr. Rhy's speech," Mrs. Tewksbury said, noticing Cleav's disgruntled visage and clearly confused at her husband's sense of humor.

"Of course not," Eula Rhy agreed. "He learned to talk that way in that school in Knoxville. That's just the way a gentleman talks. It isn't really prissy, it just sounds that way."

His mother's feeble defense exasperated Cleav further. Somehow he'd managed to make himself the butt of his own joke, and for the life of him, he couldn't imagine how it had happened.

Well, of course he knew what had happened. Esme Crabb had happened. That female was enough to give a man the hives. She'd been following him around like a bad reputation for a week. Throwing herself at him like a spinster going for the bridal bouquet, interfering in his work, and exposing him to idle talk around town. Now, finally, when she was nowhere to be seen, he found himself in the awkward situation of defending himself—and her.

"I'm delighted that I'm equally as entertaining to you, Reverend," Cleav said with a discernable edge to his voice.

Reverend Tewksbury might have continued laughing forever but for his wife's timely jab in the ribs. The Rhys were, after all, the most well-to-do family in Vader, and Mrs. Tewksbury had hopes for a match with Cleavis and her daughter.

"Sorry," the preacher told him after a pained grunt and a deadly look from his wife. He tried, without a lot of success, to wipe away his wide grin.

"Now, Cleav," Reverend Tewksbury began, forcing himself into more clergylike behavior, "I'm sure that it would be a great comfort to your mother if you would just simply tell her that all this talk among the congregation is just that, talk. Just tell us honestly that nothing untoward has occurred between you and that pitiful Crabb girl."

Cleav opened his mouth to do just that.

Unbidden, memories assailed him. Esme's long, slim leg, its soft skin so indecently bared in broad daylight in his store. The sweet, clean smell of her as she sat in his shadow beside the pond. The wild, eager touch of her lips against his own. And the hot, urgent surge of his body pressed so intimately against hers.

As he sat open-mouthed and silent, a damning flush spread across his face and neck.

The bacon popped and sizzled in the pan as Esme poured the cold cooked beans in on top of the grease.

"I don't know why we have to eat bacon beans when we've got two hams to serve," Adelaide complained.

"Because I'm the one that's cooking!" Esme replied with more than a little snap to her tone. "When you do the cooking, you can eat what you like!"

"Esme don't wanna waste that good ham on me, Sweetums," Armon Hightower said, reaching out to grab Adelaide's hand and pull her down to his side. Esme spied him giving her sister a familiar squeeze.

The young, good-looking charmer sat on the Crabbs' kitchen bench, one arm around Adelaide and the other around Agrippa. He squeezed the two girls close, causing both to simultaneously snuggle and giggle.

"You see, little pretties, your sister don't care for me at all," he told the twins, his eyes focused jovially on Esme. "I swear if she got the chance, that gal would bake me up a nice fresh ground-glass pie!"

The girls tittered daintily. Agrippa laid her pretty head against Armon's shoulder.

"Esme just don't know you like we do," she told him in a breathy whisper against his ear.

"And she ain't about to, neither," Armon whispered back, just loud enough for Esme to hear. "But truly, Esme," he said, his bright smile near blinding. "I'm enough man for the whole bunch of you. Ain't no call for jealousy among family."

Esme's grip on the spoon tightened, and she was sorely

tempted to turn around and use it to knock some brains into Armon Hightower.

"I know you can't imagine this," Esme told him between clenched teeth. "But I'm not suffering a desperate longing for your company, Armon Hightower."

Armon laughed pleasantly, clearly disbelieving.

"And you'd better watch your hands, mister," she continued sternly. "Pa comes in here, you'll find yourself a married man afore you know what hit you!"

The twins squealed at that and, if humanly possible, actually wiggled closer to the man of their dreams.

Armon paled slightly and actually did readjust the location of his left hand from the fleshy curve of Adelaide's hip to the less dangerous tuck of her waist.

Yo was, of course, not about to come in and take care of his proper responsibility of chaperoning the twins. He was sitting outside, and the sweet sound of the fiddle was drifting through the woods and down the mountain. It was a lively tune today, full of happiness and joy. Pa was still thrilled over the church basket.

"See, Esme-girl," he'd told her on the walk back up the mountain. "The Lord does provide."

"The *Lord* didn't provide this, Pa." Her voice was harsh with criticism. "It's charity from our neighbors."

Pa shook his head. "I know it don't sit well with you, girlie. But it don't just put food on our table. It provides a chance for those good folks to do good works."

Cracking an egg into the beans, Esme sighed in exasperation now as she did then. There was just no talking to Pa. The way she felt—the worthlessness, the shame—he felt no part of that. Maybe that was a good thing. Glancing over at the twins who were cheerfully trading tickles with Armon Hightower, she decided that it apparently didn't bother them, either.

Shuddering, she felt it again. Standing before them all in

her ragged dress was as if she were naked. And Cleav . . . he saw her. He saw her shame. She wondered if he pitied her. A lone tear fell unheeded into the big pot of boiling beans.

A scream of laughter abruptly halted her thoughts, and she looked toward her sisters. Adelaide was actually lying back on the bench screeching with laughter as Armon leaned over ostensibly tickling her ribs. Agrippa had her arms around the young man's chest and had pressed herself tightly against his back, pretending to be protecting her sister.

What immediately caught Esme's attention was the serious heated look in Armon Hightower's eye. The look was not playful, it was dark with passion.

Grabbing up a bucket of water, she poised it threateningly before them.

"Stop that this instant! Or I swear I'll give you something to cool you off in a hurry!"

The action froze immediately. With calm careful movements, as if not wanting to startle Esme into any drastic moves, the three disengaged themselves from their naughty little entanglement.

Esme set the water back in its place with a thud.

"Adelaide, Agrippa, you two sit on this side of the table and behave like young ladies."

The two quietly and without comment followed their younger sister's orders. Esme hurriedly turned back to the beans and gave them a quick stir to keep them from scorching before continuing her tirade. Holding the bean-splattered spoon before her like a weapon, she turned her attention to Hightower.

"Young man, I expect decent behavior in my house," she told him angrily. "If you cain't conduct yourself with propriety, you're going to find yourself real unwelcome around here." Esme's chin was raised stubbornly, and her eyes blazed with fury. Armon Hightower was five years older and twice her size, but he knew a formidable enemy when he saw one.

"I apologize, Miss Esme," he said quietly. "I guess it's this warm spring weather—it's got the sap running, I reckon."

Esme started to make a reply about not letting his sap run around here but thought the better of it.

She turned back to her beans.

"Cornbread's done," she stated with exaggerated calmness. "Best call Pa in to supper."

The meal did not set her in a better frame of mind. Armon turned his considerable charm toward her father. The bright-eyed, smiling young man had Pa laughing and grinning until Esme wanted to reach over and slap him. Armon was clearly looking to get on Yo's good side, and he was probably succeeding! Esme had little taste for her supper. How was she supposed to keep the twins respectable and safe if Pa wouldn't even scare off a no-account like Hightower?

She was more convinced than ever that her plan was the proper course of action. As long as they lived in a cave and were, as the preacher had said today, the most "bowed down" in the community, Esme knew any good-for-nothing male type with an itch in his britches was going to come looking for the twins. There must be some unwritten law that said poor women were fair game, because when fellows went looking to sow wild oats, that's exactly the girls they picked.

In a big blue house with a wraparound porch, menfolk would come courting the twins. They would woo and spark 'em on the porch swing maybe. But they wouldn't be laying 'em on the kitchen bench.

"Mr. Hightower," she said with great formality, "am I to

understand that you are interested in paying call on my sisters?''

Armon glanced quickly at Yo and then the twins.

"Well, sure, Miss Esme, your sisters are a couple of mighty fine gals.''

Esme's words were in as haughty a tone as she could project. "Then I'm sure Pa would agree to allow you to pay call to *one* of them.''

"One?'' Armon amazingly seemed surprised.

"We've always shared everything!'' the twins protested.

"You cannot share a man.'' Esme was adamant.

Staring dumbfounded across the table for a moment, Armon scratched his head thoughtfully.

"Miss Esme, I ain't got the faintest idea of how to choose between these two.''

"But you must choose!'' she insisted.

"Well, he don't have to choose right away,'' Yo said, causing Esme's mouth to open in shock and her eyes to blaze in anger.

"Pa!''

"All I'm saying is a man's got to take his time about these things.'' Pa smiled, giving the twins a wink and Armon a slight nod of approval.

"A man can't call on two women at once!'' Esme would not give on the point.

"That's right, Esme-girl,'' Pa agreed, hoping to make peace. "That why I'm saying he can call on Agrippa on Fridays and Adelaide on Saturdays.''

"What!''

"Just till he's had a chance to make up his mind.''

"Oh, please, Esme, please.'' The twins were bright-eyed with hope.

Even Armon seemed content with the compromise.

"I still don't like it,'' Esme said slowly. "But I suspect it's okay. But listen here, Hightower,'' she said, pointing her finger at him. "If you're coming on Fridays and Saturdays, I don't want to see you around this place any other time. Sunday through Thursday you find yourself elsewhere!"

"Yes ma'am!" The man flashed her a dazzling smile of compliance, and Esme wondered if she'd lost this round after all.

Armon took his leave shortly after supper, much to the whining dismay of the twins. Esme was grateful for the respite. She couldn't imagine how she was going to handle a man like Armon Hightower if he didn't choose to cooperate with her wishes.

As she cleaned up the supper dishes, Esme again thought about the big white (soon to be blue, she hoped) house with the wraparound porch. This morning in church she'd have sworn that she'd never be able to face Cleavis Rhy again. But she really had no choice. She had come to like Cleavis Rhy, maybe even want him for herself, but she *needed* Cleavis Rhy for her family.

The girls were sorting through the charity basket with excited laughter as Esme dried her hands on the dishcloth.

"I'm not going to be around much next week," she announced suddenly to the family. "I'll be spending my time down mountain."

The other three occupants of the room looked at her curiously.

"Agrippa, you're the best cook, so I'll expect you to do your best here in the kitchen. Adelaide, you'll need to go ahead and get that garden turned. Pa, you're going to have to help her."

All three immediately began to protest, but Esme continued. "Starting tomorrow I'm going to be helping Cleavis Rhy in his store, so I'll be leaving before sunup and returning after dark."

"Rhy's hired you to work in his store?" Pa looked nearly stunned with disbelief.

"Well, not exactly," Esme admitted. "But it amounts to that just the same."

"Is this more of your crazed notions about courting a man?" her father asked with a wry grin.

"I'm going to show him what a good helpmate I can be, Pa," Esme explained calmly. "There ain't nothing wrong with that."

"Esme-girl," Yo explained with a sigh of infinite patience. "If he's looking for a good helpmate, I suspect he's found it in little Miss Sophrona. She seems a fine Christian woman and more than fair looking in the bargain."

Esme felt as if he'd slapped her.

"You think she'd make a better wife than me?"

"It ain't a question of better, girlie," he answered softly. "It's a question of more likely. I love you, honey. I wouldn't see you hurt for the world." Reaching across the table, he took his daughter's hand and squeezed it. "I see what you're doing, Esme-girl. You're trying to get a better life. And I'm all for that."

"Not just for me, Pa," Esme hastened to explain. "For all of us."

"All of us are fine, girlie. It's you that cain't be content. You're like your mama, and I loved her, too." He gave her hand a warm, affectionate pat. "This Rhy fellow, he ain't for you. He's so citied, he don't know 'come here' from 'sic 'em.' He'd need to take a compass and a shovel to find his own hind end."

"No, Pa," Esme protested. "He's not like that at all. He's a gentleman and all, that's for sure. But he's got good sense. You know what he's doing in them ponds he built behind the store? He's raising fish. Raising 'em, just like theys chickens or something. He's got fish like setting hens and others like roosters, and a whole pond full of little brooder chicks no bigger than a finger."

Yohan watched his daughter's eyes as she talked. The spark of curiosity and intellect burned so brightly there.

"Trout in the river are getting overfished," Esme explained, "and the temperature of the water ain't always right for 'em. Cleav is growing more to make sure they don't give out completely."

"Cleav, is it?" Her father raised an eyebrow.

"Mr. Rhy, that is." Esme hurriedly corrected herself.

Pa gave her a long, hard look. "You hankering after this Cleavis Rhy, you think?"

Esme felt her cheeks burn with embarrassment. "Yes, Pa," she admitted in a quiet whisper.

"Hallelujah!" Adelaide shouted. Both she and Agrippa came running over to hug their little sister.

Accepting her sisters' affection, Esme still looked back to her father, hoping for approval, help, or hope. Pa only smiled and raised his fiddle to his chin and began plucking out a lively tune.

"She gets the dress," Agrippa said with certainty.

Adelaide nodded with agreement.

"What dress?" Esme asked.

"The prettiest dress you've ever seen in your life," Adelaide told her.

"It was the best thing in the whole basket," Agrippa said.

Pulling out the snowy bundle of white lawn, Agrippa shook the gown out before her. The light summer material was sewn in neat pleats across the bodice and the long skirt billowed to the floor.

"Try it on, Esme," Adelaide insisted. "Try it on right now!"

With more force than help the sisters had quickly dispensed with Esme's worn old serge, and she stood momentarily in the middle of the room, shivering in her threadbare shimmy.

Up and over her head the beautiful gown of store-bought lawn was draped over Esme. Immediately she was uncomfortable.

"What's wrong with this?" she asked her sisters in unpleasant surprise.

Agrippa surveyed her critically.

"Well, it doesn't fit," she told her simply.

The dress was several inches too short, that was clear. But there were other more serious problems.

"It's too tight in the waist," Adelaide said.

"I'm aware of that," Esme replied with a self-deprecating grin. "I can hardly breathe."

"I think we can take it out," Agrippa told her, grasping the rather voluminous folds of material that hung down past the sash.

"Look at all this wasted fabric in the bodice!" she exclaimed to Esme. "With all this a man couldn't tell if you have bosoms or you're hiding a polecat!"

Adelaide laughed along with her sister. "The gal who gave this away must have weaned the triplets."

"It looks awful," Esme stated fatalistically.

"But it's going to look wonderful," Agrippa promised her. "All this extra material means we'll be able to let out the waist and have plenty left to retrim the hemline."

"You're right. I can make it fit me." Esme's voice was hopeful.

"Of course you could," Agrippa agreed. "But you ain't going to."

"What?"

"Adelaide and I sew better than you and you know it. We just don't care for mending much." She glanced toward her twin and met a nod of agreement.

"You go on down to the General Merchandise and help

Mr. Rhy,'' Adelaide told her. ''Between chores we'll get this dress fixed up for you.''

''That's not fair,'' Esme protested.

The fiddle playing in the corner stopped abruptly, and Pa's voice was warm but firm. ''It's the fairest thing that's happened around here in a good long while.''

❧ 6 ❧

Monday morning arrived with a burst of springtime. Tiny green buds dotted the tree branches, patches of bright colors were sprinkled across the hillside, and the bright blue sky overhead heralded good things to come. Up on the mountain the snow was completely forgotten, and where the trees weren't shaded in morning fog, patches of laurel slicks dotted the horizon.

Cleavis Rhy noticed none of this. For him the day was as gray as his own thoughts. Only the fortuitous return of Miss Sophrona from tending her "windswept hair" had saved him from public humiliation yesterday afternoon. And even now it wasn't over. Although nothing was said in the presence of the innocent young woman, both his mother and the Tewksburys continued to look askance at him for the rest of the day.

With that thought clearly in his mind, it was no wonder he did not welcome the sight that greeted him when he arrived at the store.

Esme Crabb, her memorably ragged clothes covered by *his* work apron, was sweeping the store's porch.

"What in heaven's name are you doing?" The question was sharp, distinct, and to the point.

Esme raised her head and offered a bright smile.

"Morning, Mr. Rhy," she answered sweetly. "It's sure gonna be one beautiful day, ain't it?"

Cleav approached the steps woodenly. He'd lost all patience with her crush. He was clearly furious. "I asked what you think you are doing here, young woman, and I want an answer!" Standing on the first step, he was eye to eye with Esme.

Knowing it took two to make a fight, Esme simply decided not to take offense. Leaning gamely against the broom handle she propped under her chin, her eyes were bright with the hint of laughter in her voice.

"Well," she said. "You did say you didn't want me peeping at your house no more. So I come on down to the store. And I figured I might as well get started."

With a gesture Esme indicated the broom in her hand. "This is the first chore of the day, isn't it? First you dust the stock and then you sweep out."

Cleav took a deep breath and reminded himself that it was very impolite to throttle a young lady. "First *I* dust the stock and then *I* sweep out," he said with deliberate calm. "It is *my* store, Miss Crabb."

She gave him a toothy grin. "Now, I told you to just call me Esme."

He set his jaw tightly and his eyes blazed. "Perhaps, Miss Crabb, I don't *want* to call you Esme."

Stepping onto the porch, he reached for the broom, and Esme relinquished it without a word.

"Give me my apron, Miss Crabb," he ordered.

"Sure," she answered, reaching back behind her to release the tie. "But, truth to tell, it looks better on me than it does on you."

A sound came through Cleav's lips that could only be described as a huff.

When Esme handed him the apron, he hurriedly slipped it over his head and crossed the long ties behind him, then tied it neatly in the front. He gestured at her, attempting to shoo his nemesis away as if she were a chicken or a stray cat. Then he commenced sweeping where Esme had left off, purposely looking away from her.

Esme took no offense and casually drifted back toward the door.

"Thanks for taking over for me," she said easily. "I didn't eat this morning and save to graces I'm sure looking forward to a little cracker and jelly."

As she stepped through the door, she hollered back over her shoulder, "Coffee's boiled if you want some."

Cleav stopped stock still and stared at the now-empty doorway in shock. "Coffee's boiled?" he repeated to himself, as if the words were some strange foreign phrase.

Cleaning the remaining dust on the porch with a vengeance, Cleav was finished in less than five minutes. His mind was scurrying in so many directions, he barely noticed the approach of old man Denny.

"Open up a little early this morning?" the man questioned.

Cleav raised his head and stared at the man wordlessly, then turned and walked into the store.

From that very difficult beginning, Cleav saw his day grow increasingly worse.

Esme Crabb was determined to both make herself at home and to be as helpful as possible. While Cleav did his Monday book work and restocked shelves, Esme kept Denny entertained with a chat.

When the old man's checkers partner, Hiram Tyree, showed up, Esme even helped them set up the game on the front porch. "So you can enjoy the day," she told them. "They's yellow violets up on the hill already," she informed the men cheerfully. "Saw 'em myself this morning. Afore you know it, the wildflowers will be across the valley like God's own patch quilt."

The men smiled and laughed with Esme, her warmth and good humor brightening the still-foggy morning.

Cleav, however, felt no such sense of good cheer. The situation was growing very awkward, and he was convinced that if things continued this way, Miss Sophrona would surely hear gossip. He was determined to order Esme out of the store, but the time was never quite right. Customers came and went, making a private conversation impossible. He considered telling her to leave, privacy or no, but he couldn't do it. In his memory he saw her standing so bravely in the church. Her pride far too large for her meager lot in life. That was nothing to him, he quickly reminded himself. Setting his jaw firmly, he swore to himself to set this womanful of trouble out of his life as soon as possible.

Remarkably, he found she was actually quite helpful in the store. Somehow, in a few short days, she'd ferreted out where just about everything in the store could be located. And she was willing, even eager, to help out the customers.

"Since when have you been working here?" Cleav heard Pearly Beachum, the biggest gossip in town, ask her. Cold fear gripped him as he hurried over to them. What would Esme say? Whatever it was, it would be all over town by nightfall.

"I'm just helping out," Esme told the woman with a sweet smile and then whispered to her quietly, "We've run up some debt here in the past," she said in confidence. "Mr. Rhy has been so good to just forgive it, but I want to do what I can to make it right."

Cleav couldn't hear their whispers, and as he reached them, the two women moved apart. Pearly gave him a curious, but not unpleasant, look. Cleav decided that since she hadn't hit him with her parasol, Esme had obviously not said the worst.

As the morning wore on, his anger, which had ridden so strongly on Cleav when he arrived, lessened. Esme was unfailingly pleasant to the customers. He was even amused at the ingenious way she managed to make sales.

When Rog Wicker came in for his weekly supplies as well as a pack of Red Leaf, she spoke up.

"You know, Mr. Wicker, I don't chew myself, but from everything I've ever heard, Carolina Blue is a much superior jaw to that old Red Leaf."

Turning to look at the young woman, Wicker's brow wrinkled in consternation. "Course the Carolina's better," he agreed. "Costs more, too. I'll stick with Red Leaf, thank you."

"Of course." Esme nodded calmly in reply. "A penny saved is a penny earned, true enough." She sighed lightly and then added, "It just seemed to me that a man like yourself, a man who's got his farm all paid for and his children growed and married, a man who's got only one vice—and that merely being partial to a chew of tobacco— well, such a man ought to have the best. Seemed like such a man would deserve as much."

Rog Wicker's eyebrows raised. He stared after Esme for a minute as she wandered toward the canned goods. Cleav gathered the rest of the order.

"What else?" he asked the man finally.

"That's about it," Wicker answered, "total it up." The man reached for his tobacco and held it in his hand for a moment as if weighing it.

"Take this back and give me the Carolina Blue," he said without further explanation.

Cleav was momentarily stunned. Rog Wicker had been chewing Red Leaf since Cleav's daddy had run the store.

Wordlessly exchanging the tobacco, Cleav could barely concentrate on his math as he totaled up the purchase.

As Wicker took his leave, Cleav glanced across the room at Esme. Her grin was as wide as a new moon, and she raised her eyebrows in a bragging salute. The impish behavior was so infectious, Cleav caught himself grinning back. Then fastidiously he straightened his cuffs as he avoided looking at her. But he couldn't quite tamp down the smile that twitched at the corners of his lips.

The day might have taken a solid turn for the better if the next customer had not been Reverend Tewksbury. At his side his daughter Sophrona was clothed in a calico work dress and sunbonnet, and even in this modest outfit the diminutive young woman looked like a princess.

The reverend's smile was welcoming as he walked in but dimmed considerably when he glanced across the room and saw Esme Crabb apparently rearranging the canned goods.

For Esme, things were proceeding according to plan. Cleav was already seeing how much easier his job would be with her at his side. And she was surprised herself at how easily the customers were accepting her.

She'd hated her forced explanation to Pearly Beachum, but that couldn't be helped. She knew the best way to throw a dog off the scent was to give him another bone to chew on.

Now with her unequivocal victory over the tobacco, she was beginning to feel somewhat cocky. Cleav couldn't maintain his stiff behavior forever. He was coming around. A moment ago he'd smiled at her in genuine friendship. It was going to be easier than even she had expected. Her thoughts were strictly positive until she spied Sophrona Tewksbury.

Even if Esme were better wife material, physically the preacher's daughter was everything that Esme was not. And the pretty expanse of bright blue calico was headed straight in her direction.

"Esme! Good morning, what a surprise."

Although only a couple of years separated the two in age, a world of living stood between them. As children, Sophrona had played with the twins, unaware of the difference in their status. As time had passed, however, the concerns of the well-fed, well-tended young woman diverged greatly from the daily struggles of the Crabb family.

Esme, however, had always been aware of the difference. There had been no carefree childhood for her, just as it seemed there would be no careworn adulthood for Sophrona. It would have been natural to feel jealousy, envy, even hatred. But Esme had always liked Sophrona. She couldn't help it. It was hard to make an enemy of someone whose cheerfulness was legend.

"Morning, Sophrona," Esme greeted her. She saw Cleav and the preacher at a distance. Cleav looked as if he'd just taken a big bite of green persimmon.

"That's a real pretty dress you got on," Esme commented honestly. "That blue looks real nice on you."

Sophrona smiled, delighted, and then glanced down at the dress. "Do you think so?" she asked, and then with a guarded glance back to her father she added with a naughty twinkle, " 'Vanity, vanity, all is vanity.' "

Almost against her will Esme found herself smiling back. Sophrona had that way about her. She drew people to her and almost compelled them to enjoy the experience.

"I wanted to thank you for the basket we received," she said calmly, steeling herself to politeness, even as a pain clutched tightly at her. "I gathered from Mrs. Beachum that the idea and much of the gathering was done by you."

Sophrona waved away the gratitude with a pleasant word. "We all wanted to do it," she said easily. " 'A man that hath friends must shew himself friendly,' " she quoted.

Her smile faded slightly, and she glanced to the side warily. She moved closer to Esme. "Follow me," she whispered. With a guarded look behind her, she grasped Esme's arm and led her toward a deserted corner of the store.

"Have you seen the new crepe de chine Mr. Rhy has purchased?" she asked Esme with considerably more volume than was necessary. "I declare that color would be perfect for you."

Walking beside her, Esme gave Sophrona a very puzzled glance. "I could never afford to buy crepe de chine," she whispered, embarrassed.

"I know," Sophrona answered easily. "I just wanted to speak to you alone. Here it is," she began again more loudly.

Opening the cabinet into which were neatly stacked the bolts of sturdy rugged materials, Sophrona pulled out the extra-long remnant of rose crepe de chine that a drummer had thrown in with Cleav's last order.

As the two women reverently ran their hands across the beautiful material, Sophrona spoke. "There's been talk about you and Mr. Rhy."

"Oh?" Esme felt a blush stain her cheek, and she was grateful that Sophrona kept her eyes on the cloth.

"I heard a bit at church yesterday," she admitted. "Everyone was determined not to let me find out what was going on, but I know they're saying you've been seen together."

"I . . ." Esme began but immediately hesitated. Should she explain? Deny? She planned to marry Cleavis Rhy, but perhaps Miss Sophrona did, too.

"In the afternoon we took tea at Mrs. Rhy's home," Sophrona explained as she leaned forward conspiratorially. "They sent me into the house. Mother said that I needed to fix my hair." Sophrona sighed with exasperation. "Sometimes I wonder if they think I am stupid. I did fix my hair, of course," she said, "but I listened at the parlor window."

This quiet avowal was made with such seriousness, it sounded as if she were confessing to murder.

Sophrona raised her eyes to meet Esme's gaze. "I'm not sure exactly what they are accusing you two of," the young woman admitted. "But I want you to know," she said firmly, "I don't believe a word of it."

Taking Esme's hand in her own, Sophrona gave it a warm squeeze.

Cleav was never more grateful to leave the suddenly close confines of the store for the freedom of the fish ponds. When his mother arrived, she had looked even more horrified than the reverend at the sight of Esme Crabb making herself at home.

"Son," the preacher had said quietly as they had watched the two young women admiring a piece of dress goods, "just having her here in the building with you is fodder for the gossips."

"I can't throw her out," Cleav said reasonably. "If the girl doesn't steal or cause trouble, she's got as much right to be in the store as anyone else."

"You think she's not causing trouble?" The preacher looked skeptical.

Cleav couldn't argue with the man about that. In the town's eyes Esme Crabb *was* causing trouble.

"Is that girl addled?" his mother had asked. "She acts like she works here."

"She's trying to help out," Cleav explained hesitantly.

"Help out?" His mother spoke as if the idea horrified her.

"Just ignore her, Mother," Cleav advised. "She'll soon tire of this nonsense."

"I hope she tires of it before she makes us the talk of the town!"

Cleav hoped the same.

As customary, he gathered the fish food from the meat house, deliberately trying to quiet thoughts of Esme Crabb. If he had to put up with her unsettling presence across the room from him all morning, surely he earned the privilege of not thinking of her at all in the afternoon.

Feeding the brood fish, Cleav had just finished with the females and had moved upstream to the pond of smaller, more active males. The boys were swirling excitedly in anticipation of the feast when a movement to the left caught Cleav's attention. No.

Leaning up against the juniper tree, Esme Crabb was bent forward, casually adjusting her stocking.

"Would you stop that!" Cleav's voice cracked through the quiet droning of the bees and distant call of birds to startle Esme.

She jumped, dropping her skirt hastily.

"You scared me!" she complained, placing a hand just below her throat.

"Well, something ought to. You shouldn't be pulling your dress up like that in broad daylight!" Cleav shot back.

"No one's around," Esme said with conviction.

"*I* am around!" Cleav's anger was unmistakable.

"Yeah," Esme said with a naughty grin. "But you've already seen my legs."

Cleav paled. Glancing guiltily toward the surrounding hills, he jumped to his feet and hurried toward her. "Are you out of your mind?" he asked in a furious whisper. "If someone heard you, there is no telling what they would think."

Esme cocked a hip and set a fist obstinately against it. "I know exactly what they'd think," she said. "They'd think you'd already seen my legs, which you have. And I don't believe for a minute that you think they are as skinny as you let on. You liked 'em plenty well enough. You was near drooling like a starving man at a box supper."

Cleav stood speechless before her for a moment. Then he closed his eyes in a silent prayer for patience. "Miss Esme, I am sure that you are as aware as I of the indecency of this conversation."

"It's a private conversation," Esme answered him. "There ain't no use us pretending we don't know what's happening between us."

Cleav took a step backward and then spread his hands in a hasty gesture as if to wipe clean an invisible slate. "There is nothing happening between us, Miss Crabb," he said emphatically. "Absolutely nothing."

He turned from her. Why had he thought this young woman bright? She was proving to be the most thick-headed female he had ever encountered. He would simply walk away from this woman and ignore her completely in the future.

"You call that kiss you gave me nothing?"

Cleav spun around, his mouth opened in shock. "I never kissed you!"

"Did so!" she claimed obstinately. "Right here on this very spot one week ago today! Two people with their mouths together are kissing," Esme said with pretense of grand sophistication. "It makes no difference who starts it."

"It makes a world of difference!" Cleav shot back. "At least, it does to me. You can't just throw yourself against me and claim you've been kissed. Believe me, when I kiss you, you will know it."

"You *are* planning to kiss me then?" Esme was all smiles, obviously delighted.

"No! I never said that!"

"I heard you with my own ears."

"I never stated any such intention."

"You said 'when,' and when means something that's

sure to happen,'' Esme argued with the sound logic of one who usually wins such discussions.

Cleav looked directly into her eyes. ''I plan to see to it that it doesn't.''

''Why?'' Esme asked, genuinely aggrieved.

''Why what?''

''Why do you plan to 'see to it' that you don't kiss me? You want to kiss me but you're holding yourself back?''

His jaw dropped in shock. ''Where do you get these ideas!''

''From the way you look at me.''

''I don't look at you at all!''

''Now, that's a bald-faced lie,'' Esme said unequivocally. ''You watch me every day in the store when I'm tightening my stockings.''

The blush that stained his cheeks was understandable, but she suspected it was caused by fury, not embarrassment. ''Any woman who displays herself in such a wanton fashion can't complain if a man takes a look!''

''I didn't say I was complaining,'' Esme corrected as she walked toward him. ''I like feeling your eyes on me. It makes me go all tender inside, and I feel kind of dangerous.''

''You are dangerous!'' Cleav cursed under his breath.

Esme's reply was a self-satisfied smile.

Turning away from her, Cleav forced himself to continue his work. He felt her presence. She was humming lightly. The cheery tune irritated him further. He would ignore her. It was the only way. He could feel his heart pounding and the blood rushing through his veins as if he'd run a half mile straight up the mountain.

It wasn't as if kissing Esme Crabb was an unthinkable idea. In fact, that very thought had already occurred to him on numerous occasions in the last week. He remembered all too clearly the sweet, clean smell of her hair as she sat so close. And the vivid memory of her shapely, stocking-covered calf held before him almost dared his inspection. If that wasn't disturbing enough, more than one night his sleep had been bedeviled by the hot remembrance of that one shocking moment when the crux of his body had fitted itself so intimately against hers.

Cleav finished feeding the brooders and catwalked between the male and female ponds to the larger, deeper pool on the far side. Here the year-old trout were being fattened. He didn't stop to feed these fish by hand but simply scattered the meat across the top of the water like a farmer sowing seed.

Glancing back, he saw that Esme was still following him like a shadow, and he gave a sigh of disgust.

He wanted her; there was no use in denying that. But a man couldn't always just take what he wanted.

As he watched her navigate the catwalk, the slight breeze pressed her skirt, unencumbered by the usual requisite of a half-dozen petticoats, closely against her long slim legs and thighs.

Momentarily a little devil on Cleav's shoulder whispered, ''Why *not* have her?'' Even the most civilized of gentlemen sowed a share of wild oats before settling down. She made no secret of wanting him, and he was bound by no vows or even promises. It could be mutually beneficial to both of them. A bit of illicit pleasure for him; she might even enjoy it herself, and maybe a small gift when they parted? Then his thoughts took off. Some cash money could sure come in handy for her. Maybe she could buy herself some new clothes or he could help her set herself up in a little business of some kind. He'd already seen she had a good head for it.

That bit of nonsensical thinking riled his conscience. What type of business could a ruined woman set up for herself in this town? he was forced to ask himself angrily. He swore at his own lack of scruples.

Esme Crabb was a decent woman. She had spent her whole life struggling to take care of her family. What she needed was a good, steady, hardworking husband to take care of her. And she would never find one by being the storekeeper's fancy piece.

And it was not as if such an arrangement could be kept secret. If he so much as pinched her fanny, every man, woman, and child in Vader would know it. The two of them were already the talk of the town when nothing had happened at all!

She came up behind him, and he turned to look at her. She wasn't a beauty like Sophrona, but she was pretty in her own way. Her face was suntanned and ordinary, but her features were agreeable. The curves of her bosom and hip were not stunning, but they were distinctly feminine. And her legs . . . a smile twitched at the corner of his mouth. It was a good thing propriety said limbs should be covered, else Miss Esme's legs could cause a riot.

She smiled back at him, so naively, so foolishly full of hope.

Oh, how he wanted to feel those legs wrapped around his waist. Clinging, grasping, begging for pleasure from his body. A man would sacrifice a lot for that. But not everything. Cleav desired her. That was certain. He even liked her, or he would if she weren't always in his hair. But he didn't desire to marry her.

And a gentleman would protect a lady's virtue, even when the lady wasn't so keen on protecting it herself.

"You want to feed the fish?" he asked finally. His smile was the warmest and most welcoming Esme had seen from him in days. Her eyes widened with delight, and a blush reddened her cheeks. Clearly she recalled her last opportunity at the task with pleasure. "Yes, I'd like that very much." Her words were an uncharacteristically gentle whisper.

The sweet sincerity of her words nearly made Cleav discard his current plan to simply make her a friend and settle for the former, less savory option. But determinedly he hardened his heart.

"Good," he answered and handed her the bucket. "Just scatter the meat on the top of the water, and the fish will get it."

At her startled expression he continued. "The table trout aren't tame enough to hand-feed. And besides, you wouldn't want to get to know somebody you might be cutting up for the frying skillet." He looked up at the sun. "There's a world of things I need to be doing at the store."

"But—" Esme's vague protest went ignored.

"Be sure to rinse the bucket good and then carry all of the equipment back to the meat house," he said as he turned to go.

Words deserted her completely, and she could only stare open-mouthed at him as he walked away.

"Oh," he called over his shoulder before he was out of range. "If you're planning to come back inside when you're finished, you be sure to wash yourself up real good. I don't want you smelling up my store with the stink of fish."

7

Esmeralda Crabb eased her way past the mountain hobble-bush and rhododendron to the still, small pool held within the ancient roots of a towering hemlock. Careful to hold her dress back from the water, she leaned over to assess herself. She had no glass with which to judge herself, only the vague reflection of the cool water to act as a mirror.

Quietly in the silence of the late Saturday afternoon she studied herself in her new dress. Then slowly a tiny tear slipped out of the side of her eye. "Save to graces, I'm beautiful," she whispered softly to the forest around.

Wiping the tear away, a smile was next. A big smile. And then a laugh. With a hurried, happy step she made her way back to the path, where she stopped to twirl around giddily. The new white dress swirled about her, making a startling contrast to the sprouting green all around.

Esme giggled at her own foolishness. Who ever heard of a woman dancing for joy at the mere sight of herself? Still, she couldn't quite tamp down her enthusiasm.

The twins had done wonders for the dress. It fit her perfectly now. The neat little bodice pleats beautifully

accented her waist, which was attractively girded with a
sash made from the leftover material from the outrageously
oversize bustline. The kickflounce at mid-calf was also the
twins' design. The flounce not only made the petite little
gown long enough for Esme, it also served to draw attention
to her legs, which she'd just recently discovered were her
best feature.

Lifting her skirts slightly, she stared down at her old worn
work shoes. It was the only mar but couldn't be helped, she
decided. It was work shoes or barefoot, and work shoes
were infinitely better. Raising her chin in mock haughtiness,
she daintily raised one side of her skirt, the way she
imagined great ladies did, and began to promenade resolutely down the mountain path.

Raising her voice in triumphant challenge, she sang,

"Oh Katy was pretty
And so was her legs.
She sewed up her stocking with needle and thread.
The thread it was rotten, the needle was blunt . . ."

As far as Esme was concerned, this was the most
important night of her life. She'd been hoping all week that
Cleav would ask her to the taffy pull. He hadn't, and she'd
been a little disappointed about that. He was, however,
letting her help in the store and with the fish. Sometimes too
much. The jobs that would keep her away from him the
longest were always the ones that he wanted her to do.

But she'd done them uncomplainingly. Whatever he'd
asked, Esme Crabb had barreled right in and done whatever
was necessary to please him. Esme thought it strange,
however, that he never seemed too pleased.

She knew he'd be pleased tonight. How could he not? She
was prettier than she'd ever been in her life. Why, she was

just about as pretty as anybody she'd ever seen. The twins had seen to that.

They'd woken her early this morning to take her bath in the creek. Afterward they'd rinsed her hair in rainwater and crushed violets. While it was still damp, Adelaide had curled it up in rags. It had taken nearly all day to dry all tied up that way, but the result was worth it. Now dark blond ringlets flowed freely down her back like a waterfall with nothing to stay their course but the loosely tied satin ribbon that Armon had given Agrippa last Christmas.

The twins, too, had plans for the taffy pull. Since it was Saturday, Armon was to escort Adelaide, and Agrippa was coming with Pa. Pa had been rosining up the bow all afternoon, so Esme knew to anticipate plenty of music.

A pretty dress, fancy hair, and a satin ribbon. The only thing missing was a handsome beau to take her arm. Esme was confident she'd have that, too.

Her evening was laid out perfectly in her mind. Cleav would be attending the taffy pull at the church tonight. Esme would show up, as always, to follow him. As pretty as she looked tonight, he'd be pure-d foolish not to just let her walk along next to him. Once all the folks had seen them arrive together, it'd be the same as if they were walking out.

She didn't expect him to walk her home, of course. But surely he'd be wanting to see her to the woods path. If for no other reason than to finally get that kiss he'd been thinking about.

Esme knew he'd been thinking about kissing her. For herself, well, she could barely think of anything else! She had to continually remind herself that the kissing part was only a means to an end. She was marrying Cleavis Rhy and moving her family into that big house. But she had to admit that proving to him that she was worth kissing was going to be a whole lot more fun than proving she could take care of the store.

Stopping by the edge of the path, she saw sprigs of wild phlox growing in the shade of a mayapple. That's what she needed, color, she decided. She hastily pulled a handful and slipped a couple into the ribbon at the nape of her neck. Carefully she tucked a half dozen into the sash at her waist. The rest she gathered together in her hand for a small bouquet.

Flowers made a woman so feminine, she thought. And the pale purple would clear up the muddy blue of her eyes. When she reached the end of the path, she made a hasty adjustment to her drooping stockings, then set off toward the big white house.

"Mr. Cleavis Rhy," she said aloud for the birds and bees to hear. "The maiden of your dreams and the woman of your future is headed straight to your house."

If Cleav had known, he would have undoubtedly slipped out the back door.

Cleav, however, did not know and was at that moment busy thinking of his own pleasant plans for the evening and humming a ditty of his own.

"Kiss me quick! and go! my honey
Kiss me quick and go!
To cheat surprise and prying eyes,
Why, kiss me quick and go!"

The week had been a long and frustrating one. Esme had been a constant companion, and his mother's complaints had become almost frantic. "What in heaven's name is the reverend going to say about her underfoot every day?" Eula Rhy had worried. "And I shudder to even think what Mrs. Tewksbury must be imagining."

"Mother, Mrs. Tewksbury's imagination is truly not a great concern of mine," Cleav had replied.

Ultimately it had all become too much for Mrs. Rhy, and she'd taken her nerves to bed. That had been two days ago, and Cleav hadn't been able to budge the older woman.

Today, however, she had moved from the bed to her sewing rocker, happily contemplating the news that Cleav would indeed be escorting Miss Sophrona to the taffy pull.

"Why don't you join us, Mother?" he'd suggested dutifully.

Eula Rhy had smiled at her son with pleasure but refused his invitation. "I really must save my strength for Sunday. I can't be traipsing out for frolic and then not make it to the Lord's house on the Sabbath."

Cleav had expressed the appropriate degree of disappointment, but now as he straightened his tie before the glass in the downstairs entryway, he was grateful to be going out alone. The walk from the church to the parsonage was unreasonably short, but he expected a moment or two of blessed privacy with Miss Sophrona.

He checked his appearance in the mirror, both in profile and straight ahead. He was no handsome dandy, he decided, but he had the look of a well-groomed, well-tended, prosperous gentleman, exactly the image he chose to portray. He pulled his timepiece out of his watch pocket. Ten minutes before he was due at the Tewksburys'.

After setting his stylish bowler hat at a slightly jaunty angle, he picked up the bright little nosegay of flowers he'd taken from his mother's garden and headed out the door.

There was still a good bit of light; Cleav suspected it was planned that the couples travel to the party in decent sunlight. By the end of the evening it would be up to the ladies, and their fathers, who would be escorted back home through the darkness.

With a smile of self-assurance, Cleav reminded himself that Reverend Tewksbury trusted him completely. His satisfied smile dimmed slightly as he recalled that of late the reverend's attitude was somewhat less enthusiastic.

It was this worry and the woman that caused it that was on Cleav's mind as he headed past the front gate.

Unexpectedly Esme Crabb jumped into his path from behind the chestnut tree.

"Hello!" Her words were slightly breathless with anticipation.

Cleav was at first startled, and then annoyed. Was he never to be free of her constant presence?

Then he noticed there was something different about her. Something far more appealing than usual. He sensed that immediately, his body more quickly than his mind, as a surge of hot desire rolled through him. The sudden need to touch this woman was as unexpected as it was unwanted.

She stood there, staring at him as if waiting for his approval, his flattery, perhaps even his kisses. He realized the change was a different dress, a ladies' dress. For the first time she really shone to advantage. Then the image blurred. The pristine white lawn and the neatly tucked bodice pleats conjured up a different picture, a picture of the same cloth draped attractively across the lush bosom of another woman.

He was so startled he blurted out the first thing he thought. "What are you doing in Miss Sophrona's dress?" The question was harsh enough to be an accusation.

"It's not . . ." Esme began. She was so startled at his words that her face paled and the choked denial was forced from her lips.

"It most certainly is!" Cleav's tone was adamant. "I see you've tried to disguise it, but I'd recognize that dress anywhere. Miss Sophrona wore it to the Fourth of July picnic, and I brought her a cup of punch."

Cleav's words clutched at Esme's heart like a vise.

"Have you taken to helping yourself to other women's

clothing the way you help yourself to crackers in my store?''

''It's my dress,'' Esme answered, her voice raw with pain. ''It was in the charity basket. Miss Sophrona must have thrown it away.''

Esme looked down at the beautiful white lawn garment and fought back the stinging in her eyes. ''It's the nicest thing I ever owned,'' she said quietly. ''And some other woman threw it away.''

Spying the little bouquet of phlox in her hand, Esme was suddenly horrified at her own presumption. Trying to dress herself up with flowers and ribbons, she was appalled at how comical she must appear in her cast-off charity clothes.

Tears close, she flung her flowers to the ground and turned from him, raising her skirts high as she ran.

''Esme!'' he called to her, but she ran on.

Cleav was horrified at himself. He'd been stunned at his reaction to Esme Crabb prettied up. And because of it he'd been deliberately cruel.

''The charity basket,'' he whispered to himself as he watched her racing away, her shapely legs scandalously displayed. Remembering the raised chin and blush of shame as her family had accepted the handout, he knew with certainty the measure of pride she'd swallowed to wear the dress.

He looked at the scattered flowers at his feet. Squatting down, he picked up one blue-violet blossom and held it before him, examining it closely. The five little petals spread in perfect symmetry from the dark purple center. It was the natural beauty of the mountains, ungilted by human expectation. He compared the discarded phlox to the cut flowers he held in his other hand. The bright mix of roses and hyacinths was very pretty but appeared almost garish and overblown beside the simplicity of the wildflower.

When he looked up again, he could barely make out Esme

in the distance. Quickly he shrugged out of his coat and hung it neatly on one white-washed picket, topping it with his hat. The flowers he fit snugly against the rail. Scooping up the rest of the wild phlox, he hurried after the young woman in the white lawn hand-me-down.

Esme's chest was screaming for relief, but her heart wanted to run forever. She might have done exactly that had she not felt her stylish curls suddenly loose and flowing around her.

"Agrippa's ribbon!" she screamed at herself as she stopped abruptly. Frantically she began to backtrack, searching the grass for the plain piece of white satin as the tears continued to hamper her vision. Her mind was numb with pain and shame. She refused to think at all, only to search and weep. She'd crested a small hill and hurried across a just budding meadow, and Cleav's house was at last out of sight. Somehow she felt safer. As if leaving the sight of her humiliation could make her unexpected humbling less acute.

The ribbon was visible, a small expanse of pristine white amid a flourishing patch of vivid green clover. Esme pulled her skirts high out of the staining grass and dropped to her knees in the clover.

The ribbon seemed none the worse for being temporarily lost, and Esme stared at it, determinedly forcing back her tears. She was glad she'd found it; her sisters had been so generous. The dress had been meant for the twins, of course. Sophrona knew how they loved pretty clothes, and she had purposely included it in the basket. The twins would have been unconcerned with the former owner, knowing, with perfect honesty, that the dress would look better on them than any female in Vader.

Esme, however, had no such confidence to rely on. She

was a shabby hill girl in another woman's made-over dress. And Cleavis Rhy had found her pathetic, not pretty.

Looking now at the dress she had so admired, she wanted to rip it from her body. She wished she could shred it into a hundred pieces and bury it in a rat hole.

Setting her jaw with practical firmness, she knew she could not do that. Even hating the dress, it was the best she owned. Her sisters had worked long and hard to add the sash she now found tacky and the flounce which seemed ridiculous, so now she would have to wear it until it was no more than a rag hanging from her shoulders. She blinked back more annoying tears, secretly hoping that white lawn would not be a very durable fabric.

As she bravely raised her chin, resigning herself to her fate, she heard the sound of running feet on the path behind her.

Before she had time to scamper into hiding, she turned back to see Cleav topping the hill. When their eyes met, he slowed to a walk.

Esme turned her attention back to the clover in front of her. She couldn't just be sitting here, she thought desperately. She'd die if he knew she'd been sitting there crying over him. Praying that her face was not tearstained, she anxiously sought some purposeful work for her hands.

The clover was rife with young blossoms. As if suddenly returning to younger days, Esme pulled up two. Running a fingernail through the lower stem of the first, she created a narrow slit through which she threaded the stem of the second blossom. Treating it likewise, she pulled another blooming clover and wove it, also.

As Cleav crested the hill, the sun setting over the mountain in a splash of pink-tinted sky was the perfect backdrop for the young woman in a swirl of white skirts seated in the bright green clover. The vision touched unfamiliar feelings in his heart. Almost casually he approached her until he stood with her at his feet in the grass.

"What are you doing?" he asked as he watched her nimble fingers weaving the tiny white puffs of grass.

"Making a clover chain," she answered simply, as if such an occupation were perfectly acceptable for a fully grown woman on a deserted hillside on a Saturday evening.

Cleav watched her progress for a moment and then without invitation seated himself beside her. Gently he laid the handful of wild phlox on the ground before them.

When Esme saw her discarded flowers, a rush of tears filled her throat, but she forced her gaze back to the stems of clover and continued her work with diligence.

Cleav adjusted his position to make himself comfortable. He stretched out one long leg before him and bent the other at the knee. Leaning back, he was almost supine until he turned on one hip and rested his upper body on his elbow.

To Esme it felt strangely familiar to have him practically lying next to her. Without speaking they sat together for several minutes adjusting to the unaccustomed intimacy that surrounded them.

Esme glanced down and noted with surprise that Cleav had taken up the loose end of the chain and was himself calmly weaving the clover blooms.

He looked up and caught her watching him.

"Boys learn how to do this, too, you know," he told her, his voice as soothing as hot molasses on a winter night. "I was about seven, I guess," he said as he reached, not for the clover, but for one of the wild phlox blooms that lay before him. "I made what I think was the longest clover chain in the state of Tennessee." There was self-mocking laughter in his claim. "I swear I combed these hills for a week trying to find enough blossoms."

His gaze was so warm and wry, Esme found herself compelled to smile back.

"It was so long I carried it around in a sack!" he told her, shaking his head. "When it started to die and break up, I wrapped it around the barn for a decoration."

His pale blue eyes were bright with mischief. "Our old Bossy ate every piece of it, and Mama threatened to take a strap to me for feeding clover to the cow!"

Esme's peal of laughter was genuine and once Cleav had her smiling again, he proceeded toward his purpose. "I owe you an apology, Esme," he began.

She shook her head. "You did the right thing," she assured him bravely. "If you think somebody has stole something, you've got to confront 'em."

Cleav felt a stab of self-directed anger.

"I never thought you'd stolen the dress, Esme. I know that you do not steal." His eyes upon her gave her more will than she had thought available.

"No," she stated without boast. "I do not steal."

She raised her chin as if to gaze across the horizon. Cleav found himself admiring her profile, not for its beauty or femininity, but for its strength. He had wounded her, but she would not show him her pain.

"I know how you feel, Esme."

The words brought her focus back to his face. There were unspoken words of derisive disbelief evident in her expression.

"It's true," he insisted calmly. "I've been there myself." He reached for one of the phlox. The stem was not as easy to slit as the clover, but he managed to do it and added the colorful blossom to the strand, where it stood out among the more ordinary clovers.

"You know that I went off to Knoxville to school?" he asked, looking off in the distance.

"Yes."

"I was so excited about that," he recalled, his voice calm and matter of fact. "I had been wanting schooling, oh, it seems like all my life. I'd wished for it, but I never dared to hope." He wove a second phlox into the clover chain, making a companion for the first outsider.

"My father drove me to the train station in Russellville. I could hardly sit still the whole way, talking and squirming like I was six instead of almost fourteen."

Esme smiled, trying to imagine the calm, confident man before her as a fourteen-year-old with jitters in his legs.

"Mama had made me a new suit from the finest brown wool we had in the store," he told her. "It fit me perfectly the day I left and had lots of extra fabric at the seams and in the hem to accommodate a young man with a good deal of growing yet to do."

Cleav wove a plain white clover into the chain with no hesitation in his story. "The train ride was pure pleasure," he said. "I told everyone in the coach about my new suit and my new school." His grin was wry as he continued. "The porter must have thought me the greenest boy ever to come down from the mountain. But he, and everyone else, listened to my wild enthusiasm, offered words of advice on city life, and wished me well."

Esme tried to imagine herself on a noisy train heading for the city and talking to strangers. It seemed a wonderful adventure.

"Knoxville was bigger, busier, noisier, more exciting than all my wildest fantasies. I was probably close to death a half dozen times as I made my way across town to the school."

Carefully weaving another clover into the pattern, he shook his head derisively.

"I was bug-eyed at the scenes around me. I had not one thought to caution in the busy streets. That hectic flurry of rigs and wagons was intent on running me down. More than one angry driver cursed my ancestry."

Esme giggled, earning her a playful rise of his eyebrows.

"The school was just as I imagined it," he said. "I

remember stopping in front to read the name carved into the stone: Halperth Academy for Gentlemen of Good Family. I knew that I was going to learn so much there.''

Cleav's smile brightened with remembrance but just as quickly faded to a sober line.

"And I did, but not at all what I expected."

Cleav sat up. Cross-legged, he faced Esme. Her eyes were wide with wonder and curiosity. Never had he confessed his secrets to a soul. Instinctively he knew that Esme could be trusted with the most mortifying of truths. "What I learned at the Halperth Academy," he began, his voice now slightly roughened with anger, "is that a storekeeper's son from the hills is *not* considered a gentleman of good family."

Cleav swallowed heavily, tasting again the bitter gall of disgrace. Unwilling to allow himself the privilege of privacy, he raised his eyes to Esme. He had made her feel shame, so he showed her his own.

"They laughed at me," he told her quietly. "The other boys in the school, the people in the town, even the professors laughed at the way I talked, the way I ate, the things I said."

He didn't stint on the truth.

"They even laughed at the new brown suit my mama made me. Their suits were fitted at the tailor's. They called mine homemade cracker clothes. Just perfect, one of the upperclassmen declared, for Cleavis Clodhopper the hillbilly boy." Even after long years of success and achievement, the hated nickname conjured up rancor.

"At first I thought I could prove myself," he told her. "I studied harder than anyone. I perfected my manners. I was determined that I could make them see me as an equal." He sighed and shook his head. "Of course, they never did."

As Esme watched him, there was no pity in her eyes, but there was understanding.

He shrugged nonchalantly. "It wasn't all for the bad, though," he said honestly. "With no friends and resolved to succeed, I spent untold hours in the library. I would lose my unhappiness in the excitement of science.''

Smiling wryly, he added, "My biology text was so well-thumbed it looked like a risqué novel."

Esme felt suddenly closer to him. She wanted to touch him, to comfort him. She wanted to feel what he felt.

With his elbow on his knee and his chin in his hand, he looked at Esme, willing her to understand. "The people of Vader, probably even yourself," he said, "think that I am a *gentleman*. And here, well, I guess that I am. But I know that I would never have been seen as such in the city."

The statement was plain fact, not bitterness.

Esme reached across and touched his hand. The gesture surprised and pleased him.

"I'm not looking for your sympathy," Cleav told her, taking up her end of the clover chain and webbing it with his. "I'm trying to say that I do know a portion of how I made you feel. I'm sorry for what I said about the dress."

"It doesn't matter," Esme told him, and strange as it seemed at that moment, it did not.

"It matters to me," Cleav insisted. "I hurt you. That matters."

Esme felt her hand tremble as it lay against his, and she hastily removed it.

"I don't know too much about you, Esme," he said. "But what I do see in you is pride. You believe in yourself and don't allow the opinions of others to make you doubt. I can admire that. I wouldn't want to be the cause of changing it."

"You haven't," Esme assured him.

"That's good." He raised his eyes to look at her, to take in all of the vision before him. "And I wasn't honest, either. I need to apologize for that, too."

"You weren't honest?" Esme was confused.

Cleav shook his head. "When you stepped out from

behind that chestnut tree, I thought you were as pretty as any girl I'd ever seen.''

At Esme's quick intake of breath, Cleav moved closer. The sweet smell of her tempted him, but he didn't allow himself the luxury of letting his attentions forego his better judgment.

Casually he draped the clover chain around her neck. Like a wreath, he looped the chains over her head, allowing them to drop gently across her bosom.

''You are like a wild mountain princess,'' he told her, his words soft and warm. ''A true creation of Mother Nature.''

She stared down at the flowers. The two wild phlox blooms added a bright touch to the pretty green and white clover.

He sat back, his hands on his knees as his gaze wandered across her face, her strong young shoulders, and the profuse garland of flowers that flowed from her throat to her waist.

''Esme Crabb.'' His voice was a husky whisper that prickled her skin like a ghostly visage on a moonless night. ''You are as pretty a young woman as I have ever seen in my life. Any man who says differently is a liar.''

She felt her cheeks heat, but she shook her head at the compliment.

''You are kind, Cleavis,'' she answered, her own whisper sounding strange to her ears. ''But I'm sure you were right the first time. The dress is probably not too fashionable.''

Cleavis bent toward her, his eyes strangely hot and intent. With two tentative fingers he adjusted the clover chain to his satisfaction.

Esme felt a wildly charged prickle at the gentleness of his touch, and suddenly the white lawn bodice felt too tight.

''Vader is not the place for those who are slaves to fashion.''

Esme's answering giggle was as much nerves as humor. He was so handsome and so kind and so, so close.

"That I'm not," she said. "I never cared about clothes at all before . . ."

Esme didn't need to finish the sentence.

"Do you really think that I am pretty?" she asked, her voice not sounding at all like her own. In that instant her whole world seemed balanced on his answer.

His eyes darkened.

"Yes, Esme." His words were almost a whisper. "You are very pretty."

Her heart pounding within her breast, Esme looked longingly at the man before her and dared to hope. A kiss, she begged silently, a kiss.

As if he heard her mute plea, his eyes focused on her lips, causing them to part invitingly.

"Very pretty," he whispered again.

Was he going to kiss her? The dream rushed through her thoughts like a rat in a snake's nest. Here, in this tender moment, would *he* kiss *her*?

Oh, yes, please, was her silent prayer.

Esme wanted to feel his lips on hers; to breathe in the spicy smell of his throat, to be enfolded in those strong, masculine arms.

She trembled in anticipation, the way she had that day beside the pond. But Esme would not throw herself at him again. She'd wait this time. She'd wait for him to make the move.

His eyes assessed her, caressed her. She could almost feel the kiss in his gaze.

Cleav hesitated.

Esme panicked.

He wasn't ready to kiss her. Maybe he didn't really want to kiss her. Maybe he didn't really think she was pretty. Was he humoring a pitiful mountain girl?

She had to know for sure. She had to be certain. She

threw out a challenge. "Am I pretty enough to take to the taffy pull?" she asked.

Cleavis sat frozen, staring at her for an instant. It took more than a few seconds for the idyll to end and for reality to come crashing down around him. More than that before his eyes widened in shock.

"I'm late!" he exclaimed, jumping to his feet. Jerking the watch from his pocket, he glanced at its face in dismay. "I was supposed to pick up Miss Sophrona nearly an hour ago!"

8

Spring in full bloom all around them and the sweet smell of honeysuckle wafting through the air, the attractive young couple sat together on a whitewashed bench beneath the enveloping shade of a giant silverleaf maple.

"Can I get you some more lemonade?" Sophrona asked him.

The Tewksburys' parsonage was a mere stone's throw from where they sat, but it was the closest thing to privacy Cleav had been able to manage.

Glancing into his empty glass, Cleav thought Miss Sophrona's recipe for lemonade relied a good deal too heavily on sugar.

"No, thank you," he answered politely. "It's wonderful but I believe I've had enough."

Miss Sophrona was gowned in somber blue, which may have reflected her mood. It had been over a week since the fiasco of the taffy pull, and Cleav was just beginning to work himself back into Miss Sophrona's good graces. There had been no open discussion of the troubles between them. And that was fine with Cleav. He had no idea how to explain, and he was hoping that he wouldn't be expected to do so.

At least today the dangerous Miss Crabb was nowhere in sight. He wished she'd made herself equally as scarce on the previous Saturday.

After his hasty retreat from the clover-covered hillside with Esme, Cleav had arrived at the parsonage an hour late. He was not surprised to find the house deserted. Sophrona had waited as long as she could and finally gone on with her parents. Cleav had followed miserably and alone.

It might have worked out. Sophrona was so honest herself, the potential for deceit in others rarely entered her mind.

When Cleav arrived at the party, he found her gaily immersing herself in the infectious laughter that was inevitable when a dozen pairs of buttered hands are passing and pulling at a glob of hot candy.

"I'm so sorry I'm late," he apologized immediately.

Sophrona's smile was open and forgiving. "I know. I told Daddy that it must have been your mother's ill health that detained you."

Cleav did attempt not to lie deliberately. "Mother is feeling better this evening," he told her. "And, of course, she sends her love."

Scooting over, Sophrona made a place for him beside her on the bench. Within minutes Cleav's hands were washed and buttered, and he, too, was laughing and joking as the sticky sweet came his way.

As the young people worked the taffy, children ran around trying to steal a sweet bite, even though it was still hot enough to burn their mouths. The older folks stood watching and talking, some remembering the days of their own youthful exuberance, others gossiping about the current crop of courting couples. Armon Hightower and the Crabb twins came in for more of their share of the speculation. Hightower had arrived with one twin on his arm but was now sitting between both of them, apparently quite content with this double dose of feminine attention.

Yo Crabb played a lively tune that caused more than one foot to tap with an unspoken wish that dancing was not one of Reverend Tewksbury's most oft-preached-upon sins.

It was just bad luck, Cleav decided later, that the lull in the music coincided with the late, unexpected arrival of Esme Crabb. It was not so much that Esme rarely showed up for social occasions, since up to now she'd shown a patent disinterest in gentlemen callers. The problem was her altered appearance captured every eye in the place.

Armon Hightower blurted out what everyone else was thinking. "Don't you look pretty as spring!"

The made-over dress was attractive, and Esme's long ringlets were now tossed casually by her run through the meadow. She glowed with pretty disarray in the light of the Chinese lanterns. But what set off the young woman's beauty most effectively was the wild garland of clover and phlox that was draped around her.

"Oh, doesn't she look lovely?" Sophrona asked Cleav in a delighted whisper. "And in my old dress, too. I'm so pleased."

Cleav found himself unable to reply. She was pretty, but he was determined to keep his eyes on Sophrona Tewksbury. *She* was the woman in whom he was interested.

The music started up again, and a place was made for Esme in the circle. More than one of the young swains gave Esme a long, thoughtful look.

"That's a pretty wildflower chain," Elmer Crossbridge, a blond and buck-toothed young farmer, observed, giving himself an excuse to scrutinize Esme's bosom. "Must have taken you a goodly amount of time to make it." Esme glanced proudly down at the artistic creation. She thought it was pretty, too. The prettiest thing she had ever seen. And the prettiest part of it was the wild phlox that was woven in.

"Cleavis helped me," she blurted out with pleasure.

"Cleavis?" Crossbridge raised a speculative eyebrow at the unwarranted familiarity.

"Mr. Rhy, that is," Esme hastily corrected, her face flaming at her indiscreet blunder. But the damage was already done.

Cleav's face was as white as Esme's was red, and Sophrona was staring at him as if she'd never seen him before.

Now, after a week of trying to explain away the incident to Sophrona's father, Cleav found himself at last welcome in her presence.

"So what is your opinion, Mr. Rhy?" Sophrona was asking. "Do you think that the serpent in the garden walked on legs, or was he just the kind of snake we see today?"

Cleav hated thorny, Biblical catechism. Miss Sophrona, however, seemed to thrive on such. So he forced his brain to participate. "Well, the Bible does state that he was condemned to slither across the ground. That infers that it was not the serpent's original state," he said.

"Then you think the serpent in the garden was just another type of lizard?" she asked.

Cleav hesitated, hating to be pinned down.

"No," he hedged. "The serpent didn't *have* to be a lizard. It could have been any kind of creature prior to being used by the devil."

"What an interesting idea!" Sophrona exclaimed. As she postulated on the possibilities, Cleav's attention wandered.

Not five feet away from them an incongruous sight captured Cleav's attention. At the foot of the maple tree, propped neatly against the rough, dark bark, was a pair of very worn men's work shoes. Peeking out the tops were some nearly threadbare black wool stockings.

His first thought was how strange it was to find such an

item in the Tewksburys' very neatly kept yard. Then he was struck by how oddly familiar the shoes and stockings happened to be. With a sinking feeling of dread, Cleav slowly, casually, without drawing attention to himself, leaned backward and allowed his gaze to drift upward.

Dangling from a sturdy limb almost directly above them was a pair of long, shapely, bare legs that Cleav definitely should not have recognized as easily as he did.

"I suppose it would have to be some animal that no longer exists," Sophrona was saying. "Do you think it would have been in the reptile family?" she asked.

Cleav jerked his eyes and his thoughts back to the woman at his side. Struggling for an answer to her question, all he could think about was how shocked she would be to know Esme Crabb was spying on them. How could he explain it? And God only knew what Esme herself might say. The woman had about as much tact and social sense as one of his fishes.

"Miss Sophrona," he blurted out finally. "I believe I will have another glass of your lemonade."

Since he'd interrupted her musings, Sophrona cocked her head quizzically at him but recovered quickly and reached for the glass he offered.

" 'If he thirst, give him drink,' " she quoted with a cheery giggle as she rose to get Cleav another glass of refreshment.

Watching her retreat, Cleav never allowed his eyes to stray to the intruder in the tree above him. In his mind, however, the slim bare calves and ankles waved before him like a red cape before a bull.

Only when he saw Sophrona step into the house and close the door behind her did he look up into the tree.

"What do you think you're doing?"

Esme looked down through her leafy camouflage to the stormy visage of the man seated below her.

"Just enjoying the beautiful day," she answered innocently.

In truth, Esme was almost as horrified as Cleav about her present location. She'd watched Cleav hurrying to call on Miss Sophrona, and she just had to follow.

She'd just wanted to observe them, she'd assured herself. Or rather to observe *him*. The taffy pull had been a definite setback, and Esme knew she needed to regroup. Esme wanted to see this side of his nature, Cleavis the suitor. She wanted to watch and learn and imagine what it was going to be like *when* he finally came calling on her. She couldn't bear to think the word was really *if*. And she wanted to see if he was as hesitant in kissing Sophrona as he was in kissing her.

Seeing the maple tree a goodly distance from the house but within hearing of the porch, she'd scrambled. She assumed the couple would pass their afternoon on the Tewksburys' slatted swing. Esme was more than a little chagrined to find them taking their ease directly below her spying perch.

There was no humor in Cleav's grin. "You just happened to be enjoying it while hidden in a tree in Miss Sophrona's yard?"

His question didn't require an answer, but Esme gave a halfhearted one anyway. "I'm not *hidden*," she insisted with only a slight blush at the fib. "Anyone who looks up in this tree could see me."

Cleav nodded in apparent agreement. "Except that no one with any sense in the world would think to look for young women peeping from trees."

"You did!" she shot back.

"It's because I've come to know you." His explanation was terse, and his eyebrow was raised in disdain.

Esme felt the roses building in her cheeks but could think of no snappy comeback.

"Actually," Cleav continued, "it was your shoes that gave you away." He made a gesture toward her discarded footwear. "Aren't you aware that young women of your age do not go around bare-legged?"

His heated disapproval was clearly based on the distraction the sight of those legs was causing him. As Esme realized this, her embarrassment began to fade and a sly smile came to her lips.

"You can't climb a tree in shoes and stockings," she answered him reasonably. "When a woman's got a choice of modesty or breaking her neck," she told him, shifting casually on the thick tree limb, "then it's bare-legged every time!"

Cleav opened his mouth for a scathing reply, but forgot what he was going to say. Esme threw her right leg over the limb, straddling the thick brown tree branch. Her skirts bunched around her, giving an ample display of her bare legs and a tantalizing glimpse of the edge of the leg of her cotton drawers.

As Cleav's mouth hung open in shock, Esme tested the strength of her new power, casually bending forward and arching her back in what she hoped was a seductive pose.

To Cleav, it looked as if she were trying to wiggle herself closer to the hard, thick wood that she cushioned so intimately between her thighs. He swallowed the lump that formed in his throat.

"I'm not really spying," Esme said. "I'm just interested in how a gentleman courts a lady."

With deliberate casualness Cleav crossed one leg over his knee.

"Well, now that you've found out what you wanted to know," he told her, "why don't you get down from that tree and get out of here before Miss Sophrona gets back."

Esme disliked his terse order. She disliked his eagerness to be alone with Sophrona even more.

Her smile was a tease. "Leave so soon?" she asked with

mock astonishment. "Before anything has even happened? Now, that would be foolish."

"Nothing is going to happen," Cleav answered, his words cold and precise.

"Nothing?" Esme sighed loudly in disappointment. "If that's all that gentlemen do, save to graces, I can't imagine why any man would want to be one!"

"What do you mean?"

"I mean the boys on the mountain, the ones that court the twins, are always sparking and trying to steal a kiss."

She leaned forward, lying on her stomach upon the thick, burly limb. She raised her legs to drape leisurely along the rough brown bark.

"It looks to me that gentlemen don't have near so much fun."

Bending her knee saucily, she waved one long bare foot in the air. Her wide-eyed grin was downright impertinent.

"Instead of sparking, you're Bible-talking. Do you truly care about what kind of critter was in the Garden of Eden?"

As Cleav gazed up at the long-limbed beauty in the tree, there was no doubt in his mind what kind of animal the devil would have used to tempt *him*.

"Relevant theological discussion broadens the intellect and lightens the soul," he replied arrogantly.

Esme giggled, but her voice was smooth as honey. "There you go, talking prissy again."

"I do not talk prissy!" He raised his voice in anger before glancing guiltily toward the house. "I do not talk prissy," he repeated quietly.

"I'm not complaining," Esme assured him. "I told you that I like that prissy talk."

Cleav sighed loudly with exasperation. "Oh, well, thank you very much."

Esme ignored his sarcasm.

"I suspect Miss Sophrona does, too," she added, casually

surveying her fingernails. "Or she'd sure lose patience with all that talking and no kissing at all."

"What!" Cleav nearly choked.

"I said—"

"I heard what you said!" Cleav gave a hasty glance toward the house. "Miss Sophrona is a very proper young lady. A lady who can appreciate a gentleman's favor and regard."

Esme was skeptical. "I'm betting she'd consider it a favor if you'd give a bit of kissing and sparking more regard."

Her criticism of his wooing abilities stung. "Our courtship is no concern of yours."

"Of course not. I'm just trying to give you some advice."

"I do not *need* any advice."

"Well, you need something. The two of you are like to bore each other to death."

"Miss Sophrona and I are eminently suitable," he stated flatly.

Esme was not sure what he meant by that. "Suitable" was wearing a black dress to a funeral. She'd never heard the word used concerning sparking or marrying. Was courting really so different for ladies and gentlemen?

"Have you ever kissed her?"

Cleav's eyes widened in horror at Miss Crabb's complete lack of decorum. "I don't believe you are asking this!"

"Believe it," she said, annoyed at herself and wishing she could call back the foolish question. "I'm curious, that's all," she said. "Since you've kissed me, I wondered if you've kissed her."

Cleav's cheeks puffed with fury and his words were an explosive denial. "I have *never* kissed you! *You* kissed me!"

"Same difference." Esme easily shrugged away his dissent. "We've been over this before."

"You . . ."

The back door opened, and Sophrona came outside, a white wicker tray with a large pitcher of the lemonade in her hands.

"I bet she's wondering when you're going to kiss her," Esme whispered.

"I will not be kissing her with an audience," Cleav snarled back at her.

Esme couldn't have been more pleased to hear that, but she couldn't stop herself from one last prick at his pride.

"Sure wish she'd brought lemonade for me. All this prissy talk sure makes a woman thirsty."

Cleav didn't get a chance to reply. Sophrona was already within earshot, and he rose politely to his feet.

"Here we are," she said lightly as she set the tray on the bench. "All this talk is sure to parch a man's throat."

Unable to stop himself, Cleav glanced up and then wished he hadn't. Esme's I-told-you-so expression was triumphant. Cleav vowed to strangle the infuriating young woman at the very first opportunity.

For a moment he considered informing his companion of their overhead observer but quickly rejected the idea. He could never satisfactorily explain the young woman's presence in the Tewksburys' maple tree. And even if he'd had no care for the irritating little ragamuffin's feelings, Esme Crabb was fast becoming a sore subject between himself and Sophrona.

Sophrona filled his glass with the cool, sweet liquid, and Cleav forced himself to keep his eyes on her face. She was pale and pretty, polished and polite. But Cleav's thoughts continued to stray to the slim, bare legs that he knew were so decadently displayed in the tree above him.

He fixed his eyes on the warm smile of the lady at his side, attentively listening to her soft-toned chatter. He would not look up, he would not . . .

"If, of course, the serpent were some other type of animal," Sophrona continued on her former train of conversation. "Then it would be logical that such an extinct species could have actually had the gift of speech."

Cleav nodded woodenly in agreement. While before he'd tried to participate in the conversation, now his thoughts were fixed on how dull the esoteric theological discussion must sound to Esme. Certainly Miss Crabb was no expert on the affairs of the heart, but he wondered if he did seem terribly dull in comparison with the wild hill boys like Armon Hightower. This thought pricked at him.

Hightower and his like expected, and undoubtedly received, more than an occasional stolen kiss from the young women they courted. In that respect, he was certain Esme was right: It *was* more fun *not* to be a gentleman. But being a gentleman was Cleav's intent, and had always been, even if it meant going without kisses from Miss Sophrona and enduring the taunting of Esme Crabb.

Still, Cleav thought as he watched Sophrona's pouty, pale peach lips speak of the Garden of Eden, a man—even a gentleman—deserved a bit of lovespark.

In his mind he could almost hear Esme laughing at him. Was Sophrona laughing, too? Did she, as Esme suggested, long to be kissed? Was she disappointed with his chivalrous behavior? Frustrated with his highest regard?

Through his thoughts once more, the image of long, naked limbs wrapped around thick brown bark tortured him. He shifted his position carefully, disguising his very ungentlemanly reaction from both the woman at his side and the one that dangled like a sinful temptation above him. As Sophrona moved the serving tray to a small table, Cleav , made a furtive glance up through the leaves. Esme had sat up, her back against the strong tree trunk, one foot rested on the limb, her leg bent saucily at the knee. The other leg hung casually, her bare pink toes wiggling naughtily not ten yards above him.

His eyes unerringly followed the long line of naked limb upward. Those legs, those beautiful hill-girl legs, were sleekly muscled from innumerable trips up the mountain and lightly sprinkled with color from the occasional and forbidden forays into the warm Tennessee sunshine. Those legs tantalized and teased him, and he followed their length like a hound at a coon running. Oh, how they tempted him, taunted him. . . .

At last his visual wanderings led to her face, which sported a mocking grin. He was hot with desire, and she was laughing at him. To add insult to injury, she opened her mouth widely and patted it lightly in a mock yawn.

Boring, the gesture implied. *Polite, prissy, proper, and boring.* Cleav could hear her opinion as if she had shouted it.

Hastily returning his attention to Sophrona, he wondered if she thought the same. Was his courtesy and consideration a source of amusement? Did she long for the unbridled passions of rude hill boys? Worst of all, did she pick Bible discussions because she thought him stiff and unromantic?

His passions were just as ardent, just as consuming as any hill boy's. Was he being penalized for his control? His honor? Would another man, being offered the constant temptation of Esme Crabb, not succumb? Would another man, sitting on an isolated bench with Sophrona Tewksbury, steal a kiss?

By God, Esme was right to laugh at him. He must seem a peculiarly spiritless beau. Well, she wanted to spy on him! He'd give her something to see that would wipe that derisive grin right off her smudgy, freckled face!

Sophrona ceased her chatter in midsentence and stared at him, her large eyes startled. "Why are you looking at me that way?" she asked.

Without looking up Cleav could still see the long expanse of feminine nakedness that dangled so enticingly out of his reach. Before him the pale, pouty lips of Sophrona Tewksbury were accessible. And the soft, lush amplitude of her shapely bosom could so easily be pressed against him.

There was no gentlemanly reticence in Cleav's action. Turning his head slightly to one side, he pulled Sophrona into his arms for a plundering kiss. For a moment the young woman's shock stunned her into complacency, and Cleav took full advantage. Parting her lips with his tongue, he sought the essence of her mouth. His arms tightened around her, flattening her abundant feminine flesh against his chest. He could feel the tiny points of her nipples, and it fired him to moan against her lips and rub his own hard muscled chest against the softness of her own.

In the darkness behind his eyes the pale, bare legs still lured him, and he deepened the kiss to dispel the image. He would exorcise this troublesome demon. He would lose himself in the sweet-smelling warmth of the body in his arms.

Willing himself into oblivion, at first he chose not to hear the murmurs of protest forced against his mouth. Passion, he assured himself. A moment later Sophrona was clearly struggling in his grasp, and he could delude himself no longer. He released her.

As she pulled away from him, her eyes were wide in shock, and her short, uneven breathing had her bosom bouncing before him.

''How could you?'' Her question held as much hurt as anger.

''Sophrona, I—''

He wasn't allowed to finish. Miss Tewksbury, instructed in the art of dealing with cads and mashers, brought her right hand up sharply and cracked it full-force, open palm against Cleav's cheek.

His ears ringing, Cleav barely heard her furious "Good day, Mr. Rhy!" as she stomped away in fury.

Cleav sat still as a stone until he heard the back door slam. Rising to his feet with all the dignity he could muster, he, too, began to walk away at a clipped pace.

"Cleavis?" he heard the taunting tree temptress call to him. Ignoring her, he kept walking. She had seen it all. Now she really had something to laugh about!

Esme was startled by the unexpected turn of events. He had kissed Sophrona. And what a kiss! Esme's own face was a blistering red, and her heart could not have been pounding more loudly if she had been one of the principals. It was a wonderful kiss, full of passion and spontaneity.

But, Sophrona had slapped him.

Esme felt guilt swell up within her. She had teased Cleav about being a gentleman, but she had intended for him to try out bad behavior on *her*, not on Sophrona. Sophrona reaped all the rewards from Esme's flirtations, and she didn't even appreciate it.

Moving down, branch by branch, Esme carefully made her way to earth. The lowest limb of the maple was a good eight feet above the ground. Esme swung, tomboy fashion, from the bough for a moment and then dropped to the grass, rolling to deflect the fall.

Rising, she scrambled over to her shoes and stockings at the foot of the tree. Esme gathered them into her arms. Without bothering to put them on, she hurried, barefoot, after Cleav.

He was already out of sight, but Esme had a good idea where he was headed. The proud young man who had worn his homemade cracker clothes despite the cruel taunts of his peers would seek solace in nature as he always had in the past. Esme headed directly for the trout ponds.

She was right, of course. When she topped the rise near

his house, she saw him. Standing alone and lonely, staring at the trickling rush of water across the tops of the ponds.

She slowed her pace to a leisurely walk as she came up behind him.

"I'm sorry," she said as she neared him.

Cleav glanced back at her, his face devoid of feeling. "Whatever for?" he asked tonelessly. "For spying? Apology accepted." He shook his head as he continued to gaze into the depths of the water.

"I meant for getting your face slapped," she said.

There was no humor in his answering chuckle. "You were neither the kisser or the slapper," he observed. "Doesn't seem as if you have a great deal for which to apologize."

Esme took a step toward him. Wincing, she stopped abruptly.

"Ouch!" Her exclamation was like an oath whispered under her breath. When Cleav turned to see what had happened, she had raised her leg, intent on examining the bottom of her foot.

"What is it?" he asked.

"Just a goat-head," she answered, pulling at the pale blue cocklebur that was lodged in the tender flesh of her instep.

"You shouldn't be running around here barefoot."

"I've seen plenty of summers when I had no shoes at all," she said lightly.

Gritting her teeth, she grasped the painful thorn in her fingernails and jerked it free. Goat-heads were long and sharp and had a poison in them that sometimes raised a welt. Esme watched the rising blossom of a bead of blood. Relying on the common cure, she spat on the wound and hurriedly rubbed it into the soreness.

"Oh, for heaven's sake," Cleav said. "That's not the way you treat it."

In two strides he was beside her and casually swept her off her feet. "You need to wash it off and sprinkle some alum on it."

"I always use spit," Esme insisted. She enjoyed being held in his arms.

"Well, you're about to learn something new. Here," he said, seating her at the edge of the pond. "Dunk your foot in there and let me go get some alum from the shed."

Esme watched him walk away, but her mind was not on the slight sting of her instep. All she could feel was the warmth that had been his arms around her. He had held her, and her heart was still pounding from the experience.

It was only when she saw him on his way back that she remembered what he'd told her to do. Thrusting her foot in the freezing mountain water, she attempted to wash. The cold, however, raised gooseflesh all over her and dissuaded her from any thorough cleansing.

"Are you usually so adverse to washing?"

"The water's like ice!" she complained.

Cleav nodded as he sat down beside her. "It's got to be cold to raise trout," he told her. "That's the way they like it."

"Well, I'm no trout," Esme snapped. "And it's too dang cold for me!"

"Let me see if I can help," Cleav answered and began rubbing his hands together rapidly. After a few seconds he dipped them in the water and quickly brought them out to wash Esme's feet.

"Better?" he asked.

"Some."

"It's the friction," he explained. "When I rub my hands together, it creates heat. The water's just as cold as it was, but the heat of my hands makes it seem warmer."

Esme didn't answer. At that moment she was feeling much warmer, indeed. Cleavis Rhy was sitting cross-legged beside her, draping her knee casually across his own. His hands so tenderly touched her foot, stroking and strong. The warmth of it was greater than friction and rushed right up her leg to a soft and secret place.

Esme took a deep breath. Cleav looked into her eyes. A fire burned there between them. Only Cleav sought to bank it. "It's time for the alum, I think," he told her, his words strangely gruff.

After pulling her injured foot into his lap, he removed the lid from the can he'd brought and sprinkled the white powder.

Esme flinched. "Save to graces! That hurts worse than the goat-head!" she complained.

Cleav nodded like a stern father. "It draws the wound up and burns the poison out," he told her. "It hurts a lot at first, but it's over soon. In an hour you'll forget all about that goat-head."

Esme wanted to tell him that she would never forget one moment she'd spent with him, but something in his eyes made her hold her tongue.

"Let me get your shoes," he said, rising to walk away from her.

"I'm sorry that Sophrona slapped you," she blurted out when his back was turned.

Cleav hesitated an instant but didn't turn around. He went on to gather up her stockings and shoes before walking back to her. Then he dropped her things on the ground beside her. His grin was wry and humorless.

"Why be sorry?" he answered stonily. "It was quite a show for you, I think."

Esme jerked up her skirts and began pulling on her stockings. Without being asked, Cleav hurriedly turned his back.

"Truthfully, I didn't understand why you wanted me to kiss her," he said. "I guess you knew what would happen."

"No!" Esme protested. "I didn't know what would happen. And I didn't want you to kiss her!"

"You were teasing me, Esme," he replied. "You aren't going to deny that."

"Well, yes . . . I mean no," she sputtered as she hurried her shoes on.

"You suggested I wasn't a man if I didn't kiss her."

"I didn't want you to kiss *her*." Esme came to her feet and hurried to his side. Turning him toward her, she reached up and laid her palm against the strong masculine jaw that had felt the consequences of Miss Sophrona's wrath.

"I didn't want you to kiss her, Cleav," she whispered. "I wanted you to kiss me."

For a man who just minutes previous had been given a memorable lesson on kissing women, Cleav was remarkably unhesitant. Wrapping his arms around the small of her back, he pulled her tightly against him.

Esme breathed a startled little "oh" of surprise and then eagerly tried to press his lips with her own.

"Wait!" he whispered urgently. Esme quieted in his arms. "This time I want no question about it. *I* am kissing *you*."

With that he lowered his head, gently taking her mouth with his own. The kiss was brief, transient, merely a flutter of sensation, and as he drew away, Esme felt a rush of disappointment.

"Open your mouth, Esme," he whispered hotly against her ear. "Let me taste you."

The thrill of his words scattered gooseflesh across her skin, and she readily parted her lips for his. This time the kiss was neither quick nor teasing. A hot passion boiled between them as Cleav sought to ease the fire by the wet wonder of Esme's mouth.

Esme ran her fingers up the strong arms that held her, caressing his broad shoulders. Sighing against his mouth, she reveled in the illicit enticements of his lips, answering each improper liberty with accessibility.

Her knees trembled, and for a moment she feared she might drop to his feet. But Cleav held her firmly against him as his strong hands cupped her backside and raised her off the ground. Her long, slim legs seemed to wrap themselves naturally around him. She heard him groan as if in pain before he pressed her hot, feminine core against his hard, masculine counterpart.

Esme broke away from his lips with a cry, and she squirmed closer to him, aching with desire.

"Do you feel that, Esme," he whispered hoarsely against her neck.

"Yes, oh, yes," she answered breathlessly.

"That's what a husband gives to his wife in their marriage bed."

"Yes, oh, yes." She continued to wiggle against him, trying to get closer, much closer, so much closer.

It was heaven. It was hell. Cleav ground his teeth, viciously trying to regain his control.

"You know what else it is," he whispered again, rolling his hips to give her a more accurate accounting of his form and dimensions. "It's what I would give to you if I were a cad."

"Oh, yes . . . what?"

She opened her eyes in surprise to find him staring at her, his jaw tight with self-control. They were both trembling with the force of desire. But Cleav held himself rigid as he removed her legs from his waist and set her feet back on solid ground.

"I am not a cad, Esme," he said gently. "And you are not someone who should be treated lightly."

"Cleav, I want . . ."

He held up his hand to stop her words. "I know what you want, Esme." He allowed his hand to drop to her bosom.

Caressing her gently, he felt the nipples begging his fingers for attention.

"This is not what you want," he whispered hoarsely as he moved his hand up her throat to raise her chin. "A quick tumble in the grass is not what you are hoping for," he insisted firmly. "You told me that first day in the store what you really want," he said. "You want to marry me."

Esme blushed and lowered her eyes. Cleav wouldn't let her off so easily.

"You want to marry me," he repeated. "But I do not, will not, marry you, Esme, not ever."

She opened her mouth to protest, but he continued. "I know it hurts you to hear this, Esme," he said. "But it's like the alum," he insisted. "The pain is real sharp for an instant, but then the wound heals up right away. You have to understand, Esme, that I do not, will not, ever love you. And you are not the kind of woman I would ever choose for a wife."

He meant to be kinder, to add more soothing words as he broke her heart. But he still trembled from their embrace. His hard-fought battle with his own conscience was barely won. If he did not break it cleanly, honestly now, Cleav knew he might well be tempted not to break it at all.

"You deserve better than I offer, Esme," he said. "Because to a foolish hill girl like you, I offer nothing."

9

"Well, good morning," Eula Rhy greeted her son as he stepped into the kitchen.

Nodding politely, Cleav returned her greeting sleepily. "What are you doing up so early, Mother? Obviously you must feel better today."

"I'm fine," she replied and then hastily corrected herself. "I'm not *well*, of course, but I'm having one of my better days."

"I'm glad to hear that," Cleav said sincerely as he accepted the steaming cup of coffee cradled daintily in the bone china saucer she held out to him. He could remember when his mother started his day, and his father's, with hearty breakfasts of pone and sausage. These days Mrs. Rhy cooked only sporadically, more often than not for company rather than her son.

"I needed to speak to you this morning," she told him. "I waited for you last night, but you came in so late." Eula shook her head with disapproval. "What in the world do you do down at those ponds until near midnight? Shouldn't those foolish trout go to bed at a decent hour like the rest of us?''

Cleav managed a crooked grin at his mother's complaint. Last night it was the people who were restless, not the fish.

"What did you want to speak to me about?" he asked, unwilling to examine more closely his own unsettled condition.

"I spoke with Mabel Tewksbury yesterday—" Eula ended the phrase with a heightened lilt designed to convey excitement.

"Oh?" Cleav said, seemingly unconcerned.

Mrs. Rhy put out a frying pan on the stove and began stirring the cornmeal and water mixture that boiled in a pot beside it. "Mrs. Tewksbury says Sophrona won't breathe a word to her about the little spat you two had last weekend." She glanced back at her son at the table. "It's very sad for a mother when a child won't confide those things."

Cleav kept his eyes on the contents of his delicately patterned coffee cup, and Eula sighed with annoyance.

"Mabel's been trying to find out what happened, but that girl has been silent as a stone." The fat in the pan began its noisy sizzle, and Eula focused her attention on it for a moment before pouring the thickened corn paste into the hot grease. "But yesterday," she continued without bothering to look back at Cleavis, "Sophrona says that she may have been unfair and judged you too harshly."

Eula turned to face her son, hoping to see a positive reaction to her words. His face revealed nothing.

"Mabel and I think that she's ready to forgive and forget and that you should strike while the iron is hot."

Cleav looked up at his mother but didn't respond.

Eula was exasperated. "I'm coming to the store early today. You pick up a nice little bunch of flowers for Miss

Sophrona and go over there and see if you two can make it up.''

Cleav raised his eyes to his mother's, but there was no obedient young son in his look. "Mother, Miss Sophrona and I are no concern of Mabel Tewksbury or yourself."

His mother's expression was incredulous. "No concern? You are our children. Whatever else are we supposed to be concerned about?"

He looked at his mother with eyes that were not particularly sympathetic. "I will make it up with Miss Sophrona in my own way, in my own time," he said flatly.

Eula Rhy smiled at him with just the right measures of approval and condescension. "Of course you will, Cleav," she told him. "I'm just letting you know that today is the right time and this afternoon at the Tewksbury parsonage is the right place." Mrs. Rhy plopped a generous amount of the thick, yellow fried contents of the pan onto Cleav's plate and set it before him.

He eyed it with disapproval.

"Mother, you know I don't care for mush."

"It's for your stomach."

"My stomach? There's nothing wrong with my stomach."

Eula shook a finger at him in maternal correction. "You can't fool me, young man," she told him. "I heard you myself way late in the night. Moaning in your sleep, like you was set to die."

Cleav's eyes widened perceptibly, and his face flushed redder than hot coals under molasses. His gaze dropped to the unappetizing mush on his plate, and dutifully he picked up his spoon and took a bite.

He missed his mother's smile of approval, unwilling to raise his head to look her in the eye. He had been moaning in his sleep last night, but it hadn't been the dyspepsia that pained him. Esme Crabb had haunted his dreams. Since that illicit kiss beside the pond, her image had become a most frequent visitor through his sleep.

Unlike the erotic dreams of his boyhood, where he'd felt satisfied and rested the next morning, today's morning light found him edgy, restless, and plagued by thoughts that were increasingly carnal.

Night after night her long, bare legs teased and tempted him, clutching at him in wantonness. Last night she'd wrapped them around his neck, and whimpering and begging, she'd pulled him to her closer, closer . . .

He'd awakened, disappointed, with a mouth full of pillow feathers and an ache that could not be soothed with a glass of fresh milk and a bowl of mush.

Just recalling the wicked fantasy made him stiffen at his own breakfast table. Not exactly the most respectable way for a gentleman to act. Certainly very inappropriate when sitting across the table from one's mother as she chattered on about the woman one is supposed to be planning to marry.

He took no pride in his illicit imaginings about Esme Crabb. Clearly, however, the situation was out of his control. He'd warned the young woman that his intentions were dishonorable, and he'd expected, hoped, that would be the end of her girlish infatuation. Still, she persisted in following him around like a shadow, flaunting herself brazenly before him.

"Sophrona is exactly the kind of daughter-in-law that I've always wanted," his mother was saying.

"Yes, Mother," Cleav answered absently. "She is without question the perfect choice for a wife."

"Then you mustn't delay a minute longer," she insisted. "This afternoon when she agrees to forgive you, you should propose immediately!"

"Mother!" Cleav's annoyance was tangible. "I told you that I will do things in my own time and in my own way."

Eula Rhy sniffed with disapproval. "Well, your 'own time' better be soon," she warned. "That horrible Crabb girl is making you the talk of this town. Miss Sophrona may not be interested in you if this goes on much longer."

"She's not 'that horrible Crabb girl,'" Cleav said hotly. "She's just young and confused and fancies herself in love with me."

His mother raised a skeptical eyebrow and sniffed with disdain. "Seems to me she may be getting older and wiser every day."

"Mornin', Esme," Rog Wicker called as he stepped through the front door of the store. "Mornin', Cleav," he added almost as an afterthought.

"Good morning," Cleav answered, but his jaw was set in disapproval. It had been that way all morning.

Denny, Tyree, Fat Blanchard, even Brother Oswald came waltzing into his store, greeting Esme as if she belonged there. And worse yet, Esme acted as if she did. She eagerly hurried to help the customers whenever Cleav was busy, and she knew the inventory and location of almost every item.

It was clear Esme loved the store. She enjoyed the order and accessibility of everything from fabric to crackers. Having all the things that she considered so dear right at her fingertips had a compelling appeal. When customers came in, Esme was smiling, friendly, happy, and the folks who came to the store smiled right back.

They smiled at Esme. The standard approach to Cleav these days was curiosity tinged with disapproval. No one knew what was going on, why Esme Crabb spent her every waking hour in the company of a man who was supposedly courting the preacher's daughter. But they blamed him.

In the normal course of things the woman would be suspect. But human nature being what it was, people tended to root for the underdog. Esme was a good-hearted, church-going, hill girl. Cleavis Rhy had spent years establishing himself as the prosperous and genteel storekeeper. His relative affluence was *not* a mark in his favor.

Although Cleav didn't know it, every eye in town was on the General Merchandise, and every word of gossip had his name attached.

"What do you think is going on between them two?" Toady Winthrop asked Sarah Mayfield.

"Heaven only knows," Sarah had replied in a scandalized whisper, "but for sure it's something. Have you seen the way he looks at her?"

Both Toady and her friend Madge nodded resolutely.

"Why, the man can hardly take his eyes off her," Madge answered. "It just ain't decent at all."

"It's that city life," Pearly Beachum assured Madge not an hour later as the latter helped her carry in the laundry. "In Knoxville he no doubt saw them rich city men taking advantage of poor helpless girls like Esme."

Madge tutted with disapproval.

"As soon as I get this laundry put away," Pearly promised, "I'm headed down to that store to see for myself what kind of carryings-on that Rhy is up to."

"So you think he's up to no good?" Madge asked.

"He's always wanted to be one of those city men," Pearly told her levelly. "I'm thinking that he's planning on making poor, precious little Esme his *mistress.*"

The last word was more mouthed than spoken, still Madge gave a little cry of shock and covered her ears.

That did not stop Madge, of course, from repeating it to no less than half a dozen other women that day.

"It's getting worse every day," Mabel Tewksbury confided to Eula Rhy. "The talk is just getting out of hand."

Mrs. Rhy gave the preacher's wife a worried nod of agreement. "There is nothing to it," she said flatly. "I'm convinced that the only feeling my dear Cleavis has for that girl is pity.''

Mabel was not completely convinced, but she didn't say so. ''The truth doesn't matter in these things,'' she admitted. ''In matters of hearsay, appearance is everything.''

Eula knew Mrs. Tewksbury was right.

''I've tried to keep the rumors away from Sophrona,'' Mabel confided. ''But I can't lock the girl in her room. Someone is going to say something to her, that's certain.''

''The best way to squelch these stories is a very public and prompt betrothal,'' Eula said.

Mrs. Tewksbury sighed with relief. ''I couldn't agree with you more.''

''I've told Cleav that the time is right to press his suit. I can only hope that he takes my advice.''

Mabel gave a nod of sympathetic understanding. ''I've spent hours trying to impress upon Sophrona that gentlemen with Mr. Rhy's civility and resources are extremely scarce in this part of the world. My prayers are that she will accept his proposal immediately.''

Neither woman was certain that their perfect solution was on the horizon.

It was not only from the tongues of women that gossip flew that day in Vader. Across the checkerboard old man Denny asked Tyree.

''What do you think about him and the girl?''

''What?''

''I said, what do you think about him and the girl?'' Denny repeated a bit louder.

Tyree huffed with disapproval. ''I may be half-blind,'' he stated. ''But that don't mean I cain't see what's right under my nose.''

''You think those two have been frolicking in the path of damnation?''

Tyree avoided the straight answer. ''I'm thinking that if'n

I was Yohan Crabb, I'd be coming down off that mountain with my shotgun loaded!''

As the temper of the community heated up, Esme remained blissfully unaware. The thrill of Cleav's wonderful kiss could still bring a blissful glow to her cheeks whenever she thought of it. And she thought of it often. Even his wounding words about never marrying her couldn't darken her optimism. He just needs to get used to the idea, she assured herself. He wanted a wife, and one wife was pretty much the same as another. Once he became accustomed to having her around, it would just seem natural to marry up.

Any self-reproach that she felt about Sophrona, she quickly explained away. If Sophrona wanted him, and it wasn't clear any longer that she did, she only wanted Cleav for herself. Esme needed him for her whole family. Humming to herself, again she imagined the Crabb family sitting comfortably on the porch of the biggest white—no, make that blue—house in Vader.

Cleav was too caught up in handling his own errant thoughts to worry about what others were thinking.

At first he was angry that Esme hadn't run from him after his deliberately wounding comments. It had taken all of his strength to treat her so coldly, and she appeared unaffected. Then he became angry at himself because he was *glad* she was still around. Although he was a gentleman, where Esme Crabb was concerned, he couldn't keep his thoughts in check. She'd reach for an item on the top shelf, and he'd imagine running his hand from her wrist to her ankle. He would imagine moulding her soft breast with his fingertip, exploring her nipped waist and caressing the generous hip, before staking his territory on those long, luscious limbs.

He had vivid memories of the hot, secret kiss they had

shared and the eager way she had pressed her body against him.

He'd told himself that he'd been trying to frighten her, make her understand that her reputation was at risk. But he knew, in all honesty, that he'd kissed her because he'd wanted to. And he'd only stopped because in another minute he wouldn't have been able to. . . .

Clearing his throat, Cleav focused on his surroundings. Rog Wicker was still looking around the store, Esme was searching down his horseshoe nails. She'd immediately gone to the correct bin, not five feet from where Cleav was standing, to fill Rog's order. That didn't please Cleav, but what she did there pleased him a little too much.

Since the bin was nearly empty, Esme had to lean far into the wide cask to retrieve the nails. The position raised her derriere, prominently outlining the impudent curve faultlessly. Cleav's eyes flew to Wicker in anger that he made such a request. The man had continued to browse through the store, completely unaware of the vision of shapely buttocks that was being exhibited on the far side of the room.

Imprudently Cleav's gaze returned to the bountiful backside of Esme Crabb. His mouth went dry as he realized he need only take one step closer and he'd be able to touch her.

He did not allow himself to take that step, but warmth pooled to his groin as strongly as if he had.

"Damn it!" he cursed silently and slammed his fist in fury against the counter.

Both Wicker and Esme glanced up at him questioningly.

Cleav flushed with embarrassment. "I've made an error in the accounts," he explained lamely.

It was an especially lame excuse for Esme, who could see that he did not have the accounts in front of him, but rather a drummer's catalog. She looked at him curiously but didn't comment.

Cleav felt her gaze and moved closer to the counter. The last thing he needed was for her to learn how easily he could be affected by her.

Esme carefully weighed the nails at the scale, dropping two back into the bin before she got the amount exact. She folded them in paper so that none of the horseshoe nails would spill. After laying the package on the counter along with Wicker's other supplies, she returned to her dusting of the washtubs.

Perhaps his mother was correct, Cleav concluded suddenly. This was undoubtedly the perfect time to get married, and Sophrona Tewksbury was the perfect person to marry. Esme had not believed him when he'd said that he would never wed her. A betrothal to another woman would surely go a long way in convincing her.

As he surreptitiously adjusted the fit of his trousers, he decided that a betrothal was not enough. He might not sleep *more* with a woman in his bed, but he would certainly sleep *more contentedly*. And a man who was satisfied at night was surely less bothered by temptation in the daytime.

Yes, he resolved to himself. This afternoon he would propose to Miss Sophrona. And he would insist that the engagement be as short as decently possible. If he'd married her months ago when he first thought of it, this whole regrettable situation with Esme would never have occurred.

Stealing unwelcome into his thoughts was the knowledge that he didn't exactly regret these past weeks with Esme. It was a heady feeling to be the recipient of a woman's adoration and longing. Never had any female made him feel so desired, so fascinating. If only his own passions had remained uninvolved. If only the woman in question were more suitable. If only it were Sophrona, not Esme, who lusted after him.

That brought him up short. Sophrona feeling lust? It was difficult to imagine. Certainly she'd be a dutiful wife, and he would try to please her, but the hungers of the flesh were surely incongruous to a lady of Miss Sophrona's refinement.

The fantasy of Sophrona Tewksbury whining and begging as she wrapped her legs around his neck was not only difficult for him to imagine but strictly ludicrous. A good part of the reason that he had never attempted to take liberties with the young lady—except on one fateful occasion—was simply that he couldn't imagine her allowing them. And if the slap he'd received under the maple tree was any indication, his judgment had been correct.

Still, a wife would be a wife, and a wife was exactly what he needed to get Esme Crabb out of his life for good.

Rog Wicker, apparently finished with his inspection of the available goods, walked to the counter to settle up.

"Will that be all?" Cleav asked as he totaled the price of the goods for purchase in his head.

"Need some tobacco," Wicker said as an afterthought.

"Red Leaf?" Cleav asked, already reaching for it.

With a quick glance over his shoulder, the man shook his head. "I smoke Carolina Blue," he said a little louder than necessary. "It's a lot smoother than that old cheap Red Leaf."

Cleav couldn't stop himself from taking a hasty look toward Esme, then wished he hadn't. She was grinning ear to ear and looked positively ready to swagger.

As he helped Rog load the supplies on his wagon, Cleav reassured himself that, lust or no lust, he was proposing marriage to Sophrona Tewksbury this very afternoon!

The store was empty when Cleav went back inside. Well, not empty, he corrected himself. Esme was there, but she'd become such a fixture even he'd begun to think that she belonged.

She was humming to herself as she rearranged the canned goods on the shelves. A few days ago she'd suggested that since the cans with the bright-colored paintings were quicker to catch the eye than the plain tins with black lettering, putting the brightly painted ones in front would draw attention to the shelf and cause customers to make more purchases. Cleav tried, without success, to explain to her that people only bought the things that they needed. That people were too smart to be lured into buying something that wasn't necessary just because it came to their attention.

She hadn't been convinced, so he'd allowed her to change the shelving presentation however she liked, thinking she would learn for herself. To his amazement, he'd sold more canned goods in the last two weeks than in the whole month prior. And with spring blossoming out everywhere, the need for canned goods should have dropped completely.

Cleav shook his head in disbelieving approval. The woman certainly did have a head for business. Maybe after all of this was over, when he was blissfully wed to Miss Sophrona and Esme safely married to one of the hill boys, he could hire her to work for him. That would leave him more time for his trout. And a little cash money coming in regularly wouldn't hurt her family, either.

Satisfied with his solution to all his problems, Cleav almost felt like humming to himself. He resisted it, however, and returned to contemplating the drummer's catalog.

The cool quiet of the store, disturbed only by the pleasant sound of a lively tune on Esme's lips, lulled Cleav into a temporary contentment.

When the humming stopped, Cleav looked up.

As usual, with no thought to her surroundings or the proprieties, Esme Crabb had paused to jerk up her skirts and adjust her sagging stockings.

At the sight of those well-remembered, oft-dreamt-of limbs, Cleav's pulse began to pound. Heat suffused him, and the air within the confines of the store was suddenly not enough to catch his breath. This was not going to happen again, he swore to himself, not ever. He was done with her merciless teasing.

"Don't!" His shout was so unexpected, Esme actually jumped.

She stared at him, questioning and a little frightened.

"Have you no shame at all?" he asked furiously. "You flaunt yourself before me like a hussy."

"I am not flaunting myself," Esme defended herself, her cheeks blazing.

"Then what *are* you doing?" His voice was angry and dripping with sarcasm.

"I'm straightening my stockings," she explained haughtily and with a good deal more justification than she felt.

"I know you are straightening your stockings," Cleav told her. "I've watched you do it a half dozen times."

"Well, you should keep your eyes to yourself."

"If I did, you'd be very disappointed."

"Oh!" Esme felt the sting of the words as if they were a slap.

"I've seen more than I care to of those pitiful stockings of yours, and I'd like to request, if you think you can manage it, that you keep your legs decently covered in my presence."

Even knowing she was in the wrong, Esme's chin was high. She would not allow herself to be cowed by Cleav's boorish behavior. "I suppose you would have me just let my stockings sag to the floor until they trip me and I fall flat on my face!"

"Other women don't seem to suffer with that problem," he countered.

"Because other women have garters to hold their stockings up! Garters are not something that arrive in a charity box, and I'll have you know that I've certainly never had the selfish desire to spend good money buying such frivolities."

Cleav opened his mouth but couldn't think of a reply. He searched his brain momentarily for a snappy comeback and then stormed across the room. Jerking open the second drawer down in the fabric and notions section, he grabbed the first thing that came to his attention.

Striding directly to Esme, he slapped what he had retrieved into her hand. "Here! Take them," he said.

Esme gazed at her hands in wonderment. Brand-new, never-been-worn, store-bought garters. They were pristine white, but sported tiny bows of baby's-blush pink.

"Just consider them a gift from me," Cleav said cynically. "And wear them for me *every day*!"

Esme brought the beautiful scraps of dainty cloth up to her heart. Never in her life had she owned anything so beautiful, so feminine, so new.

Cleav might have tossed them to her on a whim, but for Esme they represented all that was fine and beautiful and civilized in the world. And they were given to her by the most wonderful, handsome, intelligent man any woman could ever dream of. She would wear them for him, every day. And each time she put them on, it would be as if he'd touched her flesh himself.

"Save to graces, Cleavis," she murmured. "They are beautiful." Tears welled up in her eyes until she could barely make out the beauty of the tiny pink bows. His expression was still as dark as a thundercloud, but she could no longer see it.

"Thank you, Cleavis," she managed to whisper with breathy excitement. "Thank you so very much."

The tears were now threatening to flow. Esme *wanted* to cry for joy, but not in front of him. She fled to the doorway, intending to run to the solitude of the woods with her treasured gift. Alone, with none to spy her sentiment, she could caress and kiss the pretty pink ribbons and model the feminine garments with none to see but herself and the woodchucks.

Rushing through the door, blinded by her tears, she ran smack dab into Pearly Beachum.

"Lord almighty!" Pearly exclaimed. "You pretty near knocked me down, girlie."

"Sorry," Esme answered, breathlessly, still unbalanced by the collision.

Pearly looked at her more closely.

"You crying, Esme?"

"Oh, no, ma'am," Esme assured her as the first of the welling teardrops took that inconvenient opportunity to dribble from the sides of her eyes.

"You *are* crying!" Pearly exclaimed. "Has something happened? Has *he* done something to you?"

"No, nothing's happened," Esme said, but brought the back of her hand up to wipe her eyes.

Mrs. Beachum saw a flash of pink and white within the young woman's grasp.

"What have you got there in your hands?"

The woman's voice sounded so suspicious, Esme immediately thought she was accusing her of stealing something.

"It's a gift from Mr. Rhy," she explained hurriedly.

Her curiosity unappeased, the older woman, a well-known busybody, grabbed Esme's hands and forced them open.

"Garters!" She nearly screamed the word. Pearly Beachum was clear shocked right down to her toes. "Cleavis Rhy gave you a pair of garters?"

∽ 10 ∾

It had rained all morning and the path up the mountain was soggy with mud, but Cleav took no notice. It was exactly the kind of day he expected it to be: morose, gray, and threatening. All his days had been like that lately. Ever since he'd heard Pearly Beachum screeching from the front door.

He'd hurried out to see what had happened. Mrs. Beachum had taken one look at him and slammed him beside the head with her silver-topped parasol. Then she'd put her arm protectively around Esme and had dragged the young woman away.

That was four days ago. The last time he had seen Esme Crabb, but far from the last time he'd heard about her. He'd heard little else.

"The people of this community will not tolerate such shenanigans," Brother Oswald had stated publicly. And Fat Blanchard had backed him up.

"Giving a decent woman a present of underwear is tantamount to a marriage proposal," he stated. "It always has been."

At first he'd thought he could ride out the storm. He

would get himself respectably married to Miss Sophrona and eventually the talk would die down.

He owned the only general store for miles. Even those who disapproved of him would think twice about heading over the mountains to Russellville just to buy coffee and sugar. It was simply a matter of time and the whole thing would be forgotten.

Unfortunately, he was wrong.

When he went to speak with Miss Sophrona, the preacher had slammed the door in his face. It was only his refusal to leave the parsonage porch that finally brought Reverend Tewksbury out with the word that Miss Sophrona had taken to her bed with such a malaise that her parents were worried for her health. The preacher made it crystal clear that as far as he and his family were concerned, the pink-and-white unmentionables that Esme Crabb had carried out of the store that day meant that Cleavis Rhy was now a married man.

The store remained empty, and his neighbors refused to speak to him. And his home was even worse. Eula Rhy put on her mourning complete with black satin shoes and a veil, claiming that she could never outlive the shame. Every few moments she would sniff daintily into a black lace hankie.

Only the fish continued to treat Cleav as they always had. He began to wonder if they had just not heard the gossip yet.

Slipping on the steep narrow slope, Cleav grasped a rhododendron vine as if it were a lifeline and managed to keep upright, but only just. He gave a smile that was devoid of humor.

"That's what I should do," he suggested sarcastically. "Falling face down in the mud would definitely make my new life as the local scoundrel absolutely complete."

In a normal week, Friday afternoon was certainly not the time for Cleav to be making a trip up the mountain, but he'd closed up the store. There was no reason to open it. Even

Denny and Tyree set up their checker game under the oak tree across the road.

"You've got to own up to your responsibilities," Reverend Tewksbury had advised him. "You've danced to the tune, now you must pay the fiddler."

"I haven't danced . . . or anything else, for that matter, with Esme Crabb."

The preacher shook his head. "That's not the way it looks to this town." The older man folded his arms obstinately across his chest. "A decent girl must be treated decently. Giving a girl fancy drawers just ain't decent."

"Fancy drawers!" Cleav was incredulous. "I gave her a cheap pair of garters."

Reverend Tewksbury's expression was livid. "It's bad enough that you ruin the girl's reputation. Must you brag about how little it cost you!"

"I didn't ruin her reputation," Cleav insisted.

"It's ruined," the preacher said flatly. "Are you suggesting you didn't do it?"

"It's not me that ruined her," Cleav told him obstinately. "It's Pearly Beachum and you and the rest of this town who have jumped to conclusions, conclusions that are completely untrue."

The reverend looked somewhat pacified. "I believe you are sincere when you say that, Cleav," the older man told him. "And I'm glad to think that you haven't taken advantage of the young girl's foolish infatuation for you."

For an instant Cleav thought he might win the preacher over, but Reverend Tewksbury quickly quashed that hope. "Be that as it may, Esme Crabb has lost her good name. It's only decent that you as a gentleman do the right thing."

Cleavis Rhy knew defeat when he faced it eyeball to eyeball. That's why he was slipping and sliding through the mushy damp woods on his way to the Crabb shack. He was going to Do the Right Thing.

He heard the Crabbs before he saw them. The giggly lilt of girlish voices reached him, and he hurried his pace. Stepping into the clearing, he spied the twins, who were laughing and talking as they gathered water from the rain barrel. When they spotted him, the smiles faded from their faces, and they stared in undisguised distaste.

Cleav stared them down, unwilling to allow the two hill princesses to look down their noses at him.

"Tell Esme I've come to talk to her," he said arrogantly.

Without a word Adelaide and Agrippa took their buckets into their shack and closed the door behind them.

Alone, Cleav studied his surroundings. He'd never been on this part of the mountain, and he'd certainly never seen the place the Crabbs called home.

"It's nothing but a cave," he whispered to himself, almost in horror. While he mentally postulated the significance of nineteenth-century cave dwellers, the door opened.

It was not Esme who walked toward him, but her father.

"What do you want up here, Rhy?" Yo Crabb's anger was visible, and Cleav wondered momentarily if the old fiddler might try to do him harm.

Politeness being his only defense, Cleav smiled with as much amiability as he could manage. "Good afternoon, Mr. Crabb," he said. "I've come to speak with Miss Esme, if I may."

Crabb raised a disapproving eyebrow.

"Miss Esme ain't receiving callers at this time," he answered, mimicking Cleav's prim form of speech.

"Perhaps she'll receive *me*, if you were to ask her," he suggested.

Yohan Crabb put his hands on his hips and stared down the younger man before him.

"Now, why on earth would I want to do that?" he asked.

Cleav squared his shoulders, channeling his anger into innocuous actions. "Because," he answered evenly, "I plan to ask her to go down the mountain with me to get married.''

Silence between the two men lingered to the point of discomfiture.

"So you've decided to marry up," Crabb said.

"Yes," Cleav answered civilly. "It seems the only thing to do. If she's ready to come with me now, I'm sure we can get Reverend Tewksbury to marry us this evening."

"You in a hurry to have her?"

"Mr. Crabb, I'm sure you know what's being said. I—"

"I know exactly what folks are running their mouths about. And I can tell you for damn near certain that I'm even madder about it than you are."

The fury in the old man's eyes convinced Cleav he was speaking the truth.

"But," Crabb continued, "my Esme is only getting married up one time. She's deserving better than a hide-in-a-hole weddin' with a man that thinks she ain't good enough for him."

Cleav suddenly realized that he had merely assumed that Esme would marry him. He certainly hadn't imagined any resistance from the Crabb family.

"You are mistaken, Mr. Crabb, if you do not think that I hold your daughter in high regard."

Yohan looked at him dubiously. "I'm listening," he said.

Cleav hesitated momentarily, groping for words. "Esme . . . Esme is . . . bright, yes, very bright and comely, in her own way, and a hard worker," he finished confidently. "She'll make a wonderful wife that any man would be proud to call his own."

Crabb nodded. "You're right about that, Rhy," he told him. "Trouble is, you don't believe it."

Cleav saw his chances and his reputation disappearing before his eyes.

"Mr. Crabb, I—"

Yohan held up a hand to silence him. "You want to marry up with my Esme? Then you're gonna have to do it right," he said.

Cleav nodded weakly, indicating agreement.

"No midnight marriage and sneaking her off to your house," he stated firmly. "She gets a real wedding with music and flowers and the whole town standing in the church to hear you make your vows to her."

Cleav almost choked, clearly not pleased with the prospect. "Do you think that's best?"

"I sure do! It ain't like folks won't hear about it anyhow."

"But," Cleav protested, "the need for haste is—"

Yo shook his head in disagreement. "They's haste and they's foolishness." The older man hesitated, taking measure of his prospective son-in-law. "You get a wedding set up by Sunday," Yo said finally, "and I'll bring her down the mountain to marry you."

"Fine," Cleav agreed. The day after tomorrow was surely soon enough.

"All right," Crabb said and offered his hand to clinch the deal.

"Perhaps I should speak to Esme now?"

"What for?" her father asked him.

"To formally request her hand," Cleav told him. "To see how she feels about the wedding."

Crabb shook his head. "The way I hear it, you've already seen more of my daughter than a bridegroom is entitled to!"

Cleav's clenched teeth threatened to break, but he didn't back down. "There are things that need to be said between us," he insisted.

"They'll be plenty of time for talk after she's your missus. You got anything to say before then," Yo told him, "you just tell it to me."

Cleav's next words were precise and raw-edged. "Tell her I hope that she's happy about getting what she wanted."

* * *

Wearing the white, charity basket castoff of Sophrona Tewksbury, Esme Crabb, head held high, proudly made her way down the mountain to get married.

"It'll be fine," she whispered quietly to herself. "I'll make him real happy. I'll be the best wife a man ever had," she vowed. Just exactly how she was going to accomplish that was not yet clear, but if determination was enough, she would succeed.

Her father's face was worried but determined. Yo had never told her any of the private discussion he'd had with Cleav. But he hadn't needed to. Esme could read disapproval in every line of his face.

She'd been so foolish! She berated herself, not for the first time. This wasn't what she'd wanted. Although marriage to Cleavis Rhy had been her aim for weeks, she hadn't planned on a scandal or an unwilling husband.

Pearly Beachum had caught her off-guard. With honesty as her natural bent, she'd blurted out the truth when a lie would have better served. Looking back, she'd rather have had the whole congregation believe she was stealing from Rhy's store than bring disgrace to him. Nor did she wish to tarnish the shining hope that the fancy, store-bought garters had represented. Remembrance brought a blush to her cheek and the precious pieces of pink and white to mind. She could feel them now fitting smooth and snug against her thighs. Even in her current confusion, a warmth of tenderness suffused her, and a tiny smile quivered at the side of her mouth. It was the sweetest gift she had ever received. Surely he must care for her. Surely he must care a little.

As the church came into sight, she became even more apprehensive. Her forehead broke out in beads of sweat.

"He must care a little!" she said in a desperate whisper. "Please God, I'll never ask for anything else!"

Adelaide and Agrippa, however, were bothered by neither the finality of her marriage nor the circumstances leading to her proposal. Primped and pretty, they were giddy with excitement. For them weddings were the most fun party of all, and certainly the twins had the best chance of catching the wedding bouquet.

"That'd mean that we'd marry next," Adelaide cheerfully informed her father.

Yo did not seem particularly taken with the idea. "How soon is next?" he asked with a disagreeable frown.

"As soon as Armon asks us!" Agrippa answered with a near shriek of delight. And the two young women shared a laughing embrace as they hurried ahead to the church.

Crabb hesitated, touching Esme's shoulder lightly to stop her progress. "I agreed to this wedding 'cause I's thinking it were your idea," he said evenly as he studied his daughter. "If you're afeared of this man or you changed your mind, just say so."

Even in her anxious state, Esme managed a smile for her father. Pa was lazy and practically worthless, but she never doubted his love for her.

"Marrying Cleavis Rhy is going to put us in clover, Pa," she answered with more enthusiasm than she felt at the moment. "We're going to move into that big fine house and eat regular year-round."

He shook his head dubiously. "Esme-girl, I'd never be able to choke down a bite if I thought the food was bought with your misery."

Esme managed a halfhearted chuckle. "Being married to a rich, handsome man is the kind of *misery* most girls dream of," she bantered playfully.

"But you sure ain't most girls," Yohan said. "Besides, marriage is more than dreams. Living with the wrong person, even when you love them, can be a world of grief. And truth to tell," he added, "the word *love* ain't never fallen from your lips that I can remember."

Esme forced out a little giggle that didn't quite ring true. "I love you and the twins, Pa. I *respect* the man who's to be my husband. I think that's enough."

Her father shrugged doubtfully. "Respect ain't much comfort in a wedding bed."

Her face flaming scarlet, Esme swallowed the spurt of anxiety and fear as if it were a tangible thing.

"I'll do my duty," she said bravely.

Yo nodded. "I never doubted it," he admitted. "But bedding a man ain't always easy for a woman."

Esme paled slightly.

"I never talked of such with you girls, 'cause it just didn't seem fitting," he said, showing signs of paternal awkwardness. "But if you are going to walk into that church and marry up, I want to be sure that you know what you're doing."

There was silence between them for a moment.

"I want to marry him," Esme whispered.

"You want to bed him?"

Esme nodded. "I ain't never," she confessed. "But when he kisses me, I . . . I want more."

She'd lowered her eyes with shame, but her father grasped her chin in his hand and raised it to look down into her face.

"That's where most women start their married life," he said, "half-yearning, half-curious."

"I've heard that it hurts?" Her statement was formed like a question.

There was a perceptible nod of agreement. "Your mama said it hurt some the first time," he admitted. "But I think it's mostly just so downright embarrassing," he said.

Yohan gazed thoughtfully across the meadow toward the church. "A gal is told for twenty years to keep herself decently covered, and then she stands a few moments in front of the preacher and finds herself married up to a fellow she hardly knows.'' Yo Crabb shook his head in disbelief. ''And she's supposed to lift up her nightgown for him like it was nothing!''

Esme covered her own burning cheeks at the thought.

''And the fellow,'' Yo continued. ''He's pert-near as ignorant as she is. The most of what he knows about it is stories he's heard from other men. Nearly all of which are lies and bragging. Now he's supposed to reassure her, comfort her, and please her while his own heart's a-beating so loudly he can't hear himself think and he's touching and squeezing things he's been dreaming about for years.''

With a pessimistic sigh, Crabb gently patted his daughter's cheek and carefully smoothed a stray lock of her hair. ''What I'm aiming to say, Esme-girl,'' he told her, ''is that it ain't always perfect right away. Things between a man and a woman take time. That's why God made marriage forever.''

Yo looked into her eyes seeking assurance. ''I'd feel better about this, Esme, if I knew that you loved him.''

Esme nearly choked on the words, but she knew they had to be said. ''I was thinking to marry him for all of us, Pa. I figured I could get along with just about any fellow with some money.'' She hesitated. ''Truly, I didn't expect to feel nothing special, but I think I really do love him, Pa,'' she admitted. ''I just can't seem to help myself. I just wish he loved me.''

Her father's smile brightened. ''He will, Esme-girl,'' he told her. ''How can he help himself?''

She was late. Cleav forced himself not to look at his watch again. Everybody was staring at him. Sweat beaded on his brow as a glistening accent to his florid complexion. Grandpa McCray had once told him a story about his boyhood in Scotland, where sinners were made to sit on a chair in front of the church, and the congregation stared at them as a punishment. In Cleav's youth he'd thought they'd gotten off easy. Now he wasn't so sure.

Maude Honsucker, who was every bit of ninety, was providing the music. She had warned Cleavis that she could only play the tunes that she could remember. This morning her memory was apparently not too lively as she'd been playing the same hymn repeatedly for a good twenty minutes. And her very soulful rendition of "Nearer My God to Thee" had Cleavis thinking that rather than standing to the right of the pulpit, he should be lying in a box in front of it.

Scanning the crowd, he noted, not for the first time, that it was an exceptional turnout. He'd had hopes that since his own mother refused to make an appearance, the rest of the community would do likewise. But it looked to Cleav as if Mrs. Rhy was the only living soul within ten miles that was not in attendance.

Even Sophrona, looking brave and beautiful, sat with her mother on the second pew on the left. Her head was held high, and her face betrayed no emotion. He had never anticipated that she would be there. Although there had been no understanding between them, there had been expectation. Perhaps that was why she hadn't stayed away. Community sympathy would have embarrassed her. No doubt she would be the first to wish Cleav and his new bride well.

Cleav cringed with disgust and gave into the urge to check his watch. Maybe she just wanted to be a part of the audience that watched Cleavis Rhy be left waiting at the church!

With an audible creak, the door to the church opened and the Crabb twins sauntered in. Behind him, Cleav heard Reverend Tewksbury sigh in audible relief. Apparently he wasn't the only one who'd begun to wonder.

Swinging clasped hands as they made their way down the aisle, the two pretty young girls hesitated only once to giggle when Armon Hightower gave them a broad wink. As they reached the front of the church, the two gave Cleav a haughty glance before assuming their places.

"Is she on her way?" Cleav whispered to the nearest twin, unable to tell one from the other.

"She's outside talking to Pa," she answered, pausing only an instant to watch Cleav's shoulders relax before she added spitefully, "I think he's trying to convince her to go through with this." This last was said quite loudly.

Humiliation flooded Cleav like Indian Creek in the springtime. The crowd tittered as the Crabb girl's words were hastily repeated and spread like a fire through the sanctuary. He had no idea where to direct his gaze. He didn't want to see his friends and neighbors laughing at his expense. Unexpectedly the memory of the Crabbs' charity basket came to mind. As if it were yesterday, Cleav could see Esme standing proud and strong, her eyes focused on an unseen horizon as she gazed over the heads of the crowd.

Cleav raised his chin and stared at the distant nothingness. If Esme could will herself unashamed, so could he. His mind traveled back in time to his school days in Knoxville. Again he heard the taunts and laughter of young gentlemen in tailor-made suits. Strangely the sting was not as cutting. Had time softened the images of his humbling? Or had experience taught him taunts didn't matter?

The door to the church opened, and Cleav watched the woman who would be his wife step inside. She hesitated for a moment inside the door and then squinted toward the front.

Cleav's face broke into a delighted smile. Esme's vision wasn't good enough to see him, yet, but he could see her perfectly. Her chin raised and determined, she was as ill-at-ease and embarrassed as he was. Somehow that pleased him.

The Widow Honsucker abruptly changed the sad lament she played to a rousing "When the Roll Is Called Up Yonder, I'll Be There."

Taking her father's arm, Esme led, rather than followed him, up the aisle. Brother Oswald stood, detaining her momentarily, as he handed her a small bouquet of lupins, cut from the bushes at the side of the church. The stems were carefully wrapped with white ribbons and a shield of leaves protected the blossoms, since the touch of hands would darken the petals. The sweet pungent odor already filled the room. Esme breathed in a deep fragrant breath.

Looking up, her eyes met Cleav's. They gave each other the cautious look of two people joined more by fate than free will. Esme lowered her gaze discreetly and continued at her father's side, making her way to the front of the church.

When they reached the preacher, her father at her left, his fiddle tucked neatly under his arm, and her sisters at her right, attractively and identically turned out in their Sunday best, Esme focused her attention on Reverend Tewksbury.

But Cleavis focused his attention on her.

"Dearly Beloved," the reverend began. His voice was hoarse and caught unexpectedly. After clearing his throat, he began again. "Dearly Beloved. We are gathered here in the presence of God to unite this man and this woman in the bonds of holy matrimony. An honorable estate . . ."

Cleav was not listening. His eyes and his thoughts were on Esme standing barely a yard away. He would never have chosen her, he reminded himself. But perhaps it wouldn't be so bad. He remembered the warmth of her kisses, the feel of her body pressed close to his, and—oh heaven of heavens— those long, lovely legs. He reminded himself that she was bright and hardworking. Although she certainly would not be an asset on his arm, he thought she might clean up well and wouldn't look too bad in decent clothes. He was willing to make the best of it. "Who gives this woman in marriage?'' Reverend Tewksbury boomed across the crowd as if he didn't know the person to answer was standing right in front of him.

''I do!'' Yohan shouted right back.

Stepping back, Yo placed Esme's hand in Cleav's. The two shared a brief, blushing glance before returning their attention to the preacher.

Yohan, however, was not finished. To the amazement of everyone, he put the fiddle to his chin and began to play a slow, sweet, romantic tune of the mountains.

Esme recognized it as the one he'd written the day she'd gone down the mountain to ask Cleav to marry her. That wonderful day, so long ago now, when she'd learned what sweetness was desire.

Cleav looked at his bride, surprised to see tears forming in her eyes. The song *was* tender, he had to admit. Too tender for the loveless wedding it commemorated. But then, perhaps it was not loveless for Esme. A woman who so brazenly chased, offered, and even begged for attention was without a doubt infatuated with the man of her pursuit. Maybe it was more than a girlish fancy. She could be deeply in love with him. That pleased him more than it should have.

To have Esme Crabb, with her sweet smile and seductive legs, striving to win his favor. And she'd certainly never be any trouble to him. A woman so desperately in love would be easy to handle.

''Do you, Manfred Cleavis Rhy, take this woman, Esmeralda Joleen Crabb, to be your lawful wedded wife? Do you promise to protect, honor, and cherish her, keeping yourself only unto her as long as you both shall live?''

Cleav swallowed hurriedly and then stated with conviction, ''I do.''

''And do you, Esmeralda Joleen Crabb, take this man to be your husband? Do you promise to love and obey him, keeping yourself only unto him as long as you both shall live?"

Esme turned to look at Cleav. There was fear in her eyes but resolution, too. Facing Reverend Tewksbury, she replied with calm determination, "I do."

Cleav brought out the ring. The wide gold band had been in his store for two years. He'd paid a fast-talking drummer too much for it and had never been able to sell it. Although it was too much to hope that it might fit Esme, when he placed it on the third finger of her left hand, it was perfect.

"By the power vested in me by this church and the State of Tennessee, I pronounce this couple husband and wife."

Slipping his hands around Esme's waist, Cleav pulled her close and leaned down to capture her lips with his own.

"What God has joined together, let no man put asunder."

❧ 11 ❧

There were congratulations and slaps on the back as the young couple stepped out in the churchyard for a cup of punch. Cleav had engaged Sarah Mayfield and her daughter-in-law to manage the refreshments: pink lemonade punch and white layer cake decorated with burnt sugar on the icing. Cleav had told Mrs. Mayfield to spare no expense, and the congregation considered these treats luxurious. Esme Crabb might be a simple hill girl, but her wedding would be remembered as a lavish affair.

Unfortunately, Esme had hardly had time to take stock of her surroundings when Armon Hightower separated her from her new husband. He grabbed her around the waist and forcefully pulled her from the party.

"What are you doing?" she asked, more startled than annoyed.

Armon's grin was wicked. "Miz Rhy, I suspect you'd call it being 'kidnapped.'"

Esme only allowed a second for the meaning of his words to sink in. *"Cleavis!"* she screamed.

"What's going on there?" Cleav called angrily as he

watched in shock as Armon Hightower hoisted Esme on his shoulder and began to head toward the mountain.

"Hightower! Come back here!" he hollered.

His reaction earned him some derisive laughter from Armon's fellow kidnappers. "You can buy her back for three dollars' worth of sorghum and a jug of moonshine!" one of the Roscoe brothers called to him as he followed Armon and the squealing bride.

"What are you talking about?"

"We're talking about a shivaree ransom," Will Gambridge called back with a laugh.

"Three dollars' worth of sorghum would be about a whole barrel," Cleav said incredulously.

"Rolling a barrel up the mountain with a jug of whiskey in one hand will be a trick worth any bridegroom's price," Gambridge taunted.

"Yahoo!" the Roscoe brothers called as they hurried after Hightower.

"Shivaree!" Will added as he rushed past the spectators, now over their surprise and laughing in alliance with the kidnappers.

Cleav stood staring after them, rooted to the spot. With the unusual and hurried circumstances of the wedding, the last thing he'd considered was a shivaree. Yo Crabb, his new father-in-law, hurried up behind him.

"Good Lord, son," he said. "Go after her."

Cleav started after them, but the culprits divided up as soon as they reached the cover of trees.

Wandering around without picking up a trail for the better part of an hour, Cleav decided that striking a bargain was his best chance of getting his wife back before morning.

Hurrying back to the General Merchandise, he found Mort Riggly, the local moonshiner, waiting for him on the porch of the store.

"Evenin', Cleavis," Mort greeted him amiably. "Was it a nice weddin'? Sorry I missed it."

"It was fine," Cleav answered distractedly. "How'd you know to be here?"

"Armon tole me you'd be needing another jug for the ransom when he bought his."

Cleav's eyes widened in concern. "They already have one whole jug?"

Mort heard the worry in his tone and waved it off. "Don't get yourself in a dither," Mort told him. "I admit that, drunk or sober, Will and those Roscoe boys could throw all their good sense together and wouldn't have enough to make change." Mort chuckled at his own little joke. "But Armon's up there with her. He's wild, but he ain't stupid. And he's got feelings for the gal anyway."

"Feelings?" Cleav felt the inexplicable rise of jealousy, and his question was harsher than he intended. "What do you mean by that?"

Mort found Cleav's agitation downright amusing. "I sure don't mean what you think I'm meaning," the whiskey seller assured him. "He's been courting those twins now for nigh on a half year. I suspect he's thinking your gal is practically his in-law." Mort laughed out loud. "Now, that's something I never woulda thought to see. You and Armon being practically relation."

"Armon Hightower is not a member of my family," Cleav stated tightly.

"Not yet, maybe," the old moonshiner admitted. "But when you marry up with folks like the Crabbs . . ." The man shook his head. "Hell, Mr. Rhy, you probably got shirttail relation from hear to Memphis, each poorer than the next."

"I married Miss Esme, not her family," Cleav said coldly. "Now, do you want to sell me that jug of liquor or just talk to me all afternoon?"

In full knowledge of the situation, and perhaps a bit of spite for Cleav's attitude, Mort asked three times the going rate. Cleav had no choice but to pay for the whiskey. And because he never drank spirits himself, he couldn't even threaten to take his business elsewhere in the future.

Counting his money contentedly, Mort Riggly became encouraging. "Don't you worry about a thing, Mr. Rhy," he said. "That little gal of yours is as safe on that mountain as if she was in her daddy's arms. Shivaree's a good thing for weddings. A woman getting married, well, she gets a little bit scared of her husband, that's natural. When some other men come along and steal her away, well, then she's even scareder of them. Her man comes and rescues her, she ain't nothing but grateful."

Mort patted Cleav's clean white shirt consolingly with a grimy hand. "Shivaree gets a marriage from 'him and me' to 'us and them' in a hurry." Elbowing a playful dig to Cleav's ribs, he added, "About midnight tonight you'll be downright beholden to those kidnappers."

Cleav's expression was stony.

Mort slapped his thigh with hilarity and with a lusty laugh headed off into the night. "Mark my words," he called back to Cleav. "You'll be thanking those boys afore morning."

Cleav ignored his words. Those boys would be lucky if he wasn't *killing* them before morning. What on earth was he doing tracking a gang of ne'er-do-wells through the mountain with a cask of sorghum molasses because of a pagan custom!

Attaching the handle of the whiskey jug to a piece of rope, he hung it over his shoulder like a quiver of arrows, then went to retrieve a barrel of molasses from the store.

Ransom assembled, Cleav gave a sigh of resignation and began the grueling task of rolling a full and heavy cask of sorghum molasses up one of the steepest inclines in eastern Tennessee.

The week before having been wet and rainy, the ground had reached saturation point. His shoes repeatedly slipped in the fresh mud, but he managed to catch himself each time. At least he hadn't ended up sprawled in the mud. He could imagine what a disaster that would have been with a barrel of molasses rolling over him and back down the mountain.

It was far too dark to see "signs" on the trail. Cleav just assumed, and rightly so, that the men would have taken the roughest, most difficult path.

"Is this woman worth it?" he asked himself more than once. He never bothered to answer that question, he just braced his foot in the next slippery step and pushed the cask a few feet higher.

He never did actually find them. Will Gambridge finally stepped out from behind a tree, startling him.

"You've done better than I thought," the hill boy commented with a modicum of respect. He asked Cleav for the whiskey and, after taking a good long swig, offered the jug to Cleav.

"No, thanks," Cleav answered, not even tempted. The ordeal wasn't over yet, and he needed to keep his wits about him for Esme's sake.

Will led the way to the clearing where they held Esme, laughing and talking as if this were the best game he'd ever played.

"Ahhherhea!" Cleav heard her cry before he saw her.

Esme was tied to a fallen tree, twisting and squirming in the mud. A red bandanna was tied on her mouth. Her eyes were bright and wide, but more with anger than with fear.

"Thank the Lord you made it," the eldest Roscoe boy teased. "I was worrying that this she-devil would kill us all afore you got here."

The men laughed companionably as they passed the jug of whiskey around. Even if he hadn't been told, it was obviously not their first of the evening.

"Get the gag off her," Cleav ordered with fury.

Startled at his anger, Will jumped to obey, but Armon told him to stay.

"She was spitting and squealing like a pig stuck in a blackberry bush," Armon explained casually as he leaned down to untie the constricting piece of cloth. "We didn't hurt her none, Cleavis. We's just trying to quiet her down."

"She wouldn't kiss us nohow," the younger Roscoe declared. "With no good use for a mouth, a woman's best when she's shut up."

Freezing the stupid young man with a look, Cleav went down on his knees to help Esme get up.

"Are you all right?"

"These lousy, no-account varmints," Esme complained bitterly. "You've made a mess of my wedding gown, you turd brain," she snapped at Hightower.

"You planning on getting married in it again?" Armon asked.

Esme headed for him, intending to kick him senseless. Cleav's arm around her waist stayed her. "Control yourself, Esme," he said firmly. "I won't have my wife cursing and fighting."

That stopped her, but just barely.

"You've got your jug and your sorghum," Cleavis pointed out to the captors with determined civility. "I'm taking Esme home now."

"Whew-he!" one of the Roscoes proclaimed. "He's hopping mad 'cause we delayed his honeymoon!"

The other Roscoe giggled lewdly. "Ain't marriage something wonderful. They'll be beating the ticks out of the mattress tonight!"

This time it was Cleav who nearly started a ruckus, but Esme grabbed his clenched fist. "We're leaving," she said.

"Not right yet," Armon disagreed firmly. Cleav and Esme both turned to him, challengingly.

"You've paid *your* part of the ransom, Cleav," Hightower stated, gesturing toward the jug in his hand. "But Mrs. Rhy here ain't let a one of us kiss the bride."

"And I ain't about to neither, you scheming low-life polecat!" Esme protested.

"You shouldn't talk so poor about me, now, Esme," Armon warned with a chuckle. "We're practically kin, ain't we?"

"No, we ain't!" Esme insisted. "And as God is my witness, I'll do everything I can to keep you from ever being a relation of mine."

"Not even a kissing cousin?" the handsome hill boy teased.

"Are you looking for trouble, Hightower?" Cleav asked.

"Guess not," Armon answered tongue-in-cheek, glancing around at the other fellows. "You're the one that married up with *her*."

The other kidnappers hooted with laughter at the joke. Neither Cleav nor Esme was in the mood to see the humor.

"Esme doesn't want to kiss you," Cleav stated tightly. "If I were you, I wouldn't try to force her."

Hightower raised his arms in a gesture of disbelief. "Force?" he asked. "You think my grandmama didn't raise me well enough to know not to *force* a lady?"

There were murmurs of agreement from the other men. Obviously Cleav's insinuated superiority as a gentleman was a sore spot.

"I don't want to kiss her at all," Armon stated baldly. "If I had, I'd a done it years ago."

The others laughed in agreement, and Esme blushed in fury at his boastful supposition.

"But a bride's got to be kissed. It wouldn't be a shivaree without it."

Armon looked to his cohorts, who nodded agreement.

"If we ain't going to get to kiss her," Hightower explained, "then at least we get to see you do it."

"What?" Cleav and Esme exclaimed simultaneously.

"Kiss her," Will Gambridge encouraged. "And not that sissy little peck she got in church. Let's see you buss her for all she's worth."

"Yeah," the eldest Roscoe agreed. "And put some tongue in it!"

"You—" Esme sputtered angrily again, but Cleav patted her consolingly.

"My wife and I have no intention of *entertaining* you," he said emphatically.

Armon laughed. "Suit yourself, Mr. Storekeep," he replied. "Best make yourself comfortable, then, 'cause you ain't going nowhere, and we got a night full of drinking ahead of us."

As if to emphasize his words, Hightower crossed his legs and seated himself on the ground, making himself comfortable. "Tie her back up, Will," he ordered his henchman. "If they won't pay up, they're not going anywhere."

As Gambridge made a move toward them, Cleav held up his hand. It was obvious that the drunk quartet had every intention of getting drunker. Shivarees were normally just nasty little jokes, but more than one in the hills had turned ugly.

"You want to see me kiss her?" he asked unnecessarily. "Hell, she's my wife. I don't mind kissing her one bit."

Turning to the woman beside him, he whispered, "Just play along with me, and we'll get out of here."

Esme hadn't time to reply when Cleav pulled her into his embrace, bending her backward over his left arm. With her throat so exposed, he gifted it with a breathy kiss and a gentle bite. His actions brought a startled exclamation to her lips. Then he kissed her.

His kiss was neither gentle nor sweet. It was a kiss of lust and power. A kiss of masculine domination. A kiss designed for his audience. He thrust his tongue deep into the hot, sweet recesses of Esme's mouth. His only hope was that she wouldn't fight him, that she would let him finish the lewd display that would earn them their freedom.

The last thing he expected was her response. But slowly a low, soft moan emerged from Esme's throat, and her arms wrapped around his neck. She was pressing against him and kissing him back.

Cleav forgot his escape plan and his worry about the drunkenness of his captors. He forgot Armon Hightower's scurrilous little scheme. He forgot he was surrounded by slobbering hill boys. The rough kiss melted to one of tenderness, and a moment later he, too, was moaning and pulling the woman in his arms more closely against him.

"Whew-lordy!" The oldest Roscoe brother's exclamation penetrated the hot fog of desire that had blinded him. "Is that Esme a saucy-tail or which?" he asked of no one special.

Cleav jerked away from Esme, shocked at his own loss of control. In two steps he stood before Roscoe. Without a thought to the potential consequences, he grabbed the big, ruddy blond man by the scruff of the neck and slammed him none too gently against the scrub pine at his back.

"You keep my wife's name off your lips," he said with dark fervor. "Or I'll cut your balls off and feed them to that prize hog of yours."

The Roscoe boy choked out an agreeable reply, and Cleav dropped him abruptly. Turning, he held out his hand to Esme.

"Come on," he ordered, and she followed him without a word.

He was halfway down the mountain before he realized that both his anger and his daring were born out of lust. Lust had empowered him to call the bluff of those besotted bullies. At least, he hoped it was only lust. Were there cracks in the gentlemanly veneer that barely covered his rough cracker heritage?

Either way, it didn't set well with him.

The night was black as pitch as the exhausted couple made their way down the mountain to the wide porch of the large, white house. His jacket missing, his knees splotched with mud, his muscles aching, Cleav made no attempt to enter but seated himself on the top step of the porch.

He glanced at Esme as she sat down beside him. She, also, looked a bit worse for wear. Sophrona's made-over dress was no longer white but splattered with dark, dirty stains. Her hair was loose and flying, and her shoes were missing.

"I'm sorry," she said woefully as she propped her elbows against her thighs and rested her chin in her hands. "Sure to graces, you must be just too vexed to live."

A smiled twitched at the corner of Cleav's lip. "It wasn't your fault, Esme. I should have imagined those hill boys would have to have a shivaree for us. Truth to tell, I was so busy thinking about the wedding itself, I didn't give the other even a thought."

"I never thought of it, either," she admitted. Then with fury she added, "I swear I'll kill that Armon Hightower next time I see him."

The sincerity of her words struck Cleav as outrageously funny. "I almost pity that poor man," he told her, laughing.

"What are you laughing at? There's not a thing funny about it," she declared.

Cleav shook his head. "Yes, there is, Esme. *We* are the funny thing about it."

"What do you mean?"

"Every decent hill girl that's ever been married has had a shivaree, Esme," he told her. "Poor old Hightower probably does think of himself as family. Your father thought you should have a real wedding. I guess Hightower wanted to make sure that you did.''

Esme looked at him quizzically at first, as if she couldn't quite understand. Finally she nodded. ''You're right,'' she admitted. ''If we hadn't a-been shivareed, folks would always remember it was a hurry-up wedding. Now they'll be talking about you rolling that cask of molasses up the mountain.''

The two looked at each other for a moment and then both burst out laughing.

''Was it that funny?'' he asked.

''I didn't get to see it,'' she confessed. ''I was tied up with Gambridge's dirty old handkerchief in my mouth.''

As the laughter continued, Cleav wrapped his arm around her waist and drew her closer. As he rested her head in the crook of his neck, their laughter began to fade. Tired muscles and foolish embarrassments were forgotten in the still summer quiet of the Tennessee mountains as they sat together for the first time as man and wife. Esme laid one tentative hand against Cleav's chest.

The touch fired Cleav, and he vividly recalled the lusty kiss on the mountain. She was his wife. His brain screamed the words to him joyously. There was no reason in the world for him to wait another minute. ''You ready to go to bed?'' he asked abruptly.

Esme pulled back, startled. She gave him a frightened look and then swallowed bravely. ''Yep,'' she declared daringly. ''I'm ready when you are.''

Cleav could hardly hear her for the roaring in his ears. Rising to his feet, he graciously offered her a hand, and she took it.

They moved in silence toward the door, neither having the vaguest idea of what to say. Esme's attention was momentarily drawn to a wadded gunnysack left on the porch.

"Oh, look," she said, pointing to it eagerly.

"What's this?" Cleav's thoughts were already upstairs, and in his mind he was laying Esme across his bed and throwing her skirts up over her head. Glancing inside the bag, he saw worn and faded material. "Somebody's left a ragbag on my porch," he commented distractedly, and as they stepped into the foyer, he moved to throw the gunny and its contents back to the porch.

Esme jerked the sack out of his hand. "That's my things," she explained defensively. "And my dowry."

"Your dowry?" Cleav's brain couldn't quite grasp the word. At that moment the word he most associated with Esme was not *dowry* but *legs*.

Reaching deep inside, Esme pulled out a corner of lacy white cotton that glowed in the moonlight.

"This is my mama's crochet tablecloth. By rights, it should have gone to one of the twins, since they're older. But I thought that since I'm marrying so high, I ought to bring you the best that we own."

"Oh, for heaven's sake." Cleav felt strangely uncomfortable with her confession. He pulled her forcefully into his arms, pressing the hard evidence of his desire into the softness of her stomach. "Give it to one of your sisters. Mother's got dozens of tablecloths."

A cold flash of anger swept through Esme that the warmth of Cleav's embrace could not assuage. As he brought his mouth down to capture hers, Esme struggled against him.

"*Your* mother doesn't have any tablecloths made by *my* mother!" Esme told him.

Cleav pulled back slightly and let his thoughts momentarily clear. "You're right, sorry," he answered offhandedly. "Let's forget about tablecloths right now." He pulled her against him and rubbed himself suggestively against her. "We'll just go up to bed and enjoy ourselves. We have a whole lifetime together to argue about unimportant details."

Esme found at that moment that her only desire was to "argue about unimportant details." She was an equal partner in this marriage. Suddenly she was afraid that maybe she wasn't.

"I'll have you know, my mother's tablecloth is very important to me," she stated a bit too loudly. Self-doubt fueled her anger.

"Esme, I didn't mean—"

"My family don't have much and you know that, but what we do have we value!"

"Esme sweet," he whispered against her throat. "You already know the things I value about you." He ran a hand down the length of her spine and then naughtily cupped the temptingly curved behind he found there. "Why don't we just lay ourselves down in that soft feather bed I've got upstairs"—he soothed the hot words against her throat—"and talk this out in the morning."

Her heart pounding in her throat, Esme decided that she'd made a terrible mistake. This wonderful man she thought she wanted for a husband was an insensitive, unfeeling clod who thought himself far too good for her. Did he think her some stray cat that had just wandered up on his porch? With a hasty glance at her surroundings, the shiny pine floor at her feet, and the massive, elaborate hall tree, Esme wondered if perhaps she was.

Angrily she pushed him away. "I don't care to talk to you in the morning," she claimed in a near shriek. "In fact, I don't care to talk to you at all. I'm going home."

"What?"

"You heard what I said," she snapped. "I'm leaving. I may be poor and got no learning, but I won't be looked down on by anyone. Surely not the man who's supposed to be my husband!"

"I wasn't looking down on you."

"Well, what do you call it?"

"I call it asking for my rights as a married man. This wasn't my idea, you know. I wouldn't have married you in a million years if you hadn't trapped me into it."

"Oh, you . . ." Esme raised her hand to hit him, but he caught it easily, and his expression was black.

"Don't *you* try to strike me," he said furiously. "Just because you saw another woman get away with slapping me doesn't mean you can do the same. You are not Miss Sophrona!"

Esme's eyes widened in horrified shock. "How dare you bring her name up between us on our wedding night!"

Cleav opened his mouth to make a crude comment on what should be between them on their wedding night, only to be interrupted by an anxious voice from the second-floor landing.

"What in the name of heaven is going on down there!"

The two combatants stood silently staring at each other. Neither had remembered that they were not alone in the house.

Cleav stepped away and fumbled for a match to light the lamp. "It's me, Mother," he called upstairs with a more controlled tone. "Esme and I are home at last," he commented conversationally. "How are you feeling?"

"I was feeling fine and sleeping peacefully until I was awakened by what sounded like a Saturday-night brawl in my own foyer." Mrs. Rhy's words were clipped and haughty.

Cleav managed to light the lamp and then gave Esme a beseeching glance.

"Evenin', Miz Rhy," Esme said sweetly as she stepped closer to Cleav. "We's real sorry about waking you up. I'm sure glad you're feeling better."

Cleav wrapped his arm loosely around Esme's waist.

When she started to squirm in protest, he tightened his grip.

"The wedding was lovely, Mother," he said evenly. "Everybody in town was there."

Eula Rhy peered curiously at the couple at the foot of the stairs. "You look awful. How did you get so muddy?"

Esme glanced down at her ruined dress and wanted to die with mortification.

"They had a shivaree," Cleave explained calmly. "It's a custom among the hill people to—"

"I know what a shivaree is, Cleavis," his mother replied sharply. "I've lived in these mountains all my life. Your father had to get me down out of a tree, and we both were covered with poison oak." Her eyes stared out into nothingness for a moment as if she were recalling the unpleasant incident fondly. Then, looking at the young couple at the bottom of the stairs, she actually smiled.

As if the memory of her youth had somehow fortified her, the older woman pulled up the sleeves of her wrapper and headed downstairs.

"You'll both be needing baths, no doubt," she said practically. "Esme, do come help me get the water heated."

12

What a way to start a marriage! Esme thought to herself as she helped Mrs. Rhy draw water for their bath.

"We can just have a basin bath," she had assured her new mother-in-law. But the older woman was having nothing to do with it.

"Lord only knows what kind of vermin you're bringing to my clean sheets," Eula Rhy had declared.

Esme gasped in shock. Mrs. Rhy hastily attempted an explanation. "I mean the both of you all muddy from the shivaree!" she corrected. "A couple only gets one wedding night. The *least* it ought to be is clean."

Esme thought that if a couple got only one wedding night, the least it ought to be is *alone*.

It had taken the better part of an hour to heat enough water for a tub bath. Chivalrously Cleav allowed Esme to bathe first.

The water felt delicious, and Esme was tired, but she couldn't quite relax. She was in Eula Rhy's kitchen, and the older woman showed no inclination to leave her alone with her thoughts. Esme was trapped stark naked in the bathtub as Mrs. Rhy explained Cleavis, his life and family, and Eula's own personal philosophy of marriage. "Things are different today than when I married," she told Esme. "In my day a couple really knew each other and the families were all agreed before the wedding even took place." The older woman shook her head in disapproval. "Now, you and Cleavy don't know the first thing about each other," she said.

"Oh, but we do," Esme insisted. "I've been watching Cleavis for weeks, studying him. I know everything about him."

Eula Rhy snorted in disbelief. "That's obviously not the truth, young woman, or you would have never married him."

Esme's mouth dropped open in shock. "Why do you say that?"

"You seem like a fairly intelligent girl, Esme. If you really knew Cleav, you'd have seen how totally unsuited for him you are."

Esme held her tongue with great effort.

"My son is a gentleman," Eula continued. "His life revolves around the finer things and higher thoughts. A mate for such a man should be as refined and conversant as he is."

Esme's jaw was tight as she scrubbed with diligence. Someone like Sophrona Tewksbury, she thought to herself but refused to utter the words.

"Heaven knows," Mrs. Rhy had rambled on, "it hasn't been easy for me. My late husband was a common man. He'd been to school, of course, and knew a lot about the business. But he never worried about who he was or his place in the world. Our people just weren't like that." Eula gave a tired sigh as she considered the memory.

"But, Cleavis . . ." She shook her head. "Let me tell you, Esme Crabb, that once Cleavy had been to that school in Knoxville, why, he knew everything about everything and wanted the best of all of it.''

''My name isn't Crabb anymore,'' Esme said quietly. ''It's Rhy.''

Casting a wary eye at the young woman in the tub, Eula shook her head disapprovingly. ''You are not at all what he had in mind when he thought of marrying.''

Esme raised her chin defiantly. ''Well, maybe not,'' she admitted grudgingly. ''But we's married now, and I know Cleav well enough to know he won't back down from his vows.''

''Of course he wouldn't!'' her mother-in-law agreed with a haughty tone that said such a thing was foolish even to suggest.

''I'm learning to help out about the store,'' Esme told her proudly. ''And I know some about his fish, and I'm real interested in that.''

''His fish!'' Eula Rhy chuckled with disdain. ''Those fish are the biggest bunch of foolishness that Cleavis ever involved himself with. There are fish aplenty in the river. There is certainly no call to try raising them like chickens.''

''That's probably what the mother of the man who decided to tame the first rooster thought, too.''

Eula raised an eyebrow at her daughter-in-law's unexpected defense of Cleav. But young Mrs. Rhy could apparently be counted upon to do the unexpected.

''You married my son for his pecuniary fettle and social position,'' Eula said evenly. ''I fear that you will both find that it takes more than wedding vows to make a marriage.''

Sloshing the soap from herself, Esme could think of no appropriate reply. It was not a fact that she could dispute. She'd chosen Cleav for his big white house. It was too late to deny it. Already having a glimpse of the disparity between them—Cleav regarding her mother's fine tablecloth as little more than a rag—Esme wondered if she'd made a mistake.

In all her planning and scheming, she'd never thought past the wedding. And she'd fully expected Cleav to fall in love with her and ask her to be his wife. Having a pair of garters intervene in her favor had thrown molasses in the churn. No matter how thick and hard to paddle, it seemed the combination would never turn to butter.

Esme rose to her feet. Mrs. Rhy, apparently unsatisfied with Esme's ablutions, picked up a bucket and poured the warmed water over the young woman's head.

The rush of water was not unpleasant, but it was a surprise. Esme had the bad manners to shake off the excess like a dog, splattering Eula Rhy, who gave a cry of disgust.

"Here!" she snapped, handing the young woman a towel. "Don't you even know how to take a bath?"

"I take them mostly in the river," Esme admitted. "I don't really approve of sitting in a big vat of hot dirty suds," she declared with as great a degree of hauteur as she could muster.

Clothed in Eula Rhy's soft cotton challis wrapper, Esme followed her new mother-in-law to the front hallway. The two came up short at finding Cleav seated on the stairs.

"Good heavens! What are you doing out here, Cleavy?"

His forehead was furrowed with worry. "I was waiting to take Esme up to our room."

"Oh, I can do that!" Mrs. Rhy said impatiently. "You go ahead and get your bath."

Cleav looked ready to argue, but Eula whisked past him, her arm firmly around Esme's waist, leading her upstairs.

"The furniture in this room came all the way from North Carolina," Eula told her as they stepped across the threshold. "Cleavis has very fashionable taste but an eye to quality. All of these pieces were hand-lathed from native black walnut."

Esme gazed with awe at the massive pieces of dark furniture. There were enough shelves and drawers to hide everything in the town of Vader. The huge wardrobe had a beveled glass mirror. The bed was wider and longer than any Esme had ever seen, and the headboard touched the ceiling.

"Save to graces, it's a palace!" Her whispered exclamation was so horrified, Eula Rhy turned to look at her curiously.

"Wasn't that what you wanted?"

Before Esme had time to answer, she found herself alone.

"I didn't expect a palace!" she answered the empty room. "I only wanted a good sturdy roof over my family's head." Even as she said it, the words rang false.

Somewhere between that first day in the General Merchandise and the *"I do"* she'd spoken earlier in the evening, Esme had fallen in love. But she knew, as she ran her hand along the pristine chenille bedspread, that she hadn't fallen for a man with a palace. She was in love with a man who was so gentle, he could call the fish to come eat from his hand.

She smiled as she recalled the memory. Sitting in his shadow, she'd felt so safe, so calm. It was as if the world had been lifted from her shoulders. As long as she was within his shadow, he would take care of her.

Take care of her? Esme smiled and shook her head. What a strange idea. Esme took care of everyone. She had no need for someone to take care of her.

With that, sweet memory floated in the remembrance of the other emotions of that day. The tingle that coursed through her as she became aware of his nearness. The catch in her breathing as she felt his breath on her neck. And the anxious jitters of anticipation that caused her to throw herself right into his arms.

Esme suppressed a nervous giggle and covered her pink

cheeks with her hand. From this night on she would be in his arms, for better or worse, for the rest of their lives.

With that thought Esme scrambled into her bedclothes and braided her hair. Leaving one coal-oil lamp to light his way, she arranged herself in the big dark bed and waited with trembling anticipation for her husband.

She waited.

And waited.

She awakened when the other side of the bed dipped with his weight. The lamp had gone out and the room was dark as pitch.

"Cleav?" The question was a startled exclamation.

"Who else would it be?" His tone was tight with displeasure.

"No one," Esme answered in a small voice.

He lay down beside her and sighed loudly.

Wide awake now, Esme held herself as stiff as a board. This was their wedding night. He would make her his woman. But Cleav didn't move.

Maybe she should reach out to him, she thought. No, she'd thrown herself into his arms once before. Tonight he would have to reach for her. He would reach for her. When would he reach for her?

The minutes trickled past like hours, and Esme's whole body was rigid with anticipation.

The suspense became too much, and she spoke. "Cleav, I . . ." She had no idea how to continue. He had married her against his will. He didn't love her. Perhaps he didn't even want her.

"Cleav, I . . ."

He rolled to his side, facing away from her.

"Good night, Esme," he said.

"Good night."

Cleavis Rhy yawned broadly and then shook his head as if to clear it. Glancing down to the tablet he carried, he carefully wrote in the number of tins of wool fat that he'd found on the shelf. He hadn't planned on doing inventory today. But he'd never seen a better day for it.

Apparently every soul in Vader either expected the store to be closed or weren't tempted to venture too close. Cleav would have welcomed a bustling business. He had no desire to be alone with his thoughts. His thoughts were too troubling.

"Stupid, clumsy clodhopper!" he muttered to himself. He'd thought with his trousers instead of his brain! He deserved exactly what he'd gotten! He sighed derisively at himself. He'd gotten exactly nothing!

"You have made your bed, and now you have to lie in it," his mother had declared last night.

"Lying in it" was exactly what Cleav had planned to do as he'd hurried through his bath. However, his mother had stopped him on his way upstairs.

"I wish to speak with you in the parlor, Cleavis," she'd said in her most disagreeably haughty tone.

Cleav was not a man to be bullied about by his mother, but long years of experience in dealing with Eula Rhy's snits had taught him to let her speak her piece. Otherwise, he would never hear the end of it.

"Of course, Mother," he'd answered politely and indicated that she should precede him across the threshold.

Walking across the room to lean with studied casualness against the mantel, he gestured toward her favorite chair. "Please sit," he told her. "It's very late and I'm sure that you are tired."

Eula Rhy made herself comfortable before she realized she'd been outmaneuvered. It was going to be very disconcerting—and not very effective—to scold her son while looking up at him. "You have married this young woman in good faith," she began adamantly.

Cleav nodded agreement.

"Needless to say, she is not what I had in mind for you. I very much doubt that she is what you had in mind for yourself."

"That's neither here nor there, Mother," Cleav said. "The deed is done."

"It certainly is," Eula agreed. "She'll undoubtedly turn our home into her own, as is her right as your wife. Have you thought about that?"

Cleav looked annoyed. "What are you suggesting, Mother?" he asked. "Esme is a very intelligent young woman. If you think she'll be raising chickens in the pantry and hogs in the dining room, I'm afraid you are doomed to disappointment."

Eula Rhy raised an assessing eyebrow. "I'm glad to hear you defend her. You'll undoubtedly be doing a great deal of that in the future."

Cleav closed his eyes for a moment. "I'm sure my wife and I will have our share of problems to work out," he said evenly. "Like all couples, time and familiarity are in our favor."

Mrs. Rhy gave a lofty snort that could only be described as a huff. "Time and familiarity are not usually the only things newlyweds have to base a future upon," she told him.

"There are other things," Cleav defended hastily.

"Name one?" she challenged.

One thing immediately came to mind, but Cleav was loath to speak it to his mother.

"Well . . . there's . . ." he dissembled.

"Do you love her?" The question snapped at him like a whip.

"I . . ." he hesitated. "I believe that she loves me," he said finally.

The older woman gave him a moue of disbelief. "She loves you or she loves a fine house and nice clothes?"

Cleav's mouth thinned to a line of displeasure. "Esme is

not like that, Mother,'' he said with complete confidence. In his mind's eye he could see her sitting in his shadow at the pond. Her eyes sparkling with delight as she watched the fish and then darkening with desire before she threw herself in his arms.

''She cares for me, Mother. Do you find that so hard to believe?''

Eula Rhy looked her son up and down as if to take his measure. ''I believe she might *think* that she loves you,'' his mother admitted. ''But even that won't last long if you continue to trample her pride as casually as you did her mother's hand-crocheted tablecloth.''

Even this morning, as he counted the salves and drops on the medicine shelf, the truth of his mother's words continued to haunt him. He'd pulled Esme tight against him with all the finesse of a green farm boy at a house of ill repute. His desire had led him to act crassly.

He'd been so anxious to bed her he'd insulted her, a thing that had never happened to him before. Rightly she'd foisted him off with an argument about the tablecloth.

That was why he had lain beside her last night without attempting to claim his rights as bridegroom. This morning, however, he wondered if that had been a mistake. After living through a night of sheer torture, breathing the sweet smell of her hair on the pillow, he remembered that his baser nature seemed to be one of the things she liked best.

His thoughts drifted toward a plan of action. Beginning a marriage without a wedding night was not particularly promising. Especially when in-the-bed affection was the most that he had to offer her.

As his mind conjured the possibilities, he was interrupted by the bell over the front door. ''Come on in, we're open,'' he called out.

''I know,'' a small voice answered.

Cleav turned as his wife approached him. Stepping

behind the counter, she casually made her way along the shelves, hesitating occasionally to straighten a jar or examine a tin. Slowly, almost shyly, she made her way toward him, her fingers running lightly across the polished oak countertop as if gathering strength from those things familiar.

She was scrubbed and shiny but wearing her usual threadbare attire. Cleav, however, thought only of the things he'd planned to say.

"I'm . . ." the two began simultaneously.

A slightly embarrassed giggle was shared.

"Ladies first," Cleav suggested.

"No, you go ahead," Esme offered quickly.

Cleave absently checked the shine on his shoes as he answered. "I'm sorry about last night," he said simply.

Esme's cheeks flamed bright red. Was he apologizing for his inattention in their bed? Her pulse beat so vigorously in her throat, Esme nearly choked.

"I'm very glad that you've brought your mother's tablecloth to our house, Esme."

He looked up at her then. His eyes, so deep and blue, were sincere.

Esme nearly gasped at her own foolishness. Of course he had been talking about their argument, she assured herself disdainfully.

"You were right, really," Esme answered with feigned calm. "Your mother undoubtedly has many tablecloths, and most of them will be better than the one my mother made."

"But your mother made it," Cleav answered. "That's the point after all. This is your home now, and you certainly should bring your things into it." Cleav looked at the woman before him and wondered how to proceed. "I spoke foolishly last night," he began, "because I'm a foolish man. I was thinking more about kissing your lips than about the words that were coming from them."

Esme's eyes widened, and the lips he spoke of parted prettily in surprise.

"You were?" What was she to say? She had wanted to kiss him, too. She had wanted more than kissing, she admitted to herself. She wanted to feel the strength of his arms around her again. She wanted . . . she wanted everything. Their time was not lost. Their shaky start would not set them back. Esme refused to allow either to happen.

Without giving herself a chance to think about her actions, the new bride raised herself on her tiptoes and softly pressed her mouth against her husband's.

At Cleav's startled reaction, Esme's hopes sank. "I know I don't do it right," she admitted and lowered her head shamefully.

Cleav's eyes softened. "You're a bright young woman," Cleav told her easily as his arms encircled her. "All it takes is a little practice, and I'm willing to do my part."

Bending his head slowly forward until her lips were only a hair's breadth from his own, he hesitated. "This is my part," he whispered.

Teasing his mouth slightly over hers, he captured the fullness of her upper lip between his teeth. Tenderly tugging with playful passion, he urged her mouth open. Then he captured the warmth therein.

"Mmmm, you taste so good," he murmured.

Esme didn't reply. This time she returned the embrace more slowly. Wrapping her arms around his neck, she stroked the fine brown hair that was perfectly trimmed at the nape of his neck.

Ending the kiss, Cleav pulled away only by inches. But inches was too far for Esme as she sought his lips again. The warm, lush taste of his mouth was a forbidden fruit she was suddenly free to access. Curiosity mixed with desire as she sought to know every approach and texture of his lips.

"Am I kissing you, or are you kissing me?" she asked huskily.

Quiet, tender touches suffused them with warmth as Cleav pressed delicate love bites on her neck and Esme answered them with grateful kisses to his temple.

"Once you are married," Cleav answered, "it no longer matters."

As if his words had given her permission, Esme ran her hands along the breadth of his shoulders and down the wall of his chest.

"Mmmm . . ." His murmur of approval gave Esme courage as she pressed herself against him.

The eager caress fired Cleav's blood, and he tightened his arms around her. Hungrily his lips moved from her mouth to her cheek to her neck. She arched her back to give him access. And he took it.

"Esme, sweet Esme," he whispered against her skin. Running a hand up from her waist, he gently touched the side of her breast.

"Oh!"

With Esme's startled reaction, Cleav covered her mouth with his own. As she sighed against him, he allowed his hand to skim across her bosom again, this time casually contacting the raised nipple with his thumb.

The flutter he felt in her throat might have been fear, but she ardently pressed her flesh against his hand.

"Yes, please touch me there," she whispered. "It makes me feel so . . . so . . . all over."

Her response brought a primitive growl from deep within Cleav's throat. Tightening his hold marginally, he made a tentative foray into her hot, sweet mouth with his tongue.

She jerked from him slightly, in surprise, then her own tongue snaked to meet his.

"This feels so naughty," she told him, her breast heaving with excitement.

"It is naughty," Cleav agreed. "So wonderfully naughty."

They continued their naughty exploration for several more moments until both were breathing hard. Cleav pulled away from her slightly and bent his head to rest it against the top of hers.

"We shouldn't be in here like this," Cleav told her, willing himself to take stock of his surroundings. "Let me close the store, and we'll go to the house."

Esme wanted to agree but shook her head. "Your mother is there."

Cleav gave an exasperated sigh and pulled her back into his arms.

"Oh, Esme, you tempt me so," he whispered. "But this is neither the time nor the place. I'm terribly sorry for my timing," he said. "A gentleman doesn't take liberties with a lady in a public place."

She shook her head vigorously. "Oh, Cleav, you mustn't apologize to me," she said. "And you certainly mustn't reprove yourself. It's my fault. I just couldn't wait to touch you."

His kiss was tender as he grazed her lips.

"You are so sweet," he told her as he put her at arm's length to study the line and feature of her face. "And innocent."

"Not entirely," Esme said slowly. "You know those pretty garters that you gave me?"

He nodded. How could he forget them?

"I'm wearing them under my dress," she told him.

Cleav immediately thought of how they would look on her slim thighs. Then he wondered how high up she'd worn them, but he kept that thought to himself.

"That's what they are for, Esme," he said. "There is certainly no impropriety in that."

"I came down to the store wearing them under my dress," she continued, looking up into his eyes with an expression that was far from innocent. "And that's all I'm wearing under my dress."

Cleav's eyes widened in shock. "Miss Esme . . ." he began. "Miss Esme, I . . ."

"My name isn't Miss Esme," she corrected in a low, silky voice. "I'm Mrs. Cleavis Rhy."

His nostrils flared as he struggled to breathe normally. His gaze dropped to the worn serge skirt that now was the only cloth that hid her long, luscious legs from his sight. His hands trembled with desire. No words could be said. His arms went around her waist and his palms clutched the soft fullness of her buttocks.

"I want you, Mrs. Rhy," he growled. "I want you here and now."

Together they dropped to their knees on the worn space of hardwood floor between the counter and the shelves.

With his passion overwhelming his gentlemanly discretion, Cleav pushed the offending expanse of gray serge up to Esme's waist. She hadn't lied. The slim, seductive limbs that had enticed and vexed his dreams for weeks were naked and within his grasp. His fascination flowed like hot molasses from the ankle, still clad in the worn men's work boot, up the shapely calf to the delicate curve of her knee and the whiteness of her bare thigh, encircled by the dainty pink and white garters that had changed both their lives.

Casting his better judgment to the wind, he laid a large masculine hand on the whiteness of her calf.

"So soft," he whispered as he struggled to go slowly and not frighten her.

Esme would have none of it. Fairly flying into his arms, she kissed him eagerly.

Her enthusiasm was intoxicating. It no longer mattered where they were or what social rules prevailed. All Cleav wanted was to press himself inside this woman, whose lips and tongue toyed with his own.

But there were distractions. The lips that were just learning a new fulfilling purpose required tutoring. The questing and inquisitive feminine hands nearly unmanned him with innocent curiosity. The pert little breasts that rubbed against him so longingly needed disrobing. And the secrets, so bewitchingly secluded in a thatch of brownish curls, deserved to be explored.

"Let's get this off of you," he breathed hotly into her neck as he worried the buttons on her bodice.

Once the faded garment was slipped over her head, he found himself entranced by the sight of her rosy pink nipples, hardened and straining against the diaphanous covering of her thin cotton camisole.

His mouth immediately sought contact, and as he laved and nipped at the distended nubs, he lay her back to the floor and covered her with his body. He planted his knee firmly at the crux of her thighs and felt as well as heard the appreciative sigh of relief as she squirmed ardently against him.

"Oh, it's wonderful," she whispered. Spreading her thighs more widely before him, she begged, "Push harder, it feels so good."

Cleav nearly exploded at her words. Gritting his teeth valiantly, he raised himself slightly and looked down at his new wife. Her dark blond hair was spread wantonly across the floor. Her cheeks were flushed with desire. And her heaving breasts were clearly visible within the now damp cotton of her camisole.

"Cleavis! You in here?"

The disrupting shout came from somewhere near the front door. Cleav's eyes widened in shock, and Esme struggled to rise. He stayed her easily and placed a quieting finger to his lips.

"Cleavis?" the customer called again.

Hurriedly Cleav got to his knees, straightening his clothes

and smoothing back his hair. He gave Esme a silent gesture to stay put as he rose to his feet.

"Afternoon, Mr. Denny," he answered. "I didn't hear you come in."

"Didn't expect to come in," the old man replied. "Figured you'd be holed up with that new wife of yourn." Denny gave a lusty chuckle before continuing. "When I saw the door open, thought I'd best check things out."

"I'm just doing some inventory," Cleav told him nervously. "In fact, I was just getting ready to close up. Was there something that you needed?"

Esme had scooted as close to the counter as she could get. Drawing up her knees, which she hastily covered with the serge skirt, she tried to make herself as small as possible so that she could hide better among the corn plasters and Tincture of Arnica bottles.

Her heart continued to pound like a tom-tom and she valiantly tried quiet her breathing, which sounded to her own ears like a violent roar. Still trembling with desire, the hot, sweet place between her legs was swelled and aching.

She glanced down at her disarray with consternation.

Beside her, Cleav stood, still fully clothed, speaking as calmly and controlled as if nothing had happened. As if he'd already forgotten her. . . . Glancing longingly at the strong trouser-covered leg at her side, she decided to make him remember.

Tentatively she reached out and touched his leg.

"Think we've had our share of rain this spring?" Denny asked.

"*No!*" Cleav answered, a bit more emphatically than necessary. "I mean," he continued more softly, "I think we might see more rain again before the end of the week."

"Maybe so," Denny allowed, but then glanced curiously at Cleavis. "You getting a fever, boy? You're a-looking downright flushed."

"No, I'm *fine*, um, fine," the younger man assured him.

Esme was very pleased by what she was discovering about her new husband. Not only were his legs strong and sturdy and his thighs powerful and well formed, but his buttocks were extremely shapely. She'd never paid much attention to men's backsides. Now she wondered why. Cleav's behind, so lucklessly obscured by the baggy seat of his trousers, was a work of art. Exploring the strength of the firm muscular curves with her hand, Esme discovered that her new husband seemed exceptionally sensitive to her touch. When she leaned forward to take a flirty little bite, she thought that he might vault over the counter. Her only regret was that she couldn't feel his bare flesh.

"My tomatoes ain't gonna make nothing this year," Denny was lamenting.

"Oh," Cleav choked out.

"Got cutworm," Denny told him, shaking his head sorrowfully. "It's a damn shame."

"A shame," Cleav agreed, his voice unusually high.

"But," Denny rationalized, "the taters are going to be fine."

"Fine."

"Corn ain't too bad, neither."

Esme's exploration took a wicked turn, and Cleav made a choking sound.

"What's wrong?" Denny jumped at Cleav's exclamation.

"I . . ." Cleav appeared almost breathless, his eyes wide. "I just thought of something I need to do."

Hurriedly Cleav made his way to the end of the counter, stopping only to grab the Closed sign from beneath the cash drawer.

Holding the sign in front of him, he hurried Denny out the door.

"I've really got to lock up now," he explained lamely. "You can come back tomorrow."

"Good Lord, boy. What in heaven's name is wrong?" Denny asked as Cleav discourteously shut the door in the old man's face.

13

~**13**~

After hanging the sign in the window and jerking down the shade, Cleav turned his back to the door. Flushed and trying to catch his breath, he glanced over at Esme, who was peeking over the top of the counter.

Esme's look was wary.

"I guess I shouldn't touch you like that?" she suggested.

Cleav looked at her for a moment. He was fully aroused, and his nostrils flared like a stallion who'd got a whiff of a mare in heat. His whole concentration centered not on his knowledge and good manners but on the pulsing heat at the front of his trousers.

He pushed away from the door and began walking toward Esme.

"Ladies do not touch gentlemen in that manner," he said.

Esme nodded, shamefaced. "I never claimed to be a lady," she pointed out.

Cleav reached the far side of the counter and bent forward, bringing his face close to hers. "No, you didn't," he agreed.

No woman, lady or otherwise, had ever fired his blood as

did the young innocent before him. He had ignored her, insulted her, humiliated her, but she was still there. Still there and wanting him. Esme Crabb was in love with him. Suddenly he thought himself the luckiest man in Tennessee.

They faced each other for a moment until Esme dropped her gaze. Cleav gently grasped her chin and raised her eyes to his. "No, you never claimed to be a lady, Esme," he told her quietly. "And I am just ungentlemanly enough to appreciate that."

Stepping away from her, he walked to the piece-goods cupboard. Esme watched him curiously as he rummaged through it for a moment.

"Ah, here it is," he said finally.

Pulling out the remnant of rose crepe de chine he whipped it open like a picnic tablecloth and laid it on the hardwood floor. "Ladies want romance and flowers, feather-beds and clean sheets," he said.

Esme looked at him and then at the pretty pallet of rose crepe de chine. "I only want you."

Cleav leaned against the counter and removed first one boot and then the other. Slipping his thumbs under his suspenders, he allowed them to fall loosely to his hips.

Dropping to the edge of the crepe de chine, he held out his hand to Esme. "Would you care to join me, Mrs. Rhy?"

Esme walked toward him. Just looking at him and imagining what was to happen on the pink pallet made her nipples strain eagerly at the damp cotton of her camisole.

She hesitated as she neared the makeshift bed. She wanted to join him, but she didn't want to ruin the beautiful piece of material with her heavy work shoes. "Let me take my shoes off," she said.

"Please," Cleav agreed. Leaning back, he watched her, smiling wickedly. "In fact, why don't you just take off everything," he suggested.

"Everything?"

"Well, not everything," he corrected. "Leave the garters, I think."

Esme's eyes widened in shock. Then, as his assessing look became a teasing grin, she found herself smiling back.

"You think I won't do it," she told him.

His grin widened. "Dare ya."

What hill-bred gal could ever resist a dare?

Esme hastily discarded her shoes and began tugging at the hooks at the back of her skirt. In an instant the worn gray serge pooled around her feet, and she stepped out of it.

She was reaching for the straps on her camisole when she glanced back at Cleav. He wasn't grinning anymore. His look was scorching and wild and maybe, well, maybe almost reverent.

Esme slowed her motions.

Leisurely, painstakingly, she eased the straps of the camisole off her shoulders. Her eyes never leaving his, she gently caressed her bare shoulder as if she could no longer wait for his touch.

With unhurried deliberation, she exposed the delicate curve of her bosom inch by inch as she casually stripped the damp cotton from her flesh.

Cleav swallowed visibly.

She teased him with her eyes and her lips pursed in a playful pout. Leisurely casting the damp camisole on the counter, she stood before him wearing nothing but a blush in her cheeks and a pair of pink and white garters.

Cleav reached for her.

"Why would God make a woman with legs so long?" he murmured as his strong brown hands firmly grasped her hips and pulled her toward him.

The minute Esme stepped on the pink crepe de chine, all her risqué bravado vanished. The touch of his warm hands against her bare skin made her tremble.

"I've never done this," she whispered, her voice sounding strained.

"I know, Esme," Cleav answered as his hands ran possessively up and down the bare white limbs before him. "Nobody knows about these beautiful legs but me."

His hands were almost determinedly hesitant in their caress as he pulled her forward. Standing, trembling and nude, with her husband, the man she'd fought so hard to win on his knees before her, Esme's fear melted away like mountain snow in springtime.

"I know you aren't going to hurt me," Esme told him with conviction.

Cleav raised his blue eyes to hers.

"Hurt?" He shook his head, then gently kissed her pale thigh just above the plain store-bought garter. "Hurt, no. Never hurt."

Grabbing the dainty piece of pink and white feminine fastening with his teeth, Cleav slowly pulled the garter down the length of her thigh and over her knee.

The garter tickled her leg and Esme's breath caught in her throat and her limbs turned to crabapple jelly on a warm day.

"I can't stand up!" she announced with quavering alarm.

Cleav immediately loosened the garter and brought his hands up to steady her. "Trust me, Esme," he said. "I'm not a man that will let you down."

As Esme looked down at his pale blue eyes, she felt the warm flush of desire as his strong hands so securely held her.

"I trust you."

Cleav smiled. "Then you won't mind if I do this," he answered as he turned his head slightly and leaned forward to plant a gentle kiss on the mat of springy brown curls at the apex of her thighs.

"Oh!" Esme's startled exclamation momentarily captured his attention. "Can you do that?" she asked, plainly shocked at the idea.

"I *can* do it," he said. "If you *want* me to do it."

Esme's face was flaming bright red, which in itself was miraculous, because all the warmth and feeling in her body at that moment seemed completely concentrated in the damp, heated area where his lips had been.

"I . . . I think it'd be all right, I guess," she stammered.

Not waiting for further invitation, Cleav bent his head forward to take that most intimate of kisses.

When his tongue touched the aching swollen nub hidden within her sensitive flesh, she cried out, half in astonishment, half in delight.

"What is it?" she asked him as her knees gave out completely, and he lowered her to the pallet beside him.

"It's pleasure," he told her as his hand clutched the hot, damp heaven that had felt his kisses. "Man-woman pleasure."

He moved to place light, teasing kisses on her breast and throat.

"It's supposed to hurt," she told him.

He feathered light, loving pecks across her eyes and the bridge of her nose.

"This is not the part that hurts," Cleav answered. "I'm going to try not to hurt you at all," he said. "But I want you so much. I'll try to be easy."

With that in mind Cleav began a gentle persuasion of sweet kisses and confident caresses meant to reassure rather than enflame. Esme reveled in his attention. As his hands explored her naked flesh, his teeth and tongue tutored her lips on pleasing them both.

Esme moaned low and lusciously from the depths of her throat and arched her back to offer herself. Cleav held her even closer as he wedged his thigh hard against her gentle parts.

Squirming enthusiastically against him, Esme whispered words of unintelligible encouragement as her head moved back and forth on the rose crepe de chine pallet.

Cleav unbuttoned his fine linen shirt, and Esme's hands eagerly sought to push it over his shoulders. When she finally had, she gasped with delighted surprise. She'd never imagined such a refined gentleman as Cleavis to have such a thick, silky mat of curly black hair on his chest. She ran her fingers through it until he finally stilled her hands.

"God, Esme, help me get these trousers off."

The eagerness in his voice spurred her to action. Her deft fingers easily released the buttons at his fly and underdrawers. Eagerly she peeled the fabric from his hips.

The thick phallus that pressed at her belly was disconcerting. Esme avoided it by clutching the smooth muscular buttocks that she'd so admired earlier.

A strangled sound came from Cleav's throat, and he gritted his teeth harshly.

When Esme hesitated on her sweet exploration, he tried to reassure her.

"Oh, yes, sweetheart," he whispered hotly against her flesh. "I love your touch, but I can't wait much longer. I need to be inside you."

Tenderly caressing the paleness of her inner thighs, he spread them before him and raised himself in position to take her.

Now! Esme's mind screamed to her. Now he was going to make her a woman, his woman, for all time. Now she would know all that there was to know about the dark mystery of sex. Now she would have the blessed capacity of bearing his children. Now! Now!

"This is the part that hurts," Cleav warned her as he tried to ease himself inside her.

Esme's tiny cry came from her throat as Cleav pressed his way into the outer reaches of her womanhood.

''Are you all right?'' he stopped to ask.

She nodded with more certainty than she felt.

He pushed forward again, and Esme's eyes widened in fear and pain.

''*Oh, stop!*'' she cried out as he pushed against her maidenhead.

Sweat popped out on his forehead, and he ground his teeth in near agony as he tried, without success, to move within her. The hot, wet invitation of her body was in sharp contrast to the formidable barrier of her innocence.

Cleav pulled back slightly and strained to recover himself. ''Sweet Esme,'' he choked out in tender anguish. ''I don't want to hurt you, but I . . .'' Getting control of her breath, Esme gazed up into the pale blue eyes of Cleavis Rhy and knew that she loved him. Always the gentleman, his jaw was clenched tightly against his own desire as he willed himself not to hurt her. It was supposed to hurt, everyone knew that. But this man in her arms, the man she loved, would spare her that if he could.

Wrapping her long, slim legs about his waist, Esme firmly grasped his buttocks and thrust forward, forcefully impaled herself on his shaft.

They both cried out, she in pain and he in ecstasy.

A stream of late afternoon sunlight streaked between the shade and the glass and across the hardwood floor. The quiet of the empty room accentuated the sound of the two near-naked bodies that lay between the counter and the canned goods shelf, gasping for breath.

Esme ran her hand along his straight, strong spine, feeling the quivering of well-worked muscles and the sheen of perspiration on his skin.

"I hurt you." Cleav spoke first. It was a statement rather than a question.

"No, I'm fine," Esme lied. It had hurt. More than she'd expected. But it didn't hurt now, not really. The slight rawness and the uncomfortable stretching paled in comparison to the relief she felt. Relief was definitely the word. He was inside her, a part of her, sheltering her and enclosing her. She felt so safe, so at home, at last.

Tears welled in her eyes, but she blinked them back. He'd think she was crying for the pain, and that was beneath her dignity. But joy, this kind of joy, was something worth crying about.

Cleav raised his head slightly and saw the dampness on her cheek.

"Don't cry, little baby," he whispered. "My little Hillbaby."

He tried to move away from her, but Esme wouldn't let him. Wrapping her arms around his neck and her legs around his waist, she held him fast.

"I'm too heavy for you," Cleav told her.

"Please don't leave yet," she whispered.

"I'm not going anywhere," he assured her.

"I mean," she hesitated, not sure about her phrasing, "I mean, it was such a struggle to get it inside. I don't want you to take it out so soon."

Cleav looked at her curiously for a moment and then his face was wreathed in a smile and he chuckled with self-satisfaction. Holding her as tightly as she held him, he rolled to his side and then wiggled more closely to her, securing his place.

"I'll try to stay all afternoon this way, if that's what you want, Hillbaby," Cleav told her with a teasing smile. "My spirit is willing, but my flesh may be weak."

Esme looked at him questioningly and then ran a warm

appreciative hand along the muscled length of his bicep, giving it a testing squeeze.

"There is nothing weak about you, Cleavis Rhy," she stated flatly.

Cleav chuckled lightly. "It wasn't my arms I was worried about."

When Esme continued to look at him curiously, Cleav felt awkward. His experience with women had not been among the innocent. Of course there were things that Esme wouldn't know, couldn't know, until her husband told her. He was the husband. Somehow the responsibility of educating her was a burden he was more than willing to take on his shoulders.

"My . . ." he began hesitantly. "Well . . . my . . . my . . . man part isn't always hard," he warned her.

Her eyes widened perceptibly. "It always seems to be."

He laughed out loud. "Only when you are around, Esme Crabb," he insisted.

"Esme Rhy," she corrected him, squirming slightly in an attempt to assuage the strange flutter near the place where their bodies connected.

"Just so," he agreed. "Esme Rhy."

He found himself inordinately pleased to say the name. He was suddenly sure that his decision to marry Esme Crabb was the most intelligent thing he'd ever done. No lady, he was sure, could be half as tempting. As Esme had so accurately guessed, the gentleman within him had not completely eradicated the man within him.

Dinner hostesses and esoteric conversationalists could be found among friends. It was not necessary to bed one. Esme was earthy and sensual and satisfying. Certainly those qualities were highly desirable for lifelong fidelity.

Cleav ran a lazy hand along one long, slim leg that embraced him. Those legs for a lifetime! And love, too! He placed a soft kiss on her temple as he smiled. This wild,

long-legged hill girl was in love with him. She'd chased him
and she'd caught him. At that moment he was sure that the
future would bring cause for both of them to be grateful.

"What are you wiggling about?" he asked her.

"I feel funny down there," she admitted.

Cleav's smile disappeared. "You're hurt." He attempted
to move away again.

"No," Esme assured him as she tightened her arms
around him. "It doesn't hurt exactly. It just feels funny."

"Funny how?"

"Like I need to scratch or something."

As Esme watched, the concern melted in Cleav's eyes
and a warmth of understanding crossed his face with a
pleased smile.

"Scratch?" he asked with a teasing lilt. "Have you got
fleas, Mrs. Rhy?"

"Fleas!" Esme was outraged, remembering his mother's
suggestion of vermin in her bed the night before, and she
reacted more strongly than she should have.

"I don't . . ." Furiously Esme struggled against him
with the hope of slamming her strong young fist into his
teasing smile.

"Oh, I think it's fleas," Cleav continued as he held her
fast. In Esme's anger, the teasing quality of his voice
escaped her. "No need to be ashamed, Hillbaby," he said.
"Lots of women in these mountains get fleas."

She tried to bite him, but he moved his head back just in
time.

"I do not have fleas!" she proclaimed loudly.

"I think you do," he insisted, still managing to hold her.
"But don't worry, I'm going to take care of you."

"You . . . you . . ." Esme couldn't think of words
bad enough. She continued to fume and fight as Cleav
slipped a hand between them. Luxuriantly he caressed the
length of her torso.

"Sometimes those fleas get to a woman," he told her as his hand warmed her flesh. "She gets an itch that nobody but a man can scratch," he said. "Now, with a decent woman like yourself, that man's going to have to be your husband every time."

With a sudden shocked intake of breath, Esme realized his intention, and the fight went out of her. So warm, so firm, so gentle and curious, when his hand began teasing the damp brown curls, she melted.

"I bet that flea is right about here," he said hotly against her neck.

Esme gave a cry of pleasured surprise and arched her pelvis against him.

The teasing grin on Cleav's face softened as he watched her. His body hardened inside her and his lips touched her neck with sweet kisses and naughty bites.

"Save to graces!" Esme called out as she squirmed against the steady rotating pressing of his fingers. "Oh, Cleavis! What is this?"

"This is the part that doesn't hurt," he answered. He could never remember watching a woman before. Watching and feeling such pleasure in her pleasure. Had he always done it in the dark? He couldn't remember. At that moment he couldn't remember any woman any time before the one in his arms.

Clamping his jaw against his own desire, he was fully aroused again. "Are you sore?" he asked hoarsely. "I don't want to hurt you. You tell me when you want me to stop."

Esme grasped his buttocks in her hands and begged, "Don't ever stop!"

As she pressed for urgency, Cleav stayed her as best he could, rolling her supine to take control. She was eager and earnest, but she needed guidance. He was glad he was to be the one to guide her.

"Not so fast, Hillbaby," he whispered against her ear. "Last time I lost control, but this time I'll be better."

"I'll be better, too," Esme promised breathlessly.

A humorous chuckle escaped Cleavis. "Don't try," he told her. "You're already better than I deserve."

"I am?"

"Oh, yes, sweet Hillbaby," he said as he kissed her. "You really pleased me, Esme. Last time you really pleased me. This time is for you, just for you."

But in the end it was not.

Esme squirmed and wiggled and strained for his attention. Cleav was tender and considerate, but ultimately his gentlemanly rhythm gave way to a lusty pounding that shook the floorboards.

"Yes, Hillbaby," Cleav pleaded through clenched teeth. "Come with me, fall through, let it go."

Opening her eyes, Esme meant to question his meaning. But the edges of her vision turned sunset pink, her eyes closed at the sight, and she cried out his name. She could do nothing but follow.

In the aftermath of near heaven, Cleav rocked her gently and whispered nonsense as she slowly returned to the day at hand. Their pulses still skittered, but their breathing slowed and they smiled at each other. Words were unnecessary.

He brought his mouth to hers. Opening just slightly, he applied a light pressure as he sucked gently at her sweet lips. She returned the slow seduction of his mouth and even had the audacity to flick her tongue against his teeth.

"You're a fast learner," Cleav told her as he reveled in her attention.

"You said yourself that I was very bright," she said.

"Very bright?" He gave an exaggerated look of puzzlement. "When did I say a thing like that?" he asked.

"Down by the fish ponds," she answered. "Don't you remember? The day you taught me to feed the fish."

Cleav sighed contentedly against her cheek.

"Oh, yes, Esme," he said. "I remember the day I taught you to feed the fish."

They kissed again, this time accenting the lushness of teeth and tongues with tiny pecks on noses and chins.

"Do you remember saying that I was bright?" she asked between love bites.

"I may have said it," he admitted. "But I was wrong, of course."

"Wrong!" Esme pulled back to get a good look at the laughter in his face.

"How bright can a woman be who rolls around on the floor with her husband in the middle of the afternoon?" he asked.

Esme answered his tease with a naughty pinch of his backside.

"About as bright as the man that rolls with her!"

Giggling, kissing, and exploring, the two made good use of the late afternoon sunlight to observe at close hand the partner that each had made for life.

She told Cleav about her father's warning about embarrassment. "I guess I'm nearly a sinner," Esme admitted. "But I don't feel one bit ashamed, and I'm laying here with you as naked as the day I was born."

"Not quite," Cleav corrected as he snapped the remaining garter.

"I guess it's 'cause I've been spending so much time trying to show you my legs, I plumb lost my modesty," she said.

"You've been trying to tempt me?" Cleav asked in mock outrage.

She had the good grace to blush.

"Well, I . . . that first day . . . well, I saw that you liked my legs . . ."

"Did you pull your skirt up to see if I would?" he asked.

"Of course not!" she snapped. "It was an accident. At least, it was that time," Esme admitted.

"For shame," Cleav chided. "Trying to lure me into sin just so I'd marry you."

"Well, how else . . ." she began, but as Cleav moved from her, she cut off her words.

Esme was dismayed as he pulled away from her to rise. "I'm sorry, Cleav, I . . ."

Folding his arms across his chest, Cleav leaned against the counter and raised a condemning eyebrow.

"Well, it didn't work, young woman," he stated flatly. "I resisted all your temptation and I'm sure heaven has properly noted the fact and marked it down in my favor."

"But you *did* marry me," Esme pointed out as she pushed herself up into a sitting position.

"But not because you beguiled me to it," he said.

That was true, Esme realized. All of her attempts at seducing him had been thwarted. He'd never sinned with her; people only thought that he had.

"You married me because of the town gossip," Esme said quietly.

Cleav leaned down and pulled up her chin to face him.

"Because of these garters," he said, pointing to the only clothing she wore.

Esme ran a hand across the one remaining guilty, pretty, pink and white confection of ribbon and lace.

"I guess you regret giving them to me," she whispered, a lump in her throat making it strangely difficult to speak.

Cleav didn't answer. He turned from her. Naked, he strolled to the far end of the store and opened one of the drawers in the counter.

Blushing, Esme assumed the precious moments of closeness were over and began to reach for her clothing. So quickly it was over. Just moments ago she'd felt so secure, so prized.

Cleav turned toward her, but Esme couldn't look at him. Now she felt naked. Now she felt ashamed.

Walking back to her, the counter drawer in his arms, he called to her.

"Sit still, Esme."

At his words she stopped searching for her camisole.

"Don't dress yet, Hillbaby," he said softly.

Coming to a stop beside her, Cleav stared down at his new wife, naked, on a remnant of rose crepe de chine. He gave her the smallest of smiles before upending the drawer over her head.

"What?" Esme started with surprise, then giggled with delighted laughter.

It was raining garters.

14

Cleavis stepped out of the hatching house and spied Esme lying lazily and contentedly beside the brooders' pond.

"Shirker!" he called out as he casually headed toward her direction.

Esme rolled onto her back and held an arm across her forehead to block out the sun's glare. "I'm just resting, Mr. Rhy," she told him with a teasing lilt to her voice. "Save to graces, I've only been married three days, and I swear to you, my husband doesn't let me get a wink of sleep all night!"

With a widening grin, Cleav dropped down on the grass beside her. "You bragging or complaining, ma'am?"

"Just stating the facts, sir," she responded with a snappy challenge.

Cleav reached over to give a playful tug to a loose strand of hair near her ear.

"Some of the facts, ma'am, but not all of them," he said lightly. "You forgot to mention how you wake up two or three times a night to come crawling all over the poor abused man."

Esme's smile brightened. "Us mountain folk are used to sleeping nine to a bed. Snuggling just comes natural for us," she declared.

Cleav leaned forward and placed a kiss on the end of her nose.

"It's getting to be pretty natural for me, too."

Having already decided that people didn't call the first month of marriage "honeymoon" for nothing, Cleav was content. Any hesitation he'd had about marrying Esme had evaporated like mud holes in a drought. She was loving, affectionate, fun to banter with, and eager for his touch. Surprisingly, he felt more relaxed around her than anyone he'd ever known.

There was a lot to be said for a relaxing woman. With Esme he was free to say and do what he wanted. She didn't know or care what was "proper behavior." She listened to his opinions, but she definitely had her own. But more than her good humor and her easygoing ways, she genuinely liked Cleav for himself and never hesitated to say so. That was a heady novelty.

"What are you doing out here?" he asked. "Except for grumbling about your new husband."

Esme's grin was downright naughty. "Just daydreaming a little. Wondering how scandalized the good people of Vader might be to catch a pair of newlyweds sparking in the grass in the middle of the afternoon."

Cleav raised an eyebrow. "Well, Mrs. Rhy, we will never know," he stated with firm good humor. "Not that you aren't an extreme temptation," he admitted. "But those fish are very hungry."

"Then let's feed them!" Esme agreed and hurried to her feet, holding out her hand to help him up.

He took it and kept it when he got to his feet. The two walked hand in hand to the meat house.

"I've been looking over all the fish," Esme told him. "Trying to get to know them better."

Cleav smiled.

"I still think they should have names," she said, then continued with a shrug. "But we've got more fish here than there's names in the Bible."

"Oh, I don't know. We could go through all the 'begats' and probably get enough," he said. "But I'm not about to call one of my fine trout Jehoshaphat."

Esme giggled.

Together they gathered up a bucket of the ground meat and carried the smelly mix back to the water's edge.

"These are my favorites," Esme told him as she indicated the full-grown fish swimming leisurely in the water. "They are just so pretty."

"The Rainbows," Cleav said, nodding his understanding. "They are a very pretty fish, and good fighters. But for my table, I prefer the Browns. Not much to look at, but fine eating."

"I can't even think about eating them!" Esme said, dismayed.

"That's what they're for."

"I know. No use getting sentimental about where your food comes from. But they are mighty pretty."

While he scattered in the other ponds, Cleav let her hand-feed. She loved feeding the brooders, and it pleased Cleav to watch her.

For her part, Esme thought that caring for his fish was a lot like caring for Cleav.

"What are these gray ones?" she asked him. "The ones that always run with the Rainbows." He looked to where she pointed. "That's a Steelhead," he answered. "It's the same as the Rainbow."

Esme looked up quizzically. "What do you mean the same? They look completely different."

Cleav nodded as he squatted down beside her.

"The Steelheads are the exact same fish as the Rainbows," he said as he watched a big silver gray Steelhead take a bite of meat from her hand. "They just grew up to look different."

"Why?"

"Well, you know that all the trout migrate."

"Migrate?"

"They go to other places downstream," he said. "That is, unless you've got them penned up in ponds like these."

"Why do they do it?"

Cleav shrugged. "Curious maybe," he suggested. "Or looking for the right mate. Nobody knows really, the trout just do it," he said. "But they always return to their spawning waters, the place where they were born."

Esme nodded.

"Now, all the trout travel," Cleav said. "But the Steelheads go the farthest. At one time in his life this big gray fish was swimming in the ocean."

"In the ocean?"

"Yes," Cleav told her. "It's the salt water that changes the Rainbow's pretty colors to gray."

"And his colors never come back?"

Cleav shook his head. "No, once he's been to the sea he's changed forever. The Steelhead can come back home here, stay for the rest of his days, and live among the other Rainbow trout, but he'll always be different because of where he's been."

The Steelhead came up for another bite and Esme watched him with a strange sadness in her eyes.

"He's like you, Cleavis."

"What?"

"He's like you. He'll never be a sea fish, but he's seen the ocean, and he's been marked by it."

She turned her head to face him. "You went to the city,

and it changed you, too.'' Glancing around, she indicated her surroundings. ''You'll always live here in Vader, but the city put its mark on you, and you'll never be like the rest of us.''

Cleav was silent, staring at her.

The silence between them lengthened.

Esme looked down at the Steelhead swimming in the pond. ''I'm gonna name this fish.''

Cleav's eyes went to the streak of swishing silver beneath the water.

''All right,'' he said. ''What name are you going to give him?''

A broad and bittersweet smile brightened her face.

''I'm gonna call him the Gentleman.''

Together they finished the feeding. Esme hummed softly to herself, but Cleav was quiet, almost troubled. He'd come to care deeply for Esme, but it unsettled him that she could read him so easily. It made him feel uneasy. He should never have told her about his time in the city. He'd not shared that with a living soul. But at the time it seemed right to talk to Esme. And it felt so good that she could understand. It felt too good.

He wanted to be with her constantly, to tell her everything that happened, every curious word that was said, and every foolish thought or dream he had. It wasn't natural for a man to feel that way, he was sure.

Or maybe it was natural. Looking across the room at her examining the items stored at the far end of the hatching house, he wondered if this is what it was to be in love.

Esme Crabb was not at all the kind of woman he'd thought he could be in love with, the kind of woman he'd want for a wife. But it wouldn't be the first time he'd been wrong. That was the way of natural science. Each scientist had perceptions that he tried to prove. As often as not, a scientist proved himself wrong.

Had he proved himself wrong? Could he love Esme Crabb? Maybe he could.

"What is this thing?" Esme asked as she examined a large wood rectangular contraption with a metal crank.

"That's a roller spawning box," he answered, crossing the room to show it to her.

"A spawning box?"

"It's how I collect the fertilized eggs from the trout," he said. "It's a new idea, but I like it a great deal. It seems more natural for the fish."

He turned the crank to show her how it worked.

"The fish lays her eggs here on top. Once they are fertilized, the roller carries them down to this end compartment, where you can remove them to the hatching house without disturbing the fish."

Esme examined the box more closely. It was really three boxes within a box. The top layer was a mesh screen obscured by coarse gravel. Under this was an endless apron of fine wire-cloth that passed over rollers at the ends of the box that were turned by the crank. Esme was impressed by the ingenuity but curious about the purpose.

"Can't you just leave the eggs in the ponds?" she asked.

Cleav shook his head. "There are too many predators. Birds, frogs, and lizards consider fish eggs a treat. I hate to admit this, but a lot of my fish are so dumb they don't know family from food."

Her eyes widened. "You mean they eat their own babies?"

"It can happen. That's why I keep the small fry separate from their elders until they're old enough to defend themselves."

"It seems kind of sad," Esme said.

"For me, too," Cleav admitted. "Nature isn't always

sweet and pretty the way we'd like it to be. I am a student of the natural order and have great admiration for it, but I believe there must be a balance.''

''What kind of balance?''

''It's hard to explain,'' Cleav answered, wrinkling his brow as he sought the best phrasing. ''Some men believe that only human needs are important. That trees should be cut to make farmland and dangerous animals should be destroyed routinely.''

Cleav sighed and shook his head. ''In contrast to that, there are many naturalists who would alter nothing. They believe that man should not use his superior intelligence to compete with animals and plants.''

''But you don't agree with either view,'' Esme said.

''No,'' Cleav answered with a chuckle. ''I agree with both.'' He turned his gaze to look out the doorway to the ponds beyond the hatching house.

''It's like a man with a house full of children,'' he said. ''I believe it's his duty to see that his children have bread on the table every day.''

He turned his eyes back to Esme. ''But that doesn't mean that he can ignore his neighbor's children who may be hungry.''

He reached for Esme's hand. ''Do you understand what I'm saying?''

Esme smiled at him. ''You are a wonderful man, Cleavis Rhy,'' she told him.

''I'm just a man,'' he said. ''Trying to do what I think best. That's why I prefer keeping the fish as close to their wild heritage as I can. The spawning box helps me do that. It's more natural.''

''More natural?'' Esme asked. ''More natural than what? What do other people do?''

''Well, most trout breeders simply wait till the fish are fertile and then catch them in nets,'' he told her. ''They pick a fish up in their hands and then press on its abdomen. If it's a female and she's ripe, the eggs will just pour right out of her into a pan. They can be fertilized right in the pan and taken immediately to the hatching house. The fish don't really have much to do with it.''

''But with the spawning box, they do?'' Esme asked.

Cleav nodded. ''Those trenches I've built at the far end of the ponds are called the races. When it's time for the female to lay her eggs, she wants to go as far upstream as she can and find a nice still place to leave them.

''I put this box in the far end of the races. I put lots of nice gravel on the top here for her nest and then I just leave it alone.''

Cleav's eyes were bright with the excitement and pleasure of the memory.

''The female comes up to the top of the races, finds her nesting spot, and deposits her eggs. Her mate is watching her all the time, and when she leaves, he goes behind her and puts the milt on the eggs.''

''Milt?''

Cleav hesitated. ''Milt is the . . . well, it's what the male contributes to the egg to fertilize it.''

''Is it like an egg, too?''

''No, it's more a fluid that the trout just spills on the eggs.''

Esme's brow screwed up curiously. ''Is it like people?'' she asked in a cautious whisper.

''People?''

''You know,'' she said with a blush.

Cleav's mouth opened in surprise. Ladies never mentioned such things. As his shock receded, he laughed out loud.

''Yes, Esme,'' he said. ''It's like people.''

He pulled her into his arms and gave her a warm, loving

hug. "I love being married to you," he said. It was the closest he could come to expressing his new feelings.

"Me, too," Esme admitted. "And I'm so glad we're people instead of trout."

"Why is that? Don't you know how to swim?"

"I swim just fine, Mr. Rhy," she said. "That wasn't at all what I was thinking about."

"What were you thinking?" he asked. "I'm always curious about the workings of your mind."

Esme giggled. "I was thinking that I wouldn't want us to be trout, 'cause then you wouldn't have any arms to hold me."

He immediately released her and stepped across the room.

"That's true, Esme," he said. "But it wouldn't be so bad. Sometimes a look is enough."

To prove his point, Cleav allowed his eyes to slowly travel along Esme's body. His pupils dilated with the pleasure of the sight.

"Perhaps we could create a scientific experiment," he said, "to determine if the sense of touch is absolutely necessary to create intimacy between a husband and wife?"

Without waiting for her consent, Cleav's look became a hot, fluttery caress across her skin. His lips parted as he examined the curve of her jaw and the length of her neck. Slowly he moved his gaze to the swell of her bosom, the trimness of her waist, the curve of her hip, and allowed his heart to remember the long, slim legs hidden beneath her skirts.

Esme felt her flesh quiver beneath his gaze. Forcing her chin up, she straightened her shoulders and looked back. He was so handsome, so strong, so warm and wonderful. His heart was so full and he talked with such sincerity and concern for all things. It was difficult to keep herself from running into his arms. But the challenge in his eyes stayed her.

Her nipples pressed anxiously against the fabric that

covered her. But she was not the only one who could be affected by a look.

Giving free rein to her own eyes, she watched as Cleav swallowed nervously. Her gaze wandered down his face to the broad strong shoulders that bore such care, the long sinewy arms that held her with such strength, and the large, long-fingered hands that he kept so clean and touched her with so tenderly. She felt a warmth of joy and possession as she allowed her eyes to travel the length of his masculine torso to the front of his trousers. He was already partially aroused. The sight brought a slight smile to Esme's face.

''One thing about this experiment,'' Esme pointed out. ''When the fish look at each other, they aren't wearing clothes.''

A slow smile spread across Cleav's face as he reached for the buttons on his shirt.

Sunday dawned bright and springlike as the Rhys, both the mister and missus as well as Cleav's mother, Eula, prepared to attend church.

Esme hummed with pleasure as she donned the new dress she had made for herself. The pretty pink color was perfect for her and brought out the blush of her complexion in her cheeks.

One week married, and it was heaven. Thinking back to the worries and concerns that had plagued her this time last Sunday, she laughed lightly. Cleav didn't love her, that was true. But he was such a fair and honorable man, and so tender and considerate, marriage was surely enough.

Touching the beautiful material of her new gown almost with reverence, she sighed in near bliss. He was so good to her.

''Imagine how he would treat a woman that he really loved,'' she whispered to herself and then glanced at her reflection in the glass with distaste.

She refused to long for what could never be. A lifetime of deprivation had taught her to appreciate what she had.

"You look beautiful," Cleav said from the doorway.

"Do you like it?" she asked. "I hope you don't mind that I used the material, but I knew that you could never sell it. You know how I hate to see things go to waste."

Cleav came closer to rub the fabric gently between his fingers.

"The rose crepe de chine," he whispered. He leaned closer to ask. "How did you manage to get the stain out?"

"I didn't completely," Esme admitted with embarrassment. "So I used that part for the inner facings of the yoke."

Laying a hand gently over her heart, she told him, "It's here."

Stunned by the feelings that welled up inside him, Cleav was frozen momentarily. Then gently he lay his head against the site where her hand had been.

"Oh, Esme I—" He hesitated, suddenly fearful of his own words. "I don't deserve you."

He planted a kiss on her bosom. And one led to another. Had Eula Rhy not called to them from downstairs several moments later, the Rhys would have forgotten about the Sunday service completely.

As he walked to church between the two women, Cleav was still struggling with his emotions as their light conversation finally captured his attention.

"That is a lovely dress, Esme," Mrs. Rhy said politely.

"Thank you," she answered. "I'm not the seamstress that my sisters are, but I tried to do the fabric justice."

"And beautiful fabric it is," Mrs. Rhy agreed. "I was beginning to wonder if Cleav intended for you to wear that dreary serge forever."

Esme's mouth flew open in silent shock.

"Well said, Mother," Cleav commented hurriedly. "I have been remiss about seeing to a proper wardrobe for my wife."

He turned to smile kindly at Esme. "Why don't the two of us go down to the store this afternoon and look through the materials we have on hand. I'm sure we can find several things that you like."

"I don't really . . ." Esme hesitated. "I mean . . . you don't have to give me new clothes."

Her embarrassment was clear, but Cleav refused to let the subject drop. "Nonsense, I'm not *giving* you the clothes. You are my wife. Everything that I own, you own. That's the law of God and man."

Feeling she already had so much, Esme cringed at the idea of further burdening her husband.

"I don't really need anything," she persisted. "I'm used to wearing old clothes. It doesn't bother me."

"Well, it bothers *me!*" Eula Rhy snapped in unkindly.

Cleav glared at his mother. "You must have new clothes," Cleav said gently to Esme. "Would you want the people of Vader to think I can't provide for you?"

"Of course not," she answered. "But everybody knows—"

"Everybody knows that you are my wife and that the wife of a gentleman always dresses as well as he can afford."

He was so adamant, Esme felt she had no choice but to acquiesce. But his words continued to haunt her, darkening her light mood of the morning. *The wife of a gentleman.* His mother had told it right the night of the wedding. How could plain, poor Esme Crabb live up to something like that?

They reached the church in good time. Cleav gallantly escorted both women through the crowd as he paused occasionally to have a word with one person or the next. He was proud of the beautiful woman beside him in rose crepe de chine. He felt a strength, a belonging, a completeness that he hadn't felt since childhood.

Despite his faults and foibles, almost because of them, Esme cared for Cleavis Rhy, the hill-born pisciculturist and small-town storekeeper. She saw no need for him to be anything else.

At that sweet, precious moment on a Sunday morning in springtime, Cleavis Rhy was completely happy.

Joining her new husband for the first time at his pew in the left front of the church, Esme was less jubilant. Every eye in the church was focused upon them.

Ordinarily Esme would have realized that it was natural for a newlywed couple on their first public outing to attract attention, but already worried about being a "gentleman's" wife, Esme saw it as a critical judgment.

Sophrona Tewksbury walked with studied nonchalance to the front of the church. With her smile firmly in place, she stopped beside the pew of Cleav and Esme. "Good morning," she said, sweetly offering a hand to Cleav.

He took it and came to his feet. "Good morning to you, Miss Sophrona," he said. "You look lovely as always."

Esme didn't know if she was supposed to stand up or not. Fearing to make a social blunder in front of the congregation, she hesitated a moment then stood beside Cleav.

"Don't you look wonderful!" Sophrona exclaimed sincerely. "I knew that rose color was perfect for you."

"Th-thank you," Esme stuttered.

Sophrona leaned forward and embraced Esme, planting a sisterly kiss on her flushed cheek.

"I know you are busy settling into your new home," Sophrona said lightly. "But when you have time, do come over for a lemonade with me one afternoon."

"Of course," Esme blurted out a bit too loudly.

With a warm smile Sophrona made her way to the piano, where she seated herself daintily at the bench and immediately began to play.

"She's so kind," Esme whispered to herself.

"She's a lady," Eula Rhy whispered back beside her. "You'd do well to learn to emulate her."

Esme felt a clump of fear gnawing at the back of her throat. She could never be Sophrona Tewksbury, never in a dozen lifetimes.

She glanced over at Cleavis. She wished he could hold her, kiss her, tell her that she was beautiful. But marriage, she reminded herself, doesn't take place only in the bedroom. She'd have to learn to be his wife in every way.

The preacher's words were completely lost on her as Esme continued with her own thoughts throughout the service. She turned once to see her father and sisters come in the door, late as usual. But the rest of the time she tried to look as if she were paying attention. Sitting in the front of the church did not afford a person the opportunity for wool gathering that was enjoyed by those on the last pew.

Finally it was over, and Esme hoped to make a quick escape.

"Well, don't you look just shiny as a new penny." Pearly Beachum spoke up loudly as she embraced Esme like a long-lost daughter.

"Thank you," Esme choked out. The woman's bear hug had nearly taken the breath from her.

"Come take a look at this dress, Wilma," Mrs. Beachum encouraged another woman.

As the two women "oohed" and "ahhed" over the fabric, Pearly leaned forward to whisper in her ear, "I bet those silly-minded sisters of yours are pea-green with envy."

Esme was first startled, then angered. Did these old gossips think that now that she was married to Cleavis Rhy, she was no longer one of the Crabb family?

"Excuse me," she said as haughtily as she could manage. "I need to speak to my family. I haven't seen them for a week.'' Hurriedly, almost desperately, Esme made her way through the crush to her father's side.

''Mornin', Pa,'' she said, planting a kiss on Yo's not-too-recently shaven cheek.

''Well, if it isn't my little married gal,'' her father said, chuckling. ''You're looking right pretty this morning, Esme-girl. I 'spect that old Rhy ain't taken to beatin' you yet.''

''He would never beat me,'' she proclaimed with mock outrage. ''He is a very gentle and kind man.'' Blushing with a nervous glance at her hands, Esme added, ''I'm very happy, Pa.''

The old man nodded, pleased. ''It's good to hear that, for sure,'' he said. ''You deserve some happily-ever-after if ever a woman did.''

''Oh, Esme!'' The twins greeted her with shrieking giggles and a thousand questions.

''Your dress is wonderful,'' Adelaide proclaimed.

''Do you have others? When can we come and see?'' Agrippa asked.

Esme fended off their questions as well as she could and took her leave, promising a long visit soon.

Cleav was waiting for her.

''You didn't have to hurry,'' he told her as she took his arm. ''Mother is lunching with the Tewksburys. I told them we'd prefer to be alone.''

His smile was warm and winning, but Esme was too wrapped up in her own concerns to notice.

They walked in silence for a few minutes as Esme attempted to make order of the chaos in her mind.

''When can my family move in with us?'' she blurted out suddenly.

''What?''

''When can my family move in? We've been married a

week already. Don't you think that's time enough for us to be alone?''

Cleav's brows furrowed in concern. When he'd married Esme, he'd never given her family much of a thought. Was he really expected to take them in?

"I'm not sure that your family *should* move in with us," Cleav began cautiously.

Esme's eyes widened as she turned to look at him. "Whyever not?" she asked.

Not exactly sure how to answer that, Cleav wavered. "It's not really that customary for the bride's family to move in."

"I don't care about customary," Esme said. "I'm thinking about my family."

"Don't you wish to be alone with me? I'd gotten the impression that our privacy was something you valued."

"I *do* value it," she insisted. "But my family won't make our lives any more or less private. Your mother already lives with us."

"Would you have me throw my mother into the street?"

"Of course not!" Esme was as angry now as she was adamant. "I wouldn't want to throw your mother into the street, and you shouldn't want my family to be living in a cave!"

Cleav hardly knew how to argue that. In his entire life he had never seen a home that was less habitable than Yohan Crabb's mountain cave.

"Certainly I want to help your family," Cleav began tentatively. "I guess I just hadn't thought of it."

"You hadn't thought of it?" Esme was in a genuine snit. "How selfish you must think me."

"Selfish?"

"Did you think that I would marry you to live in that big house of yours just for myself?"

Cold fear cut through Cleavis like a knife.

"Sitting up in that cave," Esme continued without noticing his darkening expression, "I saw this big old house with just you and your mother, and I knew there'd be plenty of room for my whole family."

"Of course," Cleav answered very quietly.

~ 15 ~

Once Cleav had agreed to let her family move in, Esme was genuinely startled by his rush to make that happen. Sunday afternoon he'd left her in the store to pick out whichever fabrics she liked for her new dresses while he went up the mountain to talk to Crabb.

"You are absolutely right," he'd insisted with a strange new coldness. "My in-laws cannot live in a cave in the hills. Especially with all the sacrifices you've made."

Esme wasn't sure what he meant by "sacrifices." She supposed he was talking about all the years she'd cooked and cleaned for them. She started to ask him but wasn't given time to discuss it. A moment later Cleav was off and gone.

By Tuesday her father and sisters had moved into the big house and Eula Rhy had taken to her bed with another attack.

"Bring the twins to the store to pick out some fabric, too," Cleav told her. "The three of you can spend the summer sewing up your new wardrobes."

Esme had wanted to spend the summer getting to know

her husband. "You're too generous," she protested, but Cleav ignored her.

"Your father will need clothes, also," he insisted. "We can't have him looking like a vagabond."

Esme was cut by Cleav's coldness and concerned by his quiet. With all the activity of the move, it was natural, Esme had decided, that they didn't have as much time together. But waiting alone in her bed at night while he sat up in the library made her worry.

Once she'd made her argument, Cleav clearly wanted her family better housed and better dressed. But she no longer knew his motivation. Was it because he cared for her? Or because he was ashamed of her?

As these thoughts came to her mind, she tried to discard them as unworthy. Cleav was a kind, gentle, loving man. He was not so vain that he would look down on their poverty.

Still, the thought nagged Esme. His speech, his dress, his house were all constructed to present him as a gentleman. His wife and her family, however, were a definite step backward.

Her mother-in-law's words haunted her: *If you really knew Cleav, you'd see how totally unsuited for him you are.* Esme was afraid that perhaps Mrs. Rhy was right. Maybe she didn't know Cleav as well as she thought. And maybe she really was unsuitable.

Before she married, she'd only wanted what was best for her family. Now she only wanted what was best for Cleav. Maybe a lady was what was best. She was only a half-wild hill girl.

"But I can change!" she declared to herself adamantly. With Cleav's money, she could dress as nice as anyone in town. And her family could, too. They were simple mountain folk, but they could dress and talk as fancy as they pleased. Esme was sure of it. With that as her goal Esme's life was as busy as it had ever been.

The elder Mrs. Rhy was now seemingly permanently ensconced in her bed. Esme ran errands for the older woman all day long. In part because, never having been ill herself, Esme couldn't imagine how terrible it might be. And also because she hoped in some way to prove to Cleav's mother that she could be a good wife and daughter-in-law. However, as the weeks passed, Eula Rhy seemed no closer to being won over.

With a household of six to clean for and cook for and clothe, Esme found little time to be with Cleav at the store. And even less time to help him with the fish. It seemed they rarely had a moment alone—no more quiet conversations, no more secret sharing.

Esme missed their closeness but realized it must be her fault. Perhaps after getting used to the novelty, Cleav had decided her conversation was boring. Or perhaps her manners were too crude. Perhaps she wasn't really pretty.

Perhaps he could never love her.

That thought would catch in her throat and sting her eyes. She would *make* him love her, she vowed. She would be whatever he wanted her to be.

Only those special nights gave her surcease. Those nights when he couldn't keep away from her. Those nights when they loved each other until they couldn't speak, couldn't breathe, couldn't think. Only those nights gave her hope.

No man could express such care, such tenderness, if he had no feeling, Esme assured herself.

She simply had to make herself more worthy of him. She flinched at her own words. All her life she'd held her chin high, daring the world to condemn her for her name and her poverty. Now she had finally realized that it was her own finger that pointed to her so derisively.

Shaking her head in dismay, Esme folded the wad of bread dough on the floured board and slammed it with the heel of her hand.

"You're doing it again, Esme-girl," her father warned.

Esme looked curiously at the dough for his meaning. "Doing what?" she asked.

"Taking care of everybody but yourself," Yo replied with genuine impatience.

She shook her head dismissively.

"I don't mind," she said.

"What about your husband?" her father asked. "Does he mind you working dawn to dusk with no help and never getting a minute alone with him?"

"Cleav is very understanding," she said a little defensively. "And you are all family."

"Family?" The old man humphed. "Family is family. You and your husband are the family. The rest of us are relatives."

Slightly piqued, Esme's tone picked a sharper edge. "I'd think you'd be happy to live in a clean, dry house for a change."

Yo Crabb folded his hands across his chest. "I surely am, Esme-girl," he answered. "But not at the price of you working yourself into an early grave like your mama. With four women and one old man in this household, there ain't no call for you to be doing all the work."

Esme wasn't appeased. She looked at him skeptically.

"You're right about that, Pa," she answered shrewdly. "Just what job are you willing to take on to help me?"

The old man gave her a wry grin. "I ain't much for helping, and that's the truth of it," he admitted. "I'd be right willing to play the fiddle, however, and brighten your day." His smile could have lit up their old, dark cave. And Esme understood, not for the first time, what her hardworking practical mother had seen in the "laziest man in Vader, Tennessee."

"Yes, Pa," she said quietly. "Play me a lively tune."

In minutes he began the cheerful tune to "Old Rosin the

Bow.'' Esme's foot began a rhythmic tap as she quartered the dough and rounded it into the pans.

The twins scampered in from the sewing room with a lively step and clap as they sang.

> "I've always been cheerful and easy,
> And scarce have I heeded a foe,
> While some after money run crazy,
> I merrily Rosin'd the Bow."

At least ten verses later and lots of clapping and laughter, all of them were still going strong when the kitchen door was jerked open abruptly.

"Lord have mercy!" Eula Rhy cried as she took in the scene around her. "What in the name of heaven are you doing making such a ruckus in the middle of the morning?"

Yohan ceased playing and leaned his fiddle casually against his chest.

"Oh, Mother Rhy—" Esme began, shamed at her own thoughtlessness.

"You sick?" Yo interrupted her.

"Of course I am sick!" Eula Rhy was clearly furious. "I have a serious nervous condition."

Yo nodded. "Yep, I heard that." Gazing rather calmly at his fiddle, his smile was deceptively innocent. "I've always heard that music has healing powers," he said.

"Not that kind of music," Eula disagreed huffily.

Yohan raised an eyebrow. "It got you out of that bed of yours for the first time in weeks."

Eula opened her mouth in fury, prepared to make an angry retort, when Esme waylaid her.

"Here, Mother Rhy, do sit down before you wear yourself out." Esme took the older woman's arm and helped her to a chair. "Can I get you something? Some spring water? A bit of buttermilk?"

"Tea!" Mrs. Rhy demanded haughtily.

"Of course," Esme answered and gave a quick warning look to the rest of her family as she hurried to put the kettle on.

"Pa," she said with a fine edge of authority. "Play Mother Rhy something a bit more soothing to the nerves."

Giving Eula a disapproving look, Yohan nevertheless began a soft sweet strain, and the twins sang the impromptu duet.

> "In the sky the bright stars glittered.
> On the grass the moonlight shone.
> From an August evening party,
> I was seeing Nelly home."

At first Eula Rhy's face was stony, then the music slowly seeped into the old woman's veins. By the time Yohan had reached the third and final verse, Eula's contralto had joined the sweet soprano of the girls.

"You got a right fine singing voice, Miz Rhy," Yo complimented. "Do you know 'Old Oaken Bucket'?"

The singing continued as Esme fixed her mother-in-law's tea and resumed her work. She was just bringing in the sheets from the line when Eula Rhy suddenly stood up to help her.

"Oh, ironing!" the woman exclaimed, with the excitement of a child with a new toy. "Let me do that."

"You're feeling better?" Esme asked, genuinely stunned by the woman's apparent good mood.

"It's the amusement," Yo told them both with conviction. "Now, my ladies," he continued, with the hill version of courtly manners, "I'm going to play this fiddle so well, why, your chores gonna float by like leaves on a lazy river."

And he did. Esme was sure that she hadn't heard her

father play so cheerfully since he'd moved to the house. She suspected that recently he had walked up to the mountain when the music mood struck him.

"Can you play 'The Bear That Yearned for Buckshot'?" Eula asked.

Crabb's grin was his only answer as he struck up the lively tune.

Within minutes the twins had brought their sewing into the kitchen and were simultaneously sewing and helping with chores as they laughed and clapped and jigged with the music.

Mrs. Rhy actually showed the girls some fancy clogging steps. "I used to be quite a high-stepper in my day," she confided to the group. "Of course, that was before Mr. Rhy and I became Free Will Baptists," she explained with only the hint of wistfulness in her voice. "We used to go to all the dances and just tear up the floor!"

Esme was amazed. Since dancing of any kind was considered inherently sinful by the Free Will Baptist Church, neither Esme nor the twins had ever danced a step.

As Yo had warned, the chores passed easily and quickly. And it was with genuine surprise that Esme looked up to see her husband standing in the doorway.

"What in heaven's name is going on in here?" His question was thunderous. "I could hear you all the way out at the gate."

"We're just having some fun, Cleavy," Mrs. Rhy told him. "Yohan said he would play us a tune, and I thought I'd show the twins some real country clogging."

"It's kindy a celebration that your mama is feeling more herself," Yo added helpfully.

"Oh." He was clearly at a loss for words. "Well, I'm glad you are better, Mother," he said finally.

"Dinner's almost on the table," Esme told him. "I fixed your favorite, roast chicken."

Her husband's expression was strangely cold. "Roast chicken? Is it Sunday and no one told me?"

The afternoon was a long one for Cleav. He had been as grouchy as a bear at noontime, speaking in monosyllables. He attacked the succulent roast chicken with the finesse of a mountain lion and the manners of a billy goat. Not one word of appreciation passed his lips. The chill in his own heart froze the phrases to his tongue.

The memory of his mother flushed and laughing, and the Crabbs all caught up in the gaiety, contrasted sharply with his own black mood. Since that fateful Sunday, Cleav had been chafing with the knowledge that his wife, Esme Crabb Rhy, had married him for his house. That was the fact, he reminded himself. And Esme Crabb didn't even have enough taste to appreciate the ambience of the structure he'd built. She wanted it painted blue!

Why should he care? he asked himself over again. He'd married her because he'd *had* to. Nothing less than public censure could have compelled him to align himself with a snappy little baggage like Esme Crabb.

No one in Vader should have expected a love match, least of all him. But he had. He'd thought that she loved him, desired him, needed him, for himself.

She'd needed him, all right. Needed him to support her father and sisters and put a roof over their heads.

Part of him was furious, but part of him understood. Just as he had felt obliged to give up his schooling to help his mother get through her grief, Esme felt responsible for her family's needs. She was the one who'd seen that there was a roof over their heads and food on their table. He could hardly blame her for seeking a solution that would ensure both of those things. Marriage to him was that solution.

He remembered that long-ago day when she'd come into the store and asked him outright if he wanted to marry her.

Of course she wasn't in love with him. She hadn't even known him then.

Cleav shook his head in self-derision. He'd been so fanciful.

It all made perfect sense, and he couldn't even fault Esme. She'd seduced him with her naive, countrified wiles, and he'd fallen in with the scheme easily enough.

So why did it hurt so much to think about it? Pride? Being bamboozled by a woman? Yes, that was part of it. But he'd been in business a long time and had taken his share of skinnings, enough to know that every man can be a fool at times.

There was more. Something that hurt worse than injured pride. He hesitated to put a name on it. But it was there.

Esme's duplicity hurt because he loved her.

There was no other explanation. He'd suspected as much earlier but had rejected the suggestion. But the pain in his heart could be interpreted no other way.

Remembering those first sweet days of self-deception, Cleav sighed for their loss.

Then he slammed the feather duster against the row of washtubs with a vengeance.

"Damn it!" he complained bitterly. Certainly another woman might have loved him. But other women no longer mattered.

He wanted Esme. He wanted her to love him.

And he was determined to win her. The question was how.

He could give her anything that she might want. But she wasn't the kind of woman who cared for "things" too much. They were good together in bed, he reminded himself. Was that enough to win a woman's love?

Not the way he was going about it, Cleav muttered to himself aloud.

He hadn't taken her in his arms for days. He was afraid

that in the heat of passion he would declare his feelings for her and embarrass the both of them.

But he couldn't stay away. He wanted her. Even now he wanted her.

That could be a start, but he also had to try to make her his friend—to try to understand her. To share her problems and her life.

The bell over the door jingled, and Cleav looked up to see who was the customer. It was Yohan Crabb.

"What you need, Yo?" Cleav asked him with as much patience as he could muster.

The old man shrugged. "Not a dang thing," he answered easily. "They's just so busy at the house, I thought I'd come down here and see what you were up to."

Cleav made a split-second decision and reached for the ties at the back of his apron.

"I need you to handle the store for a couple of hours for me."

"What now?" Yo asked, nearly dumbfounded.

Cleav handed him the apron.

"There's a price book in the money drawer beneath the counter. If somebody wants to buy something that's not marked, look it up in the book."

Yohan, clearly stunned, attempted to choke out a refusal. "I cain't hardly read."

"Just do the best you can," Cleav said with a wave of unconcern. "I've got something important to do."

"You going to see about them fish?" Yo's question was almost an accusation.

"No," Cleav replied as he headed out the door. "I'm going to see about my wife."

The moon was on the rise as Esme sat before the vanity brushing her hair. The fancy store-bought soap—Mrs. Rhy called it shampoo—left her hair as soft and silky as an egg wash. But Esme's thoughts were not upon the long strands of hair she pulled her brush through. They were on her husband, Cleav.

That afternoon in the sewing room, she had been laughing at a joke Mrs. Rhy had made and wondering at the sudden change in her mother-in-law when Cleav suddenly appeared at the door.

"Mother, sisters," he greeted the other women with polite nods. "If you will excuse my wife, I need to speak with her for a moment."

Esme didn't wait to hear their answers. She immediately hurried toward him.

"What is it?" she asked, but he'd ignored her and simply taken her arm to escort her up the stairs.

His silence worried Esme. She knew he'd been angry at noon. And why not? He'd spent years trying to be a perfect gentleman and live in a gentleman's house with gentlemanly manners. And in a few weeks his new wife had turned his kitchen into a dance hall and his mother remembering her own hill upbringing.

Cleav probably saw her behavior as some horrible breach of conduct. Was he angry with her? Planning to chastise her privately?

Cleav opened the door of their room and gestured for her to enter. Esme did, with some trepidation.

When she heard the door close quietly behind them, she turned to question him.

She hadn't had a chance to say a word.

Cleav's arms came around her. His mouth found hers in a kiss that was hot, passionate, hungry.

Fire leapt in Esme's veins, and she eagerly returned the kiss. Allowing her fingers to weave through his hair, she moaned in delight and pressed against him.

Cleav couldn't seem to get close enough. "Sweet Hillbaby, my Hillbaby,'' he groaned against her. ''I want you too much,'' he said.

Their kisses were as sweet and tender as they were urgent and passionate. Both speaking their feelings so clearly and neither hearing the other.

Cleav eagerly undid the buttons at her back, and Esme, her hands free, quickly lowered her bodice as a temptation for his lips.

''You're so beautiful, Hillbaby,'' he had told her roughly. ''And you're mine, Esme, forever mine. . . .''

Tonight, as Esme stared blankly at her image in the mirror, she still shuddered in remembered pleasure. This afternoon had been heaven. But all of marriage was not spent in bed.

Cleav teased and pleased and satisfied her. But the closeness of their first days together eluded them. He no longer spoke of his days and his dreams. Somehow she had pushed him away. All her life she had managed to provide for the needs of the people she loved, but she wasn't sure she knew what Cleav needed.

A throaty giggle outside the window captured Esme's attention. Although she couldn't hear what was said, she recognized the voices of her sister and Armon.

It had been Agrippa's night to walk out with him, and she and Adelaide had worked furiously that afternoon to finish her new blue percale.

Her sister had looked positively charming when she'd come downstairs. Esme hoped that a rakish, overbearing clod like Armon could appreciate all their work.

The sounds from the yard ceased. But Esme didn't hear the door open. Curiously she made her way to the window.

Looking down, she saw Armon and Agrippa locked in a passionate embrace on the front path. He was holding her far too closely for a couple who were not engaged, and her sister was not complaining.

Disapproving, Esme was just about to call out a sisterly rebuke when the kiss ended and Armon set her at arm's length. Although their conversation was spoken too softly for Esme to hear, apparently Armon bade her good night. With one last longing look, Agrippa hurried to the door.

"For heaven's sake," Esme muttered to herself. "That was entirely too close."

She would definitely have to speak to Agrippa about her behavior. Certainly this time Armon had acted like a gentleman, but Esme was pretty sure that he could not be counted on for continual chivalrous behavior. She was just about to move away from the window when a movement behind the chestnut tree caught her eye.

"What are you up to?" She heard Armon's voice clearly. "Spying?"

With a naughty giggle Adelaide emerged from behind the tree. Esme couldn't hear her sister's reply but watched in horror as the other threw herself into Hightower's arms.

Adelaide's kiss was much like Agrippa's. Too close, too intimate, too long, and far too dangerous.

"Save to graces!" Esme exclaimed to herself. This had to stop. If someone didn't do something soon, those two would be planning a double wedding before she knew it, and with only one groom!

She was so stunned, Esme didn't hear Cleav come up behind her until he touched her on the shoulder.

"What are you looking at?" he asked.

When she didn't answer, Cleav leaned forward out the window.

"Hmm . . ." She heard him spot the object of her interest. "Good night, Hightower," he called out calmly.

The couple in the darkness of the chestnut tree jumped apart guiltily.

"Come on in the house, Agrippa."

As Adelaide rushed down the path and into the front door,

Esme almost corrected him. Cleav still could not tell the twins apart. Then she saw the very cold glare that Cleav was offering Armon. He'd stated more than once that he didn't approve of the twin spark.

"I'm sorry, Cleavis," she told him as they watched Hightower disappearing into the night. "I swear I'm going to have a talk with those twins tomorrow. I won't have them making a scene on your front lawn."

Cleav shook his head and chucked his wife affectionately under the chin. "Don't worry about that, Hillbaby. I'll have a talk with young Mr. Hightower," he said. "Sometimes a man needs a bit of prodding to make his choice."

"Oh, you don't have to do that," Esme said, horrified. After she'd forced him into an unsuitable marriage and made him support her entire crazy family, did he think she expected him to help raise and marry off her two foolish sisters? "The twins are my responsibility. I would never ask you to take that on."

Cleav placed the palms of his hands on Esme's cheeks and tilted her head to look at him.

"I know you'd never ask me to take it on, Esme," he whispered. "But I hope you'd ask me to share it."

∾ 16 ∾

Like the renewal of crops and trees all around them, spring was also the time for renewal of the soul. The Reverend Wilbur Boatwright, an itinerant evangelist, arrived for the annual Vader revival, known as a week of nightly hellfire and brimstone preaching.

Because the church could be a mite stuffy, and revival meetings were famous for running long into the night, the men of the congregation constructed a brush arbor on the little knoll overlooking the church.

Six sturdy posts were driven into the ground and connected to each other with two-by-fours. A few crosswise slats were nailed as roofing and were covered with fresh-cut pine, fern, and sumac. The open area allowed cooling breezes to pass over the congregation and the makeshift roofing shaded them from the late evening sun.

Usually Esme found the sweet smell of freshly cut brush soothing, but this time she was too excited and wary to appreciate the setting. Revivals were times for reunions with old acquaintances, high entertainment, and spiritual reevaluation. While she looked forward to the fun and friends, Esme was not anxious to look closely at her life.

She'd accomplished what she'd set out to do. Her family now had a decent roof over their heads and new clothes and plenty of food. But the man she loved, the person who was now most important to her, had she made him happy?

"Why should he be?" she asked herself as she brushed his good black suitcoat. "He was tricked into marrying a woman whose ignorance and countrified ways would surely weigh him down for a lifetime!"

Esme was doing her best to learn ladylike behavior. She listened avidly to her mother-in-law's directions on keeping the house up to fashion. And she severely rebuked her sisters and father for bringing "cave manners" into Mr. Rhy's fancy house. With her sisters she pored over the ladies' magazines to ensure that their new clothes were neither immodest nor out-of-date. But the fact was, she couldn't change herself. She was still Esme Crabb, the same Esme Crabb that God had created. And she hated to face her Maker so disappointed with the job he'd done.

"Are you about ready?" Cleav asked from the doorway.

Esme nodded. "I'm just brushing your coat."

Cleav shook his head and looked at her curiously. "I wasn't planning to wear it. It's quite warm out tonight, and the crowd will be very close."

"Of course," Esme answered, blushing with embarrassment at her own stupidity. She'd thought gentlemen always wore coats. "I'll just hang it back in the wardrobe."

Cleav could see that Esme was upset.

"Do you want me to wear the coat?" he asked her. "I'd be happy to do it, if it pleases you."

"No! Certainly not."

"I just want to make you happy," he said quietly.

"I just want to make *you* happy," Esme answered him

with a curious look. "I should have known that it was too
hot to wear the coat."

Cleav reached out and took her hand. He held the palm in
his own for a moment and then squeezed it encouragingly.

"I don't expect you to know everything I want, Esme,"
he said.

Esme nodded. He didn't expect her to know what he
wanted, she thought, because he realized a woman like her,
an ignorant hill woman, could never understand his needs.

"Come on, you two," Eula called from the hallway. "If
we don't hurry, we'll be late for the foot washing."

Free Will Baptist, usually abbreviated with the initials
FWB, were oft referred to in the mountains as the "foot-
washing Baptists." The denomination, founded in Tennessee, was more famous for its insistence on foot washing as
part of the communion service than for its adamant oppo-
sition to the concept of predestination, for which its name
was taken.

The foot-washing ritual was performed much as it was
done on the night of the Last Supper. Men and women were
separated for the task. Each participant brought two clean
towels: One towel was wrapped around the waist and the
other hung down from it in front like a long sash. One by
one the members of the congregation would perform the
humbling task of washing the feet of another in a shallow
basin and then drying them with the towel they wore.

Eula wasn't afraid of missing the event, rather she wanted
to get the washing done before the "foot water" got too
dirty. As usual, she was not the only one with this idea.
More than half the congregation was better than a half hour
early.

"Come on now, Esme," Mrs. Rhy urged. "I don't want
a dozen people ahead of me."

"I'm not going to wash feet tonight," Esme told her and then glanced at her husband.

"All right," Cleav answered, patting her reassuringly on the shoulder. "Go on ahead, Mother."

As Mrs. Rhy hurried down the aisle, Cleav turned back to his wife. "Are you feeling all right?"

"I'm fine," she told him easily. "I just thought I'd skip it this time."

Cleav nodded his agreement and gave her a chaste good-bye kiss on the cheek.

"I hate to leave you alone up here," he said, glancing over his shoulder at the circle of men already forming in the clearing, their water buckets and towels in evidence.

"I'll be fine, go on," she said.

"You sure, Esme-girl?" her father interrupted.

"Yes, Pa," she said. "Go on now with Cleav."

As she watched the retreating backs of the men, she heard a giggle behind her. Turning, she saw the twins coming up the hill with Armon. He had one arm around the waist of each.

Seeing Esme, the two broke away from their sweetheart and hurried toward her. "Are you waiting for us?" one asked.

"What are you *both* doing with Armon?" Esme asked, looking over her sisters' shoulders to the culprit, who was now leaning so negligently against a tree trunk.

"Armon says that since we're going to the revival instead of walking out, the rules don't count," Adelaide answered with unconcerned openness.

"The rules *always* count," Esme said firmly. "Adelaide, this is your night, so I'll expect you, Agrippa, to walk home with me and Cleav."

"Oh, for heaven's sake." Agrippa gave her sister an exasperated look. "Well, can't I at least sit with them?"

Esme started to say no and then held her tongue. "All

right,'' she said finally. ''But you find me as soon as the service is finished.''

''Thank you.'' Agrippa gave Esme a grateful kiss on the cheek.

Esme hugged both girls warmly. ''Now, you'd best hurry or you'll be late,'' she told them.

''You're not coming with us?''

''Not tonight.''

As Esme stood on the hill watching the twins scamper toward the women's group, she folded her arms across her chest. Her sisters were sweet and pretty and such precious little feather-heads. She'd always thought that she would provide for them. But it was Cleav who had given them a decent place to live and furnished them with clothes to wear. Could she expect Cleav to protect them from the human dangers in life as thoroughly as he protected them from the elements? Cleav wanted to share her responsibilities, but she still felt that she should handle this one herself.

Turning, she looked at the object of her sisterly concern. Armon Hightower stood, like a wolf in waiting, grinning at her. She felt the rise of powerless ire inside her. Oh, how she'd like to slap the self-satisfied smile right off his face! But she'd never slapped a man in her life.

Suddenly an idea came to mind. As her plan hastily took shape, she slowly made her way toward Armon Hightower.

He stood, a sprig of straw stuck in the side of his mouth, and his movements were lazy and casual as he watched Esme approach. ''Evenin', Miz Rhy,'' he greeted her politely. ''What you doing up here with us sinners?''

With a hasty glance around Esme realized that virtually everyone who had chosen not to go foot washing was either a mother with a quartet of children or a wild young man.

''Actually, I wanted to have a word with you,'' Esme lied.

Armon raised an eyebrow warily. ''If you're fit to be tied

about me escorting both them gals up here," he said, "I warn you that I already mentioned it to your pa, and he didn't care nohow."

Esme accepted his statement with a nod. "This has nothing to do with the twins." She stated the bald-faced untruth without flinching. "This is something else entirely."

Pushing off from the tree, Armon stood straight before her, his interest obviously piqued.

Allowing the suspense to gather, Esme hesitated. "There is . . . I have a friend here who . . . well, has indicated an interest in you."

His eyebrows raised in surprise, and then he shrugged with studied unconcern. "Lots of young gals hanker after me," he admitted without an overabundance of pride. "I choose the gals I want, they don't choose me." His words were accompanied by a slight tilt of his head toward the circle of men, where her husband now stood ready to take his turn.

If Esme had any qualms about her plan, Hightower's implied criticism of Cleav quelled them. She nodded slowly. "This young woman," she said with careful reluctance, "the one I'm speaking of, is not one that would be considered 'one of the bunch.'"

"Oh?" Armon wasn't exactly sure what she meant. His expression was now openly curious. "Well, who in the world is she, this special female?"

Esme smiled slyly. "I'm really not at liberty to say."

"Why not?"

With a deep, heartfelt sigh, Esme continued with feigned hesitance. "This young woman confessed to me how she has loved you from afar for years."

Esme stopped momentarily to let her words sink in. "For years she's been dreaming of you, but you've never approached her."

"So now she wants to approach me?"

Esme appeared horrified. "Oh, no! She's much too genteel to ever speak to you herself."

Armon's eyes brightened. "So she asked you to speak for her?"

"Certainly not!" Esme's tone indicated that she was appalled at the suggestion. "She would be horrified if she ever learned that I'd mentioned this to you." And then more quietly she added, "You must never breathe a word of it."

Armon began to tire of the game. "How do you expect me *not* to tell her, when I don't even know *who* she is?"

"Well, you don't expect me just to blurt out her name, do you?" Esme asked.

"How about a hint, then?"

Esme considered his suggestion carefully, as if she'd never thought of it herself. Finally she sighed, as if losing a battle with her conscience. "All right," she said. "I'll give you some hints, but I will not tell you if you are right or wrong."

"Fair enough." Armon struck the bargain easily.

"Let's see," Esme began. "She's a young woman who is exceptionally attractive."

"Must not be from Vader, then," Armon joked. When his chuckle was met by Esme's stony look, he backed down. "Okay," he said noncommittally.

"She's not seeing anyone at the present time, but she suffered a very recent loss of a sweetheart."

Armon's brow furrowed as if deep in thought. Esme looked at him hopefully, but the young man shook his head.

"Could be a lot of gals," he said.

"She—" Esme tried to think of something else to hint. Armon was dense. "Oh, she plays the piano."

Armon's grin was wry, and his answer was sarcastic. "Half the women in these hills *think* they can play the piano. A man don't look at the piano when he's thinking about a woman.''

"Oh, for heaven's sake." Esme was clearly getting frustrated.

"She has red hair," she said with an edge of temper. If he couldn't get that, he must be a complete dolt.

"Red hair?" Armon looked at her as if she'd lost her mind. "I don't know any gals with red hair," he said.

"Of course you do!" Esme insisted.

"Well," he said, after thinking a moment, "there's that old whore down by Collins Crossing. But I'm pretty sure her red hair come out of a bottle."

"Do you think such a woman would be a friend of mine?" Esme asked with fury.

"No, ma'am," Armon answered. "But you're the one that brought up the red hair, and she's the only red-haired woman I know."

"You *do* know another young woman with red hair!" Esme told him.

"Nope," Armon replied obstinately. "Can't think of nary a one."

Esme gritted her teeth with frustration. "All right," she said between clenched jaws. "One more hint. If you can't get it this time, I'm giving up."

Armon shrugged.

"She's the daughter of a preacher."

Armon stared dumbly at her for a moment, then his eyes widened in shock. "Tits Tewksbury?" he whispered, the tone of his question incredulous.

Esme frowned at the vulgar nickname.

Glancing down the hill toward the women's foot washing, Armon's expression was one of disbelief.

"I cain't believe it, Miss Esme," he said sincerely. "That gal ain't never give me so much as the time of day."

"I'm not saying a word," Esme told him, reeking of

guile. "A lady's heart is involved, and I wouldn't want to in any way cause it to be broken."

Shaking his head in disbelief, Armon was clearly pole-axed. "Miss, uh, I mean Miz Rhy," he said, "I'll never breathe a word of what you tole me. But I do thank you for letting me know." His smile was joyous.

"Them ladies, they ain't like gals," he said. "You cain't even get a inkling of what they's a-thinking."

The crowds were breaking up, and Esme took her leave quickly.

If Armon couldn't get an inkling of what a lady was thinking, that must mean she was a lady, Esme thought to herself. Because Armon surely wouldn't have been smiling if he could have read her mind.

Esme hummed a cheery tune as she hurried to join her husband. If Sophrona had slapped Cleav for a gentle kiss, she'd probably break Armon Hightower's jaw.

The idea appealed to her.

The Reverend Wilbur Boatwright was a short, balding man with a florid complexion and a pure white handlebar moustache. What the middle-aged evangelist lacked in pulpit presence, he managed to make up for with a booming set of vocal cords.

Cleav and Esme found seats near the middle of the third row. Yohan deserted them for the male camaraderie of the hastily constructed "amen corner."

Only a couple of dozen benches were available, and with everybody within ten miles showing up, the place was crowded. Esme was jostled more than once as worshipers shoved into the row and she found herself plastered right up against her husband.

"Do you mind?" Cleav asked as he slipped his arm around her to give her more room.

"It's fine," Esme whispered, and they both heard a titter from behind them.

The twins sat on either side of Armon, and he was holding both snugly at the waist.

"You don't have to ask permission, no more," Armon told Cleav. "You're a husband now, and husbands do what they want."

The twins sighed adoringly and leaned even closer against him. It was all Esme could do not to pull away from Cleav's light embrace.

"Pay him no mind, Hillbaby," Cleav whispered.

The sweet endearment brought a bright blaze of color to Esme's cheek.

Cleav grinned.

The teasing lightened the tension between them, and Esme found herself leaning against him even more closely than necessary.

There was no piano in the brush arbor, so Miss Sophrona was not in sight. There were no songbooks to follow, but when Brother Oswald led the singing, Esme felt the warm spirit of shared harmony enfold her.

Cleavis, his arm still encircling his new wife, felt peaceful for the first time in days.

When the evangelist, Brother Wilbur, took his place behind the pulpit, he quickly read the scripture before stepping down by the altar and surveying the crowd.

"*You are farmers!*" he screamed at them. "*When you put seed in the ground, you expect it to grow!*"

He had clearly caught the attention of the crowd, who were now all silently staring at him.

"Why?" he asked more quietly. "Why do you expect it to grow?" He indicated an old man in the front row for his question, but then answered it himself. "*You expect it to grow,*" he shouted again, "*because the Lord promised you that it would!*"

Cleav's moment of serenity had passed abruptly, and he was now wishing that he'd chosen to sit farther toward the back. He considered himself a religious man, but evangelical fervor always seemed a mirage of righteousness rather than evidence of it.

Righteousness, he decided as he sat politely watching the little preacher pace frantically back and forth across the room at top volume, was nothing more than doing what you know is right. Even when doing it hurts you.

No, righteousness was no big mystery. It was love that was so difficult to understand.

He looked down at his wife beside him. Esme's hands sat idly in her lap and without thinking, Cleav allowed his right hand to join them.

Esme glanced up with surprise that quickly turned to pleasure. She gently caressed her husband's palm and held on to him with both hands.

The congregation was obliged to rise for prayer. Cleav and Esme, still clutching hands, bowed their heads with the rest. As the preacher droned on about the needs of the world and the people in it, both Cleav and Esme tried to concentrate on something besides each other.

When the prayer was over and the amens were spoken, both took their seats, but Brother Wilbur's tirade from the pulpit continued unflagging for well over an hour. Carefully manipulating the emotions of the crowd, the preacher had them yearning for the gentle "shepherd of men" one moment and fearing the wrathful king determined to cast sinners into the "lake of fire" the next.

Notes were passed from one youthful hand to another. Babies, their sleep disturbed by the noise and excitement, fussed and squalled in turn. Old Man Tyree fell asleep and began snoring loudly. And Garner Broadwick carved his name in the right rear arbor pole.

As the service reached a crescendo, the frequent "amens"

were joined by shouts. Youngsters on the back rows eagerly watched the proceedings in hopes of seeing a fainting zealot or hearing someone speak in tongues. Jimmy Milo bet Noch Gingrich his best cat's-eye marble that when the women fell on the floor, they pulled up their skirts. Noch bet eagerly, feeling, right or wrong, he could hardly lose.

On this first night of the revival the boys were doomed to disappointment. When the invitation was given, only three people went to kneel at the unfinished pine bench that served as the altar.

A seven-year-old girl was seeking redemption from sin. Tearfully, the cotton-headed child confessed that her life of sin so far had led her to hide in the cellar when her mother called her to help with the laundry.

A thin, frightened young mother was worried about her sick baby. The child was the only one of her three that had been spared the measles last fall, and now he was looking mighty peaked. Pearly Beachum got up and put a consoling arm around the woman and promised her that they would take the child to see Old Grandma Woolsy the next day and get the baby a tonic.

The other mourner at the bench was the ancient, half-crippled Nola Hightower. The distraught woman, not a day under seventy, cried until little puddles seeped along the raw blond pine.

"Dear Sister, dear Sister," Brother Wilbur said as he attempted to help the old woman to her feet. The matron was amply nourished and hadn't been down on her weak, aged knees in a month of Sundays. Not even with the help of the preacher and her two canes could she rise to her feet. Finally a man in the first row rose to help, and they managed to get her to a standing position.

"Dear Sister," Brother Wilbur began again, "tell us your name and the burden that's on your heart tonight."

"Speak up, Miz Hightower," another admonished. "We're all brothers and sisters here in the Lord."

Poor old lady Hightower could hardly speak but managed to choke out her name as she gained her composure. She was no public speaker, but she was far from shy and had lived too long to be intimidated by a crowd.

"Your message, Brother Wilbur," she said finally. "Lord, it really touched my heart tonight."

"Amen!" was heard throughout the crowd.

"You're a-talking 'bout the promises we make to the Lord," she said. "And the promises he makes to us."

The woman shook her head sadly and looked over the room. "Well, the Lord made a promise to me, writ right thar in the Good Book," she stated. "I know he keeps his promises."

"That he does, Sister," Brother Wilbur agreed.

"Tonight, I'm praying that he'll keep this one while I'm still alive to see it."

A murmur went through the crowd. Speculation. What could the Good Book have promised Nola Hightower?

"We can't know the time or the season that God works his miracles," Brother Wilbur warned. "The Bible says we must 'wait upon the Lord.'"

The old woman nodded. "I know that's true," Mrs. Hightower admitted. "But I've been waiting nigh on to twenty years. I ain't sure I got much wait left in me."

Brother Wilbur gave the woman a comforting pat on the shoulder. "You may outlive us all," he told her.

Nola Hightower ignored him. She raised her eyes to the crowd. "When my boy Ephraim died," she began, "I was plumb tore up with grief."

Other women among the congregation who'd lost children of their own made sympathetic noises.

"I promised my son," Nola Hightower continued, "to take care of his baby boy, a motherless orphan."

A strange hush came over the crowd. Cleav swallowed and gave Esme a nervous look.

"I done all I could for that boy," the old woman said. "I weren't young anymore, but I raised him same as I did my own." The old lady's sigh was pitiable. "Now, the Bible done promised me," she said, "that if I raised up a child in the way he should go, then he'd sure enough go that way when he got growed."

Surreptitiously numerous members of the crowd began to glance toward the center of the fourth row.

"Tonight I'm praying that heaven will touch the black, sinning heart of my grandson, Armon Hightower, and lead him to get right with the Lord. I ain't going to live forever, and before I go to meet my Maker, I want to see that boy on the straight and narrow."

Cleav and Esme joined the rest of the crowd in turning to look at the young man behind them. The twins were both sober and flushed. Between them, Armon sat uncomfortably as a vivid red stain crept up his neck.

Even Esme felt sorry for him.

~❧ 17 ❧~

A large black cloud had formed on the western horizon, but the moon still shone bright enough to illuminate the summer night as the crowd dispersed down the little knoll and through the tiny town. Esme walked beside Cleav, her hand on his arm in the proper position of the escorted. Behind them, Yohan and Eula were muttering together about the surprising end of the first night of the revival. Agrippa seemed stunned into silence.

When they reached the turnoff for the house, Cleav hesitated.

"Why don't you all go on home," he suggested to his mother and in-laws. "Esme and I are going to check on the ponds."

"Check on the ponds?" Eula asked incredulously.

Yohan chuckled. "What in tarnation can you do for fish in the middle of the night?"

"Looks like a bad storm coming in from the west, and I don't want any of the dams to give. I'd surely hate to lose half my trout downstream."

As they separated from the group, Cleav cast an eye to his

wife. Neither knew exactly what to say. Though they'd flirted with each other during the revival meeting, this was different. It seemed so long since they'd truly been alone together. The silence between them continued for several yards.

"You don't have to come with me if you're too tired, Esme," he said, hoping she'd stay.

Esme smiled at him shyly. "I was hoping we'd have a moment."

Cleav nodded with appropriate gravity. "It does seem we are somewhat short on those these days."

She agreed silently.

The moonlight shone across the water like a path to another world. The wind had picked up, and the smell of rain floated on it. They walked together quietly along the shore, lost in their own thoughts. Cleav stopped to inspect each of the earth, wood, and screen constructed dams that he'd built between the ponds.

Having constructed the system with his bare hands, it was solid and strong. Still, because he was a man who took his responsibilities seriously, Cleav tried to check the water-breaks carefully before each rainstorm. He'd learned the hard way that one weak-jointed corner could destroy a whole season's work.

Esme followed along with him, occasionally helping, but mostly just observing. In tonight's thoughtful mood she was amazed to find herself married to Cleavis Rhy.

Only last winter she had hardly given him a second look. Now she couldn't take her eyes off him.

Carefully he made his way from one pond to the next. The ominous rumble of a thunderstorm could be heard now, but it was still far away. And he was so near.

He was quiet again tonight. He'd grown too quiet these days, and Esme worried. When he came to her at night, there was warmth and wonder, but he held himself from her—she felt it.

Was it because she was so unladylike? She feared it might be so. Surely a lady didn't caterwaul until her husband had to cover her mouth to keep her from waking the house.

Still, Cleav never complained about the way she acted. In fact, she got the distinct feeling that he actually liked it.

A tiny thrill of desire spiraled through her. He hadn't sent her on to the house ahead of him. Maybe he had plans for tonight.

"Save to graces," Esme said abruptly, hoping to side-track her wayward thoughts with an attempt at lively conversation. "That Grandma Hightower was sure a spectacle tonight, wasn't she?"

Cleav looked up from the wire screen he was inspecting and smiled. "I swear, I don't think I'll ever feel more sorry for Armon Hightower than I did this evening."

They laughed together in remembrance, and their humor bridged the uneasy distance between them.

"He did look a guilty sight, didn't he?"

Cleav agreed.

"Wonder why she did it?" Esme asked more seriously. "Surely she knew it would embarrass the daylights out of him."

Cleav shook his head. "She thought she'd give a little push. People do that sometimes."

Esme nodded thoughtfully. "I'm even guilty of that myself," she admitted, thinking of all the deliberate glimpses of her legs that she'd given Cleav. If she'd waited for the spirit to move Cleavis Rhy, she'd have died an old maid, living in a cave with Pa.

"We all are," Cleav answered, squeezing her hand gently in reassurance before releasing it to wrap his arm familiarly around her waist.

"You can want something so much," he said, his eyes caressing the curve of her jaw, "that you forget that it's what *you* want, maybe not what's meant to be."

Uncomfortable with her own thoughts, and not wanting to pursue this line of conversation, Esme rushed to return to the original discussion.

"You'd think Miz Hightower'd know better," Esme insisted.

"She does," Cleav replied. "But she also knows that sometimes it works. Sometimes it's part of the plan after all."

Esme turned to face him. The silvery moonlight lit his face in handsome heights and hollows. In the distance the rumble of thunder was premonitory.

"Do you think *we* are part of the plan?" she asked, a tremor of concern in her voice. "Do you think our marriage was meant to be?"

Cleav gazed down at her, the eyes so wide in worried question, the cheeks so hollow without hint of smile, and the lips, so sweet in his remembrance that he didn't even try to hesitate as he brought down his own for a gentle kiss.

"Our marriage *is,* Esme," he whispered softly.

Esme wrapped her arms around his neck and buried her face in his throat. He'd spoken so sweetly she'd felt overwhelmed, though she wasn't sure if he was happy or sad.

The two embraced tightly, so tightly, as if each could enfold the other to his heart. Both thought the limbs they felt trembling were their own.

With a determined sigh, Cleav released her and attempted to steer the conversation to a lighter vein.

"Well," he began, his face sober, "at least I know that something good will come from Granny Hightower's words."

Esme swallowed, bringing her thoughts back to the

present. "You think what happened tonight will lead Armon to salvation?" she asked him, slightly startled.

"No," he answered, the hint of laughter in his eyes. "I think it will lead him to let the twins escort themselves to the rest of the revival meetings."

Esme stared dumbly at him for a moment, and then they both broke into laughter. They began walking again, hand in hand, this time with a more lively step.

When they reached the path that led to the house, Cleav hesitated.

"Are you ready to go in?" His question revealed his own reluctance.

Esme shook her head. "There's no hurry. Though we may end up a little wet."

Cleav glanced into the darkness at the ominous cloud bank coming on them from the west.

"We've got a few minutes," he said.

Walking to the smooth, dry grass near the water's edge, Cleav seated himself cross-legged on the ground and held his hand out for Esme to join him.

She dropped to her knees and scooted up close beside him. He wrapped his arm around her, and they sat companionably together.

They gazed into the gentle ripple across the top of the pond. "What do you think your piscean friend, the Gentleman, is up to tonight?" Cleav asked.

Esme glanced with mock concern at the depths of the water. "I suspect he's sound asleep by now."

"Asleep?" Cleav's question was incredulous and he chuckled lightly. "Do fish sleep?"

Esme gave him a shrug. "Everything sleeps, doesn't it?"

"I don't know," Cleav admitted.

"Folks think that river critters aren't like the rest of us, but I suspect they pretty much are."

She sighed thoughtfully. "We're all made by the same God, so more than likely we're pretty much the same."

Cleav looked at her approvingly. "I'd never thought of 'river critters' that way."

Pulling Esme closer, he set his chin lightly on the top of her head. "You're very likely correct. We are probably pretty much the same."

Smiling proudly at his agreement, Esme snuggled against the man at her side.

"That old Steelhead is sleeping for sure," she said.

"Do you think he's dreaming?"

"Sure enough." Then curiously she asked, "What do you think fish dream about?"

Considering the question, Cleav's lips finally curved into a smile, and he placed a gentle kiss in the sweet-smelling hair on the top of her head.

"I bet that Gentleman has some long-finned female Rainbow swimming through his dreams."

Esme giggled for a minute and then sobered. "Wouldn't he want a Steelhead?" she asked. "A woman more like himself?"

Pulling back slightly, he raised her chin to look into her eyes.

"Is that what you think?" he asked her softly. As she nodded mutely, he shook his head. "No, Esme," he said. "The Gentleman's memories are for bearing, not for sharing."

A tensionless quiet settled between them.

"Are we still talking about fish?" she asked.

"No," Cleav replied again.

"I—" Esme forgot what she meant to ask as his mouth came down on hers.

His lips were soft and warm, but they were demanding. No sweet, gentle pressure, but hot urgency guided him. The persuasive movement of his mouth teased and tempted her to respond in kind.

Esme twisted against him, holding his broad shoulders, trying to bring herself as close to him as possible. Side by side was not nearly intimate enough.

Cleav pulled her into his lap facing him. The new position forced Esme's dress indecently upward, baring her legs to him. Cleav's hands took advantage. Possessively, he ran his strong hands along the length of her calves and thighs, making her feel hot and sweet all over.

"Kiss me, Hillbaby," he murmured softly before he plunged his tongue deeply into her mouth.

She did. She was as eager for the taste of him as he was for her.

Cleav moaned in appreciation as Esme teased him even more immodestly to demonstrate her gratitude.

She ran her hands through his hair. She thrilled at its smooth, silky sleekness and breathed deeply of the spicy masculine smell.

He bit her lower lip, teasingly, and she traced the sensitive curves of his left ear with her tongue.

The low mellow sounds of her pleasure could no longer be distinguished from his own.

Cleav's mouth strayed down to her throat.

Esme reveled in the feel of his slightly scratchy beard against the flesh of her neck and wiggled unchastely in his lap.

Moaning, Cleav allowed his hands to explore her long, lusty legs, as her hand boldly guided his up to her bosom.

Cleav was thoroughly caressing her, but Esme was eager. Anxiously she pulled away from his kiss and raised her arms to undo her own buttons at the nape of her neck.

"Help me," she begged him. "I can't wear these clothes another minute."

Unwilling at first to release the warm, silky flesh of her

legs, Cleav finally reached up to pull away the fabric covering her bosom. He, too, wanted her naked to see her curves exposed in the moonlight.

The two began pulling at each other's clothing in a rush of youthful abandon. Shirt, suspenders, chemise, and stockings, nothing was seen as necessary covering. Within minutes both were naked and clinging to each other.

Cleav laid Esme out on the cool grass. He placed tiny kisses on her eyes and her chin, before putting one distended nipple in his mouth. She parted her legs, impatient for more. He drew himself up and pressed his shaft coaxingly at the crux of her womanhood. But he held back, wanting to prolong the closeness.

Their kisses became deeper and more urgent. Esme squirmed against him, and Cleav nearly lost control like a boy half his age.

The boiling black clouds covered the moon above them, and Cleav could no longer see Esme's face beneath him. Then the first cold drops of summer rain splashed against his back.

"It's raining," he whispered hotly.

"Oh, yes!" Esme pushed her pelvis against him, eager for him to be inside her.

"It's raining," he tried again. "You'll catch a chill."

The droplets of water were now soaking the parts of her his body didn't cover, but she didn't care.

"I want you to always keep me this warm," she begged, pressing her body against his.

Her actions, more than her words, encouraged Cleav to ignore the increasing tempo of rain that pelted his back, trickled down his limbs, and soaked his hair.

But finally she shivered.

"You're cold," he said, pulling away.

"No!" she declared and pulled his lips back against hers.

Cleav couldn't help but agree as he spread her legs with

his knee and ran a loving hand along the swelled sweetness of her sex.

Hearing her plaint of desire, Cleav embedded his finger within her, reveling at the tight heat that surrounded him.

Her jolt of pleasure was mirrored by flashes of fire in the sky above them, and her cry was lost in the crash of thunder.

The rain poured down upon them but failed to put out the fire that blazed. Cleav was hot and hard, and knew she was ready for him.

A wild streak of lightning passed just above them, touching its fiery tip to the juniper tree across the pond. The loud crack of the tree was like a scream of pain.

Instinctively he huddled Esme protectively beneath him. "We've got to get away from here," he said.

With more strength than he would have believed he possessed, he pulled away from Esme.

"No!" she cried forlornly.

"It's lightning, Hillbaby," he explained to her hurriedly over the increasingly loud torrent of rain. "We can't be out in the open like this."

He had moved from her embrace, and Esme felt a loneliness that was completely tangible.

"Please!" she pleaded.

Slipping one arm beneath her shoulders and the other behind her knees, Cleav scooped her into his arms. Holding her tightly against his naked chest, he raced through the night and pouring rain to the shelter of the hatching house.

He unlatched the door, and the wind slammed it open. Stepping inside, he stood holding her securely in his arms as water dripped from their bodies to the rough wooden floor beneath his bare feet. The storm beat a staccato rhythm upon the tin roof.

The tiny room was crowded with tanks and tools and machinery, and there was no place to lay her down. The hatching house, when not in use, was the logical place to store nets and cranks and lumber curing with tar. Jars and buckets, gloves and fish-gutters covered every square inch of the tables.

Cleav set Esme on her feet and tenderly wiped the long strands of rain-soaked hair away from her forehead. Her knees still trembled in passion.

"Touch me, Cleav," she whispered. "I need you to touch me."

"I need you, too," he told her longingly. "When this rain lets up a little, we'll make a run for the house. You'll not get a wink of sleep tonight, ma'am, I promise."

Esme smiled, shivering, as she wrapped her arms around his naked form and rubbed the tips of her breasts against the thick dark fur of his chest.

The feel of her body, her hardened nipples, made his loins tighten again.

"No, Hillbaby," he said with a sharp intake of breath. "Don't tease me now. It's torture to taunt me with what I can't have."

"I'm tortured, too," Esme murmured. "I'll be tortured to death before we make it back to our proper marriage bed."

Leaning forward, she grasped the sleek muscles of his arms as she searched his chest with her tongue. Finding a small, brown nipple with a point as hard as a two-penny nail, Esme nipped him gently.

Moaning, Cleav grabbed her shoulders firmly and turned her away from him. If he continued to look at her breasts, her lips, he would have to touch her. And he was aching for her already.

Holding her away from him so that his jutting arousal could not find soft haven in the curve of her buttocks, he spoke gently.

"You've got to stop, Hillbaby," he insisted.

"No!"

"Yes! I can't take much more."

"Make love to me," she begged.

Taking a deep and controlled breath, he tried to explain. "This is clearly a moment that calls for"—his voice cracked slightly—"civilized behavior."

A quiver went through Esme's flesh at his words.

"You're chilled," he whispered tenderly. "And we haven't even a blanket in here."

"Keep me warm, Cleav," she beseeched him desperately. "Your body can keep me warm."

Cleav swallowed with difficulty. "There's no place in here," he explained painfully through teeth clenched against his own desire. "Not enough room to lie on the floor, not even enough wall to lean up against."

The frustration in his own voice mirrored her own.

Esme looked back over her shoulder at him with despair. "There must be some way." Her tone was frustratingly forlorn.

"Maybe there's no room to lay down on or lean against, but there's plenty of room to bend over."

Against his will, Cleav reached out and ran a trembling hand along the soft, perky backside so prominently displayed before him. "Esme, put your hands against your knees," he whispered.

Cleav had seen French postcards with pictures of men and women doing this exact thing. He, however, had never imagined he would be participating. It was strictly night-dream fantasy.

Tenderly he reached out and stroked the firm young flesh of her backside. When he allowed his hand to wander down between her slightly spread legs, she gave a deep sigh of pleasure.

"Do you really want this, Hillbaby?" he asked, shaking with desire.

Esme worried that she'd asked too much.

"Do you think I am very wicked?" she asked, dismayed at her own inability to practice ladylike behavior.

"Nothing between *us* is wicked, my love," he whispered as he leaned over her, stroking the sides of her breast and waist as his sex pressed against her.

She purred like a cat against his caress.

"Cover me, Mr. Rhy," she said with a naughty inflection. "Cover me like the stallion covers the mare."

Cleavis did not require a second invitation.

❧ 18 ❧

The morning sun was just peeking over the top of the mountain. Cleav, impeccably groomed and ready for the workday, detoured along the banks of the trout ponds looking for any damage caused by the thunderstorm.

The memory of that wild collection of rain, wind, and lightning lingered just below the surface of his thoughts, evidenced by the naughty little ditty he hummed to himself as he made his survey.

Several of the screens were clogged with leaves and debris, which he quickly scooped out so the appropriate running ripple in the water resumed.

The screen at the lower end of the brooders' pond was blocked with more than branches and vegetation. Reaching down to clean it, Cleav brought to the surface a pair of windswept, rain-soaked, white muslin ladies' underdrawers.

The find brought a warm smile to Cleav's lips.

"So that's what happened to these."

Carefully wringing out the fabric, he let his thoughts roam back to the previous night. Their lovemaking had been as sweet and satisfying as ever, but the added excitement of the clamorous storm and illicit acts made it even more memorable.

It was near dawn when the rain finally let up. Cleav had wandered along the banks of the pond collecting their sodden clothing.

Giggling like naughty children, they'd covered themselves with as little of the cold, damp cloth as decently as possible and sneaked into their own house like thieves.

They hadn't bothered with sleep but warmed each other beneath the luxury of clean, fresh-smelling sheets and bedclothes.

The lack of rest should have left Cleavis exhausted. His jaunty walk, however, indicated otherwise. He took the scanty evidence of their wicked behavior to the hatching house. With a sly grin, he was tempted to hang the drawers from the tin roof, like a conqueror displaying a captured flag.

Propriety still had its place, he conceded, and carefully draped the unmentionable garment across the end of a hatching tank to try. He had no intention, he decided then and there, of ever returning these underdrawers to his lawfully beloved wife. Dried and hidden in one of the drawers of the cabinet, they would be a souvenir of a very thrilling night together.

Whistling again, Cleav latched the door to the hatching house and headed for the store. He was late. Tyree and Denny would already be there wondering about him. With a shrug of unconcern, he found that punctuality no longer held much of a place in his heart. There was too much love there, and it crowded out the non-necessities.

"Morning, gentlemen," Cleav said as he came around the corner of the store and spied the two older men waiting impatiently for him to open up.

"Where on God's green earth you been?" Tyree asked

him, clearly disgruntled. "It's pert-near noon, and we ain't even got our checkers laid out."

Casually slipping his watch from its pocket, Cleav checked the time. "It's precisely seven twenty-five," he told the men calmly. "No doubt there will be time for a game or two before luncheon."

Within five minutes Cleav had the store swept and open for business. The still-grumbling older men were only half-engrossed in their checkers as they speculated on what could have made the storekeep an hour and a half late that morning.

With complete unconcern, Cleav continued his tasks with a smile on his face and a whistle on his lips.

"Guess that preachin' last night was good for you," Tyree suggested.

Cleav looked up. His smile broadened. "Yes," he answered. "You could say I've been communing with heaven."

By midafternoon Cleav had already had more business than was typical for a weekday. With the revival in town, more and more families from the hills would be coming down to camp out in the valley. By Saturday night of the "homecoming," every soul in east Tennessee who'd been "saved," married, baptized, or had kin buried at the First Free Will Baptist Church would be in town for the service.

Cleav had his usual "revival days specials," but this year he couldn't make himself concentrate on business.

In his mind all he could see was the beautiful woman that he'd married, and all he could think about was how much he loved her.

When the small bell over the door tinkled, for perhaps the dozenth time in the past hour, Cleav glanced up to see Sophrona.

Strangely she glanced guiltily in both directions, before entering the store. A hasty, uncomfortable perusal of the occupants of the room apparently reassured her. Hurrying to a deserted corner of the store, Cleav watched her uncharacteristically enthusiastic examination of the several types and sizes of washboards available for purchase.

Puzzled, Cleav finished his business with his current customer and then headed across the room.

He'd hardly spoken a word to his former sweetheart since his marriage. It wasn't that he felt he should. His break with Sophrona had been clean and well understood between them both. He knew she'd been embarrassed by his apparent fickleness, but she was clearly not pining away for him. He wondered, in fact, if she'd cared for him at all. They really had very little in common and even less to say to each other.

"Afternoon, Miss Sophrona."

"Oh!" The young woman startled as he reached her side. As she turned and quickly recognized him, she sighed with relief.

"Oh, it's you, Cleav," she said softly. Recovering herself, she made a swift restatement. "Good day, Mr. Rhy. It's so pleasant to see you."

Cleav gave her a polite bow. If she preferred to act like an acquaintance, Cleav was certainly courteous enough to allow her to do so. "It's a lovely afternoon," he commented.

"Yes," Sophrona agreed and quoted piously, "'This is the day the Lord hath made.'" Then halfheartedly she added, "That is, if it doesn't rain."

"Of course," Cleav answered politely and secretly reminded himself that he'd developed a new appreciation for rain.

Miss Sophrona seemed distinctly uncomfortable and that distressed Cleav. More than likely they would both live in Vader for a long time. It was best for all concerned if they could forget their courting. Or at least to look back at it as a useful folly.

"Were you looking for something?" Cleav asked her. He was almost certain that she intended to answer negatively when the customer bell rang softly behind him.

An anxious, almost frightened look came over Sophrona's face. She rubbed her hands together nervously and then focused on the floor, the walls, the ceiling, Cleav, as if unsure where to look next.

"Yes, I want to purchase this!" she declared with more decisiveness than was necessary.

Hurriedly she directed her attention to the merchandise on the shelf behind her. Cleav followed her gaze. Puzzled, he glanced back to her face. "You want to buy a washboard?"

Sophrona's cheeks were flaming, and Cleav sensed that she was looking at something behind him. Glancing back, he saw only Armon Hightower, totally absorbed in the week-old newspaper lying on the rack across the room, oblivious to them.

"Yes, I want a washboard," Sophrona said, capturing Cleav's attention once again. "Our old one is nearly worn out."

His expression even more mystified, Cleav replied, "I can't imagine why it's wearing already. Mrs. Tewksbury bought it just last month. A washboard's meant to last a lifetime." Nodding firmly, he added, "Tell your mother to bring it in, and I'll make good on it."

A chuckle from behind him made Sophrona's cheeks flush even more scarlet. Cleav looked back at Hightower. Still reading, Armon had obviously found something amusing in the newspaper.

The week was a busy, hectic one. The store was so crowded, Cleav had to call upon both his mother and Esme to help him.

His mother's neuralgia was much improved. But rather

than being more help in the store, she became increasingly less. To her son's amazement she had taken a sudden interest in planting flowers all around the house. That was where Cleav discovered her one afternoon, wearing an old faded calico dress and a straw hat that was easily as old as Cleav himself.

"Surely, Mother," he said, "you don't have to spend your days crawling around on your hands and knees in the dirt."

She looked up at him, slightly bemused. "I've always loved to garden. I know it's not as genteel a vocation as embroidery or tatting, but truth is, I never was much good at either one." Sighing, she added, "Growing things was always a special gift to me. But if it truly embarrasses you, I won't do it."

"Embarrasses me?" Cleav was dumbfounded.

"I know you want me to be the lady and all," she said. "And I've truly tried. But all this beneficial conversation and delicate living can wear a body down." Mrs. Rhy wiped the sweat from her brow with the back of her sleeve.

"I was just the helpmate that your father needed me to be," she said. "After he died, I tried to be the partner that you needed, also. I gave up my way of living to follow yours. I knew that you needed me to do that." Eula Rhy reached a dirty-gloved hand toward her son, and he didn't hesitate to take it.

"You needed me but not anymore. You've a woman of your own now to be beside you," she said. "So if it's all the same to you, I'd like to get my life back to where it used to be."

"Mother," Cleav said, genuinely appalled. "You know I would never ask you to give up anything. I only want what's best for you. This heat and the dampness of the ground could ruin your health."

Eula waved away his concern. "I've never felt better in

my life. Besides," she added, "Brother Yo tells me it's a sin in this world to go counter to my own nature."

Cleav's eyes widened in shock. "Since when has Yohan Crabb become your spiritual adviser?"

"I am my own 'spiritual adviser,' young man," his mother snapped. "Now, if it shames you to see me with my hands in God's earth, say so."

Disconcerted, Cleav answered contritely, "Of course I'm not *ashamed*, Mother. If you truly enjoy gardening, certainly you should do it," he answered her honestly.

Giving his mother a kiss on the cheek, he started back toward the store, wondering if he could have said the same thing a few months ago. Somewhere in the last few weeks the demons that had plagued him since his days in Knoxville had gotten misplaced.

Even when trying, he could hardly conjure up any concern at all about the opinion of people who hardly knew him.

With Eula otherwise occupied, Esme was called upon more and more to help out in the store. She didn't seem to mind; in fact, she seemed to thrive on talking and joking with the customers, sorting and stacking the merchandise, and delighting herself with a difficult sale.

On Thursday and Friday she'd worked right beside Cleav from daylight until dark, even spelling him when he left to take care of the fish.

Cleav worried that she was working too hard.

"Your father could lend a hand down here," he suggested gruffly.

Esme shook her head. "Pa's just Pa," she told him. "We've got no right to expect him to be anything else."

Cleav looked at his wife and thought about his mother.

"That's really the way you feel, isn't it?"

Esme looked at him curiously. "That's the only way

there is," she told him honestly. "People are just who they are. The only one you can change is yourself, and it takes a good deal of sweat and worry to make even any inroads there."

Cleav reached over and pulled his wife into his arms. Tenderly he brought his lips down to taste the sweetness of her own.

"Ain't it a sight!" Denny hollered to Tyree, who dutifully squinted at the embracing couple.

"Who's it?" he asked.

"The newlyweds!" Denny yelled back.

The revival's finale on Saturday night had all the makings of a true camp meeting. A half hour before the singing started, every seat under the brush arbor was filled, and all around the space outside families sat together on blankets covering the grass to hear Reverend Wilbur Boatwright's sermon.

Eula, who had arrived early to visit and gossip, saved half a pew for the rest of the family.

Esme and the twins had hardly sat down before Mrs. Tewksbury approached them. "Have you seen Sophrona today?" she asked.

Esme was momentarily startled. "No," she answered. "Well, maybe," she said thoughtfully. "She might have been in the store this morning. I'm not sure. Why?"

"Oh, no reason," the preacher's wife said. "She left early this morning to visit a sick friend. I just expected her to be back by now."

"Who's sick?" Agrippa asked tactlessly. "I ain't heard of nobody sick with the revival in town."

"I'm sure she'll be here shortly," Mrs. Tewksbury replied, carefully dismissing the question as she turned to return to her seat.

Esme's curiosity was piqued, but after several nonchalant

perusals of the crowd, she gave up. Sophrona was probably there, she decided. She just had the good sense to get some visiting in before the sermon started.

The sermon did start, on time. And to Esme's mind, it ran on forever. It was clear, almost from the start, that the evangelist was not in his best form.

As is sometimes the case, the freshest, clearest, most important sermon can be presented at the wrong time and fall flat upon its face. Esme was quite sure that that was what was happening.

The crowd stirred restlessly. Babies cried. Toddlers whined. Several boys in knee-pants were called away from the service by fathers, presumably for a visit to the woodshed.

The crowd out on the grass, who would have had trouble hearing the best of orations, quickly lost interest in this one and began to visit among themselves. The low buzz of consistent whispering soon escalated to a clatter of voices that even distracted the "amen corner."

Having seen a preacher lose a crowd before, normally Esme would have felt sorry for Brother Wilbur. It was difficult, however, because the stout, red-faced little man refused to accept defeat. On and on his sermon went. Screaming at the top of his lungs, one hour passed and then two. It was as if he was punishing the congregation for their inattention.

Esme squirmed uncomfortably in her seat and glanced over at the twins. Both sat with elbows on their knees, bored but bravely holding their chins in their hands.

She glanced over at Cleav. He carefully stifled a yawn by turning it into a little cough. Their eyes met and silently communicated their agreement that a week of fine sermoning had fizzled into a final fiasco.

Though the evening got later, the temperature seemed to grow hotter. Esme was handed a fan, a triangular piece of paper attached to a stick. One side read "Moreley Undertaking and Mortuary; Russellville, Tennessee." The other side had a Bible verse: "Whatsoever ye ask in prayer, believing, ye shall receive." Esme began asking that the service would end. She didn't, however, believe that it ever would. So it didn't.

As if sensing Esme's annoyance, Cleav sneaked his hand into her lap to grasp her fingers. Esme looked up at him, but his gaze was focused straight ahead and his expression was one of rapt attention.

Slowly the softly callused pad of his thumb began making lazy circuitous rounds across her palm. The tender touch had a strange, sensual effect on Esme. As if the hot room had suddenly become chilled, she felt her nipples tighten and glanced down quickly to assure herself that no evidence of that effect was visible.

She tried to pull her hand away, but Cleav's stayed her. With a quick glance down into Esme's eyes, he gave her a knowing smile that flushed her cheeks as bright as berries.

He was teasing her! The reality was simply shocking. Right here in the middle of a sermon, he was doing this on purpose!

Esme couldn't quite stop the naughty grin that curved her lips. Slowly, surreptitiously, she crossed her legs in a very unladylike fashion and began to stealthily caress the back of his calf with the top of her new high-buttoned shoe.

Cleav looked at her again, his eyes wide with surprise at her attempt to turn the tables.

Esme immediately turned her attention to the preacher, seeming to hang on his every word as her husband squirmed somewhat uncomfortably beside her.

She should be ashamed of herself, she thought with a momentary flash of guilt. But the self-reprimand quickly faded.

Whyever would heaven give the evangelist such a boring sermon if they were expected to actually listen?

The Rhys' momentary diversion lightened the evening to some extent but could not eradicate the long, wearying evening completely. The increasingly loud sound of a quartet of snores from the "amen corner" was the only other diversion.

Esme spied Mrs. Tewksbury in the first row, nervously making an almost continuous survey of the crowd.

Pearly Beachum also seemed to have her eyes constantly scanning the rest of the congregation. Probably taking notes for tomorrow's gossip, Esme thought unkindly.

Eula Rhy was carefully examining the cloth on her second-best black silk gown.

The lantern to the left of the pulpit sputtered sporadically, threatening to give up the meager amount of light it was throwing on Brother Wilbur's insistent pacing back and forth.

It was nearing midnight when the exhausted, sweating, and genuinely petulant preacher finally called for the invitational hymn. "Just As I Am" had never sounded so good.

The old men in the "amen corner" came awake with the typical coughing and hacking of aged lungs. Esme almost giggled as she watched Pa, bleary-eyed, shake his head like a wet dog, trying to clear his brain.

As the congregation raised their voices in song, the preacher compelled any sinners present to come forward and "make themselves right with the Lord." Esme almost groaned. That type of invitation could last for hours if enough people felt led to make their way to the altar. Even nonsinners could be moved to come forward to confess troubles and ask for prayers and guidance. A good sermon could set dozens of repentant feet in motion.

With tonight's message, however, even the most pious among the crowd didn't budge.

The congregation, standing, was pitifully warbling out the third verse:

> "Just as I am! Tho tossed about,
> With many a conflict, many a doubt . . ."

when a stir started in the back of the crowd.

Like everyone else, Esme turned. Could someone be coming forward? Esme couldn't imagine it after that sermon, but the Lord did work in mysterious ways.

Craning her head to peer around the dozens of others straining for a look, she finally saw the instigator of the excitement: Armon Hightower.

Her mouth dropping open in surprise, Esme heard a little huff of disbelief from Cleav.

With Sophrona Tewksbury at his right, Armon was making his way down the outside aisle to the front of the brush arbor. Speculative murmurs ran through the crowd.

The singing slowly faded to silence as Armon reached the front and spoke a word to Brother Wilbur, who seemed as surprised as everyone else. Sophrona stood in the background looking distinctly ill at ease, avoiding a glance to the side of the room, where her parents sat.

The preacher nodded at the younger man several times during their discussion and then stepping away from him, raised his arms. "Brothers and Sisters," the preacher began, "this young man has come forward this evening, wishing to address the crowd."

The stunned silence was broken by a whispered flurry of voices, each asking the person beside him, "What does it mean?" "What's this about?" "Young Hightower getting saved? Unbelievable!"

As the rustle of quiet questions began to fade, Armon

gave a hasty glance at Miss Sophrona before stepping forward.

The handsome young man cleared his throat nervously. "Lots of you folks were here on Monday," he began. "And those that weren't, well, I suspect you heard that my granny got up here to ask you all to pray for the salvation of my soul."

There were nods of agreement throughout the room.

Armon's darkly attractive good looks were enhanced by the bright blush of embarrassment that flushed his cheeks.

"Truth to tell," he admitted, "I never really thought much about getting saved. It always seemed kind of contrary to my nature."

A chuckle of agreement was heard from the "amen corner," and Esme gave her father a disapproving look.

Running a worried hand through the thick hank of hair that crept toward his brow, Armon forced himself to scan the crowd bravely.

"I've been studying on it a bit more lately." His eyes stopped at the sight of the bent and aged woman who sat on the far right end of the second pew. "Granny," he said, his voice lowered slightly in tenderness, "I know you been praying for me, steady, for a lot of years now."

He swallowed visibly. "I want to thank you for that. And for everything else I got in this world," he added. "You done kept me clean and fed most of my life. And that ain't easy for a widow woman, and we all know it."

Catching his upper lip between his teeth, he rubbed his hands together as he contemplated his next words.

"I'd like to tell you, Granny, that I've done made a decision for the Lord," he said. "But it'd be a lie."

A ghost of a smile curved his lips as a memory wafted across his thoughts. "If you remember, I promised you years ago, when you told me your old arms were too tired to take a switch to me no more, that I'd never lie to you again."

The old woman smiled back at him with love.

"I ain't been saved yet," Armon declared honestly.

A strange sigh went through the crowd, as if a hundred people had been holding their breath.

"I'm thinking on it, real serious," he said. "And I want you, and everybody else here, to remember me when you're a-praying to God. I'm sure going to need all the help I can get."

Another chuckle filtered from the "amen corner," and Armon, himself, was able to bring forth a slightly jittery smile.

"The good Lord seems to know that," he continued more calmly. "'Causing he done sent me the best kind of help that a man can have."

Turning his head, he gave Sophrona a glance.

"I ain't been saved," he told the crowd. "But I have decided to change my ways."

With a warm smile he held out his hand, and Reverend Tewksbury's daughter stepped up to his side. The big-bosomed beauty was flushed and pretty as she shyly kept her eyes down, holding Armon's hand tightly, as if for strength.

"I done give up being a wild hill boy," he announced. "No more liquor, cards, or ladies for me. Now I'm just another dour-faced old married man."

Sophrona grinned broadly.

"I want you all to be the first to meet my new bride, Sophrona Hightower. We was married in Russellville this afternoon."

If the boys in knee-pants on the back row had been waiting for excitement all evening, they got it now.

Granny Hightower clapped her hands above her head and cried, "Hallelujah!"

The Crabb twins screamed in harmonic horror.

And Mabel Tewksbury fainted dead away.

❦ 19 ❦

The next few weeks in the biggest house in Vader, Tennessee, were seen differently by different people.

The twins, Adelaide and Agrippa, could only be described as in mourning. Armon Hightower's fickle heart and unexpected marriage was their only subject of conversation. The two cried in each other's arms and vowed off men for a lifetime. Esme quashed their hastily made plan to join the sacred sisters in Bletherton when she advised them that they had to be Catholics to become nuns.

Pa settled into "life in town," as he called it, with ease. Mornings he began joining the old men at the General Merchandise. Too lazy to play, he spent hours watching the endless games of checkers. Afternoons, between naps, he sat on the shady side of the porch and played his fiddle until suppertime. Typically, he was content to accomplish nothing.

Eula had strangely taken up a liking for the old man. His laziness only seemed to bother her in the abstract. She'd leave her flowers when the sun was the hottest and sit on the porch with him. Yo would continue his music, unconcerned.

And Eula would ponder aloud whether she should weed out the canna bulbs on the south side of the house and plant impatiens.

Cleav and Esme were a little too self-absorbed to worry much about the changes occurring. Daytime they worked together as often as they could. Esme would rush through the housework to join Cleav at the store. Cleav hurried through the fishtending to return to her side.

Evenings they sat together in the fresh coolness at the ponds and named all the brood fish. Holding each other's hands tenderly, they talked of the future. The improvements they could make on the ponds, the added attractions they could bring to the store, and the changes they could make in the house.

"It ought to be blue," Esme told him, not for the first time.

"Hillbaby," he answered her, gently rubbing the nape of her neck as he sat behind her on the grass looking up at the house. "Houses are meant to be white. Someday I'll take you to Knoxville and you'll see. Practically all the fine houses in town are white."

Esme shrugged unconcerned. "I couldn't care a flip about houses in Knoxville," she told him. "That house ought to be blue like the sky, not white as death."

Cleav shook his head and laughed lightly. "You are not getting your way on this, Esme," he said with mock severity. "If you want to paint something blue, we can paint the store. My house is going to be white and nothing else."

"The store can be blue," she said, nodding. "At least for now. I suspect we'll be building a bigger store in a few years anyway. It will have to be brick, of course."

Cleav nuzzled her neck and gave her a playful bite on her throat. "Of course," he agreed with a chuckle.

Since the night of love in the hatching house, Cleav had given up his late evenings in the library. As soon as it was decently dark the young couple hurried to the privacy of their room. Romping like children, they wore the bedsheets thin.

If in the still, sated silence of the darkest part of night Esme doubted she could make him happy, she never let it show.

If the dark circles under his eyes indicated a habitual lack of sleep, Cleav never complained. But he did wonder to himself if having her love him could be any better.

Cleav could no longer even imagine life without Esme. And Esme felt that she had never lived before she lived with Cleav.

They were easy together.

Sorting the barrels in the store together, their conversation strayed to both commerce and fish breeding.

"If we could figure out a way to keep the ice from melting, we could take a wagonload of fresh trout down to the city and make a pretty penny," Cleav suggested.

Esme, standing on a small stepladder beside the shelves, looked down at her husband.

"And if we had wings, we could just fly over the mountains, too," Esme replied with feigned impatience.

Cleav refused to be daunted. "We could store the fish in a mesh sack and drag them downriver in a boat," he said, his eyes thoughtful as he considered the possibility.

Esme nodded hopefully. "And what the gators didn't eat, the folks in the city could?" she suggested.

"There are no gators in the Nolichucky River," Cleav answered.

"Well, save to graces," Esme exclaimed. "Let's raise some and put them in there!"

That remark earned Esme a gentle slap on the fanny.

With a snort of disapproval, Pearly Beachum stopped examining the nickel powders and stormed out of the store in protest.

The two, finding themselves unexpectedly alone, glanced at each other guiltily before good humor overwhelmed them.

Laughing, Esme jumped down into her husband's arms, wrapping her long, stocking-clad legs around his waist.

"We are shocking the neighbors," she declared as she rubbed her bosom wantonly against his chest.

"It isn't the first time," Cleav answered, his hands cheerfully cupping her bottom. "That's how we got together in the first place."

"Are you sorry?" Esme asked, surprised at her own candid question.

Cleav's expression momentarily turned serious and then a mischievous smile brightened his face. Rubbing himself lewdly against her, he answered, "Only if you're going to make me wait until after supper."

Esme playfully reprimanded him with a slap on the shoulder. "I most certainly am going to make you wait. You have got to get back to work, Mr. Rhy. You've got a family to support."

Cleav shook his head in mock solemnity. "You're right about that," he said. "I've got a garden-grubbing mother, a fiddling father-in-law, a set of lovelorn twins, and a positively wicked wife with the longest, lustiest legs in Tennessee."

Esme giggled and then gave a flirty swipe of her tongue to his ear.

"I do promise, Mr. Cleavis Rhy, my dear husband," she stated baldly, "to make myself absolutely worth the wait."

And she was.

It was on a Thursday when the mail arrived that Cleav, brimming with excitement, left the store in the not very dependable hands of his father-in-law and rushed to the house.

"Esme!" he called, banging open the front door with atypical unconcern for the fine piece of oblong beveled glass in its middle. "Esme! Where are you?"

Her hair tied up in a kerchief, Esme stepped out of the back parlor, feather duster in hand. "Save to graces, Cleav. What has happened?"

As if in answer, he held up a long, slim envelope.

Esme looked at it curiously.

"What is it?"

"A letter from Mr. Simmons of Springfield, Massachusetts," Cleav replied, his eyes bright with enthusiasm.

"Who?"

"The gentleman of the American Fish Culturists Association." Cleav's face was wreathed in smiles that were instantaneously contagious.

"Oh, yes," Esme said finally. "One of your trout friends from up north."

"Well, he's not a *friend,*" Cleav corrected her modestly. "Although the gentleman is a frequent correspondent." Smiling broadly, he added, "And today he sent some very thrilling news."

Esme grinned. "Well, are you going to tell me or make my bile choler trying to guess?"

"Mr. Simmons is coming to Vader," he said, hugging her to him.

"What?"

Cleav laughed out loud at his wife's expression.

"Mr. Theodatus G. Simmons of Springfield, Massachusetts, is coming to Vader, Tennessee, to"—Cleav opened up the envelope and read from the letter inside—"'survey the trout-breeding experiments of a fellow pisciculturist'—that's me."

Esme's face paled and she stood speechless before him.

"Surprised?" he asked but continued without waiting for a reply. "There's more. On his way down here he'll be stopping in Washington, D.C., to meet his friend, Mr. Benjamin Westbrook of the U.S. Deputy Fish Commissioner's office, to accompany him."

Cleav laughed with genuine joy. "Can you believe it? Two of the most important gentlemen in the fish-culture movement are coming to Cleavis Rhy's little trout farm in Tennessee!"

"That's wonderful," Esme said. Her words rang flat and toneless, but Cleav was too excited to notice.

"I suggested such a visit months ago," he explained. "But never in my most optimistic dream did I imagine that they would actually accept my invitation."

Laughing again, he pulled Esme close and held her tightly. "Do you realize what this means, Hillbaby?" he said. "It means recognition of my accomplishments, validation of my work." He shook his head with delighted disbelief. "It means that maybe, just maybe, my achievements will see acknowledgment. Pisciculturists all over the country"—he raised his arms in a broader gesture— "maybe all over the world will hear about my experiments, my ponds, my trout."

"That's wonderful," Esme tried again more enthusiastically, but something about her reply still didn't ring true.

"Three weeks," Cleav told her excitedly. "Just three weeks and we'll have those esteemed gentlemen right here in this very house!" With his arms wrapped tightly around her waist, Cleav lifted Esme right off her feet and spun her around like two children playing Whirling Dizzy.

"Yes!" Cleav hollered as he spun.

Esme found herself pushing back the block of cold fear as she tried to join her husband in laughing at his foolish antics.

When he finally stopped, they both weaved in place for a moment as the room continued to spin. Then Cleav lowered his lips to hers in a sweet, joyful kiss that, with a quick flick of the tongue, turned to naughty loveplay.

Esme basked in the hot sensuality for a moment before hearing a giggle from the doorway of the sewing parlor. Pulling away from her husband, Esme gave Adelaide a disapproving look.

"Mind your own business!" she told her huffily.

"Business!" Cleav said and slapped his palm against his forehead as if his brain didn't work perfectly. "You mind *your* business, Miss Snoopy Crabb," he told the twin. "And I'd best get back to minding my own," he added to Esme with one last hasty kiss. "Your daddy is probably fiddling as the store burns!"

With a wave and a promise he was off.

Esme closed the door behind him and watched him take the steps down two at a time as he hurried off toward the General Merchandise. There was no smile on Esme's face as she watched him go.

"Three weeks," she whispered aloud. "In three weeks two of the most important gentlemen in the fish-culturist movement will be coming to Vader, Tennessee, to meet Cleavis Rhy." Tears stung her eyes, and she bit her lip to hold them back.

They were going to find some fancy ponds and some dandy fish, she thought. And they were going to discover that their friend—no, their correspondent—Mr. Rhy, was married to an ignorant hill cracker.

"Oh, Cleav." She sighed aloud. "You've wanted this so long. You've wanted to be one of them."

Weaving her hands together in a double fist, she placed them earnestly at her chin.

Oh, please. *Don't let me ruin it for him.*

Two days later Esme determinedly reminded herself that "the Lord helps those who help themselves" and sought out her mother-in-law.

Eula Rhy was not hard to find. A large floppy hat on her head, her voice was raised in a loud off-key rendition of "Why Are You Weeping, Sister?"

Esme interrupted her right in the middle of "I was foolish and fair and my form was rare."

"Mother Rhy," she said. "I need to talk to you about something."

The older woman looked up from the impatiens she was carefully replanting in the shady spot next to the house. "Why, what's wrong with you, girl?" the woman asked. "You're not looking quite yourself today." The older woman eyed her up and down curiously. "You're not in a 'delicate condition' already?"

"Oh, no," Esme assured her quickly. "It's just that . . . well . . ."

Eula Rhy sighed loudly with impatience. "For mercy's sake, child, say what you have to say. These plants don't have time to waste on your nonsense."

"Well," Esme tried again. "I'm not really sure what to say."

Mrs. Rhy snorted in disbelief. "If there's one thing no one would accuse you of, it's not being able to speak your mind!"

Tightening her jaw bravely, Esme finally blurted out, "You know that these fancy fish folks are coming to visit my Cleavis."

"Lord, yes," Eula answered with an unconcerned wave of her arm. "I may be old, but I'm not deaf. That's all that boy can talk about these days."

Deciding that Esme's interruption was unimportant, the older woman kneeled forward again and began working the dirt through her hands.

Esme raised her chin in shameful defiance and admitted the worst. "This-is-very-important-to-Cleav-he's-been-waiting-for-a-chance-like-this-ever-since-he-came-back-from-Knox-

ville-and-these-gentlemen-just-have-to-like-him-and-accept-
him-as-a-gentleman-too-and-I-don't-know-one-blame-thing-
about-being-a-lady-or-how-to-serve-gentlemen-or-what-to-
serve-gentlemen-and-it's-just-like-you-said-I-won't-be-any-
good-as-a-wife-to-Cleav-and-I'm-going-shame-him-and-
ruin-it-for-him-and-I-just-can't-do-that-to-him-and-you've-
got-to-help-me.''

It was enough to capture her mother-in-law's attention.
The older woman studied her curiously. "You're worried
about being an embarrassment to Cleavy?'' she asked.

Biting her lip painfully, Esme nodded.

Eula Rhy shook her head in disbelief and chuckled
lightly. "Esme,'' she said. "Dear girl, there was a time
when I worried about just the same thing.'' With a smile of
amused remembrance, she continued. "I told you the night
you married that you weren't the wife for Cleavis.'' The
older woman's smile was broad now. "But you've proved
I was wrong.''

Esme looked up, startled. "What?''

"I said you've proved me wrong,'' she repeated. "I
thought my son wanted—no, *needed* to be a gentleman.''
She sighed heavily. "Lord only knows what happened in
Knoxville to change him so, but he did come back a very
different boy than the one I sent.''

Picking up one of the flowers, she examined it for insects.
"He came back so stuffy and proper,'' she said. "Truth is,
I didn't quite know what to make of it. But I love that boy,
and like you, I didn't want to let him down.''

Leaning back on her knees, Eula Rhy pulled off one very
dirty glove and held her hand up to Esme. "Help me up,''
she ordered. "One thing about getting old, no matter how
much you enjoy doing a thing, your bones do get stiffened
up by the time you stop doing it.''

Esme helped her to her feet, and the two walked together
to the front of the house. In the distance could be heard the

rhythmic melody of tree felling. The smell of fresh-cut pine was in the air, wafting along with honeysuckle in bloom.

The piece of sky overhead was exactly the color Esme wanted to paint the house, and a couple of high white clouds floated along it.

Down near the river Yohan had found a piece of shade and was playing a soft summer tune that had the power to bring a smile to anyone's face.

It almost brought a smile to Esme's until she remembered the errand she was on and the danger and disappointment she saw for the man she loved. For herself, she didn't care. She'd been facing shame for who she was since she was big enough to walk under a wagon. She'd learned how to ignore it, accept it, make herself stronger for it.

But Cleav was different. Cleav fought it. Like Esme, for years pride had stuck in his craw. But unlike her, he'd never swallowed it.

This time, for his sake, Esme wasn't swallowing it, either. She was as good as anyone else, she'd told herself from childhood. Now, for Cleav, she was going to have to prove it.

They'd walked to the front of the house, and Mrs. Rhy removed her other glove and tucked both carefully into her gardening apron. Reaching the shade of the porch, Eula untied the ribbons on her hat and gestured for Esme to sit with her on the swing.

"Just like you are thinking," she said, as if no lull in the conversation had existed. "I wanted to be a help to Cleav. I wanted to see that he got the kind of life that he wanted.

"He built this big old house, too big by half, when we'd been living fine for years in the one his granddaddy built. He filled it up with city things and talked about city people and city ways until it nearly scared the life out of me."

Eula shook her head and patted Esme's hand in comfort. "I'm really just a hill girl, not much better off than you," she said. "I've probably had more book learning, but I never thought about being a lady or taking up fancy ways until Cleav came back from Knoxville."

The woman sighed wistfully.

"I hated for him to give up his schooling like that, but after my man died"—Eula looked off into the distance, her expression one of remembered pain—"I just couldn't seem to make it on my own."

Eula's expression was one of self-contempt. "I made him come home from school. Everyone thought it was because I couldn't run the store and didn't have money."

Eula shook her head, and her next words were low and had the ring of sincerity. "I could have managed by myself. But I didn't," she said firmly. "Because I didn't want to."

The confession was hard won. Never having voiced her shameful truth aloud, Eula's eyes momentarily misted, and she wiped them quickly on the cleanest corner of her apron.

"Here was my quiet, confused only son," she said. "He was no longer a boy and not quite a man. And I thought only of what *I* wanted. He tried to do the right and honorable thing."

Eula shook her head with both sadness and pride.

"Not only did my boy lose the daddy he loved, he lost the life that he loved, too. I stole it from him."

"Oh, Mother Rhy," Esme interrupted. "I'm sure . . ."

Eula turned to the younger woman as if to will her to understand. "You're Cleavy's wife now. Let the others believe the kinder lies, but we need to have truth between us.

"When I finally realized how spoiled and selfish I'd been," she continued solemnly, "it was too late to change things."

There was a sad, quiet moment of silence as Esme tried clumsily to comfort the mother of the man she loved.

"I wanted to make things up to him, you see," she

explained. "I wanted to do those things that would make him happy. So," she said evenly, "I tried to be a fancy lady."

With a toss of her hand, Eula laughed lightly in self-derision. "Lord knows, I wasn't much good at it."

"You *are* a lady!" Esme protested.

"No, girl," the older woman insisted. "I pretended to be one. It worked, more or less, but it made me miserable."

"Miserable?"

"Clearly, I admit it," she said. "There were days after days that I couldn't even get up and face myself in the mirror."

"You were sick," Esme insisted.

Eula nodded. "Yes, I think I was," she said. "I was sick in my heart. I was living the life of a pure hypocrite. I couldn't be who I am, and I couldn't be who I tried to be, either."

She gave Esme a hopeful smile. "I was just waiting for the day when Cleavy would marry himself a real lady."

Esme's cheeks stained with fire, and she looked down with shame.

"I wanted him to marry dear little Sophrona," Eula said, "because I thought she was what he needed. She'd never have to pretend the way I did."

"She was perfect for him," Esme whispered dejectedly.

Mrs. Rhy laughed at her words. "Seems that you're as wrong about that as I was," she told Esme, chucking her lightly under the chin.

"Wrong?"

"Completely, totally, a mile off, wrong."

Esme considered her words for a moment. "You mean because Sophrona fell in love with Armon?" Esme asked.

With a spurt of mirthful laughter Eula wrapped an arm around Esme's shoulder and squeezed, "Now, that *was* a sight, wasn't it? Lord, I thought I'd die laughing for sure

when Old Man Tyree threw that bucket of water on Mabel
Tewksbury, and she came up spurting like a hog in vermin
dip.''

Laughing with Eula, Esme recalled the last evening of the
revival vividly. Armon had quickly gone to his mother-in-
law's aid, but after he'd helped Mrs. Tewksbury to her feet,
she'd taken one look at her rescuer and slugged poor Armon
in the stomach like a prizefighter at the county fair.

As their laughter faded away, Eula said, "That isn't why
I was wrong about a wife for Cleavy."

"Then why?" Esme asked.

Eula smiled brightly, and Esme noticed for the first time
that the mother's eyes were just exactly like her son's. They
were the eyes that Esme wanted to give to her own children.

"Because Cleavy's done fallen in love with you," Eula
said simply.

"What?" Esme was momentarily stunned to silence.

"Can't you see it? It's right in front of your nose, young
lady. Have you taken a good look at that man that you've
married lately?" Eula asked.

"Cleav doesn't . . ." Esme sputtered with embarrassment. "I mean, it's not like . . . well, I know he has the
highest regard for me and—"

"Regard!" Eula hooted with laughter. "That boy is
calf-eyed crazy about you, and everybody in town knows
it."

Staring mutely at her mother-in-law, a vehement denial
came to Esme's lips. She forced herself, however, not to
voice it. Eula Rhy loved her son. No matter how she'd acted
in the past, it was clear the woman genuinely cared for
Cleavis Rhy. Undoubtedly it eased her mind to think that he
was blissfully happy in his marriage.

Esme would not, could not, be so cruel as to dampen
Cleav's mother's contentment. Especially since she'd been

so cheerful and healthy these last couple of months. It would be the worst type of unkindness to reveal the sad truth.

"Still," Esme began tactfully, "I do feel that I should properly entertain these city folks when they're here," she said. "They probably eat special food, on special table-cloths with special utensils. And what they must talk about is a pure-d mystery to me. I plainly have got no idea about any of it, and I really need your help."

Eula laughed and shook her head with determination. "Don't you give that nonsense another thought," she said. "I don't want you trying to be anybody but Esme Rhy," she stated firmly. "If those northern gentlemen are offended by a sweet, open young woman like yourself, then heaven knows, I want to be around to watch when that son of mine and husband of yours kicks their fancy behinds right out his front door!"

~ 20 ~

"This is a passel of foolishness, if you're asking me!" Yo Crabb's words were adamant with disapproval, but they only garnered a warning look from Esme and a sweet throaty giggle from Sophrona Hightower.

"Now, Mr. Crabb," the young woman answered him patiently. "Good manners are never foolish."

The old man tried to scowl, but it was difficult when looking into such a pretty face.

"Got no quotation, do ya, Miss Sophrona?" His question was presented as a statement. "That's 'cause the Good Book don't care a tinker's damn about such foolishness."

The young woman placed a tiny, delicate finger to her temple near her neat reddish-blond hairline, as if thinking momentarily. A smile suddenly lit her face, and she raised it to the older man.

"Mr. Crabb, Paul does state that God *suffered* the manners of the children of Israel in the wilderness for forty years," she said. "How old are you now, sir?"

The question was rhetorical, and Yohan chose to answer

it only with a disgusted "humph!" However, he made no further complaints.

"The flatwear is laid out by order of its use," Sophrona explained. "Working from the outside toward the plate. It's the latest in etiquette to place the knife at the top of the dinner plate. That reminds the diner not to use it."

"Why in tarnation do ya have it, if you ain't going to use it?" Yo asked her.

Sophrona smiled politely. "You may use it to cut your food. But you can't use it to eat."

Yo glanced down at the mock meal before him with a dismal sigh. "There's enough metal around this plate to forge a good-sized plow."

Esme, seated across the table from her father, found herself reluctantly agreeing with him but hastily stifled the thought. She should be grateful to have someone teach her and her family the proper way of things. Although Eula Rhy had encouraged her to be herself, Esme had wanted what was best for Cleav. She still believed what was best was a ladylike wife. And if Esme wanted to learn to be *like* Sophrona, the person to teach her was Sophrona herself. With that in mind Esme had issued an invitation to the new Mrs. Hightower. Terrified that she might not come, Esme scribbled a personal note in her carefully penned block letters that read: *"pleese come. we mus tawk."*

But Sophrona showed no hesitation, eager to let bygones be bygones.

"I'm so glad you've invited me over," Sophrona had greeted her, throwing her arms around Esme like a long-lost friend. "I've been wanting to speak to you, to thank you, but I've just been so busy."

"Thank me?" Esme was more than curious.

"My dear, beloved Armon told me how you put the idea of courting me into his head," Sophrona explained.

Esme's face flushed a bright red. She'd forgotten about

that trick, and it came back to her in a rush of guilt. She could almost hear Armon calling this lovely, sweet young woman "Tits Tewksbury."

"I'm sorry . . ." Esme began.

Sophrona hugged her. "How you knew that we loved each other," she said, "when we didn't even know ourselves has got to be one of God's great miracles."

Esme stuttered. "I didn't . . . I mean, I didn't actually think . . . I . . ."

A delighted giggle escaped Sophrona's throat. "Of course you didn't think," she said cheerfully. "You spoke from your heart, just as the Lord intended." Reaching for Esme's hand, Sophrona squeezed it lovingly. " 'The Lord works in mysterious ways.' "

Esme couldn't help but agree. And bringing Sophrona to her side for this onslaught of important company was surely a reprieve from heaven.

They'd spent the morning devising the menu.

"Of course, you'll want to serve trout," Sophrona guessed accurately.

"Yes," Esme said, though she looked uncertain. "But if I'm in the kitchen, how am I supposed to be a hostess?"

Sophrona nodded in agreement.

"Well, you certainly can't be cook and lady of the house at the same time," she said. "So we'd best devise a dish that can be fully prepared and ready when you announce dinner."

They went through a year's worth of back issues of *Home Companion* before Sophrona found the perfect recipe. Baking the fish in mushrooms and mussels would definitely heat up the kitchen, but it would free Esme to be the gentleman's lady at the dinner table.

Sophrona reached into the top of the cabinet and retrieved a large two-part serving plate.

"Lord, what is this?" Esme asked.

"It's a chafing dish," Sophrona explained. "You put boiling water in this outer part and it will keep your main course warm throughout dinner."

"You put this right on the table?" Esme asked doubtfully. "Save to graces, it looks like a chamber pot! I'm supposed to serve these folks food out of it?"

Sophrona couldn't hold back a delighted giggle. "It does look somewhat like that other vessel," she admitted. "But it is all the rage in the cities now. With only the rich being able to afford servants, a normal family must find a way to serve elegantly without the hostess popping up to play scullery maid every second."

Esme nodded at the reasoning but still couldn't quite get past her first impression of the chafing dish.

The two women sorted the linens, both exclaiming over the abundance and quality.

"This tablecloth is beautiful," Sophrona said, pulling the slightly worn white crochet out of one of the drawers.

Esme glanced at the cloth in her hand and blushed with shame. "My mother made that," Esme stated with deliberate quiet. "I'm sure Mrs. Rhy has more lovely things to use."

Sophrona looked at her curiously. "But this is beautiful. And it's older and more sedate." Running her hand gently across the material, she added softly, "It was obviously made with love."

The young woman's smile was warm and winning. "That's what's truly important in a family. Love is the ultimate in quality."

"It was the nicest thing my mother owned," Esme said without emotion.

"And it's the nicest thing you will own, also," Sophrona said easily, running her hands along the fabric. "Because she made it."

Esme, too, tenderly caressed the work of her mother's

hands. "It's too small for the table," she said, practically. Sophrona shook it out and agreed with a sigh. "What a shame," she said. "Well, perhaps you can save it for a special dinner for just Mr. Rhy and yourself," smiling as the young woman let her fancy take her away. "Maybe you should save it for the night you announce to him about your first child."

"Sophrona!" Esme exclaimed in a harsh whisper. "Ladies don't talk about such things."

"I thought you didn't know how ladies act," she said.

With menu, dishes, and linens chosen, Sophrona had agreed to make suggestions for the family wardrobe.

The twins were lovely in identical designs, one in pink, one in blue. Sophrona fairly gushed over them.

"No wonder you two turned my dear husband's head," she said. "I declare, no man would be safe with this much beauty around."

Adelaide and Agrippa, who had formerly declared their adamant dislike of "the red-haired cow-teated man stealer," discovered their resentment quick to melt in the warmth and sincerity of the new Mrs. Hightower.

Esme was still worried.

Sighing as she stared into the doors of her wardrobe, she turned to Sophrona with dismay.

"It don't seem to matter what I wear," Esme told her sorrowfully. "They's no way on God's earth that I'm going to ever look as pretty as you and the twins."

Sophrona waved away Esme's foolishness. "Obviously Mr. Rhy does not share your opinion," she said. "All women have blessings and curses. Why, this horrible red hair has been a veil of shame to me nearly all my life!" She leaned closer and confided to Esme in a whisper, "But my dear Armon says the sight of it just makes him 'pure weak in the knees.'"

Esme's startled expression set both women to giggling.

Discussion of marital secrets was something new for the both of them and quickly formed a strong friendship from what was formerly just a pleasant acquaintance.

"Tell me, what do you think your best features are?" Sophrona insisted finally.

"Well," Esme admitted, still smiling, "Cleavis is mighty fond of my legs, but I don't think he'd be wanting me to show 'em off to company."

With a trilling giggle, Sophrona agreed. "You probably shouldn't serve dinner skirtless," she said with mock civility. "But there is no reason why the right gown shouldn't be able to accent your hidden beauty."

And accent it, she did.

Sophrona pinned the seams of a plain prim white gown narrowly against Esme's thighs. "The straightness will emphasize the length of your legs," she said. "And you are so lucky, this is absolutely the latest style. No woman in the city will be more up-to-date."

The only real argument Sophrona received was from Esme's father.

"I look like I'm about to be buried!" the old man complained of the fine broadcloth suit of dignified black.

"Pa!" Esme snapped waspishly. "I won't have you looking like you just stepped out of a cave."

Yohan raised his chin defiantly. "Well, Esme-girl," he said, "the fact is, I did just step out of a cave, not more than a month ago. I'm a poor, simple man and trying to look like anything else is the same as lying."

"Pa!"

Sophrona quickly intervened in the threatened father-daughter fireworks.

"Surely it is not a lie to show yourself as a sober and attractive man of middle years," the pretty redhead suggested.

Yo Crabb immediately puffed up as proud as a bantam

rooster. Smoothing down the perfectly cut lapels, he asked, "You don't think I'm reaching beyond myself?"

"Indeed not," Sophrona insisted. "Sackcloth and ashes doesn't make one humble. Humility comes from the heart."

Yohan pursed his lips, thoughtfully considering her words before finally nodding. "I suspect you're right, Miss Sophrona."

Esme marveled at Sophrona's ability to maneuver her family. Assuming that such ability was part of being a lady, Esme could hardly wait for the conduct portion of Sophrona's lessons.

Now sitting at the table with her family and Mrs. Rhy, who was observing the lesson skeptically, Esme decided that it was not as easy to act like a lady as it was to look like one.

"The important thing," Sophrona stated firmly, "is to make everyone at the table feel comfortable and relaxed."

"That shouldn't be too difficult," Esme stated. "Why, fancy northern gentlemen like these probably always feel at home."

"Not necessarily," Sophrona told her. "Everyone feels out of place at times. Tennessee is a completely new world for these men. They are strangers here, and you'll have to do whatever you can to make them feel welcome."

"Welcome is one thing," Esme said. "But they're going to be here near to ten days. We've only got the first one planned."

Nodding with agreement, Sophrona took her hand encouragingly. "Making a good first impression is all that's really important," she said. "The men are here to meet Cleavis and discuss those horrid fish after all."

The twins giggled.

"Once the gentlemen are favorably impressed by your home and your lifestyle," she said, "they will relax and fit right in."

Esme worried the nail on her index finger with her front teeth. "But just how am I going to 'favorably impress' them?"

"You won't be alone," Sophrona assured her. "Your entire family will be here to help."

Esme looked around the table. The twins were like fancy meringue, pretty and inviting, but with nearly no substance at all. Pa was just Pa. A fiddle-playing ne'er-do-well who was almost proud of being the "laziest man in Vader, Tennessee."

Looking back at Sophrona with desperation in her eyes, Esme entreated, "Teach us!"

Glancing around the table, Sophrona cleared her throat and began. "The most important thing about gentility is fine conversation."

"You mean just talking?" Pa asked skeptically. "I suspect we can all manage that."

"Fine conversation," Sophrona corrected, "is not the same as simply speaking to another person."

"It's talking prissy like Cleav," Esme suggested.

Sophrona was unable to stifle a giggle. "No, no," she said. "It's not the *way* you talk. It's the things that you say."

"Like quoting the Bible all the time, instead of speaking for yourself?" Agrippa asked.

A pretty blush suffused Sophrona's cheeks. "No, not really," she admitted. "I find myself falling back on Bible verses when I'm nervous and lack anything substantial to say." With a self-deprecating smile she added, "The art of fine conversation is something I haven't quite mastered, either."

"Well, if you don't know how to do it," Yohan said, "I don't suspect these gals and I can learn in a few days."

"Oh, I do know *how*," Sophrona corrected. "Though I must confess that I am far from competent at it."

"You always seem to have the right thing to say to Cleavis," Esme said.

Smiling across at her, Sophrona's eyes lighted with mischief. "These days he does seem significantly more interested in what *you* have to say."

There was a chuckle of good humor around the table. It was clear that no hard feelings existed between the two women.

"The key, I believe," Sophrona said, "is to allow the men to talk about the things that they want to talk about."

"What kind of things will that be?" Esme asked.

Sophrona shrugged. "I really couldn't say. The interests of gentlemen vary. At least we know that, like Cleavis, these men are interested in pisciculture."

The twins moaned in unison.

"You mean we're going to fix a fancy dinner and get all dressed up so we can sit around the dining room table talking about some smelly fish!" Adelaide's words were incredulous.

"Well, perhaps fish will not be their only interest," Sophrona suggested hopefully. "Conceivably, gentlemen from the city will have an interest in art and music."

"We don't know anything about either," Esme complained.

"Speak for yourself, youngun," Pa interrupted. "I know dad-blamed everything there is to know about fiddle-playing."

"That's true," Sophrona agreed delightedly. "Your father's musical abilities could make fine parlor discourse."

"Sure enough," Yohan stated with a nod. "Don't you worry about a thing, Esme-girl. If these city-shoed starched collars start looking antsy, I'll just take up my fiddle and have them cutting the rug in a shake."

Hugging each other and giggling, the twins quickly made

their own plans. "When Pa plays them the fiddle, we can teach them how to clogg."

"Clogg?" Esme somehow couldn't imagine two northern gentlemen in fine suits stomping their heels against the floorboards.

"Sure!" Agrippa said. "And we can take them up on the mountain and show them how to pick lupin."

Adelaide nodded enthusiastically. "Maybe Agrippa and I can take them swimming down to the river," she suggested.

"No!" Sophrona and Esme spoke with immediate harmony.

"That kind of thing shocks folks here," Esme told her sisters. "You'd probably give these city men apoplexy!"

Sophrona nodded gravely. "It's very important," she told the twins, "to behave within the proper limits of genteel society."

"Well, that's not going to be a whole lot of fun," Adelaide protested. "These fellers ain't gonna feel welcome, they're gonna feel downright bored."

Tut-tutting lightly, Sophrona disagreed. "Ladylike behavior is never boring. Gentlemen find it fascinating."

As if her words had suddenly become flesh, a light tap was heard on the front doorframe.

"I'll get it," Mrs. Rhy said, easily pulling herself up from the chair and hurrying into the front hall.

"Well, come on in," they heard her call in welcome. "I do swear marriage must be agreeing with you. You are looking mighty fine."

"Why, thank you, ma'am." Armon Hightower's voice could be heard from the hallway.

Both twins paled and then flushed as they glanced hastily at Sophrona. Her eyes lighted with anticipation.

Armon followed Mrs. Rhy into the dining room. His smile was broad, his face relaxed, and his expression content.

"Afternoon, Mrs. Rhy," he said deferentially to Esme. "Mr. Crabb, Miss Adelaide, Miss Agrippa."

The young man's proper manners made him strangely unfamiliar and conversely unthreatening to the inhabitants of the room.

"Well, good Lord!" Yo exclaimed. "Miz Rhy's got the right of it. You look downright gratified, and talking that way, too. Marriage must agree with you."

"The right woman can change a man's whole outlook on life," Armon said easily. Then, as if suddenly realizing the unintended censure of his words, he gave an apologetic nod to the twins. "Although for certain I've been a fortunate man in all my *friendships*."

The twins appeared more confused than embarrassed, and Sophrona, sensing their disorientation, hastily stepped into the breach. "I didn't expect you to come down from the mountain to get me," Sophrona declared with pleased surprise.

The formerly arrogant young man actually blushed. "Ah, Phronie honey," he said. "I was calculating how much longer we'd have to be parted if'fen I was to let you walk home by yourself."

The pretty young redhead tittered shyly. "I do declare, Mr. Hightower," she said. "You have words that could charm the birds out of the trees."

The twins sat staring at their former sweetheart in disbelief. They couldn't have been more surprised if he'd suddenly grown a second nose right in the middle of his forehead.

"Well, I do believe that I'll go on and take my leave," Sophrona said to Esme. "I'm sure you'll do fine on your own."

"You *must* come back," Adelaide said. "We haven't learned even half of what we need to know."

"I swear," Agrippa added, "if you'll come back and

give us another chance, I'll listen to every word you say.''

Sophrona looked at the girls curiously and then exchanged a puzzled glance with Esme.

"Well, of course," she said. "If you want another lesson, I can come back tomorrow." She turned politely to her husband. "That is, of course, if it suits you, Mr. Hightower."

Armon's expression was that of a faithful puppy. "I could walk you here and back home," he said with unreasonable delight.

When the two had taken their leave, Esme turned questioningly to her sisters.

"What made you change your mind?" she asked. "I thought you were all ready just to be yourselves and let Cleavis be embarrassed if he must."

To the twins, the answer was obvious.

"Did you see Armon?" Agrippa asked.

"If being a lady can get a carousing man like him pulled up on a short leash," Adelaide stated, "give me ladyhood and give it to me quick!"

21

"Oh, he's wonderful!" Adelaide sighed blissfully as she leaned precariously out the front window.

"Yes, he's perfect!" Agrippa agreed, joining her sister to stare at the two gentlemen who were exploring the trout ponds with Cleavis.

Leaving at dawn for the train station at Russellville, Cleav had hardly had a moment to speak to the family. And after only perfunctory introductions all three men had eagerly headed out to examine the Rhy experiments in pisciculture.

"And the spectacles just add that special something," Adelaide declared dramatically.

"Spectacles?" Agrippa turned to stare at her sister. "I'm not talking about the four-eyed one," she said. "It's the handsome feller I've got my eye on."

Adelaide looked back at her sister, incredulity written across her face. "The one with the spectacles *is* the handsome one!"

Her sister laughed. "Adelaide, I'm thinking you might be needing spectacles yourself."

The argument exploded as Esme stepped into the room, amazed at her sisters' unusual bickering. "What are you two doing in here?" she asked.

"This is the best view of the ponds," Agrippa answered, as if that explained everything.

"The ponds?" Esme put her hands sternly on her hips. "Neither of you has ever shown so much as a gnat's life of interest in the ponds. It's those two young gentlemen you're interested in, and I just won't have it."

"What do you mean, 'you won't have it'?" Agrippa questioned belligerently.

"You've been telling us to forget about Armon," Adelaide reminded her. "That gent with the glasses is the first lick of interest I've had in a man in weeks!"

"For mercy's sakes, Adelaide," Agrippa implored her sister. "I tell you the one to set your cap for is the blond."

Adelaide shook her head. "He just looks like another washed-out farmer," she told her sister. "The other fellow's got dignity."

"Dignity?" Both Agrippa and Esme found that word strange on Adelaide's lips.

"Well, it doesn't matter," Esme stated sharply. "I won't have either of you throwing yourself at these gentlemen."

"Whyever not?" Agrippa protested. "They ain't married?"

"No, they aren't," Esme admitted. "But when they do marry, they'll for sure be wanting ladies for wives," she said.

Both young women raised chins in defiance.

"I'll have you know," Agrippa said, "that Adelaide and I have been living and breathing every word that Sophrona's been telling us."

"We can act just as ladylike as any of 'em," her sister proclaimed with confidence.

"Acting like isn't *being*," Esme answered sharply. "Folks

can't just change the way they are, no matter how much they want to.''

"Whyever would we want to change?" Adelaide asked. "You've been telling us ever since I can remember that we was just as good as anybody else. That we've got to hold our heads up high and know that nobody can make us less in our own eyes but ourselves.''

"That's right," Agrippa piped in. "You're always saying that it ain't the outside things that makes a person worthy or unworthy. It's what's in the heart and mind.''

The twins gazed at their sister curiously.

Esme stood staring at the two women she had loved, and worried about, and felt responsible for since her mother's death. She had taught them to believe in themselves. Should she let her own failings tarnish their hopes?

"I'm just a little nervous," Esme hedged awkwardly. "You just be careful around them city men. I don't want either of you being talked out to a deserted barn.''

Both girls giggled mischievously.

"Not unless we're doing the talking," Agrippa said. "And Pa's waiting in the barn with a shotgun!''

"We learned a wealth of knowledge from your dreadful circumstances," Adelaide added.

Esme's mouth dropped open in stunned shock, and the twins grabbed her in a three-way sister hug. Their joy and happy chatter soothed her frayed nerves and nurtured her tender feelings.

"If I don't get down there and see to those dad-gummed fish," she told the two, "we'll have to feed those gentlemen salt pork and poke salad!''

Esme tried desperately to get everything perfect, but the afternoon went by quickly. And perfect was not easy.

The mushrooms she'd picked the night before had gotten damp and turned a very unappetizing black. And the mussels had a peculiar odor that Esme found somewhat worrisome. The yeast rolls stubbornly refused to rise, so Esme was forced to mix up baking soda biscuits. And she could hardly glance at the "chamber pot" chafing dish without losing her own appetite.

By the time Esme finally was certain that perhaps she would have something to serve, the gentlemen had already returned to the house to dress for dinner.

Rushing upstairs, she prayed that she'd have time to whip her tired, flour-coated, sweat-stained body into shape before anyone saw her.

With all the angels in heaven watching out for her, Esme made it unnoticed to her room and hastily slipped through the door.

Before she had a moment to offer thanks for her reprieve, two strong arms came around her and Cleavis pulled her tightly into his arms.

"Cleav!" She startled at the unexpected embrace.

"You feel so good," he told her, pressing his body closely against hers. "I've been dreaming of holding you in my arms all afternoon."

Esme raised her head with surprise. "You certainly haven't." She pulled away from him and hurried to the washstand. Gazing dismally at her reflection in the mirror, she hastily poured water into the bowl and began stripping down to her chemise.

"What do you mean I haven't been dreaming of holding you?" Cleav asked her.

Esme found a towel and turned to give her husband a tolerant grin. "You've been hoping those men would come to Vader all summer. I venture to say you haven't had a thought of anything else in a week."

Raising an eyebrow, Cleav looked at her skeptically. "I beg to differ, dear wife," he said. "I *have* been excited about finally having someone with whom to discuss trout breeding," he admitted. "But it's you, Hillbaby, who've had nothing on your mind but this visit since the moment I told you about it.''

"Well, it's very important," Esme said. She was scrubbing her face and neck now, removing every vestige of her long day in front of a hot stove.

"Important?" Cleav's expression was openly curious. "*Pleasant* is a correct word, I'd think," he said. "Even *interesting,* but *important?* This visit is not *important.*"

"Well, it's not important in that sense," Esme agreed. "But it's important to you, so I want to make a good impression."

Cleav chuckled out loud. "I can't imagine how any gentleman could be other than favorably impressed," he said, stepping up behind her to wrap his arms tightly about her waist.

Pressing a gentle nip-kiss into the crook of her neck, he said, "I don't want the gentlemen *too* impressed, however, so keep those pretty legs of yours decently hidden."

Esme paled and jerked away from him, her expression hurt, her eyes stinging with unshed tears. "Of course I would never shame you like that, Cleavis," she said quickly. "Surely you trust me not to make a spectacle of myself."

"Esme? What's wrong?" he asked her. "I was joking with you, of course."

He reached out to run a comforting hand along her arm. "What is it?" he questioned curiously. "Are you ill?"

"No, no, I'm fine," she answered, trying to regain her composure.

"You are *not* fine," Cleav said firmly. "Something is very wrong and has been for the last several days."

Esme shook away his concern hastily. "I'm just worried about the evening," she said. "Would you mind looking in on the preparations, the dishes and linens and such?"

"If you want me to," Cleav said.

"I'd just like for you to make sure that I've chosen everything correctly," she said. "The salt cellar and spoons don't match the celery vase. I don't know if that will do."

"Esme? What—" he began.

"Please," she interrupted. "I need to dress or I'm going to be very rudely late. Could you please have a look at the table, just to make sure that everything is proper and appropriate?"

Cleav agreed with a nod and headed toward the door. With his hand on the brass knob, he turned back to look at his wife. Esme scurried around nervously through her toilet.

"Proper and appropriate?" he whispered to himself. With a shrug that lacked understanding, he headed downstairs.

"So you've been living in these mountains all your life, Miss Crabb?"

It was the blond gentleman's question that caught Esme's attention as she stepped into the front parlor.

"Oh, please call me Miss Agrippa," the pretty magpie replied with a chirpy twitter. "Miss Crabb sounds like an old maid schoolteacher."

The gentleman's pale face flushed with bright color and his eyes seemed glued to the vision in blue before him.

"No one could ever mistake *you* for such," he told her. "And because you've given me such honor, I must implore you to call me Theodatus."

"Oh, Mr. Simmons," she teased. "I should never do that."

"Oh, please, Miss Agrippa," he said. "I'll go down on my knee to beg if necessary."

Agrippa giggled. "You'd best not be doing that," she warned. "Pa's liable to get all kinds of strange ideas about it."

Simmons laughed gleefully, as if the young woman's comment were funny.

"Esme, dear." Cleav captured the attention of the room as he acknowledged his bride.

Standing beside the mantel, Cleav looked the part of the relaxed gentleman at leisure. The two young men stood, also, brandy glasses in hand. Yohan was seated on the divan with Mrs. Rhy, both passing occasional knowing looks. The twins were seated in identical fireplace chairs as if posing for an artist's portrait.

"Gentlemen," he said, addressing the two city fellows. "Although I made introductions this morning, I know you have hardly had a moment to greet my wife, Esmeralda."

Bespectacled Westbrook grasped her hand immediately and bent over it.

"It is truly a delight to meet you, Mrs. Rhy," he said.

Simmons stepped up and took his turn. "Yes, it is a pleasure," he agreed. "Your husband brags incessantly about your knowledge and interest in trout breeding. Ben and I have both been positively virescent with envy at his good fortune in finding a wife who shares his interest."

"How could she not be interested?" Adelaide piped in with a hasty glance toward dark-haired Westbrook in the thick gold-rimmed spectacles. "Trout are such fascinating creatures, I swear I can hardly hear enough about them."

Eula Rhy nearly choked on her lemonade.

"Oh, really?" Westbrook bit the bait, turning to examine the pretty twin in pink more closely.

"Oh, yes," Agrippa agreed with her sister. "We just love to hear that fish talk."

Cleav barely managed to hide his grin as he took Esme's arm and led the conversation into the direction closest to everyone's heart—fish breeding.

Esme hardly heard a word that was said. Her mind kept tumbling over lists. What to say, what to do, how to act, how to think, and dinner. *Dinner!*

"Esme?" Cleav asked curiously as she hastily pulled away from him.

"I must check the food," she said and managed an extraordinarily polite request to be momentarily excused.

The okra was slightly scorched and the corn not quite done, but the fish smelled very good, and Esme swallowed down the nausea as she carefully spooned it into the "chamber pot."

She checked everything at the table four times before deciding that she could safely invite the honored guests into the room.

"We descend to dinner," she whispered to herself. It sounded funny to her ears and she tried again. "*We* descend to dinner." That wasn't much better. "We *descend* to dinner."

She nodded approvingly to herself. That was undoubtedly it.

Stepping quietly across the foyer to the front parlor, she stopped formally at the threshold.

"Ladies and gentlemen," she spoke up distinctly, "we defend the dinner."

The twins looked up puzzled.

"Defend it from what?" Adelaide asked.

"It's time to eat," Cleav announced quickly. "Theo, why don't you escort Miss Agrippa."

Esme's face was bright red as her husband reached her side. "It smells wonderful, Hillbaby," he whispered. "And the dining room never looked prettier."

Esme nodded but couldn't quite shake the embarrassment of her foolish misquote.

Directing the gentlemen to their places, Esme regained some of her composure as she ignored dagger looks from the twins, who found themselves seated next to Eula and Pa rather than the gentlemen.

"This is certainly beautiful country. These peaks clearly

take one's breath away," Theo offered politely. "Even my own Massachusetts doesn't compare."

"It's all we've ever known," Cleav explained easily. "I spent a few years in Knoxville, but the mountains are the mountains."

"I ain't never been nowhere," Yohan stated with matter-of-fact evenness. "But ain't never been nowhere I've wanted to go."

"That's understandable," Theo acknowledged.

"Are you a farmer, Mr. Crabb?" Ben Westbrook asked.

An unexpected hush fell over the group.

Esme held her breath.

What would her father say? What could he say? I'm the laziest man in Vader, Tennessee?

"I don't farm much," he answered honestly. "I play the fiddle."

"Oh, really?" Westbrook's expression broke into a delighted smile. "My grandfather was a musician," he said. "He played the French horn with the Philadelphia symphony for twenty years."

"What else did he do?" Adelaide asked.

"What else? Why, nothing. He was a musician."

The twins shared a delighted glance before Agrippa said firmly, "That's what Pa is. He's the best musician in this part of Tennessee."

There were smiles and nods as Yohan half-heartedly attempted to dispute the compliment.

"I wondered if you were from a musical family, Mr. Crabb," Theo told him. "With a name like Johann, a man should definitely be involved in magical blending of tones and rhythms."

"You must play for us while we are here," Ben entreated.

"I planned on it," the older man said easily. "Why, I

intend to have you two city boys cutting up the rug afore morning.''

Esme was stunned and shocked by the direction that the conversation had taken. This was not going to be nearly as difficult as she had thought. If she'd known that lying was so easy, why, she'd have started doing it years ago.

The last of the fish was being separated from the still-warm chafing dish as the conversation turned once again to pisciculture.

Esme rose to retrieve the peach crisp, allowing the twins to continue their concerted attempt to pretend that they knew and were interested in the subject of fish.

Feeling herself relax, Esme began to gain confidence. The gentlemen were not so different from the people in Vader. The twins had made no horrific blunders, and even her father had managed not to make himself a family embarrassment. Cleav seemed quite pleased with her, and she could only sigh a thankful prayer for Sophrona's help.

Passing around the dessert, she began, at last, to get caught up in the conversation.

"Trout need cold running water to live," Theo was explaining. "That's why the ponds must be set up to drain into each other, keeping the temperature and oxygen level adequate.''

"Once the fish are raised to fingerlings," Westbrook continued, "they can be let out into the river or transported to areas where trout have not been or are now unavailable.''

"It must be hard to move those little fish across country," Adelaide said. "Looks like there would be an easier way.''

"Some have tried easier ways," Theo told her. Then, with a teasing glance, he turned to Cleav. "What do you think of the Reverend Dr. Bachman's experiments?''

Cleav's grin was infectious. "I think they worked best in his own imagination.''

"What were Reverend Bachman's experiments?" Agrippa asked.

Theo leaned forward slightly to get the pretty young woman more fully in his line of vision.

"The gentleman from South Carolina insisted that he managed to fertilize eggs that were kept dry for ten days and actually produced offspring."

At the twins' puzzled expression, Cleav explained. "A trout egg can't live more than a few hours without water. Still, Dr. Bachman assures us that he managed to fertilize dead eggs."

"Don't you have to have fish to make fish?" Adelaide asked Mr. Westbrook, her eyes wide open with sweet innocence.

"Of course you need fish to make fish," Esme answered the foolish young woman easily. "Cleav uses a natural method of propagation, but many trout breeders simply strip the ripe females of their eggs, throw them in a pan, and then cover them with milt."

"Milt?" Agrippa asked curiously. "What in heaven's name is milt?"

"Milt is the stuff that comes from the male fish," Esme explained easily. "It's like the man's—"

Stopping abruptly in midsentence, Esme glanced in horror around the table. Pa was staring at her curiously. The twins looked puzzled. Eula Rhy's expression was sympathetic. Theodatus Simmons sat stone still, his mouth hanging open in shock, and Ben Westbrook seemed ready to choke on the spoon that was frozen in his mouth.

Finally her eyes met Cleav's. As her final humiliation, her husband looked ready to burst out laughing.

"I . . . I . . ." Esme struggled valiantly for a way to save her disgrace but failed miserably. Giving in to tears, wordlessly she fled the room.

Down the hall, out the back door, Esme had to get away.

She was running to the hills. She had never run from humiliation, but she was running now. She was running and she was never coming back. She had embarrassed herself. That she could stand. But she had shamed her husband. He deserved better. She was going to keep right on running forever more.

A strong brown arm encircled her waist, capturing her before she made it past the azalea bushes.

"Esme, Esme," he whispered, pulling her against his chest. "Don't cry, Hillbaby, it wasn't that bad."

"I'm so ashamed," Esme managed to choke out before she buried her face in the warm, familiar shirtfront of the man she loved.

"You shouldn't be ashamed," Cleav told her, rocking her slightly back and forth. "Embarrassed, maybe a little, but never ashamed. When we're talking about fish breeding, it's hard to remember to be delicate."

"I'm so sorry, Cleav," she moaned. "I'm so sorry."

"What in the world are you sorry for? A few silly words aren't anything to make a fuss about."

"I'm not just sorry for that," Esme admitted. "I'm sorry for all of it. I'm sorry that you had to marry me. I'm sorry that I'm not the wife that you needed. I'm sorry that I'm not the woman that you wanted."

"The woman that I wanted?" Cleav held his wife at arm's length and looked down at her.

"Esme, my sweet Hillbaby," he said softly, "you *are* the woman that I wanted. The only woman that I've really ever wanted."

Esme shook her head.

"I don't mean that way," she insisted. "I know you want me that way. I mean the woman that you wanted for a wife."

"You are the woman I want for my wife," he said firmly. "I want you *that* way and every way."

Clasping his hand under her chin, he raised her face to look at him. "I love you, Esme Rhy."

"Don't joke about such a thing," she admonished him as another tear sneaked out of the corner of her eye. "It may be just funning to you, but a gal can take such a declaration plumb serious."

"I mean it 'plumb serious,'" Cleav replied. "I've never said it before because I didn't think that you loved me back."

"Loved you back?" Esme looked confused. "You know I love you, I've never made a secret of it."

"You *did* make a secret of it. A secret that got out of the bag tonight."

Esme looked puzzled.

"You said you married me to get this house," he reminded her.

"This house?" she asked, not quite recalling the conversation.

"Yes," he insisted. "You said you wanted to marry me to get this house for your family."

"Well, sure I wanted *this house* for my family," Esme tried to explain. "But I wanted *you* just for myself. I was downright selfish about it. I didn't think about Pa or the twins, or even poor Sophrona, your sweetheart. I didn't even care about your feelings. I just loved you so much, I said I was going to have you by hook or by crook."

"By hook or by crook?" Cleav repeated, a smile stretching across his face. "Or by garters."

"Cleavis!" Esme protested. "How could you believe that I married you for your house?"

"I don't anymore," he said. "When I saw you this evening, my proud, imposing Esme, who knows she's just as good as everybody else, trying to hide her light under a bushel of meaningless manners, I knew you loved me."

Reaching for her, he pressed her tightly against his shirt as if he wanted to fuse her self with his own. "Nothing but real, true love could have made you humble yourself."

"I am humble! I failed you," Esme whispered against his chest. "I've embarrassed you in front of your friends. I know how much their opinion matters to you."

Cleav shook his head. "No, you don't, Esme," he said. "Because it doesn't matter. You love me for myself. That's a hundred times more fulfilling than having the whole world love me for something I can pretend to be."

"Oh, Cleav," Esme wailed. "You deserve to have a lady, a real lady."

Cleav smoothed her brow with one long finger.

"I have a lady, Mrs. Rhy," he whispered. "I have you."

"I'm no lady! You saw that tonight."

"You *are* a lady, and you always have been. I saw that one morning in church."

"In church?"

"The day they gave your family that charity basket," he said. "We humiliated you. But you never cowered or cried or hid your face. You raised your chin and just looked right past us. You knew you were as good as anybody. And you've taught me that I am, too."

His lips found hers, and he tasted her gently.

"All this to-do about being civilized and proper," he said. "It's kept me in a stew for too many years. Finery and genteel conversation don't make us ladies or gentlemen. City folks have their ways and we have ours. When we try to be what we're not, we only shame ourselves."

"You mean you want me to be just Esme Crabb?"

Cleav smiled. "I want you to be Esme Rhy," he said. "I want you to be the lady that I love."

He kissed her then, and the sweetness was such that Esme couldn't let it go. She answered his lips with urgent exploration of her own.

Their bodies strained against each other in passion both remembered and renewed. Esme felt the now familiar warmth melting her loins, and she eagerly squirmed to meld that fire against the evidence of his response.

"I love you," Cleav whispered. "I've wanted to tell you that every day, every time I've touched you. I've wanted to say it and now I can't stop."

"I love you, Cleav," Esme answered. "I don't know if it was that first day in the store or later when I got to know you. But I couldn't live without you, and I would have done anything to keep you, to help you, to make you happy."

"Even pretend to be something you are not," Cleav said accurately.

"I'd swim like a fish if it was what you wanted," she declared.

Cleav's smile was naughty. "Swimming was not quite what I had in mind," he said. "But if I take you upstairs, will you promise to wiggle like a trout out of water?"

Esme giggled and then shook her head reprovingly. "Only if you promise to give me another of those no-hands fish looks."

"Can't promise that, ma'am," he answered. "Tonight I'm planning to put these hands all over you."

"Well," Esme suggested. "How about prissy talk? Can I expect some of that at least?"

"My dear Mrs. Rhy, I vow to eloquate with such magnificence that you will find yourself incapable of resisting supine repose for the remainder of the evening."

"Mmmm," she replied appreciatively.

Cleav grasped her hand, and they hurried to the house like eager children.

"Wait." Esme hesitated at the doorway. "Can we go upstairs?" she asked him. "We have guests in the house."

"Mrs. Rhy," he said smoothly. "In this house *you* make up the rules of etiquette. What do you deem proper?"

Esme was thoughtful for only a moment.

"Our guests might be scandalized," she told him. "And I always try to keep a watchful eye on Pa and the twins."

Cleav acquiesced easily. "Whatever you think, Mrs. Rhy."

Esme's thoughtful expression slowly became a confident grin. "But I think I've been taking too much care of my family," she said. "It's time that Pa and the girls start facing the world all on their own."

"Now, that's a very good idea," Cleav said.

"And your gentlemen friends from up north should really get some opportunity to find out about real Tennessee people."

Cleav nodded. "So we go straight upstairs?"

As if suddenly remembering what happened, Esme sighed in dismay. "No, after making such a fool of myself, I'd better go back in there and face them tonight."

Cleav placed a strong arm around her waist and grinned at her.

"Just stick close to me, Mrs. Rhy," he said. "It's a husband's right to rescue his wife from social blunders."

"Who made that rule?"

"I did," he replied easily.

Esme walked nervously beside her husband as they entered the house. The company had left the dining room for the informality of the back parlor, and she could hear Pa fiddling a happy tune.

Reaching the doorway, she saw the twins gleefully instructing the gentlemen from up north on the proper steps of mountain clogging. There was much laughter and clapping, and the two somewhat bookish gentlemen were clearly having the time of their lives.

"Excuse us," Cleav interrupted their revelry.

Every eye focused on them, and Esme felt her courage

drifting away. Only the strength of Cleav's arm kept her beside him.

"My wife and I would like to apologize for our abrupt departure from dinner," Cleav began civilly.

"Quite all right," Theo said eagerly.

"We're perfectly fine," Ben insisted.

"Wonderful," Cleav replied with a pleasant smile. "Do go on and enjoy yourselves," he said. "Mrs. Rhy and I must retire early, it seems."

Esme glanced up at her husband in surprise.

Cleav smiled at her before he said calmly, "You may find this difficult to believe, but my wife and I have both suddenly developed an unprecedented infestation of fleas."

Theodatus G. Simmons
Springfield, Massachusetts

My dear brother-in-law Theo,

As always, we enjoyed receiving your missive, especially the good news of your addition. Esme sends her love to your new son and our dear Agrippa with hopes for an eventless recovery.

I accepted the salutation on your last letter as jest. Believe me, the degree is strictly honorary and I certainly have not taken to calling myself Dr. Rhy, despite the governor's fine words about my modest contribution to natural science.

Esme and I did, however, truly enjoy the trip to Knoxville. After so many years it was quite strange to return and discover things so unchanged and yet so different from the memories I had held. Esme charmed the dignitaries, one and all. I believe the headmaster at Halperth Academy was near ready to write odes to her eyebrows. As per usual, my dear wife remains unaffected by the unique effect her wit and humor have upon the male species.

Esme wanted me to be sure to mention to Agrippa that Reverend Tewksbury has retired and his son-in-law, Reverend Hightower, is now pastor of the church. The new reverend was a friend of the twins when they were children. The man is actually a very exceptional preacher. I was quite surprised myself, but Esme was not. She assures me that the worst sinners always make the best preachers.

Yohan is doing better now that the weather is warming up. The cold bothers the arthritis in his *knee, but he rarely complains. He continues to talk about his visit to Ben and Adelaide in Washington, D.C. Meeting President Cleveland and playing with the gentlemen of the symphony now figure largely as the highlight of the old man's life.*

Mother is doing well, the twins keep her busy. Not just playing with them but replanting all the flowers those two manage to trample.

I'm sure you heard the story about when the boys were born and Esme named them Herbert and Hubert. I felt, and continue to feel, that the names are far too prissy for a couple of Tennessee storekeeper's sons. Esme disagreed with me completely and declared that I knew nothing about naming children. She stated before the whole company at the visiting that were I to name the boys I'd undoubtedly call them Catfish and Crappie. To her horror the names stuck. She was especially disheartened when the boys returned from their first day at school with their nicknames written neatly on their slates.

I do hope that perhaps late in the summer you will come again to visit us. The trout spawning was extremely successful this year, and I am eager to show you my new design for races.

I must cut this letter short as the boys are waiting upon me. We are doing a little project together this spring. I'm allowing the boys to help me repaint the house. White is such a lifeless color, I've decided it should be blue. In the mountains there is just simply not enough sky.

As ever,

Cleav